"PUT ME DOWN!"

"I'm about to. Of all the foolish—"

He plunked her on the bench and knelt to unfasten her boot. She jerked away, tucking her foot behind her where he couldn't reach it without creating a scene. "This is totally unnecessary. I'm not helpless. It's a very small pebble."

"My dear, take it from a soldier who's been on many a long march. Pebbles are nothing to laugh at. Infection can follow a cut swiftly. Now," he said, staring into eyes that'd turned stormy, knowing his were just as threatening, "let me see that foot."

"No," she bit out. "I am *not* made of crystal, sir. I do *not* shatter at the slightest touch. And I'm not a complete simpleton. I'm a grown woman with as much experience of the world, in my own way, as you."

The breeze twined the soft folds of her gown against a form as lithe and graceful as a young sapling's. It was all he could do to refrain from reaching out to touch her. "Damnation, I just couldn't bear the thought of you, well—you see to everyone, and there's no one to see to you, and there should be."

He prayed she'd forget circumspection for once, and speak her heart so clearly there'd be no pretending not to understand— though what he would do then he had no notion. Recklessly sweep her into his arms, thereby creating precisely the situation he was determined to avoid? Entirely too possible.

"There could be," she said, looking directly into his eye.

* * *

"Readers will revel in this unforgettable Regency tale."
—*Romantic Times* on *The Colonel's Courtship*

BOOK YOUR PLACE ON OUR WEBSITE AND MAKE THE READING CONNECTION!

We've created a customized website just for our very special readers, where you can get the inside scoop on everything that's going on with Zebra, Pinnacle and Kensington books.

When you come online, you'll have the exciting opportunity to:

- View covers of upcoming books
- Read sample chapters
- Learn about our future publishing schedule (listed by publication month *and author*)
- Find out when your favorite authors will be visiting a city near you
- Search for and order backlist books from our online catalog
- Check out author bios and background information
- Send e-mail to your favorite authors
- Meet the Kensington staff online
- Join us in weekly chats with authors, readers and other guests
- Get writing guidelines
- AND MUCH MORE!

**Visit our website at
http://www.zebrabooks.com**

DAUNTRY'S DILEMMA

Monique Ellis

Zebra Books
Kensington Publishing Corp.
http://www.zebrabooks.com

For Ann, Pat, and Chris,
and for Mike and Tim, too—
you're the greatest!

ZEBRA BOOKS are published by

Kensington Publishing Corp.
850 Third Avenue
New York, NY 10022

Copyright © 1999 by Monique Ellis

Zebra and the Z logo Reg. U.S. Pat. & TM Off.

First Printing: April, 1999
10 9 8 7 6 5 4 3 2 1

Printed in the United States of America

One

Quintus Dauntry, the younger son of Viscount Harald Dauntry, bent low over his flagging mount's neck, urging him on. The lathered gelding scrambled over the sun-struck ridge, then started for the broad valley through which the lane passing by Combermere ran. Only a mile to the valley floor, another to the lane, then three more to the gates.

It'd been hard traveling.

Dauntry'd done the two and a half days from Danescroft in a day and a half, much of it cross-country, stopping only to change horses, pushing himself and his mounts unmercifully and paying dearly for the privilege.

It was not the first time he'd traveled like this—cheeks shadowed, togs caked with sweat and dust, eyes burning—but that was before he'd taken a ball at Salamanca in July of '12. It had been almost a year, and still his thigh troubled him when pressed too hard. He'd be stiff for days following this escapade.

The twenty-eight-year-old former major slowed the dun, taking the steeper part of descent at a reasonable pace.

What the devil sort of disaster had overtaken the family this time? The only thing of which he could be certain was Combermere still stood, and that the viscount had roared, "I want him instanter, d'y'understand? Instanter!" at the groom sent to find him.

Instanter had taken close to a fortnight, given Voit didn't hurry once he was beyond the gates, apparently intending a holiday. His lordship wouldn't be pleased, one of the reasons Dauntry had pressed on without meals or sleep. The young fool was cooling his heels at Danescroft. By the time Pugs Harnette permitted him to leave, Dauntry hoped to have his father mellowed. Otherwise, Voit risked dismissal without a character.

They reached the valley floor. Dauntry cut toward a stream beside which a farm track meandered, its edges sprinkled with wildflowers. The track would offer surer footing. Exhausted as they both were, that made sense. First he guided the dun into the stream, and gave the poor beast a chance to drink. No reason it should suffer because he daren't risk dismounting. The temptation to strip off his clothes and join it in a good wallow was close to irresistible. Instead, once the dun had had its fill he forced it back up the bank and onto the track, and encouraged it to a slow trot.

"Just a bit more, fellow," he murmured as they turned onto the lane a few minutes later. "Then it's the best stabling you've ever known, and the most deserved rest."

The gelding's hooves raised puffs of dust as they passed the fork leading to Bittersfield, the nearest market town to Combermere and its neighboring village of Coombe. Suddenly lane and verges were pocked with holes left by last winter's ice and eroded by spring rains, the high hedgerows lining the fields overgrown.

What the devil? Pruning hedgerows might be the individual farmers' responsibility, but the stretch between the Bittersfield fork and Coombe was Combermere's. He'd never seen it like this—not in July. Of course, he hadn't been here in years, but such careless inattention was unheard of. Suddenly the trouble at Combermere, whatever it was, became very real.

Dauntry crested a small rise, resisting the urge to give the dun a flick of the crop and wring a last bit of speed from him. Well ahead, a slip of a girl limped along the side of the lane. He slowed the gelding, frowning at her uneven gait. She tripped, almost stumbling into the overgrown ditch between lane and hedgerow, then disappeared around the next curve. Probably the daughter of some nearby farmer, or even one of his father's tenants. She couldn't be going far. It would only cost him a minute or two to take her up.

He trotted around the curve, guiding the job horse past the potholes and ignoring all but the deepest ruts chaining from the crown, and stopped just behind her.

"Wait," he rasped past his parched throat.

She froze, silhouetted against the sun's glare, then turned, back to the verge's lip, her eyes widening. Whoever she was, he didn't recognize what he could make out of her features, even granting the changes in face and figure seven years would have wrought. Given her dusty gown, she'd come farther than he first thought, and she was definitely no farm girl despite her reddened cheeks and mussed hair. That air of self-assurance came from generations accustomed to command.

"Search out a more likely victim." She retreated a step. "I haven't so much as a farthing about me."

"Didn't ask if you did. You were limping." He squinted into the sun, discerning little beyond an impression of youthful delicacy.

"Which makes me an easy target for thieves and vagrants? Think again."

"That what you believe I am? Good Lord! Not very perspicacious—but then, given your age, I suppose that's no surprise."

The girl scrambled into the ditch and up the other side, shawl snagging on deadwood deposited by spring runoff. She twitched it loose, then turned to face him, clinging to a branch poking out from the hedgerow. The little idiot was covered with weeds and burrs now, as well as dust.

"That was foolish," he said. "What d'you think it gained you?"

"You come one step nearer, and I'll scream."

"Which will do you precisely how much good in the middle of nowhere?"

"Not much, but perhaps it'll frighten your mount."

"In case you haven't noticed, it's spent. Couldn't take to its heels if its life depended on it. Now, be a sensible child, and get back over here. You shouldn't be walking on that foot. I haven't got all day, and I can't come after you as I'm not willing to risk this slug in the ditch."

"I'm well able to take care of myself."

"Not given the evidence, young lady. What are you—a runaway?"

"Hardly. A runaway would have a bundle. I don't."

She edged farther into the tangle of briars and shrubs, disturbing a sparrow who scolded her more effectively than ever he could.

"Indulging in a forbidden tryst, then." That had to be it—a clandestine encounter with some local sprig whose taste for petticoats had outstripped his common sense. "I won't nark and I won't lecture, I promise."

She laughed. "Gowned like this, and with my hair falling down? What an odd notion you have of the conventions of romance."

"I've never indulged in the pastime."

"Yes, that's clear."

She was still giggling, clearly not half so afraid of him now as she was amused.

"For God's sake," he croaked, returning to the main point, for time was wasting, "I don't care who you are, or why you're all the way out here. Take my word for it—traveling on an injured foot can lead to infection. Then you'll be in worse case than ever, no matter what your other problems."

"Far more acceptable than permitting you an inch closer. If I learn you're in the vicinity tomorrow, I'll inform Squire Burchett you attempted to accost me, so you'd best put as much distance between Coombe and yourself as you can before your mount founders."

Who the devil she might be he still hadn't the slightest idea. Possibly just a hoyden out berrying in her oldest gown, though what she was doing so far from the village, and without a basket, remained a mystery. She'd doubtless receive a drubbing once she got home. Well, with the exception of attending his grandmother's funeral in the bleak winter of '06 shortly after Pitt's untimely death, he hadn't been at Combermere since he attained his majority. No doubt he'd find more changes than just a new family or two in the neighborhood and a rutted lane.

"Don't be a fool," he snapped. "I'll take you up, but I can't dismount. Bad leg."

"A likely tale. I don't accept assistance from strangers."

"I'm perfectly trustworthy, devil take it!"

"Yes, may the devil take you, indeed, for I shan't."

As he watched, the little minx forced her way through the hedgerow, almost becoming trapped, then disappeared into the hidden fields beyond.

"Show your keeper that foot when you get home," he shouted past his raw throat. Dear Lord, he'd gone hoarse. "I'm serious about the possibility of its causing you problems. If it throws off pus, summon an apothecary immediately."

Silence greeted his words. Well, he'd tried. She looked to be healthy enough despite her slight frame. She'd make it home. That was what mattered.

Less than half an hour later, Quintus Dauntry scowled at Combermere's open gates, wishing he was back at Danescroft with Pugs Harnette, and the rest of the informal band dubbed North's Irregulars by the *ton*. Well, he wasn't. He was very much here.

He glanced about, mouth in the downward curve that'd set his subordinates quaking not so many months before.

Sunlight glinted on distant farmhouse roofs, gilding mellowed thatch. From the rise, the spire of St. Martin the Lesser, hinted at three miles down the valley, seemed shorter, the village smaller, the lane leading there narrower than he remembered. Lesser, indeed. It was as if everything had shrunk during his military years.

He shifted in the saddle, easing his leg.

He hadn't worried overmuch when Voit'd ridden up—with Harald Dauntry, disaster too often consisted of a family squabble, tempers flaring, and dinner arriving late and cold—but the last time he'd been ordered home from a distance was shortly after Duncan'd taken a tumble when his mount refused a jump, suffering a concussion and subsequent inflammation of the lungs.

His father had feared for the line's continuation, for Duncan's son Bertram hadn't been born until seven months later. When the old gentleman learned Dauntry'd taken a ball barely two weeks after Duncan came a cropper, he'd ordered him to sell out

and then forced the issue with the assistance of several cronies
at the Horse Guards.

Danescroft wasn't as far as the Peninsula, but it was far
enough. His brother might've actually cracked his skull this time.
Duncan could even be dead, rather than lying semiconscious for
close to a week while wife and mother wrung their hands and
wept but took no part in nursing the neck-or-nothing nodcock.

After a moment Dauntry passed through the open gates. The
drive might've been filled and scraped that morning. The park
was in excellent repair, the trees perhaps a bit taller and thicker—
unlike the diminished village of Coombe and St. Martin's mini-
aturized spire—and the lane still rutted from winter storms, for
all it was midsummer.

He noted with approval the widening and deepening of the
trout pool below the ornamental falls his father had had constructed. There were other improvements. The mossy grotto was
overdone, though the ferns surrounding it were pretty enough.
The gothic folly just beyond was an abomination, and appeared
dangerous. His lordship would be regretting that expense once
little Bertram was old enough to scamper about. Selena was sure
to have the vapors if the apple of her eye so much as scratched
an elbow. Bertram bid fair to become a man-milliner if his mother
were given free rein.

Dauntry broke into the sunlight at the park's edge. The house,
as always, was a monstrosity, and had been since his father disguised its clean Tudor lines with a Palladian façade that might've
suited the banks of the Tiber if glimpsed from a distance between
stands of cypress. In England? Another abomination. At least the
gardens his grandmother'd laid out with the assistance of Capa-
bility Brown remained untouched.

Potts, head groom at Combermere for as long as Dauntry could
remember, ambled around the corner of the house, hand shading
his eyes as he peered toward Dauntry and his exhausted mount.
Uncanny as ever, apparently.

Dauntry continued along the drive that curved to form a circle
in front of the pile, halting as he arrived at the foot of the steps
leading to the overblown portico.

"Afternoon, Potts," he said, as if he'd been absent for hours rather than years. "There've been a few changes."

"Bound to, given you been gone so long. Welcome home, sir."

Dauntry nodded, pretending not to hear the tone of reproof. The house was always a shock, for he tended to remember it as it had been in his grandfather's day.

He eased from the saddle, wincing as his feet struck the gravel, handed Potts the reins, and unbuckled his portmanteau from behind the cantle. Then he turned to face the bandy-legged old fellow, eyes narrowed, ignoring his throbbing thigh.

"All right, Potts, what's put my father in a pelter this time? I won't bolt now I'm here, but Voit wouldn't tell me a thing."

"His lordship wanted you. Instanter. Eben was to tell you that."

"But why now? I haven't been here in years. His lordship and I agreed it was better that way." The customarily voluble Potts played boulder, a game at which he'd always excelled when the notion took him. "Well, it *is* best."

"If that's how you see it, sir, then that's how it is."

"My father's in good health?"

Potts nodded. "Isn't a one of the family isn't thriving."

"No discord among the staff?"

"Not so's you'd notice, sir."

"Haven't sailed up the River Tick, have they?"

"Your father's purses was deep in London?"

"So far as I could tell."

"Well, however it was then, that's how it be now. Where's this glue-bait from, Bittersfield, or the Bear in Chiverton?"

"Chiverton. See he's well rested before he's returned."

"And here I was thinking you'd want me to send him back foundered, just as I always do." They eyed each other for a moment, neither giving an inch. Then Potts tugged his forelock and grinned. "Will you be selecting a mount from his lordship's stables this afternoon, or in the morning?"

"Won't be selecting anything. I'll be here just tonight."

"Y'think so? Not likely. Not likely a'tall. Hope that starched-up Longtree fellow's following you by coach with the rest of your toggery."

The gleam in the groom's eyes gave Dauntry pause. There was knowingness there. Strangely, there was also an air of pleading. Potts had never sported that particular look, that Quintus Dauntry could remember.

At least there was no hatchment over the door. Fury at the way he'd pushed himself vied with relief, relief winning. Whatever imbroglio had caused his father to summon him, it couldn't be serious. Possibly merely his mother taking to her deathbed again, convinced she'd been felled by the latest fashionable indisposition. That, or someone with an injured sense of self-consequence. Anything short of death or destitution wouldn't take long to sort out. He'd clear the matter up, leave smoothing ruffled feathers to others, and make his escape by the morrow. As he'd told Potts, better that way, no matter what the old fellow thought.

"Any new families in the district?" he said in afterthought, remembering the graceless hoyden with the injured foot.

"Nary a one."

He shrugged, then climbed the steps as Potts took off with the job horse. Probably a visitor briefly in the neighborhood—though where she'd be staying he hadn't the slightest notion, unless it might be Beechy Knoll. She had mentioned reporting him to the squire. The joke would be on her if she tried it.

The door opened before he seized the knocker. Behind Mayhew an unfamiliar dark-haired footman hovered, clutching a sweaty tankard.

Dauntry glanced about, nose wrinkling. Combermere's ornate entry rotunda had been transformed. Bedraggled vegetation draped niched busts intended to hint at a Roman villa, the classical scenes between them hidden by mirrors and crucifixes. The place had an earthy, cellar-like aroma he couldn't identify. Then he caught sight of his reflection. Good God—he resembled a hedgebird of the most villainous sort. No wonder the girl'd taken to her heels.

"What the devil's going on, Mayhew?" he croaked.

"Glad you're home, sir." The butler, who'd headed Combermere's indoor staff for over a generation, relieved Dauntry of portmanteau, hat, gloves, and crop, then nodded for the strange footman to hand him the tankard. "Took some finding, I gather, or Eben Voit would've had you here sooner."

So—another retainer on the alert, and given to uncharacteristic circumspection. Interesting.

The cider was as crisp and tangy as a November day. Dauntry took three small swallows, waited a moment to see how it sat, then drained the lot and returned the emptied tankard to the footman.

"Ran me to ground at Pugs Harnette's," he rasped.

"Ah, that's it, then. We assumed you were in London, or else with Mr. Sinclair."

"Well, I wasn't. What's all this, Mayhew?" He pointed to several trunks by the door, and the odd decorations.

"His lordship will explain. If you'll follow me, sir?"

"Like this? My mother'd have palpitations. I'll just take myself to my old suite, if that's where Mrs. Ford's put me, and—"

"Not here."

"Who's not here? Mrs. Ford?"

"Her ladyship. Brighton, sir. They all are, excepting his lordship. It was considered wisest. Mr. Longtree didn't accompany you?"

"No need for a valet. I'll only be here a day or two at most. Hope you've been keeping well, by the bye."

Mayhew's brows rose, though he made no comment.

That was strange. Mayhew'd commented on Dauntry's every action from the time he shed leading strings—generally with disfavor laced with not a little humor. Except for occasional fits of temper, Duncan had been the placid one, rolling through life like a ball of dough. No imagination. No sense of adventure. No curiosity. Little intelligence. And, generally no trouble to anyone except when he mounted a horse. Then he was a deal of trouble for everyone, including the horse.

The dark-haired footman took his portmanteau and headed for the stairs, casting glances over his shoulder. The fellow appeared scared to death—that, or curious. Possibly both. Mayhew, who always saw everything, including things one would much rather he didn't, appeared not to notice.

"His lordship's this way."

Dauntry shrugged and followed the butler toward the rear of the house. "Looks like they're trying to turn the place into a compost heap. Everyone vying for incarceration in Bedlam?"

"Hardly that bad, sir."

Mayhew's chortle had a hollow ring. More musky vegetation draped the library door. The portraits of the viscount's favorite hunters had been replaced with mirrors. Pastilles burned in dishes. Another crucifix, this one flanked by stubby candles, graced the mantel. Open Bibles littered every surface. The library smelled like a cross between a damp bivouac and a Portuguese brothel. Still more vegetation festooned the open French doors leading outside.

"Is there sickness in the neighborhood, Mayhew? Brain fever, possibly?"

"Oh, no, sir. A very healthy summer it's proved so far."

"Then what's all this?"

"Precautions, sir. If you'll go through to the terrace, you'll find his lordship waiting."

"What—you trust me so far unescorted?"

Mayhew's look of reproof had Dauntry flushing. With a cough and a, "Yes, well," Dauntry headed for the terrace while Mayhew hovered inside, apparently anticipating something.

Bathed in sunlight, Lord Harald Dauntry lounged in an antiquated Bath chair, milky complexion protected by a broad-brimmed straw hat, eyes closed, figure slumped, gouty foot elevated, hand gripping a tumbler of port. A garland of bulbous white objects hung about his shoulders.

"What the devil?" Dauntry muttered.

"Wha-what?" The viscount's eyes almost sprang from their sockets as he stared about him.

"Good afternoon, Father."

Lord Dauntry squinted, face paler than ever, shoulders hunched. "Who's there?" he yelped. "That you, Quintus? Don't hide in the shadows. Show yourself, by damn. It is you, isn't it?"

"For better or worse. How are you faring?"

"Abysmally. No—worse. By God, I'm glad you're here—

though you took your time coming, and now you're here y'got the air of a scarecrow an' the voice of a jackdaw. Told 'em I wanted you instanter. This ain't instanter by any stretch."

The viscount paused, gulped, and drained his glass.

"She's back, Quint!" he wailed, refilling the tumbler from the decanter at his side. "And the way y'look and sound, y'won't be the least use. Not near impressive enough."

"The dirt's removable. Who's back? Not Great-aunt Persephone. Letter from her found me only last week. Said being surrounded by sun-baked antiques was rejuvenating, and she'd never leave Crete. Can't think of anyone else who'd put you in such a state."

"No-no, it ain't her. Minor annoyance, m'mother's sister, harpy though she is."

"Who, then? Cousin Gertrude hasn't turned up with her brood, has she?"

"No, blast it. Destitute hangers-on ain't a disaster. A few pounds gets rid of 'em."

"Who then, Father?"

"It's the girl in white," his lordship whimpered. "She's back. Everywhere!"

"You don't say." Dauntry strode over to the balustrade to hide his grin. There wasn't much he could do about his shaking shoulders. So this was the great disaster that'd had him galloping cross-country for over thirty-six hours straight—the damned family ghost. No matter what the fellows had come up with to explain his father summoning him to Combermere, they'd lose their wagers.

"I do—I do! Your mother saw her. Selena too, and your brother. Heard her m'self, come to that, though I ain't seen her. Has chains this time."

"Buttered crab and a surfeit of sweets, doubtless spiced with laudanum in their case, and an excess of brandy in yours and Duncan's."

"What's that? M'hearing's not what it used to be."

"Nothing, sir." Dauntry schooled his features and faced his father. "You're certain it wasn't indigestion, or a drapery blowing in the wind?"

"Nothing of the sort. She's everywhere, I tell you. Constantly. Course it can't be a real ghost, can it?—no such thing as ghosts—but someone's up to something. Scared your mother and Selena out of their wits. Had Duncan a bit green about the gills, too."

"Fearing for Bertram's life? And his own, I suppose."

"Course he is. And Selena's increasing again. She don't want to die in childbed any more'n he wants to die of a choking fit, so he whisked 'em off to Brighton. Dreadful commotion they was raising, with your mother running 'em a close second. No hope of sleep, or anything else. Vapors everywhere day and night. Dreadful thing—when a grown man has the vapors."

"Most disconcerting, I'm sure."

"Now you're here, I'll be joining 'em. You ain't heir to anything, and you certainly ain't increasing, so you ain't in any danger."

"Neither're you, Father. Girl in white? Phah! A hoary legend to make children stay tucked in their cots at night, and not go where one doesn't want them to by day."

"I will when Aunt Persie finally cocks up her toes—be heir to something, I mean. Why I had that stuff put about. Has a tidy packet, Aunt Persie does, and that place in Kent. Never has cared for Duncan, so if I ain't alive to inherit, Lord knows where she'll leave it all. Can't have that."

"Mirrors and garlic—that's what's hanging around your neck, isn't it, garlic? Mirrors and garlic and crucifixes're for vampires, Father, not ghosts."

"Few onions too, as garlic wasn't easy to come by. Been thinking you should have the vicar up, do one of those popish things. Examination? Excoriation? Ex-something."

"Exorcism," Dauntry muttered. "What next?"

"Might be best to stay at The Garter—not that you're not welcome to your old apartments. Y'could come over at dawn, leave at sunset. Much safer. Course night's when she appears, and you'll need to be here to catch her at her tricks, so maybe that won't do."

"Father, we agreed when I sold out that my summers were to be my own."

"Not when disaster strikes. I want you t'get rid of her."

Dauntry sank onto one of the marble benches lining the terrace and stared at the old gentleman in disbelief. "You want me to do what?"

"I want you t'get rid of her. Permanently."

"But you admit there's no such thing as ghosts."

"Maybe not, but there's *something*. I want that something gone, whatever it is. Dreadful bother, all that wailing and moaning and clanking. Happens most every night. Won't any of us come back 'til it's gone. Not safe."

The sun was as bright and the sky as brilliant as they had been moments before, the air as filled with the scent of roses and the warbling of birds. It was only his own mind that'd gone murky, Dauntry decided. Folly had to be contagious, for he was actually considering his father's demand rather than laughing.

"How're things in the village?" he said after a moment's reflection.

"Much as ever."

"And here? You've dismissed no one of late?"

His father shook his head. "Had to hire some new girls, come to that, now Selena's proving a healthy breeder. Footman, too."

"I see." Only he didn't. "They came well recommended?"

"All spoken for. Girls're from the village, mostly. One's from a farm up by Bittersfield. New footman's Mayhew's youngest nephew."

"Duncan behaving himself? No fathers with a grudge?"

"Selena keeps him on a tight rein, and doesn't spare the crop. If he's larking, he's circumspect about it these days. No, there's none in the neighborhood with a burr under the saddle. You'll have to look elsewhere."

The viscount drained his glass, lowered his bandaged foot, and seized the cane hooked over the chair's arm.

"It's a troublemaker," he insisted. "Sure to be. Well, you were in the army. You're supposed to know something about ferreting out troublemakers, and seeing to it they stop plaguing honest people. What you were doing over there, after all—ferreting out Boney's troublemakers, if one stretches the point. Might as well put your training to use, was my thought. Never got any other good out of all those years y'were away. An inconvenience, more like, what with your mother having palpitations day and night for fear you'd be killed. Only right I should get some good of you now.

"Mayhew!" he shouted. "Mayhew, send for the carriage. I'm ready to go."

"A moment, Father." Dauntry stood, shoulders squared, chin firmed. "If I agree to stay, I want a free hand."

"Anything, m'boy. I'll even increase your allowance. Just chase her off, whatever she is."

"That includes any necessary changes or expenditures. I want Nace given instructions to that effect before you leave. I can't have him referring to you constantly if I'm to accomplish anything, or Mayhew or Mrs. Ford, either."

"Y'can empty the attics. Y'can tear down that tower I had put up a couple years back t'give us some dignity. Y'can even redecorate the place if y'think it'll help," his father wheedled. "Wall up those old passages. Change our bedchambers about. Tear out your grandmother's roses. Selena thinks that's where she's hiding—the tower, y'understand, or Merlin's grotto, not the attics—and only comes to the house when she's bored or it rains. Your mother thinks it's the roses, and it's not the girl in white at all. She thinks it's m'mother come back to devil her. Utter nonsense, that last, of course. Tower's not such a dotty notion, though, if one gives the matter a thought or two. Just the sort of place a ghost'd find congenial."

"I see." That was as much as Dauntry could manage without choking on the words. "You don't fear it'll be considered craven—your leaving like this?"

"Craven? Not a bit of it! Sensible, more like."

Despite an occasional quibble, Harald Dauntry formally affirmed before the senior staff and his bailiff that his younger son was to have *carte blanche*.

If the boy were so foolish as to insist on staying at the house, that was his affair.

If he didn't believe summoning the vicar was the best course, that was his affair, too.

He could make any changes, incur any expenses. No need to send to Brighton for permission. The important thing was to rid Combermere of the girl in white, no matter what it took, and no matter who or what she was.

His lordship, chest puffed out, tone blustering, gave his library a last, wary glance and lumbered from the oak-paneled room, leaning heavily on Dauntry's arm. It took some doing and several false starts, but at last they got him ensconced in the carriage, his luggage loaded in the boot and lashed to the roof, his valet settled across from him. The coachman seized the reins as an armed groom leapt onto the box and two more fell in behind, mounted on sturdy cobs. They were off.

Shoulders slumping, Dauntry headed for the columned portico, trailed by the household staff. Blast the silly upheaval when one of the family departed for somewhere. Blast the girl in white, whoever she was. Blast being torn from the routines he'd constructed for himself since selling out. How he'd bear this sort of nonsense the rest of his life he had no notion. Escaping to the Colonies held more appeal than ever, if only he could come up with passage money and enough extra to tide him over until he found employment of some sort.

"Quintus!"

He turned. His father leaned from the carriage as he hurled his garland to the drive.

"Put that 'round your neck!" his lordship shouted over clopping hooves and creaking wheels. "I remember my grandfather's tales. Ware your back!"

And then he was truly gone, the carriage raising a cloud of dust as it rumbled down the drive and disappeared into the park.

Dauntry retrieved the garland and tossed it to Mayhew as they entered the house. "Tell Mrs. Ford to get rid of this. Have the rest of the mess cleared away, and any rooms my father protected aired. This place will be back to normal before anyone goes to bed tonight. Once that's begun, I want you in the library." There was as much menace as good humor in his smile. "Something doesn't ring true," he muttered as he strode across the rotunda. "I'm just not sure what."

Mayhew was there by the time he'd stuck the Bibles back in

their cases. The new footman followed close on his heels, toting a pitcher and a platter of sandwiches. The fellow made a ceremony of pouring Dauntry a tankard of ale, handed him a napkin and plate, then presented the sandwiches. Dauntry gave the fellow a courteous thank-you that he knew would gain him another ally in the household, then watched as he gathered up the library's unaccustomed decorations and stomped off, broad shoulders straining his livery.

Stifling a grin, Dauntry turned to Mayhew once the door closed.

"That's quite the raw recruit. What's your nephew's name, old friend?"

"Alphonse," Mayhew murmured, eyes fixed on the middle distance.

"Not the one my mother assigned him. His real one."

"Nick, sir. Nicholas Beetle."

"Nick could do with felt soles, I believe."

"Not until he enters a room so quiet God Himself couldn't hear him, begging your pardon, sir. Felt's earned where I'm in charge."

"God might understand a certain assertiveness when heel meets floor. I doubt my mother or sister-in-law do."

"Naturally not. Don't permit the lad abovestairs when the ladies're in residence. Meantime, he learns his duties where he's no bother to anyone, and relieves the others of tasks they consider beneath them."

"I see. No problem, then, so long as his lordship doesn't object?"

"None, sir. If that will be all?"

Mayhew eased toward the doors, clearly anxious to escape. Dauntry's grin faded.

"You bloody well know it's not, Mayhew. What's been going on here?"

Did Mayhew's gaze flick to a particular spot on the carved paneling surrounding the fireplace? Dauntry couldn't be sure, but he suspected it had, if only for a moment. The fellow looked almost guilty. Amazing.

"The girl in white has reappeared, sir, just as your father informed you."

Dauntry snorted, picked up a sandwich, took a bite and chewed, one brow soaring.

"It's true." Mayhew's hands twitched, then stilled. "Several of the maids've seen her. Even Mrs. Ford and I've heard her wailing. Most disconcerting, happening as it does in the middle of the night, waking one from a sound sleep, and making one think one's descended into hell."

"Yes, I imagine it must be off putting. Well, why?"

"Sir?"

"Why's she come back after all these years—not that I believe there's a girl in white, or ever was. You must have some notion what's caused it."

"I'm afraid not, sir."

Mayhew shifted his bulk as Dauntry speared him with a steady gaze and consumed sandwich after sandwich. Not another word did the man say. Apparently the tricks that had served in the Peninsula were useless in a place where one'd been known to slip frogs in tutors' pockets and tadpoles in the ewers of visiting dandies.

"How'd my father happen on the notion of sending for me?" Dauntry said at last. "Not that he hasn't done it before, but this isn't that sort of situation."

"I suggested it, sir—after consulting with Mr. Potts, Mrs. Ford, and Mr. Nace—when his lordship appeared puzzled as to how best to proceed."

"At his wits' end, was he? But, why me? I haven't been here in years, and have no notion how you all go on. This is sure to do with some petty domestic disturbance."

Mayhew glanced away. "You've always had uncommon sense, sir," he said on a strangled note, "if you'll pardon my being so forward—raids on Cook's larder and a predilection for appearing in odd crannies at odd moments aside. And then, you're a military gentleman. Military gentlemen have a reputation for solving problems with expedition. We felt that was needed, and I was deputized to propose you be summoned to take charge."

"I see." Dauntry sighed and set his plate aside. "Well, that's all true enough, I suppose—odd crannies and larder raids aside. See here, what d'you want me t'do? I've no desire to linger longer than I must, and I doubt my father'll be pleased if he's forced to stay in Brighton above a week or two. Expensive place, Brighton. One or another of them's sure to tumble into the briars."

"We have every confidence you'll do what's needed, sir, once you determine what that is. In the interim, if I may be so bold, there's those hereabouts who remember you with fondness, and'll be glad to find you in residence again. I doubt you'll lack for distractions or entertainments."

Some time later—the ache in his leg eased by a bath, his spirits restored by fresh clothes and the warm smiles with which he was greeted wherever he turned—Dauntry wandered through the library, across the terrace, and down the broad marble steps to the gardens, intending to walk out the lingering stiffness.

It had been these scents and sounds to which he'd clung as the surgeon dug the ball from his leg after Salamanca, and the memory of his grandmother's roses, glowing like jewels against the yew maze in which he'd tormented Duncan as a boy. Pull out those roses to placate the girl in white? Not bloody likely. His mother might try to seize on the event to rid herself of despised reminders of the mother-in-law with whom she'd constantly brangled. His father, for all his faults, had foiled her in the past. Dauntry would foil her now.

He circled the maze, following the path to the sundial and fountain banked with still more roses. There, surrounded by his "ladies," was another touch of the familiar.

"Afternoon, Mr. Heater," Dauntry called.

"Hisself's come back, my lovely, just like they said," the crabbed gardener crooned to a glowing pink bloom. "See him standing there? That's Master Quintus Dauntry hisself, what doesn't think Combermere good enough for him, and never visits his old friends anymore. 'Member him well, if you think on it. Cut off all your buds when he was but six years old, the scamp, and give 'em to old Potts's youngest acause he thought she was pretty."

"You still prefer the conversation of flowers to that of mere mortals, I see," Dauntry chuckled.

"Y'never talk back, do you, my bonnies? Course you don't, and course I do. Roses got a deal more sense'n people, an' a deal more couth. Roses know their place, and don't stray from it."

Heater cropped an overblown blossom, revealing a tender bud behind, the first touches of crimson showing at bright green seams that would soon burst. As the petals unfurled, the red would fade to pink. Dauntry remembered the bush well, and the swift retribution for plundering it. Like Heater, it was more gnarled than ever.

"How're the rheumatics?"

"An' he's still asking witless questions, just like he always did. Not changed in the least, for all he's grown so tall and proud, and calls hisself a man. Even a fool'd know rheumatics don't trouble this time o' year, 'cept when it comes on to rain."

"Glad to hear it."

"Got a bit of a limp, though, he does. Can hear it in his step." The old gardener turned, eyeing Dauntry directly for the first time. "Y'all right, lad? They said as how you was hurt sore bad over there."

"I'll do."

"Wonder Potts ain't told him he's got a concoction what works wonders for men as well as cattle," Heater muttered, turning back to his roses. "Think maybe he should ask for some? Might be just the ticket to set him to rights."

"I will. My thanks for mentioning it. I wonder," Dauntry said, turning to address a bush of heavy-headed yellow blooms just reaching their peak, "if Mr. Heater knows anything about the girl in white. D'you think he does? Perhaps we should ask him."

"That'd be telling, wouldn't it?" Heater snipped away at more blooms past their prime. "There's things as we're meant to be told, and there's things as we're meant to tell. Then there's things we're meant to learn for ourselves. Don't it seem t'you that's something hisself should be learning for hisself, rather'n asking others to take him by the leading strings an' show him where to walk safe?"

"Perhaps he should, at that," Dauntry agreed, "not that he

won't go on asking questions. That's why his father had him
come—to ask questions."

"Sure and enough, his father asked questions. Asked a mort
of 'em. Didn't do a bit o' good. It's not questions what's wanted.
It's being about and doing. Been a dearth of being about and
doing in these parts of late, hasn't there, my lovelies?"

Heater clipped a last faded rose, dropped it in the basket at his
feet, and stomped off. After a moment Dauntry retrieved the basket and followed toward the greenhouses, just as he had as a boy.

That night, after a dinner fit for a returning prodigal, Quintus
Dauntry settled at his father's desk in the library, gave it a bit of
thought, and took pen in hand.

Dear Pugs—he began, gave it some more thought, then
added—*and all, including Amelia*—as Amelia Peasebottom had become an unofficial member of North's Irregulars following her marriage to Val North only weeks
before.

You've lost your wager—he continued—*you would
never have come up with this one. I've been summoned
to banish Combermere's resident ghost. The place was
littered with crucifixes and garlic when I arrived—all removed once my father decamped for Brighton to join the
rest of the family, who had run off in fear of their lives.*

*I'm convinced Potts (our head groom), Nace (my fa-
ther's bailiff), Mayhew (who's butlered here since time
immemorial), and possibly Heater (my grandmother's old
gardener), know a deal more than they're saying. I did
my best to loosen Potts's tongue this evening, but neither
brandy nor stern looks were the least use.*

*Likeliest culprit is a hoyden I encountered on the road
just before arriving. She's of an age for such pranks, and
has precisely the character. Snaffling her's another matter, especially if the staff's cheering her on while looking
the other way.*

*In sum, I appear to be trapped for a fortnight at the
least, depending on what—and who—lies at the bottom*

*of this. My apologies for any inconvenience to you and
the fellows, and my respects to your mother.*

*Also, my respects to everyone at Hillcrest, including
Lady Katherine, and a pat on the head for Val's wards.
With any luck they aren't driving you all entirely to dis-
traction.*

*If you haven't already, please give Lady Katherine and
Amelia my apologies for not taking proper leave of them
before haring off.*

That duty seen to, he settled in a comfortable chair and waited
far into the night for the girl in white to appear. She never did.

Two

"Dear merciful heaven—Master Quint?"

Quintus Dauntry glanced over his shoulder. The slender woman in faded cotton hiding beneath a deep-brimmed, chip straw bonnet might be a stranger, but not plump Mavis Twitchell, a pair of baskets set in the dust at her feet.

One did not forget someone who had grilled fat trout one caught with one's hands in the squire's stream, the excuse for such a lark being that one adventured with the squire's only son. Such splendid meals those had been, spiced with laughter and sunshine, when he, Harry Twitchell, Geoff Cairns, and Josh Burchett appeared at the inn kitchens, their treasures nestled in cress to keep them fresh.

He had envied Harry his mother in those days. Given the fool's errand on which he had just been summoned to Combermere, he still envied Harry. Harry had employment. Harry had sensible parents. Harry had a soul to call his own, a home, and a future.

The noon sun hot on his shoulders, the breeze ruffling his dark hair as he doffed his hat, Dauntry quitted the back of the chestnut he had selected from his father's stables. The stranger curtseyed, features still hidden by her bonnet, and scurried off, either painfully shy or not wishing to intrude on the reunion. He watched her for a moment, frowning in puzzlement, then held out his arms, reins in his gloved hand.

"Mrs. Twitchell, you're blooming."

He gave the innkeeper's wife a hug reminiscent of his boyhood, ignoring her babble as he buckled her baskets on either side of the saddle. Then, tucking her hand in the crook of his arm, leading Argus, he set off toward The Garter.

"How's Mr. Twitchell been keeping himself?" he said, cutting through her effusions. "Still as ready with a joke as ever?"

"You haven't heard, then."

Bloody hell. His heart sank. Yes, he'd known there'd be changes in Coombe, just as there had at Combermere. Not that one, though. "No, no one informed me. Don't know much about what's been happening here since my grandmother died. He was a fine man. When? How?"

"Two years ago this spring. Heart gave out. Wasn't as if we'd had no warning, for we had. I'm not complaining, mind, though I do miss him something fierce."

She took a breath, then smiled, eyes a touch overbright. "Harry and I're doing well. He'd already taken over the inn. His father insisted, as we knew what was coming. Married Joan Croft from Bittersfield just afore himself died. Lived to see that, at least. Joan's as tall and thin as Harry's short and stout. A widow bit older than he is, and a blessing she's been. Has a boy, Peter, kept us lively through the bad times, and they've a girl of their own now, Heather. Still in leading strings, but she's bright as a new penny."

"You're a grandmother?"

"Twice over, for I make no difference between the pair. Fair worships our Harry, Peter does. Already helps about the place, and feels he's quite the little man. Harry's the only father Peter's known, for his own died of the typhus just afore he was born, and he may be the only son Harry'll have. Joan's lost two, poor thing, and'll never see the sunny side of thirty again."

"Then thank heaven for Peter." Harry Twitchell, snared in parson's mousetrap and with a stepson who, from the sound of it, was older than they'd been when they started roaming the woods together? Not even Val North's recent marriage had been so disorienting. At least he'd met Amelia Peasebottom before the fact, and watched Val tumble top-over-tail with not a little amusement. "How's Polly?"

"Waited for Geoff Cairns to come to his senses, just as she swore she would, and turned down many a fine offer while she did." Mavis Twitchell grinned. "Our Polly and Geoff'll be married after harvest. Has his own carting business, and is doing right well."

"Good for him. Polly used to follow Geoff like a foal its dam. We couldn't imagine how he bore it."

"Geoff was the oldest of you lads. Three years makes a deal of difference at that age. All of you spoken for, yourself excepted—and poor Josh Burchett, of course. Pity about him, but there it is. Always had more bottom than sense, Josh did."

"It wasn't Josh lacked for sense, but my brother—and I for not managing to stop it."

"Fiddlesticks! Didn't wash then. Doesn't wash now."

He'd heard that tone at the time: from Mavis Twitchell, from the former vicar, from his grandmother, from Great-aunt Persephone, from his cronies, even from the squire and Mrs. Burchett. He'd never agreed. No wonder he'd avoided Coombe once he was able. A place where one had been a lad held layer upon layer of experience. Not all those experiences could be happy ones.

At Mavis Twitchell's sudden tug on his sleeve, he glanced down.

"Stop gathering wool. Doesn't do a bit of good, 'specially when it's dyed black," she snapped as if he were still a lad of fourteen rather than a man of twenty-eight. "And yourself—any young lady got you dancing? You're of an age for it, and then some."

"No, I'm heart free, and careful to remain so." He shrugged. "Nothing to offer a lady, nor females of the other sort, either."

"A strapping fellow like you, with a touch of the devil peeking out of his black eyes and an angel in his heart? Nonsense!" The lecture trembling on her tongue evaporated at his sharp glance. "Y'need feeding, though. Got the look of a Gypsy. Cheeks're hollowed, and your nose's like a beak," she scolded instead. "Nothing but muscle and bone. I suppose being wounded does that. How d'you find things at the great house?"

"The gardens're much the same, and the people."

"Keeping your father company, are you?"

"No, his lordship left for Brighton yesterday. I'm surprised you hadn't heard, given the way news travels here."

"Didn't know you'd come, let alone he was gone. Not as much

traffic between great house and village as there was in your grandmother's day." Mavis Twitchell's snort was as telling as her expression. Then she gave an unexpected girlish giggle. "So— she chased his lordship off as well, and you've been called in to learn what's to do? Not a bad notion."

"Some traffic, then."

"The girl in white? Yes, we heard. Hard not to, what with your brother pounding on the vicar's door in the middle of the night, making enough noise to wake the dead. Started by ringing the church bells. We thought there was a fire at first, and more likely the Day of Judgment on us."

"The bells? I know you wouldn't joke about such a thing."

"Master Duncan was always excitable when his moods hit. Insisted the vicar go and say some prayers so her ladyship and young Mrs. Dauntry'd return to their beds."

"Now, I wonder why that doesn't surprise me."

"Acause of your father's suggesting you try the same thing, knowing him. Once his lordship takes a notion in his head, he don't let go of it easy. Sometimes that's a good thing. Sometimes it isn't. Having you come, now that's a good thing."

"Perhaps, perhaps not. Then what? I presume there's more, given my brother."

Mavis Twitchell broke into laughter, though there was an edge to it.

"Nothing'd do but they go where the poor girl's supposed to be buried, for all it'd come on to rain, and that Mr. Gardener say more prayers. Still had him at it when the sun come up, with them all snug in the carriage and him without so much as an umbrella, and looking like death for days acause the rain begun in the middle of the night and he wasn't dressed for it, for neither his lordship nor your brother thought to offer him the carriage when he was done, and he had to walk back to the village. Three miles and more in the wet? Shameful! Took to their beds without so much as a word of thanks, or a penny for the poor box, either."

"Why didn't—Mr. Gardener, you say—take his gig?"

"Hasn't got one."

"But Mr. Killmartin always kept a—"

"Mr. Gardener don't."

Dauntry paused, gazing toward the church at the other end of the village. The roof barely peeped above the trees, but there appeared to be more than a few slates missing. "How does he go about his parish rounds? The neighborhood's extensive."

"Lines his boots with pasteboard, and pushes a barrow with anything he has to distribute. Claims it's healthful, and misses nary a one he should call on, no matter what the weather. Not your fault by any stretch—though 'twouldn't've been this way had you stopped more often the way her ladyship intended when she left you Three Rivers Farm."

His frown had her eyes snapping. The entire village knew he'd ceded Three Rivers to Duncan at their father's insistence. Duncan'd thrown a tantrum that lasted for days when he realized their grandmother'd left him only a few trinkets and a thousand pounds, while the valuable property he'd anticipated owning had gone to his younger brother. In recompense, their father purchased Dauntry his colors, and eventually his promotions, except for the last one—a *quid pro quo* whose brief delay was intended to make the arrangement seem less like a bribe, and lasted only six years in any case. Everyone probably knew he'd returned the price of his commission to his father after he sold out, as well. Things got about in places like Coombe.

"Gone to ruin in your brother's hands," she nattered. "Turned the tenants off. Uses the place for hunting. Gamekeeper lives in the house, the fields lie fallow, and the barns're a disgrace. Pity, but there's no help for it, I suppose."

"No, there's no help for it."

She paused to hand horehound drops to a pair of ragamuffins driving a flock of geese toward the village pond. As he had long ago, the boys suffered tousled hair to garner the treat. Then, as Argus tossed his head and jibbed at the bit, they scampered off.

"That was Peter," she said. "The littler one with yellow hair. You'll meet him, but today I want you to myself. Besides, too many explanations needed. You've become a legend, for the lads've credited you with every prank any of you ever pulled."

"Dear heaven," he muttered as they started toward the inn once more, Argus—after one last snort in the direction of the routed geese—prancing at his side.

"Point is, Mr. Gardener's a fine gentleman, and his sister's his equal. That was her I was chatting with—Cecelia Walters. Mrs. Walters, that is. Widow lady with a small lad, just like our Joan. Tragedy of some sort there, though no one's sure what, for they're that closemouthed about it. Joined her brother shortly after her ladyship died, which is why you aren't acquainted."

"I see."

"Keeps to herself, though she rides gooseberry between him and Miss Burchett often enough, and does her duty by the parish. Sad case, that. Squire's offered to frank 'em, but Mr. Gardener won't hear of it. You haven't forgotten Rebecca Burchett, I'm sure? Josh Burchett's sister. Golden-haired moppet, more determination in her little finger than most men have in their entire selves, and a bundle of mischief when she took it in mind to be. Grown to a fine young woman. Make an excellent vicar's wife."

"She always cleaned her own fish," Dauntry murmured, remembering.

"Still does, in a manner of speaking, and never a word of complaint if they aren't as fresh or easy to clean as she might like."

"So little Becky Burchett's enamored of the new vicar?"

"And he of her, but he won't cast his sister off—not that Miss Burchett'd hear of it, for she's that fond of Mrs. Walters—and Mrs. Walters's penniless for all her husband's supposed to've had grand London connections. Not new, though—the vicar, I mean—unless you're a stickler, and anyone not born here's new 'til the day they die. Been at St. Martin's eight years and more."

"Oh yes, of course." He glanced over his shoulder in the direction of the church as they entered the inn yard. There definitely were slates missing from the roof. "The living supported a family of five and three servants when my grandmother was alive."

"Doesn't now. There's a war, in case you hadn't heard, and things're dear. That precious living your father controls might keep one person from starving these days. Three, and one of those a growing boy? A pure disgrace, it is. The village helps as best it can, but most times what's given Mr. Gardener he passes on to those in even worse case. Asides, the Killmartins had other income. Mr. Gardener don't."

He thought of the improvements his father'd made at Combermere. Then he considered Gardener, the church, and the vicarage. No wonder the girl in white had reappeared. The only question was why she'd been so long about it.

Mavis Twitchell guided him toward the back of the inn. "You'll stop, won't you? Harry'll be that pleased to see you. Been maundering about how you should be sent for—not that he'd've presumed to do it, but the thought was there."

He nodded, handing Argus's reins to a stableboy he didn't recognize, then unbuckled the baskets.

"There's nothing I'd like more. Any visitors in the neighborhood?" he said, thinking of the hoyden he'd encountered the day before—the most likely candidate he'd uncovered for the high jinks at Combermere.

"Not a soul," she replied.

Clouds scudded across the afternoon sky by the time Dauntry arrived at the vicarage. Three hours guiding village gossip at The Duke's Garter had only partly prepared him. Banishing a scowl that threatened to become permanent, he grinned at the solemn, freckle-faced lad who responded to his knock on the weather-beaten door.

"Master Walters, I presume?"

Candid eyes the hue of flawed emeralds met his, only partly masked by carroty hair tumbling over the boy's brow. "Sir?"

"Quintus Dauntry, at your service. I've come to call on your uncle, if that doesn't pose an inconvenience."

Young Walters cocked his head, eyes widening. The assessing gaze would've done Wellington proud, though the triumph lurking behind it would've confused even him.

"Mr. Gardener's in, I presume?"

The vicar's nephew nodded, the glow in his eyes lingering as he thrust a tattered Latin grammar higher under his arm, then seemed to collect himself.

"Yes, sir. If you'll follow me?"

The little house was as immaculate as Dauntry remembered it, but a glance proved that the hand of time had pressed on it as heavily indoors as out since he last called, following the death of his grandmother. Frown once more in place, he trailed the slender lad across the entry and down the narrow hall to the study, noting crudely repaired spindles on the stairs, and floorboards that shifted beneath his feet.

He pretended to ignore the stained walls as a tall, angular man unpleated himself from behind a table strewn with schoolbooks.

"Mr. Quintus Dauntry to see you, Uncle Robert."

Keen, brown eyes assessed him as carefully as alert green ones had moments before. Dauntry did his best to come up with a disarming smile as he strode over to the table, extending his hand.

"Vicar, a pleasure to see you."

"Mr. Dauntry." The other's grip was firm and dry. "The pleasure and honor are mine. How may I be of service?"

"I need counsel, that's certain, though it's hardly a spiritual matter unless we stretch the point farther than such points should be stretched." Dauntry glanced from the scarred table with its welter of papers and books to the vicar. "It appears I've arrived inopportunely, however."

"Nonsense. Thomas'll be glad of the liberty. The subjunctive grows dull when God's Creation sings its siren song, doesn't it, my boy?"

Thomas's grin transformed the youthful scholar into the urchin he doubtless was. "Too right, Uncle, and declining nouns is its equal."

"Not too far afield," Gardener cautioned as the boy set his grammar on the table, marking the place. "Your mother'll want your help when she returns, for we'll be having an early supper."

Thomas Walters nodded, then turned and gave Dauntry a punctilious little bow. "It's an honor to have you in Coombe, sir. You've been both missed and needed."

Then, coloring at his temerity, he fled his uncle's book-lined study.

"You'll forgive Thomas, of course." The vicar's eyes twinkled as he pointed to a pair of much-worn wooden chairs flanking a window at which mended cotton curtains stirred like wraiths in the breeze. "Anyone who's battled the Corsican is a hero in his eyes, and thus capable of performing miracles."

"A hero?" Dauntry snorted. "Not I. Say rather continually exhausted, often bored, and occasionally terrified. Also, generally speaking, ill from one cause or another. There're few who understand what goes on over there, or care, so long as their comforts aren't encroached upon by the exigencies of war."

"Lengths of silk and casks of brandy counting for more than victories? Yes." Gardener sighed as they sat. "I know. A disgrace. Well, how may I help?"

Dauntry stared at his hands, commanding them to lie still on his knees. Fidgeting was the mark of a johnny raw. He was blessed if he'd give the vicar the satisfaction—not that he expected the man to laugh at him outright, but he'd come on the most preposterous of errands.

"You know about the recent to-do at the great house, of course."

"The girl in white?"

"Yes, none better, according to Mavis Twitchell. I do apologize for my brother's importuning you at such an hour, and on such an errand."

"He was, ah, distraught."

The vicar's eyes were twinkling again.

"Distraught? Wonderful word. Yes, I suppose you could say he was. Behaving like a blithering idiot, is more like it." Dauntry leaned back, wincing as the seat's edge cut the old wound on his thigh. "I've been summoned to straighten things out. You know—make an investigation, chase whoever's responsible from the place. At least that's how I see it, though my father's requirements are a bit different. You were there close after the fact, so to speak. Any reconnaissance possible?"

"Hardly." Now the vicar was chuckling openly. "Nothing would do but we go directly to the woods once I'd prattled a bit to reassure the ladies. Then it came on to rain—a most uncomfortable affair. Rather akin to what you suffered in the Peninsula, I imagine. Soldiers for Christ also have their less comfortable moments."

"I imagine they do, here at least. So you didn't see her?"

"The girl in white? Not a glimpse."

"I suspected as much." Dauntry grimaced. Thus vanished the

sole potentially rational witness. "Still, you must've reached some sort of conclusions."

Gardener's expression became guarded. "In such situations, I generally espouse the more prosaic," he said.

"Which, in this case, would be a surfeit of buttered crab perhaps past its prime followed by too much trifle, a superabundance of sweetmeats, and a laudanum-laced composer to end the evening."

"Something along those lines—meaning no disrespect to Lady Dauntry or Mrs. Dauntry. They were genuinely terrified, and there's no question in my mind but what they were intended to be so. A most unfortunate affair. I was only too glad to do what I could to reassure them."

"A servant with a grudge?"

"That was my conclusion—not that I voiced it. Or a prank. It's summer. The sprigs in these parts are restless. That's equally possible."

Dauntry nodded, then rose, pacing the room where he'd spent many a challenging hour playing chess with old Horace Killmartin, lured by Mrs. Killmartin's superior lemonade and the Killmartins' mellifluous-voiced and unattainable eldest daughter—elegant nineteen saw bumbling fourteen as an insect to be avoided, and bumbling fourteen viewed elegant nineteen as the *sine qua non* of female perfection. For a miracle, no one ever guessed what truly drew him there. At least, he hoped they hadn't. All that had ended when Josh Burchett was killed, of course.

The stained walls, betraying a roof in desperate need of repair, depressed him. So did the absence of the bright Axminster carpet that used to grace the floor. There was no excuse for it, any more than there was a reasonable explanation for the absence of the other furnishings that came with the living, or the slates missing from the church roof.

Dauntry turned to Gardener. "Where's the desk?"

"This table is ideal for composing sermons—more than enough room for as many references as I care to consult—and Thomas would inform you it's a wonderful place to construct kites. Much more practical than a desk."

"You don't say? And I'd swear these chairs used to be in the kitchen."

"Straight backs and hard seats are far more conducive to intellectual endeavor than softer ones. Discourage napping, you see. Make one more efficient."

"An ascetic? I hadn't thought that of you. Who's got the ones that used to be here?"

Gardener hesitated, coloring about the ears.

"Come now, where are they?"

"Something was mentioned regarding the servants' quarters at the great house. It was necessary to hire more staff when Mr. Dauntry wed."

"Even the desk?"

"I believe so. We're perfectly comfortable. You mustn't concern yourself."

"We'll see about that," Dauntry muttered.

Even the pious engravings he'd found oppressive as a lad were gone, pale rectangles marking where they'd once hung. Of course those might've belonged to the Killmartins, but he didn't believe so. He seemed to remember them when he'd called following his grandmother's death. More likely Gardener had taken them down for safekeeping when the roof began to leak.

Well, time to come to the main point—though he suspected the two might in some way be linked. Certainly he intended to pretend they were when he wrote his father. "I presume you find the notion of an exorcism as ludicrous as I do."

"Naturally. Whoever the girl in white may be, I'm convinced she—or he—is mundanely corporeal. It's only the apparition's purpose that puzzles me, unless mischief's all that's intended."

"I'll get to the bottom of it, that I promise." Dauntry forced a grin, returned to the chair across from Gardener, and eased his wounded leg over the other. "When I do, you'll be the first to know."

"You'll not be too hard on whoever it is, I hope?"

"More likely to reward 'em." Dauntry shook his head at Gardener's questioning look. "No, I'm not going to explain myself—at least not yet. Tell me how things are in the neighborhood. It's been years since my last visit."

"Times are hard for some," Gardener said, echoing Mavis Twitchell.

"So it would appear. How do Squire Burchett and his wife go on? I remember them with particular fondness. And their daughter—Hepzibah, Hesther, something biblical of that sort."

"Rebecca—Rebecca Burchett. A lovely young lady." Gardener flushed at the reference. "The squire and Mrs. Burchett are thriving."

"Rebecca, too?"

"Miss Burchett does well, yes."

"Glad to hear it. Always chose her own path, and never complained if there were brambles along the way. Admirable in a chit. Beyond price in a woman—if she's continued as she began."

"She has."

Amazing that a gentleman five years his senior—a supposedly staid vicar, no less—would color up like a mooncalf. One could hardly term Gardener bloodless. For what it was worth, Dauntry approved. Still, as soon as the opportunity offered he'd learn for himself how Becky Burchett regarded her clerical swain. She was Josh's little sister. That placed a certain responsibility on his shoulders.

The sun was tickling the treetops by the time Dauntry took his leave, for their conversation turned general and animated after his perhaps not so subtle interrogation regarding Rebecca Burchett. Gardener had proved an amusing companion with a keen eye for the human condition and an understanding far above the ordinary. Coombe was fortunate in its new vicar—something Dauntry had suspected when he encountered the man briefly at the time of the dowager viscountess's death. It wouldn't be just a duty to regularize matters at vicarage and church. It would be a pleasure.

He let himself out, claiming previous acquaintance obviated any need for ceremony.

The vicar's nephew had returned from his adventures disheveled and flushed, and was lingering on the verge conversing with Argus. Dauntry paused, watching. Either the lad had encountered the chestnut before, or he had a way with superior cattle. Perhaps both. Given the gentle whuffling to which Argus was subjecting the lad's carroty hair, the powerful animal was as taken with Master Walters as the lad was with *him*. Interesting.

"Friends, I see," Dauntry said, striding up with a trace of a limp.

The boy spun, hand still tangled in Argus's mane, eyes glowing. "He's a fine one, sir. Carry you day and night, and never flag."

"He would that."

And so was Thomas Walters a fine one, unless Dauntry had lost his ability to judge youthful sprigs. He didn't believe he had.

He eyed the boy as carefully as he'd been inspected earlier. *Wiry but strong* was his assessment, *and agile*—with a certain kinship to the tough little drummer boys who survived a forced march wearied but unflagging, and needed only a bite of supper and a word of praise to set them caracoling.

Creative, at a guess. Only children usually were, fashioning imaginary playmates with whom to explore the world because the adults in their circle were too preoccupied to join in the fun, or else had forgotten how.

And as fearless as he was active—witness the jagged scar on the boy's cheek. An old one, by the look of it, fading but still visible, especially against the sun flush of an afternoon ramble.

"One of the best in my father's stables," Dauntry continued, "though not the showiest. Showiest isn't necessarily best, in horses or in people."

He hoped he didn't sound too pompous, but the lad seemed to understand, for he gave a sunny grin, then unlooped Argus's reins.

"Good thing you're going home for supper. Wouldn't've been enough, no matter what Uncle said or Mama did, and I know he must've asked you to stay."

"He did, but I suspected as much. Unexpected guests are the bane of every lady's existence."

"Wouldn't've mattered if you'd been expected or not, unless Uncle'd given me the whole day, and I caught more trout than I've ever caught before. You enjoy your visit?"

"I did that. A fine gentleman, your uncle."

"The finest. So's Mama—the finest lady, I mean. Prettiest there ever was, too, and she sings like a lark, and even makes that old pianoforte in the parlor sound like it was Mozart's own. You'll see. Course, Miss Burchett's nice. She's showed me where the sweetest raspberries grow, and she knows the name of every bird God made. She can recognize them, too, and even whistle like some of them. And the squire and Mrs. Burchett're top-of-the-trees. Always making too much for dinner and sending it over, but not so often it's an insult. That's when you ought to stay— when the Burchetts send things over. There's usually enough then, unless someone's come asking Uncle for help. When that happens he gives it all away instead of just most of it."

The boy started to lead Argus toward a crude mounting block.

"It's all right. I can manage," Dauntry said behind him.

"You're sure, sir? I know you were wounded in the leg over there. Mercury would've hobbled about like Vulcan if he'd had to sit in one of those chairs, and I doubt Uncle took you in the parlor as his study's more private, given it's off by itself and hasn't anything above it. Course the roof leaks something fierce, but one can't have everything. Mama saves the parlor for best. We live mostly in the kitchen, especially in winter. It's cozier, and it doesn't leak as much except around the door."

"I imagine it is cozier."

Dauntry took the reins and clambered gracelessly into the saddle, white-lipped by the time he had himself settled. The lad was more right than he knew. The chair's assault on his leg had set him back again. He'd have to ask Potts for some of his concoction.

"What do you think of Coombe?" he said, forcing a smile over clenched teeth.

"Everybody likes Mama and Uncle, and so everybody's kind to me. I wouldn't want to live in a city, that's certain. They're dirty, they smell bad, and nasty people live there—ladies with mean eyes who talk sharp. Besides, I can't remember any place well but here—not really. Just scraps that don't mean much, and I don't like to ask. When I do, Uncle frowns and Mama looks sad. I don't like her looking sad."

"Understandable."

Dauntry's brows rose as he waited. Young Walters scrubbed his toe in the dust, glancing back at the vicarage, then along the lane. There was a determination to the set of his jaw incongruous in one so young.

"Things were better before. I know that much. And I know they'll be better again. We've just got to get through this part. Uncle says we're like Sisyphus, pushing our rocks up the hill. He says we're never to get discouraged, or give up. I think it's more like we're in the Slough of Despond, because they got through that, didn't they? But Sisyphus is still pushing his rock up the hill if the legends're true, so I'd rather this was the Slough of Despond."

"Couldn't agree with you more. I imagine you have the right of it, too, and it is the Slough you're slogging through, not toiling up Sisyphus's hill. Well, *buenos tardes,* sprout. If I don't return soon, they'll be sending out search parties."

"They do that for people as old as you?"

"Especially for people as old as I. Ware the snakes in the slough, sprout," he murmured, and set off for home.

A bit over half an hour later Dauntry, the abstracted scowl he'd sported since quitting the vicarage deeper than ever, slipped into the estate offices. Old Nace was hard at it, surrounded by stacks of crop and market reports. A pair of clerks labored over ledgers, legs tucked around their stools, shoulders hunched, pens scratching. It might have been any counting house in the City, complete to a fly buzzing among the rafters. Only the scent of roses spoiled the illusion, and the sound of cow bells.

Architect's plans lay on a worktable under an open window, most neatly rolled, one spread out, weights holding it at the corners. It appeared to be a scheme for extending and refurbishing Combermere's ballroom—which had been extended and refurbished only two years before.

One of the clerks, a youngish fellow with thinning hair, glanced up. When the ensuing confusion died down—the viscount never descended to the offices, preferring to summon his bailiff rather than seek him out—Dauntry strode over to the worktable trailed by Nace as the clerks returned to their high desks. A quick glance confirmed his suspicions. With a grunt of disgust, he rolled the thing up and put it with the others, then gestured at the uneven pyramid.

"More of the same?"

Nace nodded.

"Which rooms?"

"Drawing and reception rooms, and the wing housing Mr. and Mrs. Dauntry and their son."

"No expense to be spared, I assume, and a decorator imported from London to oversee the whole?"

"The ladies find the wallpapers no longer in the latest style, and the hangings and carpets to have faded beyond what is acceptable for a noble gentleman's country seat."

"How lowering. Nothing's been ordered, has it? No work's begun?"

"The appearance of the girl in white has delayed matters temporarily."

"Good. They'll be delayed a bit longer—at least a year or two. It's clear the girl in white doesn't approve their taste." The narrowed look he gave Nace was met by one so bland it almost had him laughing. "I'd like to see the estate books, if it wouldn't be too much trouble? The annual summaries'll do."

Mouth downturned, he scanned the pages, not so much searching for one particular item as struggling to satisfy himself it wasn't to be found. Only it was, thanks to Nace. The vicar's living had been reduced by first a third, then a half—ostensibly his share of reroofing the vicarage and church. Nace had been meticulous in detailing the viscount's purported intentions. He'd also been meticulous in assigning the uses to which the vicar's living and the funds customarily allocated to upkeep of vicarage and church had been put, among them Merlin's grotto.

Finally Dauntry slammed the heavy book closed in disgust. The clerks were gone by then, the sun sinking toward the horizon.

"It's clear the viscount has been distracted by the pressures of family life and affairs in Town," he said. "An oversight, I'm sure. Repairs to the vicarage and the church will begin Monday. If the roofs can't be repaired, have 'em replaced. I want the estate carpenter and crews of plasterers and painters, as well. I'll give you a list. The work at the vicarage's to be done a room at a time, to least inconvenience the family." He turned, glancing at Nace in the deepening gloom. "What became of the furnishings?"

"Her ladyship borrowed some, as she said Mr. Gardener was a bachelor, sir, and had no need of so much furniture."

"I see. To what purpose?"

"Servants' quarters, sir. And then your brother's gamekeeper wed, and had need of some things."

"Even the desk?"

"Mr. Dauntry insisted on furbishing tutor's quarters as soon as Master Bertram was born."

"It's in the schoolroom gathering dust?"

"Yes, sir."

"Bloody hell," Dauntry muttered. "What condition is it in?"

"Not good, sir. The vicarage roof had already been leaking for some time when Mr. Dauntry sent the stable lads to collect it."

"How long? No, don't tell me. I don't want to know. All right, then. Item, one desk, best to be found. Item, two chairs, two hassocks, a decent table, and a divan of some sort, all for the vicar's study. Highest quality, greatest comfort. Consult him. Say the instructions come from my father.

"The old pianoforte from the Killmartins' time is still there, I gather. Have it tuned, and place an order for sheet music. From what Tommy Walters claims, I assume the vicar's sister not only plays, but plays quite well. Be sure to get some of that German fellow's stuff. You know the one I mean—von Bay-something.

"In short, I want the place returned to its condition in my grandmother's day. I'll be conferring with Mrs. Burchett regarding any other refurbishing the place requires—draperies, household goods, and such—another gift from my father. I assume she and her daughter will be willing to assist Mrs. Walters in her selections, and will contrive not to let her know the cost."

The delighted sparkle in Nace's eyes had Dauntry grinning.

"The girl in white'll approve, don't you think?" he said.

"I'm sure of it," Nace replied, "and all the countryside into the bargain."

"Good. The vicar's to have his full living. All that'll be in your hands permanently. No need to trouble my father or brother about it. We'll have to devise a manner for Mr. Gardener to receive the arrears he's owed, as well. That'll take some thought, for both his pride and my father's must be considered. There'll be more.

"Now, let's quit this dreary room. I'd be grateful if you'd join me at table. I despise dining alone, and we've other things to see to for the vicarage, such as gifts of food, fruit from the succession houses for Mrs. Walters, and several bottles of wine and some good brandy for the vicar. My father's pre-war vintages. That'll require Mayhew's and Mrs. Ford's assistance."

Three

That night, pleased with his progress, Quintus Dauntry took pen in hand to inform his father he'd initiated the first steps to placate Combermere's troublesome ghost.

The girl in white was a proud creature conscious of tradition, he wrote tongue-in-cheek, and was sure to have been mortified by oversights regarding parish church and vicarage. While undoubtedly caused by demands on the familial purse engendered by the advent of Bertram, the vicar had need of the usual furnishings and his full living.

He'd taken steps. Both church and vicarage were receiving the repairs their dilapidation required. In addition, he'd seen Mrs. Ford about resuming the usual gifts of food—all this in Lord and Lady Dauntry's name. He'd arranged things, he said, so Nace and Mrs. Ford would be the active parties in the future, thus relieving lord and lady of onerous effort while ensuring all credit for beneficence was theirs.

He concluded by saying while he doubted these problems were the sum of the girl's quarrel with the family, they went far toward explaining her sudden reappearance after so many generations of circumspection. He'd see what eventuated, take further action as advisable, and report when necessary. In the interim, he sent his dutiful best wishes, hoped his mother and Selena were sufficiently recovered from their upset to enjoy the delights of Brighton, and that young Bertram was thriving on the sea air.

It was, he felt, a superior example of the epistolary art, saying neither too much nor too little and relying on his father's credulity to ensure neither church, vicarage, nor vicar ever again suffered neglect.

Infinitely pleased with himself, he sought his bed and waited for the girl in white to give him an approving moan. She proved uncooperative. At last he drifted off to dream of sheet-draped bailiffs, hoydens limping by the side of the road, and ginger-haired sprouts toting trout the size of whales, the whole inter-twined with conversations with roses that proved both loquacious and argumentative.

Two days passed, boring and eventless. On Sunday, putting himself together as best he could given he'd left most of his clothes at Danescroft, Dauntry presented himself at St. Martin the Lesser for morning prayer, his grandmother's admonitions regarding participation in communal gatherings echoing in his mind.

Horace Killmartin had been a soporific shepherd, as gentle as he was genial, and as convoluted in his homilies.

Gardener, by contrast, was impressively economical. No plati-tudinous exhortations culled from published sermons for this vicar, or incomprehensible ones of his own devising. He spoke instead of cathedrals formed by soaring beech, of feathered cho-risters whose hymns needed no words, of seasons of renewal and rebirth. And then, eyes pointedly trained on Dauntry, he spoke not of the prodigal's return as old Killmartin would've done, but of salmon struggling to reach ancestral headwaters.

When, at the end of it, Gardener recited the Doxology with fervent simplicity, the congregation rose as one, joining him softly at first, then at full voice.

During those moments Dauntry's gaze traveled from crudely patched pulpit to cracked altar rail, then to the boarded window above the baptismal font. Something would have to be done about those, as well.

Then it was over, the last prayers said, last hymns sung, the blessing given, and Dauntry was on the porch shaking Gardener's hand and being presented to the vicar's widowed sister. The voice was that of the hoyden he'd encountered near the Bittersfield fork, modulated by place and circumstance. It'd been her slight frame that fooled him. She seemed to have no recollection of him, thank God—probably the fact that he'd resembled a hedge-bird and sounded like a catarrhic crow.

The world turned unwelcome somersaults as his gaze met the clear, gray eyes lifted to his. He hushed her thanks for the baskets delivered from Combermere, then moved on, cursing under his breath. Val North's confusion when he first encountered Lady Amelia Peasebottom no longer seemed quite so amusing, nor his tumbling top over tail at the mere sound of a voice.

He had no notion of the color of Cecelia Walters's hair, the style of her gown, or how her features might be modeled. There'd been a willowy figure, cheeks that turned first pale and then rosy, a slender-fingered hand in his. She might be a beauty. She might be a platter-faced fright. Either way, she'd done for him.

"Damn," he muttered, staring past the lane where carriages and farm wagons waited, trying to drag his heart back from his boots, or his throat, or wherever that inconvenient organ had taken itself in the last few moments. "Oh, bloody hell!"

The worst of it was, he couldn't avoid her, not even until he had a chance to indulge in a stern lecture regarding impossibilities. He'd informed Mayhew he intended to invite the vicarage family to spend the day at Combermere. He'd even had the landau his mother used to drive guests about the park brought to the church. If he failed in the invitation, Mayhew might guess why. He couldn't have that.

With a low growl he stalked across the churchyard, pasting a smile on his features, answering warmhearted hails and pausing to exchange greetings and accept winking references to the girl in white and his father's departure like an automaton. At last he fetched up beneath the thick-leafed oak where he'd tethered Argus in the shade.

And he'd always been so punctilious about avoiding females, whether of good or ill repute, confound it. Well, it hadn't done him much good in the end, had it?

Society had very few unbreakable rules, so long as one broke them with circumspection. That a penniless, untitled, landless gentleman lacking either profession or prospects was never to wed, no matter how great the temptation, was one of those that couldn't be broken without sinking beneath contempt.

"Damn," he repeated.

Tommy Walters tugged on his sleeve. He glanced about. The churchyard had all but emptied while he stared at the oak's mossy trunk, cursing his father, Duncan, the girl in white, fate, and himself. The squire and Mrs. Burchett were striding up, followed by the vicar with Rebecca on one arm, Cecelia Walters on the other.

Dauntry gave Tommy a smile he prayed would pass muster. He beamed at the Burchetts, accepting the squire's hearty clap on his shoulder without demur. He bussed Mrs. Burchett's cheek. He bowed to the two younger ladies, doffing his hat and fixing his gaze on Rebecca.

"What, no sun-reddened nose or healing wounds?" The grin accompanying his words was so forced he thought his face would crack. "I'm amazed."

Rebecca blushed, blue eyes twinkling. "Only when Thomas and I go on one of our rambles. Then anything can happen. Beyond that, I try to pretend I'm a lady these days. It's time for it, don't you think?"

He tweaked one of the golden curls peeping from her bonnet. "Not too much of a lady, I hope."

"Let's say I scurry up the back stairs when I return."

"Berry stains?"

"Among other things. Brambles are attracted to me, or I to them, I've never been certain which. Sundays, however, I put my best foot forward."

Was that a trace of a frown on the vicar's brow? Ridiculous! Dauntry'd known Becky Burchett from the cradle, blast it. Her brother had been one of his closest boyhood friends. That permitted him a certain license, didn't it? Still, it wouldn't do to have Gardener believe him a poacher—or, worse yet, suspect himself of appropriating coverts belonging to another.

He turned to the vicar, employing the plural to what he hoped was good effect. "You must forgive us. If I didn't tease Becky, I doubt either of us would know how to go on." Was he sufficiently disarming? At least the vicar's look of displeasure was fading. "Becky's always stood in stead of the sister I never had. Josh deviled her as unmercifully as she plagued him. I do the same in his memory."

Gardener murmured something innocuous through thinned lips.

"You remember how it was, Robert."

Cecelia Walters was smiling at her brother, even giving him a saucy wink, by damn. And she wasn't a fright. Far from it. Hers might not be the features that launched a thousand ships, but they caused his breath to catch in his throat. Intelligence was there, and humor, and sweetness, and a lingering sorrow he longed to banish. So was the independence he'd witnessed near the Bittersfield fork.

"You couldn't bear to have me forever about," she pressed, "but if one of your chums commented on my outrageous larks, his nose was never the same."

"You're a devotee of the Fancy, Mr. Gardener?" Dauntry grinned. "I'd never've suspected a vicar of a taste for pugilism."

"Schoolboy fisticuffs—rather to the peril of my immortal soul."

Gardener's eyes were clearing, for all his expression remained guarded. Good.

"Don't be silly, Robert. You know perfectly well you saved every penny to attend Gentleman Jackson's salon when you were at school, and pleaded with Papa to take you. He did, too, and later you boasted you'd been told you had a punishing right."

"Afraid I was something of a heathen in those days."

"We'll have to go a round or two, then—when the ladies aren't there to faint at the sight of two gentlemen good-naturedly pummeling each other," Dauntry threw in, blessing Cecelia Walters for smoothing over what had promised to become a difficult situation. "Perhaps even this afternoon? We could use the gallery, or even a secluded spot in the gardens. I'd hoped you and Mrs. Walters—and your nephew, of course—would join me at Combermere for the day. Cook promises a dinner of splendid proportions in your honor, and a superior trifle in the lad's and mine."

"How kind," Cecelia murmured, "but I'm afraid—you see, customarily we—"

"We always go to the manor Sundays," Tommy broke in. "That's what Uncle likes, 'cause then he can spend the afternoon with Miss Burchett, only Mama and Uncle're embarrassed to tell you. Wish we could come, though." He paused, an odd look coming over his face. Then, frowning slightly, he said, "Playing gooseberry gets wearisome for Mama. At Combermere, it's Uncle would be *de trop*. Certainly it's his turn."

Then the graceless scamp spun to the squire's wife, ignoring his mother's agonized, *"Hush, Thomas."*

"I know!" Tommy caroled. "Why doesn't Mr. Dauntry come to Beechy Knoll? Then *I* could play gooseberry, for Mama'll need one too. You always have extra, and eating alone is the worst punishment there is. Everything tastes horrible, no matter how good it is. I'd be glad to have my dinner in the kitchen to make room. Mama'd be sure to find Mr. Dauntry a more interesting table partner than me."

Mrs. Burchett overrode Dauntry's babbled protests—which were at least as incoherent as Cecelia Walters's apologies for Tommy putting himself forward in such a manner.

The vicar expressed his gratitude for Dauntry's offer of the Combermere landau to cover the four miles to Beechy Knoll and later return to the vicarage with an incoherence that matched his sister's and Dauntry's.

Rebecca blushed furiously and ducked her head.

Their mismatched quartet could've formed the basis for a superior farce, he decided—if any of them had a taste for such things. Then, giving herself a shake, Rebecca rescued Tommy from his mother's gentle scold, soothing the lady's mortification, and so her own. Things began to go better after that.

Escaping conversation that became general, Dauntry directed Mayhew's heavy-footed nephew to inform his uncle of the change in plans, and extend his apologies to the household for putting them to so much trouble for naught. Those items that would keep so long were to be delivered to the vicarage that evening. The staff were to regale themselves on those that wouldn't.

Nick Beetle nodded, and clomped to the estate wagon, where those of the staff who'd elected to attend services waited. Gregory Heater was staring at Dauntry, hands crossed over the head of his crude walking stick. Then the old gardener's gaze traveled just beyond him.

Dauntry turned back. The company was preparing to clamber into the carriages. Tommy glanced at Argus during the inevitable fuss, longing in his eyes. The chestnut blew gently through velvet nostrils, and tossed its head in invitation.

"This won't do at all." Dauntry grinned at the boy, then the others. "I'm sure you and your brother would prefer Becky's company to a lad's prattle, Mrs. Walters. I, by contrast, have an overwhelming desire to become better acquainted with the imp who rescued me from a solitary Sunday, and would be honored if you'd grant me permission to take him up. Argus is dependable despite his bulk, and dining solo *is* tedious, as Tommy says."

The sudden silence, the frowns, the startled glances, the lad's embarrassed shrug had Dauntry wondering where he'd put his foot wrong that time.

"Thomas is unaccustomed to—that is, I shouldn't wish for you to be inconven—"

"Nonsense," the squire broke in. "Wonderful treat for the lad. Should've thought of taking him up years ago, but there, I've detested seeing sprigs mounted ever since Josh—that is, I, ah—"

"The cases are different, my dear." Mrs. Burchett placed a plump hand on Cecelia's arm. "I know you've heard tales, but Quintus was in no way responsible for Josh's breaking his neck in that foolish race, no matter what he believes, as anyone with more intelligence than a worm will tell you. I've always thought that's what made Quintus such a stranger—misplaced guilt, for which I've scolded him every chance I get.

"Now, enough of this silliness. Let Thomas go. You grip the reins too tight, and he'll snatch at the bit. Then you'll truly be in the suds, for boys develop the oddest kick to their gallop when one attempts too much coddling or curbing."

The glowing hope in Tommy's eyes as his gaze flew from one to another was a knife in Dauntry's chest.

"Quint was always the best rider in these parts," the squire coaxed. "Soul of responsibility. Was from the time he crawled into the saddle. Wouldn't let anyone put him there, you see. Had to do it for himself. Knows how to care for his mounts, too.

Besides, Quint's a highly decorated officer. Mentioned in count-less dispatches."

Dauntry's cheeks burned, but he held his peace.

"I truly don't believe—" Cecelia Walters turned to her brother.

"I'd be no bother, and we'd be ever so careful," Tommy pleaded. "Sober as judges, Mama. No larking about."

"Then why do it?"

"Look at him!" The boy sighed, turning to Argus. "He's just about the most perfect thing I've ever seen."

Dauntry and the vicar exchanged a measuring glance.

"He'll come to no harm. That I promise you, Mr. Gardener."

"You'll not let him encourage you to play the fool?"

Dauntry snorted. When that appeared insufficient, he added, "I'm well aware of the tricks striplings employ to bring one around to their way of thinking. There were several little older than Tommy under my command in the Peninsula. Always up to what we more staid types considered no good. Seeing they didn't come to harm while not crushing their spirits proved a challenge, for it was their inventiveness brought us out of harm's way more than once when Boney's fellows proved overfractious." Dear God, but he sounded pompous. Was this how it took some—with an irrationality of thought and an intemperance of speech to rival a bloated toad's croaking?

Gardener nodded. "It'll be all right this once, I think."

Cecelia Walters turned to Dauntry. He steeled himself. There was nothing for it but to meet her eyes.

"You'll keep to the lanes, and not go above a walk?" she said.

"Why, madam, I'd thought to order Argus to sprout wings so we could take to the air. A grand adventure for the boy, flying across the sky. Highly educational."

The gasps had him blanching. Damn this damnably impossible situation!

"My apologies. No, I don't intend to eat your dust, or force you to eat ours, Mrs. Walters. Either would be unpleasant." He managed what he hoped was a convincing smile, not the rictus of a death's head. "In the woods one's forced to proceed at a decorous pace. While traveling cross-country is shorter, it can take a bit longer."

Too many words. Too much explanation. Blast! But it seemed to've done the trick. She was smiling slightly now, rather than according him a troubled frown.

"The woods, then, rather than the sky? I shouldn't like your feathers to be melted, and it is a warm day."

"The woods it'll be." He answered her smile. He couldn't help it. And no one must know—that was the damnable thing. No one must suspect there was the slightest thing amiss, or that everything would be amiss for the rest of his life.

"Mama," Tommy breathed, "I'll be good for a year of Sundays, not just a month of 'em."

"Don't promise more than you can accomplish." Cecelia's gray eyes were twinkling now. "I'll be satisfied with surviving the afternoon with no more displays such as the one to which you just treated us."

"Not to worry, Mama."

"Oh, but I do! You're not to prattle interminably, and you're not to ask Mr. Dauntry a thousand questions about his Peninsular experiences. I've been told military gentlemen don't care to speak of them, except possibly among themselves. With civilians they feel they must soften the horrors, and so are forced to invent innocuous tales bearing no relation to reality. That's tiresome for them."

"Yes, Mama."

"And you're not to dawdle. We don't want to spoil Mrs. Burchett's excellent dinner."

"No, Mama."

"And you're not to—"

"We'll be fine, both of us," Dauntry broke in with a genuine laugh. He gave Tommy Argus's reins, then turned to the widow. "My thanks for your trust, Mrs. Walters. With the exception of your brother, who's waiting to hand you up, everyone's ready to leave. Handing you up, however, is a pleasure I believe I'll reserve for myself."

What the next moments cost him he was never certain, nor whether the rewards were worth the penalties. Then he was playing groom as he lifted the step and closed the landau door after

Gardener, latching it firmly. The squire's carriage had already set off.

"Drive on," Dauntry ordered.

Then he stood in the sunny lane, hat in hand, watching until both carriages disappeared around a curve.

"Where'd you learn an expression like *de trop,* sprout?"

They'd been picking their way through the woods, ducking beneath branches, and pausing now and then to observe a creature scurrying about its business, Argus with his ears pricked forward, Tommy with delighted catches of breath.

"I heard my father say it once, I think."

"Because you employed it perfectly."

"Thank you."

Dauntry grinned in response to the pride in the lad's voice. Being told one possessed an elevated vocabulary had its attractions at Tommy's age—a modest *douceur* for what was to come. And then he sobered. Best get on with it. They had only a mile to go.

"You said the other day things were better when your father was alive."

There—it was done. He'd put a question in his voice. With such a trusting child it should've been enough, but the only response was a slight stiffening of the slender frame perched before him. They went on for some distance, Dauntry waiting, Tommy Walters clearly considering.

"Mama and Uncle say it's best not to talk about when Papa was alive, and so I don't." Tommy glanced up at him. "Told you that. People repeat things, and they usually get them wrong— even the nicest ones, like Mrs. Twitchell and Mrs. Burchett, though they don't mean any harm by it—so when somebody asks, even in the politest way, or supposes, I just say I don't remember. It's not a lie, not really. I was awful young then."

"I suppose you were, though you're not so very old now."

"I'm *much* older. Three times as old. I was almost still in leading strings back then."

The lad was incensed. When one considered it that way—the

thought of being three times his own age made Dauntry shudder—Tommy was indeed older. *Much* older.

"You're right," he said. "I stand corrected."

"But you don't really live here, do you?"

"No, I don't. In fact, I live everywhere *but* here. My presence in the neighborhood is an anomaly—an anachronism, if you wish—and not likely to be soon repeated."

"And you're not the sort who goes about flapping his tongue just to make sure it's still there, are you?"

"No," Dauntry replied with a chuckle, "I'm not."

"Didn't think you were. Hard to imagine the real Julius Caesar or Mark Antony flapping their tongues, even if Shakespeare does have 'em giving everyone bear-garden jaws every chance he gets, and you're a military man, just like they were."

"Was, not am. I sold out almost a year ago."

"Makes no difference."

They were on Burchett land now.

Dauntry guided Argus past the gnarled oak Josh had insisted marked the grave of an apostate druid priest. Here the green-tinged shade was so dense it might've been twilight. There was an expectant hush. Even the woods waited to hear what the boy might say, the birds' voices stilled.

"I suppose it'd be all right to tell you, then." Tommy's voice, when it came, seemed to echo from a great distance. "There's times I want to talk about it so much I feel like I'm going to burst."

"Well?" Dauntry said, hoping he infused the word with just the right touch of encouragement.

"I don't know if it was better exactly, except for Papa being alive, but it was different."

"Different? In what way?"

Another pause, as if the boy were considering what he might say, and what he should not.

"There was a big house, and a dovecot, and rabbits and deer in the woods. There were lots of rooms—almost as many as at Combermere—and gobs of servants. I had a nurse, and a puppy. Papa read to me a lot, and Mama and I played counting games. I don't remember much—I told you that already, too—but Mama didn't have to cook or clean, and there were things, pretty ones. Shiny. Gold, maybe, or brass, I suppose. Brass would be more likely, don't you think?"

"Possibly. One can never be sure."

They broke into a small clearing, slender saplings arching over their heads. The lad didn't notice the rabbit frozen beneath a bush, or the fairy ring formed by puffballs.

"Then there was a March storm, and everything got dark." The boy shivered. "The storm came on all of a sudden. It wasn't Papa's fault."

Dauntry guided Argus past the terrified rabbit, and back under the thick canopy of trees. "A real storm?"

Tommy nodded. "There was a lake, too. At least I thought it a lake, though I suppose it might've only been a pond. Things look bigger when one's little, but we could row on it. I liked that—when Papa'd take me out on the lake in a boat. I'd sit very still, and we'd fish. We caught things, too, only the last time it got too cold. The wind started gusting, and the rain came down in buckets. There were even waves. The weather'd changed that quick."

Dauntry held his breath.

"Papa rowed for shore like anything because he was afraid I'd take a chill and Mama'd scold him. He was joking about it. We hit a snag and tipped. I fell out. Papa jumped in after me. I couldn't swim, you see. At least, they tell me that's what happened. There're parts I don't remember. They say Papa wrapped me in his coat, and ran for the house. Three days later he was dead, and I was fine."

"Dear Lord," Dauntry murmured. "I'm sorry, Tommy."

"It was a long time ago. But you see, it's my fault Papa died and we had to come live with Uncle because he's Mama's brother and one of my guardians. I've always known I had to do something to make Mama happy again, everything the way it was, but I've never been sure what. And now there's Uncle and Miss Burchett. They want to get married, but they can't because Mama and I have to live with Uncle. I ruined everything for everyone."

"It wasn't your fault, and you're not burdened with making things the way they were." Dauntry's arm tightened around the sprite. "It was an accident. You're not to blame yourself."

"I know what I know, and what I know is if I hadn't fallen out Papa wouldn't've caught a chill that descended to his lungs and died, and Mama would still be wearing silk, and Uncle would have enough money to marry Miss Burchett. He can't see to two families—not here. Mama's been trying to find work, even though she'd have to leave me behind, but she's had no luck. I've heard her crying about it. I'm not supposed to know about any of that, but I do."

"Neither your father nor your mother ever counted the cost. You mustn't, either. Any father would've done the same."

"Would yours?"

"The cases are different. I doubt my father's ever set foot in a boat, and he certainly can't swim."

"People tell you not to blame yourself for Joshua Burchett's accident, but you still do."

"Again, the cases are different."

"How? I can't see any difference, except mine's worse. I should've held on to the sides tighter. I *made* my father die because I was young and stupid, and didn't obey him because I was pretending to be Lord Nelson at Trafalgar. You didn't make Joshua Burchett break his neck. He just took chances he shouldn't've in a silly race your brother goaded him into. Your brother was the older by far, and should've known better, but he was in one of his moods, and had no more sense than a slug. Everybody says so."

"I see."

"If I shouldn't blame myself, then you shouldn't blame yourself, either. You were the youngest of all of them. Taking blame when one shouldn't is self-puffery, Uncle says, and utter foolishness."

"He may be right about the foolishness, at least in your case, but trying to make oneself seem more important than one is? I'd argue that point until the Day of Judgment, and beyond. Who's your other guardian?"

"A gudgeon," Tommy replied with a strangely adult chuckle. "Fat as a flawn, Nurse said when Papa died, and twice as dull. He never came. We had to go there, and once we had we couldn't go home again."

"And you've no other family to whom your mother could turn for assistance?"

"There're those swells in London, but I've seen 'em only once." The boy shrugged. "Don't care if I never see 'em again, either. I don't like ladies who gush one minute and sneer the next, and wear rings that cut one's cheeks." The boy shuddered. "There was no way I'd say what that lady wanted me to, no matter how many times she slapped me. Grandmother and Grandfather Gardener're dead. Mama says someone else lives in their house now. There's Uncle. There's Mama. There's no one else."

In the event, Tommy wasn't forced to dine in the kitchens, or even make a picnic of it in the garden—which he insisted he wouldn't mind at all—for Mrs. Burchett cared nothing for a balanced table when enjoying a family party.

"The lad's family, Thomas—and to me you're still a lad, begging your pardon, Quintus, for all you're a man grown." She ruffled Tommy's hair and patted Dauntry's arm. "Y'used to lead Rebecca in, but that's Mr. Gardener's place now. It'll be Mrs. Walters you'll take in, and no fuss either, for I remember how you balked at the thought of doing the pretty for anyone's sister."

"I was a graceless scamp in those days, wasn't I?" Dauntry returned with a grin. "I just hope I won't put you to the blush, for there're those who'd say I'm as graceless as ever, and not be so kind as to call me a mere scamp, either."

"Those fine friends of yours in London? Yes, we hear things. Your family comes, and while we may not see 'em above a time or two each summer and exchange only the commonest civilities when we do, there's still a bit of news gets about if one plays ferret. Clever stableboys, don't you see? I doubt those friends of yours'd say any such thing. Rather the opposite. Thomas, take your mother's other arm, if you please."

They paraded into the sunny dining parlor where Dauntry had first had the adult duties of dinner partner foisted on him by Josh's mother. Carpet, draperies, and wallpaper were new, but so similar to those he remembered that it was primarily the brightness of their colors that betrayed their recent acquisition. The massive table and other furnishings were the same, thank heaven.

"I've always liked this room," he murmured to Cecelia.

"Happy memories despite being forced to take a schoolroom miss on your arm?"

"Becky wasn't bad for a girl. She never made a fuss if she skinned her knee or tumbled from a tree," he said with a chuckle. "Best of all, she never prattled of balls or gowns. She never put on airs. She never expected one to grovel at her feet mouthing idiocies about her superiority to every other female, and to my knowledge she never once requested a London Season, let alone demanded one."

"Your list of female failings seems rather particular."

"It is." He held her chair. "The chit I describe is to be found in the hundreds, and with other and far more irritating failings than I've bothered to mention. One who breaks the mold is a prize beyond compare. I have a friend who lucked on such a one, and is now happily wed. It's clear both your brother and your husband had equally acute vision, and equally discriminating taste."

"Thank you on all our behalves," she said, neither simpering nor pretending to misunderstand. Instead she colored up prettily.

"It's not really a compliment, you know." He gave Tommy a wink and took his place beside the widow as the rest settled themselves. "Telling the truth isn't paying a compliment, is it, Tommy?"

Light and bright—that was the ticket. Slightly roguish. Treat her as he treated Rebecca Burchett: a beloved cousin too well known to be of romantic interest. Play the dangerous fellow with a hint of rakishness to him—though never a danger to her or her son—the sort who, if he married at all, would do so unsuitably, and at such an advanced age that marriage was a laughable folly.

He'd get through the rest of this day without setting a foot wrong again—that he'd sworn during the ride to Beechy Knoll—and consider the problems presented by Cecelia Walters later. He'd solve them too, no matter what it took.

At least he'd solve all but the insoluble one, and as he was the only person who knew it existed, that one didn't count, did it? A quick glance had revealed her wedding band firmly in place, a warning to any gentleman with aspirations. That'd keep her safe from him as nothing else could.

"I think it's the very best kind of compliment there is," the boy returned.

"I happen to agree." Dauntry's grin was broad and—he hoped—a trifle wicked. "It would appear your mother concurs."

He reached for the glass of wine before him, ready for the toasts to king, country, and master of the hounds that always preceded meals at Beechy Knoll in lieu of grace. The squire coughed. He glanced up. All heads but Gardener's and Burchett's were bowed.

Gardener winked. Dauntry flushed. Somehow he'd managed to forget the fellow was a vicar, perhaps because old Killmartin'd sported snow on his roof, and been past temptations of the heart. One didn't tend to think vicars prone to jealousy like common mortals. So much for not setting a foot wrong the rest of the day.

With tantalizing aromas from the sideboard attacking their senses, Gardener was as efficient in his giving of thanks as he was sincere. No long-winded perorations for him while stomachs rumbled, auditors became restless, and food chilled. It was quickly and neatly done, and raised Gardener even higher in Dauntry's estimation.

"Rebecca's told me of her father's old custom," Cecelia Walters murmured under cover of the conversation that broke out as the first course was served. "Please don't let the change distress you. The toast comes at the end, now—not at my brother's request, but at the squire's insistence."

"Understandable. That's how it was done when Mr. and Mrs. Killmartin came to dine, even at Combermere. I'd forgotten. Such niceties as beginning a meal with a prayer of thanks are rarely honored beyond the family circle, and I've had little to do with family circles of late."

She glanced at him, frowning, then shook her head. "It's not that, then. And I thought I was so clever! What troubles you? You seemed curt after services. Even now you're frowning. Did my brother say something to offend you? That wasn't his intention, believe me. He only meant to thank you publicly for your exceptional kindness to us."

"I doubt Mr. Gardener would know how to give offense, but rectifying the omissions of others is hardly worthy of thanks." Dauntry steeled himself, then faced her directly. "I was merely distressed by the changes I discovered at St. Martin's. It's a beautiful old place, or at least it was in my grandmother's time. I intend to remedy the worst as soon as possible, of that you may rest assured."

"People are of more importance than buildings. A church, like a body, is only a shell."

"Don't worry, I'll see to the rest, as well. That's what I'm here for, I suspect. The girl in white, you know—she's miffed." Then he sobered. "I appear to've put my foot in it earlier, though. There was an odd moment in the churchyard as we were preparing to leave."

"Thomas," she murmured, clearly understanding what he meant, "not Tommy."

"I beg your pardon?"

"My son's permitted no one to call him Tommy since his father died. That was his pet name for Thomas, and mine. Thomas insisted he had to become a man and take care of me, and that Tommy was a name for a baby. There was no reasoning with him. You shouldn't use it, for all he's been very patient with you."

"I see. Thomas, it will be."

"No, it's all right," Tommy piped up. "When Mr. Dauntry says it, that's different. I don't mind. In fact, I rather like it, but you're still not to call me that, Mama."

"But, Thomas—"

"It's all right, I tell you. He didn't know us before."

"But neither did anyone else in the village, dear, and you won't permit them to call you Tommy."

"They knew Uncle. That's the same as knowing us."

Four

Quintus Dauntry stared at the decanter, trying to decide whether a third portion of brandy would make the world appear less bleak. So far he'd attempted a brief conference with Nace, reading, billiards, a moonlit ramble among his grandmother's roses, a chilly dip in his father's enlarged trout pond, and the brandy. None had served.

"Damn and blast."

He ran his fingers through his damp hair as he glanced around the dark library. A single candle not far from guttering flickered on the table beside him. The rest of the household was long asleep—and good riddance to them, with their knowing smiles and pointed questions about his afternoon at Beechy Knoll. Old Heater had been uncharacteristically busy—that, or he'd conversed too loudly with his roses.

"May my mother indulge in so many Brighton extravagances she drives my father mad," Dauntry growled. "Why the devil did he have to call me home? Why the devil couldn't the girl in white've kept to her place in the woods? Why couldn't I've been a slugabed this morning, rather than attending services?"

He could've done very well with never knowing that such a person as Mrs. Cecelia Walters, widow, existed. Or, her son. Yes, indeed—he could've done without that, too. For the rest of his life. Gladly.

Why?

Because, against all logic, and discounting the devastation she'd wreaked in his heart with those glorious gray eyes, he felt

responsible for them. The closest he could come to paralleling
the sensation was the moment when he'd seen Major Jordan fall
at Albuera in May of '11, and read in the man's dying eyes that
command had passed to him.

Nonsense, of course. Then, and now. Especially now.

It must be his old failing reasserting itself. No gentleman of
the *ton* castigated a jarvey for flogging his nag, not even a very
young gentleman, or rescued mongrels from their guttersnipe
tormentors. His tutor had insisted on that. Still, he'd persisted in
such solecisms, despite his mother's horrified pleas and his
brother's disgust at the mortifications he forced them to suffer—
undoubtedly the reason he had had the worst of the johnny raws
foisted on him in the Peninsula. He'd made something of them,
too.

He was attracted to Tommy Walters by his own lamentable
predilection for rendering the innocent not quite so defense-
less—nothing more complicated than that.

As for the boy's mother, she wasn't that lovely. Or that clever.
Or that gentle. Or that witty. Or that entrancing. Or that coura-
geous and uncomplaining. Or that delightful. She was quite ordinary, when one came down to it. So were her eyes.

Nothing to recommend her—nothing at all.

Why, she probably wasn't even a widow. Tommy's tale, with
its hints of luxurious isolation, had all the earmarks of a *ménage
à carte blanche*. The heavy band of gold on the woman's finger
was mere window dressing. He was the worst kind of idiot.

Dauntry reached for the decanter with a groan.

If he managed to convince himself of that claptrap, he'd be
able to convince anyone of anything.

A long pull of brandy had him recognizing the error of his
ways. No sense mourning impossibilities. The best way to get
through this was to consider himself a casualty. If a mangled arm
had to come off, quick and clean was best—the surgeons had
the right of that, at least. He'd worry about the healing later, just
like any other soldier. Survival was the point.

First order of business: Two females in a single household was
an impossibility, no matter how delightful those females indi-
vidually, and no matter how excellent the terms on which they

appeared to be. With the vicar and Becky as good as seen to, the goal now was to establish Mrs. Walters—and he was going to have to think of her that way, not as Cecelia—and her son separately.

She wanted either a husband or employment.

Well, he'd see she had one or the other. A woman of her charm shouldn't have any trouble attracting droves of suitors, empty pockets and impedimentary son or not. One of the fellows might do nicely for her once the golden band was removed. Pugs Harnette and Tony Sinclair were both superior horsemen, and they would take to Tommy on the instant. The lad really needed a father. It was a notion worthy of consideration.

And then he'd disappear from their lives. In a year's time Cecelia Walters and her son would barely remember him. If there happened to be one friend of whom he saw less and less, he'd manage it with such circumspection that no one noticed.

It was a good plan—if he could keep to it.

The only puzzle was why, if Cecelia Walters had been wed—and he'd swear she had—she was destitute. Given Tommy's descriptions, his father had been comfortable at the least. Gardener was no fool. He would've husbanded his sister's resources with care.

Of course it was possible Walters had lived beyond his means, but that didn't ring true. Besides, even then a modest competency should've remained. He had a sense of what Walters must've been from meeting his widow and son. He'd've liked the man. Better yet, he'd've respected him. Walters would never have left penniless the son for whom he gave his life. The solution had to lie elsewhere.

Dauntry refilled his glass and raised it.

"Rest easy, friend," he said, knowing it was the brandy talking, and not caring in the least. "Not certain how I'll do it, but I swear I'll straighten this mess out for you. Your wife and son'll be back in their home by the lake when I'm done, or in one equally fine, and Tommy'll never be forced to hang on anyone's sleeve the way I am. It's the worst fate a man can suffer. Then I'll make my exit."

He drained the glass and reached for the decanter. He'd have a ferocious head in the morning. He didn't care about that, either.

Then he froze. The hidden hinges in the paneling were complaining.

He grinned, set his glass down, slumped in his chair, closed his eyes, and gave vent to a theatrical snore.

The cool air, the dank odor rising from cellars, took him back to his childhood. The moan came next, naturally—a pathetic thing that would've raised the hairs on the back of his neck were he not convinced its source was vibrantly alive. Then came the clank of chains. Potts, Mayhew, or Nace? That was the only question, given the hoyden he'd encountered along the road was an impossibility—with Potts and Nace the front runners.

He produced another hearty snore.

What the devil could be so amiss at Combermere that they felt justified in terrifying the family to get him there? Church and vicarage roofs, dilapidated though they were, could hardly be the answer.

The ghost moaned again and again, but whether its tone was hopeful, laudatory, or disapproving he couldn't tell. He kept up his snoring, damned if he'd give it the satisfaction of a reaction. At last it ceded the field. The hinges squealed. There was a sharp click as the latches caught. He waited a few moments so it could make good its escape. Now wasn't the time for confrontations.

Then, with assurance born of experience, he crossed to the chimney surround and pressed the third boss on the left just below the mantel, opening the entrance to the warren of passages he'd explored as a boy. Dauntry lifted his candle high. The dust of years had been disturbed—no question there. Unfortunately, it'd been disturbed more than once of late. There wasn't a single clear footprint to betray the ghost's identity. As he listened, scurrying steps echoed from below, followed by the creak of a heavy door and a bolt sliding home.

Definitely Potts or Nace, then. That was the vine-masked door giving on the gardens at the back of the house, not the one into the picture gallery on the same level as the library, or any of the ones into the family bedchambers on the floor above. Mayhew must be opening it when necessary, and relocking it after the girl in white departed.

Dauntry frowned, set his candle on the mantel, then swung

the section of paneling flanking the chimney surround closed, pressing firmly. It took less effort than he remembered. For all their complaints, the hinges had been recently greased, and the counterweights rebalanced. What in blazes was going on?

Nace had been efficient, but then his father's bailiff always was.

When Dauntry rode to the village the next morning to call on Gardener, intent on learning as much of Cecelia Walters's history as he decently could, workmen were unloading slate and erecting scaffolding at both church and vicarage. As he dismounted, the carpenter's wagon from the estate pulled in with a load of fine walnut for the altar rail and some superior oak for the pulpit. Repairs to the window over the baptismal font would take longer. Nace was making inquiries. He suspected they'd have to send to a cathedral town. The stained glass wanted a true artist.

Wondering how Gardener could hear himself think in all the din, Dauntry led Argus around to the shed hidden behind some trees where the Killmartins had kept horses, gig, and carriage—another thing in need of attention—then went to the door giving on the lane and knocked.

He expected Tommy, schoolbook tucked under arm, or even Gardener. Given the hour, Cecelia Walters would be running errands or seeing to parish duties, just as Mrs. Killmartin had done—that was the essential.

Only she wasn't. She answered his knock, patched gown covered by a coarse apron, chestnut curls hidden under a cumbersome cap. They stared at each other in confusion. At least, he hoped it was confusion he portrayed. Her expression was so guarded he couldn't read it.

"Mr. Dauntry," she almost shouted over the din. "And so early? Why, it's before noon. Goodness!"

"Military habit. Seems a pity to waste the best part of the day serenading one's pillow, don't you think?" He smiled, indicating the sunny lane, the daisies blooming on the verge, the butterflies flitting about, the puffs of fair weather clouds on the horizon. If he must play a part, he'd play it well.

"There is that. I must thank you for the wonderful treats awaiting us yesterday evening." The words seemed to take tremendous effort. "Robert was as delighted with the trifle as Thomas. Nothing would do but that they sample it immediately. And for the loan of the landau, of course."

"Think nothing of it. A minor matter." He glanced about. "I seem to've arrived at an inopportune moment. Your brother isn't here?"

She shook her head, blushing as she wiped her soot-stained hands on a rag. Were those traces of tears on her cheeks? Certainly they were streaked. He supposed it might be sweat. The day was already hot, the air sultry. By evening those distant clouds might produce a thunderstorm or two.

"Please forgive me—I've been cleaning lamp chimneys, and I'm a trifle distracted. No, Robert found it best to make his rounds now, rather than waiting for afternoon."

A pair of workmen lumbered past, dragging a small sledge of slates. From the roof another shouted he wanted a bucket of nails and some timber. He'd found a rafter that required strengthening. If there was one, there'd be more.

"And Tommy?"

"Robert's given him the morning to do with as he pleases. Neither could bear the noise—not that I'm complaining. How uncivil that would be." She blushed even more furiously. "We're extremely grateful for the repairs. Things should be quieter once the scaffolding's up."

"You think so? What an innocent you are. It'll be worse—like living in a drum. Sure to develop a megrim. Surprised you don't have one already."

He cocked his head. Perhaps those were tearstains, an aching head their source. The temptation to brush them away and be as much in her company as he could manage was overwhelming, and the price he'd pay for it go hang. Accomplishing that was easy.

"Why don't you spend your days at Combermere for a bit? There's plenty of space, and heaven knows I'd be glad of the company. Lots of toys and games in the old schoolroom for Tommy, even if they're outmoded. Your brother would find the library a peaceful haven, and then for you there're the gardens and morning room. A maze, too. One can be private for hours."

She was blanching at the notion. What ailed the woman? Most females would've been babbling their gratitude by now, and dashing for their bonnets and shawls. Opportunities to visit Combermere were rare, and greatly prized. Being given the run of the place never occurred, at least when his parents were in residence.

"You'd be doing me an immense favor by agreeing," he insisted, "for you'd rescue me from dining alone." He tried a smile. It didn't help. "There're few things I detest more than being restricted to my own company when faced with a meal. Puts me off my feed. Why, I'm likely to fade away to nothing if you don't come."

"Oh, dear, but—I mean, we couldn't put you to such—"

"What, more incoherencies, Mrs. Walters? It would seem that's how you greet any attempt at kindness or courtesy."

She blushed again. The rosiness became her.

"It's not to be thought of," she said with a primness he hadn't seen before, and didn't in the least like, "delightful though it would be. People expect to find Robert at the vicarage. They'd be intimidated seeking him out at Combermere, and wouldn't come no matter how great a need they had of him."

"Certainly they'd come. Word's already spread that I'm here, and the rest of the family isn't."

"And then there's the housework."

"I could easily send a couple girls to see to that for you."

"And give them a megrim in my stead? That wouldn't be kind, tempting though the prospect is."

"Then let the blasted housework go, for pity's sake."

"It multiplies like rabbits if one does that, Mr. Dauntry, and becomes equally uncontrollable. You've no notion."

"No, I suppose I don't. The closest I've come is routing vermin from a Spanish barn. In the rain, too. They were most incensed."

"Why do you think there're so many servants at the great house? The lack of one increases the burdens of all. Being treated to tardy service, even truculence, would be your reward for such lack of consideration. That's not what you have in mind, surely?"

"Where did you learn so much about managing servants?"

From above came the sound of vigorous hammering, then a stifled curse. Hammer striking thumb rather than nail? Likely. "You speak with the authority of one who has considerable experience."

"Servant problems are a favorite topic among the parish ladies. To hear them, one would think there wasn't a footman in the district who didn't view every maid as—well, let's just say there're difficulties in large households." Her attempt at a disarming smile didn't quite do the trick. "And then, I visited here and there as a schoolgirl. Some homes were well regulated, others not. The discomforts of those that weren't were myriad."

Her response was glib. Too glib. And stilted where it wasn't forced. She'd recited it before. Tommy's memory of a house with almost as many rooms as Combermere was probably accurate.

"It's deucedly uncomfortable conversing on the stoop like this," he said, loath to leave as convention mandated.

"Were we conversing? Yes, I suppose some might call it that, though I suspect the term might better be making polite, if rather loud, noise, mostly about nothing—or at least not on topics of interest to a gentleman. Of course some information *was* exchanged. Still, it must be a dreadful bore. Please don't let me detain you."

He laughed. He couldn't help himself. Well, in for a penny, in for a pound. After all, he had to learn everything he could about Cecelia Walters if he were to help her, didn't he? "The point is, aren't you going to ask me in?"

"I don't think—that is, Robert is away from home, and I'm afraid it wouldn't be proper. Even if it were, I'm busy. The lamp chimneys must be seen to, and then there's tonight's stew, and the laundry. It is Monday."

"You've such a high regard for Mrs. Grundy?"

"For Mrs. Twitchell, at least. I believe that's she, just down the lane."

"Nothing could be simpler." He turned in the direction of the estate carpenter, who was still unloading his wagon. "Briggs," he roared, voice soaring over the roofers' clatter, "I'm going to check the vicarage. I spotted some loose floorboards in the entry last week. There're sure to be other problems. I'll confer with you later."

Parade ground experience had its uses. Briggs raised his hand, indicating he understood. Mavis Twitchell paused in the lane, glancing at them. Dauntry gave her a jaunty wave, then turned back to Cecelia Walters.

"And if every soul within miles doesn't know why I'm coming in, they're deaf. Now, are you going to permit me the honor of assisting you with lamp chimneys?"

"Oh, but—"

"And I'm a dab hand at stews. We often had to do for ourselves in the Peninsula. Rabbit, hare, squirrel—it matters not so long as you've an onion or two, and some carrots or turnips. Pepper and salt're handy, too."

"You can cook?"

Good. He had her off guard.

"It's preferable to starving. I picked up a trick or two while cadging kitchen treats as a boy, and Mrs. Twitchell was always talking about what she did to make trout taste like heaven when Harry, Josh, Geoff, and I arrived on her stoop with our catch. Cress—that's one of the secrets of trout, even roasted on a stick over an open fire. Keeps 'em moist. If you can't find cress, there're other wild greens that'll do."

"Dear heaven—a gentleman who cooks?"

"One who likes to eat as well as he can, no matter what his circumstances. Don't you know all the great chefs are men?"

"But they're French."

"And what makes you think a Frog's capable of things an Englishman isn't?" He grinned, then. He couldn't help it, her expression was so comical. "Simple things, at least. I insist you let me prove myself. You must, you know, for the insult of those doubting words, and that even more doubting tone. Most unfair not to. My prime specialty was a sauce made from any wild berries we happened on. Good with everything but fish."

"Dear heaven," she repeated, her tone one of awe.

Taking that as an invitation, he gave her a bow with as many flourishes as an eighteenth century courtier's. "Let's leave the door giving on the lane open, shall we? That should reassure any doubters of my honorable intentions. Besides, you'll need an extra pair of hands to finish the chimneys. I've detained you making polite noise an unconscionable time."

Her laughter had as much unease as humor to it, but she stood aside.

The vicarage kitchen was stifling despite the open door. The sun beat on walls and stoop. Not a breath of air stirred.

"Good Lord," Dauntry blurted, tearing off his coat, loosening his neckcloth, and rolling up the sleeves of his shirt as the first drops of sweat trickled down his neck, "is it always this bad? How can you bear it? This might be Spain at the height of August."

"You would insist on coming. In midwinter it's quite pleasant."

"Why haven't you opened the windows?"

"They won't—open, that is. Nothing Robert's attempted loosens them. Would you care for tea? We keep it for guests."

"No, thank you. I'm fine as I am. So he's the one who's been playing carpenter. At the church too, I gather?"

She nodded. "Rebecca wanted—that is, Squire Burchett offered to send a man to see to the worst things, but Robert insisted he and the sacristan could manage. There may be some port in Robert's study. Would you prefer that?"

"At this hour? No, thank you all the same. An independent sort, your brother?"

"We both are," she said, lifting her chin.

"Has he ever attempted to prepare a meal in this kitchen in the summer?"

"Of course not."

"The experience might prove beneficial. Your brother should stick to vicaring. At that he excels. Carpentry, however, appears beyond him despite his Master's example. What's he trying to do—recreate the climate in which He lived as penance for some imaginary transgression?"

"As I said, we prefer to do for ourselves."

"False pride."

Dauntry glanced around the well-remembered room. Mrs.

Killmartin's gleaming copper pots were gone. Her Wedgewood plates no longer graced the shelves. That was to be expected, but clearly any small personal luxuries Gardener might've once possessed had been disposed of to support his sister and nephew. The straggling geraniums, the wilting wildflowers on the mantel, were acts of defiance in the face of penury.

"I assume you've a pencil and a scrap of paper? I'm serious about that list. Your brother can't object to Briggs, who should've been seeing to things here all along, whatever his opinions concerning someone coming over from the squire's."

She nodded and backed from the room, hope warring with doubt in her eyes, then disappeared in the direction of her brother's study.

He strode to the table where three lamp chimneys awaited cleaning and seized a rag, uncovering an open letter. His brows rose as he picked it up, stifling a twinge of conscience.

Tommy'd had the right of it. The curt denial of employment was addressed to Candace Witherspoon, Spinster, in care of the *poste restante* in Bittersfield. So that was what she'd been doing trudging along the lane—collecting her mail where she wouldn't be known.

She lacked, the thing claimed, both the experience and the superior accomplishments requisite to guiding the young in a gentleman's household. The engraved, highly embellished direction indicated Hans Town.

Hans Town? Dear God! London's Hans Town was inhabited by Cits and shopkeepers intent on mimicking their betters while pinching every penny, and treating their few overworked servants like scum. Those likely *had* been tearstains, both today and almost a week ago. She'd just had even the forlorn hope of a life of servitude snatched away.

Well, he'd grant her points for pluck—but then he already realized she possessed that quality in abundance, didn't he.

Dauntry strode to the open kitchen door and stared into the rear garden, slapping the letter against his thigh. Not a one of the chickens he'd had sent over from Combermere was in evidence. A mass of linens soaked in a tub under a tree.

Bloody hell! A slip of a thing such as she had no business with heavy work. She'd made an attempt at a vegetable plot, too. Stunted cucumbers vied with wilting cabbages and what might've been turnips under a more skilled gardener's care. Here they hadn't a prayer of being more than barely recognizable as the poorest examples of their sort.

Not a weed in sight, of course—those she and Tommy could control so long as they recognized them.

"So—you were a spy in the Peninsula?"

He froze, then turned from the door, not bothering to hide her letter for all he could feel his face burning.

"I've always skirted the gentlemanly accomplishments. That's expected of a younger son in a *tonnish* household. We're black sheep by definition, unless someone has a need of us. Then we're heroes for a bit, before we sink back to our usual condition of being beneath contempt. Does your brother know about this da—cursed thing?" He held out her letter.

"In general, if not in particular."

"Does he approve?"

"I don't see how that's any business of yours," she snapped.

"I intend to make it my business, however. He doesn't like it, does he—but I'll wager you've taken the bit in your teeth, and there's not much he can do to stop you short of chaining you to your bedpost. Don't you understand I'm trying to be a friend to you all?"

"No one asked you to involve yourself."

"No. I invited myself in, didn't I?"

Their voices had been rising, hers in what he assumed was indignation, his from exasperation. Now he took a deep breath, attempting to steady himself. Brangling wouldn't serve, however oddly natural it seemed. Safer than what he wanted to do, certainly. One couldn't kiss a vicar's penniless widowed sister silly—not if one were penniless oneself, and in no position to combine those kisses with an honest offer.

"Things weren't like this when my grandmother was alive," he said, forcing his tone to soften. "It's not that my father's a cruel man. It's just that he's careless. If he takes a notion in his head, it gets worse. He seems to've had more than a few of late, doubtless encouraged by my mother. See here, were you truly intending to go so far away? Tommy'd be devastated."

"Children are resilient. He'd forget me in a week."

"I doubt it. He hasn't forgotten his father, and that's near on seven years, not just seven days."

She clamped her lips. They glared at each other again, Dauntry clenching her letter in one fist and the damp rag in his other, while she clutched the tablet of paper and pencil she'd brought from her brother's study against her chest like a breastplate and sword. Above them the steady thud of hammers echoed like distant cannonades.

She might've been North's Amelia. Same determination. Same courage. Same fire. Same humor. Same loyalty. Same tenderness when touched. Same temper when roused.

That was it, by heaven! What a nodcock, not to've thought of it immediately. North's wards. They'd require a governess.

Better employers she'd never find. Amelia would adore her. So would North's mother. Knowing Lady Katherine, she'd take Cecelia under her wing, make her a member of the family. Best of all, they'd insist she bring Tommy. He'd see to that.

And Cecelia'd like them, for they'd treat her with respect and Tommy with deep affection. Why, North might go so far as to pay for the boy's schooling. Lord knew, he could afford it.

And the fellows would be there, or at Harnette's neighboring estate, most of the summer. One of them would evidence sense. Cecelia'd find herself at the altar before she knew it. Tommy would have a father, and she'd no longer struggle with lamp chimneys, cabbages, and sodden sheets. The point was to get her to Hillcrest, no matter what it took.

"You're really determined to find employment?" he said, coming forward.

"I must."

"Then let me help. I can, you know, surprising as that may seem. The girl in white's given me a certain authority."

"Your nephew's too young for a governess."

"I'm not thinking of Bertram, though if you'd prefer to remain in the neighborhood I suppose I could arrange that just as easily."

"No, it would be more comfortable for everyone were I at some distance. Two ladies in one house is impossible, especially a house this size. A lady who's had charge of the parish remaining in the district when another should take responsibility for those functions is the equivalent. When one is actually the vicar's sister? Breaking old habits is difficult. Were I nearby, Rebecca would find life intolerable—with justification. We'd soon both be striding about with fists clenched and lips pursed, finding insult where none was intended, and spitting like angry cats. Poor Robert!"

"What about your comfort?"

"I, too, would prefer it now Tommy is old enough to be left in their care."

"You would? See here, why don't we attack those lamp chimneys? We can discuss this while we work."

"Military efficiency?"

"Something like that. I won't apologize for reading this," he said, handing over the letter and taking the tablet and pencil from her. "I found it by accident, and someone has to do something. Why don't you throw it on the grate where it belongs, rather than letting it distress you?"

"You've a penchant for direct action, I see."

"And the devil take the hindmost, which he generally does. Why waste time prevaricating? Direct is simplest. Besides, deviousness smacks of the infernal, no matter how it's disguised. The few times I've attempted it, I've suffered disaster."

He sat on one of the stools at the table, wrote *shed, kitchen windows, loose floorboards, staircase spindles,* and *needs Heater* on the tablet, set it aside, picked up a chimney, dipped a rag in the basin, and started scrubbing.

"I have a close friend who's recently wed—a sterling fellow by the name of Valentine North. One of the ancient, untitled families. Very wealthy, pays excellent wages. He has a pair of wards. Robby's seven, Tibbie five. Excellent playmates for Tommy. He'd steady them down, and they'd liven him up. He wants a bit of livening, don't you think? And they definitely want a bit of steadying."

"I think Thomas's welfare is my concern, not yours."

"North's wife's delightful, and his mother's her equal," he continued as if she hadn't spoken.

"To their equals, perhaps. To one such as I? I doubt it."

"You're determined to find fault with the project. Why?"

She turned crimson, crammed the letter in her apron pocket, then sat, putting the full length of the table between them, and crossed her hands. Crossed them? She'd balled them into most unladylike fists. Interesting.

He glanced again, eyes widening. The heavy band of gold was missing. Of course she could be afraid of losing it in washtub or garden, and have put it aside for safekeeping when seeing to household duties.

"I've had a bit of experience," she said more mildly. "It's taught me to regard the great world with skepticism."

Interesting? Fascinating. Who *was* the female with the sharp rings that cut Tommy's face, the one who'd turned nasty? The boy had mentioned her twice. She must've made quite an impression on him.

"North tumbled top-over-tail for Lady Amelia when she was playing governess," Dauntry explained. "It's a long story—one they'd probably prefer to tell you themselves. Point is, you'd be perfect for them, and they'd be perfect for you."

"I doubt anyone of that sort would want a governess who lacks either references or experience." She picked up a chimney, eyes fixed on her hands, and attacked the soot. "They generally require credentials of the most exalted sort."

"I assume you share Tommy's tuition with your brother. That's experience enough with children that age. As for references, my word'll suffice."

"Thomas has been busy. I'll have to speak to him again, I see."

"Don't. He was definite regarding careless talk, and only considered me trustworthy because I'm not at Combermere as a usual thing. In fact," he said with a chuckle, "he questioned me pointedly regarding propensities for idle chatter. Had some interesting observations on the failing, too."

"Oh, dear—I hope he wasn't uncivil?" She looked up then, her eyes meeting his.

"Tommy, uncivil? I doubt he'd know how to be."

He scowled as he took a dry rag and began polishing the chimney.

Cecelia Walters, cursed with Val North's wards? Most of the time Robert and Tabitha Tyne were untutored, ill-mannered, selfish, self-centered little monsters, their flashes of humanity rare, engaging though they could be at their best.

Good Lord—what was he thinking? She'd believe she'd been sent directly to hell. He should never've opened his mouth. How the devil to caution her without making her believe he thought she wasn't competent to have charge of the little villains? This was what came of interfering in the lives of those around him. When would he learn? Never, he supposed.

"There is one problem, however." He set the sparkling lamp chimney aside and retrieved the last one.

"There always is. I take it you've thought better of the matter."

"Only for your sake. The children were dubbed 'the Spawn of Beelzebub' by their father. The sobriquet remains more or less accurate."

"Mischievous?"

"If that were all. No, totally undisciplined. Little better than wild animals when they arrived from the Colonies, though Amelia's done her best with them, and quite good her best has been. At least they no longer howl like wild Indians, Tibbie doesn't cast up her accounts to get her way, and Robby doesn't hurl food at the walls."

"They did that? And it was effective?"

"With their parents, it would seem. Not with Amelia, however. And then there's the spaniel Robby and Tibbie named Beezle because of *his* undisciplined characteristics—such as treating gentlemen's boots as tree stumps."

"Warning me off, or presenting me with a challenge?"

"I don't like the thought of your contending with them, and that's the truth."

"Thomas is no angel, you know. He can be difficult."

"Not like these hellions. There's no need to do anything instantly, is there? Other possibilities exist. Let me make inquiries." The solution that appealed to him most was Aunt Persie, but Crete was out of the question. "I have a friend whose great-aunt could do with a companion. That'd be no sinecure either, but Lady Farnsworth *is* civilized, even if she's something of a Tartar.

It might be possible to take Tommy with you there, as well. Unfortunately, she lives primarily in Town or Bath. The Norths offer the advantage of an immense country estate. Summer in London and children don't match. Too much disease. Bath's worse. Nothing but rain, invalids, and down-at-the-heel cheese parers desiring to cut a dash more cheaply than in Town."

"I've sworn to be gone by September. I had my chance at happiness. Robert must have his."

"September, it will be, if you'll promise me there'll be no more Hans Town foolishness."

"Why should I trust you?"

"Tommy does. That's recommendation enough, I would think." He glanced up. "Speaking of Tommy, I'd like to ask you a favor. There—this one's done. Have a care—if you keep scrubbing that chimney, soon there'll be nothing left of it."

Another blush. What ailed the woman, for pity's sake? He'd said and done nothing out of the ordinary since he arrived on her doorstep—if one didn't count his claim to a passing acquaintance with the culinary arts, that was, and his assisting her with cleaning lamp chimneys.

"Yes?" she said.

"Given yesterday, he appears entranced by horses. Rather typical for a lad his age. Would you consider permitting me to teach him to ride? It'll be an essential accomplishment should you accept a position at Hillcrest. Both Tibbie and Robby are learning. Given those rotters, if Tommy's incompetent they'll make his life miserable."

"But there's no assurance—"

"My father keeps a pair of ponies for the entertainment of visiting children, but they haven't seen much use of late. Tending to fat, which isn't good for them. I've already spoken with Potts. He thinks it's a sterling notion. You'd be doing us all an immense favor by agreeing."

"But Thomas knows nothing of horses. Children can be injured, and—"

"Not with me in charge, and Potts overseeing the whole."

"It would cut up your day. Soon you'd lose interest. One must be faithful where children are concerned. I shouldn't like to see Thomas disappointed."

"You wouldn't."

"And you'd find it a dreadful inconvenience once the novelty'd worn off."

"With a lad as delightful as Tommy?" He snorted, brows rising. "You don't have a very high opinion of him, do you?"

Again, the blush. "Of course I do! But you aren't intending to remain at Combermere very long, are you?"

"When I leave, Potts will take over. He suggested it himself."

"Oh."

"So, you see, there's no reason not to say yes, and every reason to do so. Tommy could do with the activity, and a bit more time in the outdoors. It's summer, after all. Even those attending the most elevated schools are on holiday. You truly don't intend to rob your son of such a treat, do you?"

She shook her head. "I just don't think—that is, it's not for me to say. You must discuss the matter with my brother. He's one of Thomas's guardians. I refer such decisions to him."

"And who might Tommy's other guardian be?"

She hesitated, then shrugged, set the clean lamp chimney and rag aside, rose, and took the basin of sooty water to the door to empty it.

"I suppose it doesn't matter if you know," she said, her back to Dauntry, "though I'd rather you not bruit it about, for I treasure my privacy. It's Thomas's paternal grandfather. He involved himself only once, and then only at his wife's insistence.

"Now I must ask you to leave. I've laundry to see to, and I doubt you'd enjoy scrubbing dirty sheets as much as you did lamp chimneys. Far messier. Good day, Mr. Dauntry."

She went into the garden without a backward glance. After a moment he pulled himself together, shrugged on his coat, slammed his hat on his head, shoved his list in his pocket, and showed himself from the house. Blast the woman for her independence. He'd intended a superior stew for their supper.

Five

The sun was at its zenith when Dauntry stormed through the open terrace doors an hour later, muttering under his breath. He hurled hat, gloves, and crop at his father's desk, and jerked the bellpull.

What the devil had been going on at Combermere since his grandmother's death? For it wasn't only the living, or the church and vicarage. From what he'd just learned—and most reluctant Gardener had been to say anything, blast him, probably for fear of giving offense—it was the entire neighborhood, not that it had happened all at once. It'd happened a bit at a time, so that at first no one noticed.

No wonder the girl in white had decided to reappear, no matter if she were the family ghost or an incensed retainer, or even a villager intent on punishing heartless inattention to need.

Nick Beetle plowhorsed in as Dauntry was reaching for the bellpull again, heavy steps announcing him well before his arrival. Dauntry turned on the novice footman with a growl. The poor fellow lost his goodhumored grin, blanching and opening and closing his mouth like a fish.

"Sir?" he gulped.

"I want your uncle. I want Mrs. Ford. I want Nace and Potts. While we're at it, I want old Heater. Instanter. And something in the way of food. A slice of last night's pigeon pie'll do, or some bread and cheese if there's none left, and some fruit."

"Wha-what kind of cheese, sir? And would it be peaches, or grapes, or—"

"Anything that's to hand," Dauntry snapped. "Don't stand there gaping like an idiot. Hop to it! And it's not you I'm ready to tear limb from limb, nor anyone else here, so stop looking as if you were about to be dragged to the scaffold. You're not."

"Y-yes, sir. Right away, sir. Soon's I can, sir."

The fellow backed through the doorway, steps whisper soft.

"Hisself's in a state," Dauntry heard him hiss to someone invisible from the library. "Have a care. I'll get t'others, an' t'vittles."

Mayhew glided in, brows slightly arched, cheeks a trifle pink.

"Is something amiss, sir?" he said.

"Yes, something's amiss! Why the devil didn't you write me? Why the devil didn't you write Miss Blaire, if you didn't know my direction? You knew how to reach her easily enough when Grandmama died, and my father decided things'd go easier if she wasn't alerted. Got her here in record time, too. Of course Shropshire's a bit more convenient than Crete."

Mayhew braced himself as if for a blow and held his peace.

Dauntry sighed, the rage draining from him. No sense railing at these poor sods. They had done what they could when the situation became intolerable, witness the girl in white. He had to hand it to them—it was an inventive ploy, and had enjoyed a success informing absent family members wouldn't have.

When his father was terrified—and God knows his lordship had been the other day—he'd agree to anything. That wouldn't've been the case had Persephone Blaire descended on him, brandishing a stick and threatening to call the hounds of hell down on his head for ignoring family traditions her sister had followed to the letter. Gotten his back up, more like than not. His lordship with his back up was as immovable as the Alps. No, they'd done the right thing in playing the game as they had.

Mrs. Ford bustled in, Nace hard on her heels. Dauntry gave them a curt nod. Smiles were beyond him, for all he had a grudging admiration for their initiative.

Potts and Heater would take a bit longer. Nick'd either have to think of sending the potboy to the stables and the scullery maid to the gardens, or else he'd have to go himself. Nick hadn't appeared to be thinking clearly when he quitted the library.

He considered taking the chair behind his father's desk, then discarded the idea as ridiculous. One didn't appropriate the trappings of power if someone else had used that power so inappropriately even his servants held him in contempt. Well, perhaps not contempt. Say rather that they were dismayed. That felt better, even if it probably wasn't quite the truth.

Heater and Potts came through the terrace doors, red of face and somewhat out of breath. Dauntry nodded again. Good for Nick. He'd kept his wits about him, after all. Mayhew's nephew might never make a proper footman, but he'd make a valuable and proper something else, if only Dauntry could figure out what it was.

"Council of war." He strode over to the library table and leaned against it, doing his best to present an air of informality. "You all know what one of those is, I presume? Good. Let's get on with it, then."

He needed their enthusiastic cooperation. He needed them to feel as indispensable to his plans, as they indeed were. He needed them to feel as if they were his equals. Perhaps, given the steps they'd taken to get him there and chase his father off, they were. Certainly they were the best friends anyone in the vicinity of Coombe had.

"I stopped by the vicarage this morning to see how things go on there." Dauntry looked directly at his father's bailiff and forced a smile. "You're to be commended, Mr. Nace. At the cost of a few days' inconvenience, the vicar and his family are going to be far better housed. I have a list of additional repairs for Briggs. I'll give that to you when we're done. Briggs is to go over everything at the vicar's convenience and make his own list of what needs to be done in addition. I'll want to review it, but I can tell you in advance that I'll approve anything he deems necessary."

"Thank you, sir."

Dauntry nodded, then paused. There was really no delicate way to put the next three items, and no way to compliment anyone about them. He glanced at Mrs. Ford, then at the others.

"On my way home, I noticed the vicar's barrow in front of a cottage. I stopped. Turned out he was visiting the Crays. On foot, of course. That's going to change. Potts, what's available in my father's stables that he doesn't care for, and that I could afford? Something that'd pull a gig over the countryside in good weather and foul without flagging, and could also be ridden? Nothing showy, mind you."

"There's nothing, sir. Mr. Gardener's already refused the gift of a horse and gig from the squire. Said he couldn't afford the tax or the feed. Wouldn't accept the loan of 'em, neither—not even if the squire gave him the feed, which he offered to do."

"That's changing. Mr. Gardener'll be able to afford to maintain them, if not purchase them. All right, find out what Mr. Burchett wants for that gig and nag."

"T'isn't a nag, sir. It's a prime bit of horseflesh what Miss Burchett drives. She's that fond of it."

"Better yet. In time they'll be reunited. Guess I'd better see the squire about that personally."

He grinned. They grinned back. Good. Now they were conspirators under his command rather than their own, and he could get on with it.

"By the bye, Potts, I gained Mr. Gardener's agreement to our teaching Tommy to ride. Hard for him to refuse given what'd gone before, which I'll explain in a moment. We'll be starting tomorrow. You can have the ponies brought in from pasture today."

"Very good, sir."

Was Potts reddening about the ears? Certainly his eyes were everywhere but on Dauntry. Well, grooms weren't generally summoned to the main house. That probably explained it, though the man'd been himself moments before. The others' expressions remained as good-humored as ever. In fact, they appeared to be suppressing cheers.

"Mr. Heater," he continued, "Mrs. Walters is massacring her kitchen garden. She needs help. What do you think of the notion of an experimental plot at the vicarage? You'd have to convince her she's doing you a favor by letting you try things out there, and not the other way around. That wouldn't be easy, for the lady's no fool. And, you'd have to persuade her to report to you on the quality of your vegetables, that that's part of it. It'd take a deal of cleverness. Think you're up to it? I'd propose it, of course, but it'd be up to you to convince her she's really doing you a favor."

"Vegetables?" Heater gulped, not attempting to pretend he was talking to anything but another mortal. "Not flowers? I ain't mucked with vegetables in dunamany years."

"Flowers'd be nice, but vegetables are what they need."

"So long's it can be both."

"It can be both. You might want to assign one of the lads to work there daily."

Heater nodded. "Little late to start things. End o' winter and early spring's the time for planting, or fall. I'll see what I can do."

"Take plants that're already bearing if you must. Just provide the vicar with a flourishing garden—that's all I ask. If anyone can do it, you can.

"Now, Mrs. Ford—there're some new girls in training, am I right? And," he said with a grin, "one of them's a bit shy, uncertain how to go on in a grand household. Am I right about that, too? Of course I'm right. She needs extra training. She needs a smaller household in which to accustom herself to service, and learn her duties. And, don't you agree the ideal person to give her that training would be Mrs. Walters? Naturally we'd have to pay the lady for her efforts, though that would never get about."

"Now that's a bonny notion, sir." Dauntry could've sworn Mrs. Ford gave him a wink. "I've just the one. Farm girl from up past Bittersfield. Willing enough, but wants her speech improved and her manners smoothed. Mrs. Walters'd be doing me the greatest favor by taking her on, for she's something of a problem, yet so sweet-natured I'd hate to turn her off. Be doing Rose a favor, too. Cries herself to sleep nights for want of her little brothers. Wouldn't cry near so much at the vicarage with young Thomas to spoil, I'll warrant."

"I'll warrant you're correct. And, I doubt not her family has great need of her wages."

"That they do, sir, and that's the plain truth."

"Good enough. Be sure you stress that to Mrs. Walters. Tell her you're at your wits' end, and she's rescuing the girl from being sacked. I'll lay the groundwork. There. The worst problems at the vicarage're well on their way to being solved."

He looked at each in turn. "Now, there's Coombe, and the entire neighborhood. Mr. Gardener was delivering the food we sent to the vicarage to others he considered in greater need. He was so embarrassed by my catching him at it that he granted permission for Tommy to learn to ride."

"Mr. Gardener's been doing that a long time," Mrs. Ford said.

"So I gathered. Every last one of the chickens're gone without one bite going to the vicarage family," Dauntry fumed. "The wine, the fruit, everything but Sunday's trifle, and I'm not so sure about that. Gardener was confused when I asked how he liked it. What the devil's happened to Combermere's charitable traditions? Assistance to people like the Crays would've been automatic when I was a boy. Dear God, he's doddering, she's bedridden, and their only son was pressed into the navy years ago. If it weren't for Gardener taking food from his own family's mouths, they'd starve."

"It was the dowager viscountess saw to all that." Mayhew studied his feet, then reluctantly lifted his eyes. "When she died, the new Lady Dauntry gave orders applications were to be made directly to her. Then she refused to see those who came, for they had the misfortune to appear at inconvenient moments. There were a few who tried again when young Mrs. Dauntry arrived, but she had no desire to be taxed with overreaching herself, and so she sent them packing without seeing them, too. Squire's family's been doing what they can, but they have their own responsibilities."

"I see." No time for dependents, but plenty for visitors anxious to cadge free meals and a bed. His grandmother must be spinning in her grave. "That's going to change. Mrs. Ford, from now on the vicar'll be coming to you with lists of those in need. At all seasons, whether the family's in residence or not. You or Mr. Nace're to provide anything he requests. Mr. Gardener and his sister will see to the distribution. Of course, they'll mention my parents' names as the source of such generosity."

They were beaming their satisfaction.

"Are Christmas baskets still distributed? I couldn't make sense of Gardener's prevarications."

"As best we can, sir," Nace said, "but not like they were."

"Everything is to be as it was in my grandmother's day," Dauntry snapped. "Everything, do you understand? I'll write his lordship explaining what I've arranged, and blame the girl in white for the changes. That should satisfy her, don't you think? Clever chit," he added, "getting me here the way she did, then making sure I'd learn all this. I doubt she'll trouble anyone now matters've been rectified."

Blank expressions met his knowing look. Well, sooner or later he'd confront them with it openly, and congratulate them on a game well played.

The murmured comments of Mayhew and Mrs. Ford as they'd made their departure still rang in Dauntry's ears minutes later, making writing his father close to impossible: "He's still himself, for all he's a man grown." "Not a bit of it—he's *more* himself than ever. Something's got to be done, though the dear Lord knows what or how."

Well, he'd always supposed one became ever more intensely oneself as time passed. Certainly his father's à-la-modality had burgeoned into a determination to cut a dash from which all Combermere's dependents suffered. If Dauntry were more himself, that was probably to be expected, whatever it signified.

Full of apologies regarding the delay, Nick Beetle finally arrived with his nuncheon well after the others scurried off. Dauntry set the letter to Brighton aside, beaming his thanks as Nick placed the tray on the desk and slipped from the library without so much as a single clomp or rattle.

He sighed, and attacked the food. Once he'd written his father he'd reward himself by answering Aunt Persie's letter. That would be a delight. He'd regale her with the tale of the girl in white, the garlic and crucifixes, and the problems he'd uncovered in Coombe, while assuring her things were now well in hand.

The letter to his father was the problem. No matter how he phrased it, the dratted thing kept turning into a diatribe on seignorial responsibility. That simply wouldn't do.

The pigeon pie was succulent, the peaches perfection. The ale, given the warmth of the day, seemed to have gone to his head by the time Dauntry—*sans* coat and neckcloth, and with his waistcoat and neckband unbuttoned—returned to his letter writing. Now it was too great an emphasis on the girl in white from which the crumpled pages suffered, rather than pompous lectures regarding family duty.

Playing on his father's superstitions for the good of the neighborhood was one thing. Playing the old gentleman for an addlepated fool was another. Lord Harald Dauntry was no dimwit, whatever his other failings. He merely simulated it for his own convenience.

Dauntry had just discarded what felt like his thousandth attempt, and was considering seeking inspiration in his father's trout pond, when vigorous pounding on the door followed the clatter of wheels on the drive. Tossing his latest attempt on the cold grate, he shrugged into his coat, made a sketchy business of his neckcloth, and headed for the entry. At this point any distraction was welcome, so long as it signified no problems for others.

Five grinning faces greeted him in the rotunda. Beyond the open doors, Mayhew directed his nephew and a pair of grooms in unloading a pair of dusty curricles as Potts led Pugs Harnette's road-grimed mount toward the stables.

His heart sank. It was going to happen sooner than he'd planned or wanted. Well, he was damned if he'd play dog in the manger. One of the fellows was luckier than he deserved, for all he didn't know it yet.

"I see you've decided on a progress," he said with a chuckle. "Welcome to the family monstrosity."

"Not a bit of it." Pugs Harnette tossed crop, hat, and gloves on a bench, sat, pulled out a handkerchief, and wiped his face. "We've come to see how our wagers're faring, and lend a hand with this ghost of yours. Course Val didn't come, but then one couldn't expect him to, could one?"

"We're to report back." Stubby Clough grinned his thanks as he accepted a tankard from one of the maids, who'd appeared from the nether regions. "He's as curious as the rest of us, but it wouldn't't've been fair to burden you with Lady Amelia and the rug crawlers, 'specially as there's a ghost involved, so he stayed at Hillcrest. Lady Amelia's curious about your ghost, by the bye.

Wants all the particulars. Robby says—well, you probably ain't interested in what Robby says."

Dauntry grinned. "Doubtless insists it's a kindred spirit, and is incensed he wasn't given an opportunity to either befriend it, or howl it into submission and take its place."

"Something like that. Takes a terror to terrify the terrible. Almost brought him with us, but then Lady Katherine said it wouldn't do, and Val played stuffy *pater familias,* and so we discarded the notion." Clough raised his tankard. "To your ghost."

"Robby'd find this one too sedate for his tastes, I'm afraid. Nothing but a bit of chain and the occasional moan. It's a female, after all, not a swashbuckling pirate. Still, she's very caring in her own way. I've developed something of a fondness for her. No—I'll explain later."

He glanced at the fellows, trying to see them through a lady's eyes as they downed their ale, arguing good-naturedly about the race they'd made of it from Chiverton to Combermere. Tony Sinclair had won, of course. Sinclair always won their curricle races. When it was horseback, it was Sinclair or Pugs Harnette.

Sinclair's ginger hair and green eyes would make people believe him Tommy's father rather than his stepfather, but there was something about him that warned he might prove a stern disciplinarian once parental responsibilities were thrust on him. Dauntry was damned if he'd see Tommy's originality stifled.

Dabney St. Maure would never stifle anyone, and possessed the advantages of a long head, deep pockets, and an enviable sense of the ridiculous betrayed by his laughing eyes. Better yet, Lady St. Maure would take to her new stepgrandson on the instant. Unfortunately, the St. Maures were gossip-prone. *She* wouldn't like that—not in a husband, and not in a mother-in-law.

Ollie Threadwhistle probably wouldn't tumble—still wearing the willow for the fiancée he'd lost to consumption three years ago. A pity, but it couldn't be helped. Threadwhistle'd make any woman a fine husband, and any lad a fine stepfather.

That left Pugs Harnette and Stubby Clough.

Harnette might do. Certainly he had the advantage of having already come into his inheritance. Danescroft was a prime estate, though nothing so extensive as Hillcrest. And he was solid, if somewhat unimaginative. Unfortunately, his mother ran his household with a grip she'd be reluctant to release, and did her best to run Harnette and the estate into the bargain—one of the reasons he escaped whenever he could. Matilda Harnette would make any daughter-in-law's existence a living hell, no matter how comfortable her physical surroundings or secure her place in her husband's affections.

As for Stubby Clough, he claimed he'd never wed. He might, but Dauntry suspected Cecelia Walters wasn't the one to fell him. Besides, at twenty-six he was too young to have charge of Tommy. They'd be forever leading each other into the briars, and Cecelia would be forever forced to rescue them.

Which left no one. Perhaps a position at Hillcrest was the best notion, after all.

"What's the matter, Quint? Measuring us for coffins?"

Dauntry's laugh sounded hollow, even to him. "No, Dab, nothing like that. Beds, rather." Or, a bed—which none of them fit. He turned to Mrs. Ford, who was hovering in the background. "What can be made up quick as possible?"

"We want to be together," Ollie Threadwhistle said. "Cots'll do."

"Because of the girl in white?"

Threadwhistle's flaming features provided a nice contrast to his curly blond hair and blue eyes. "Course not," he spluttered, "but we don't want to cause trouble, arriving unannounced and uninvited like this. We've even left our men behind. Longtree, too, though we did bring your toggery. Ghost hunts and spoil-sport valets don't mix."

"In other words, you bolted, every last one of you. Too close proximity to marital bliss giving you a sense of the impending dooms?"

"Only female we're interested in is your ghost." St. Maure's sober expression was more telling than any grin. "All *she* wants is a bit of shroud. Living ones want silks and laces and things— and oh, dear heaven, are there a lot of 'things'."

"That doesn't sound like Amelia."

"It's Lady Katherine," Stubby Clough explained, chuckling.

"Wants to rig her new daughter in style. Val's given his mother her head, and is watching the process with no little amusement. The place is crawling with seamstresses. That was bearable. Then Pugs's mother took it in mind to have a house party and invite all her unwed nieces. Got a passel of 'em. Didn't tell Pugs what she was about, of course. They descended on us three days after you left. It was to be open season on bachelors, and winner take all."

"No wonder you bolted."

"And have no intention of returning for at least a fortnight," Harnette snapped, chin outthrust, "so your ghost'd best keep us amused that long."

Dauntry's brows soared. Pugs Harnette's bolts rarely lasted more than a week.

"I may be an easygoing fellow," his friend bit out, "but enough's enough. I warned Mama if my house's still littered with my fubsy-faced cousins when we return, we'll stay at the Crowing Cock until I've shown them the door and packed her off to Tunbridge Wells. I don't think they'll be there. M'mother detests Tunbridge Wells."

"Somehow I suspect you're right. Tunbridge Wells isn't such a bad notion, though." Pugs Harnette might be a possibility, after all. Dauntry turned to Mrs. Ford. "Put them across from me. That suite's got two bedrooms and a sitting room. Easier for the staff, keeping us together."

"Safer, too," Dabney St. Maure murmured. "See here, who is this girl in white? What does she want?"

"Later."

Dauntry turned to the still open door at a small sound. Tommy Walters stood on the threshold, face sun-reddened, hair on end, stockings falling down, collar crumpled, a string of five under-sized and very limp trout clenched in one grubby fist, a makeshift fishing pole in the other.

"Tommy! Well, come in. We're about to have tea, and not a lady's tea, either. Lots of solid things such as gentlemen prefer." He gave Mrs. Ford a quick glance. She nodded, and headed for the service stairs hidden behind a particularly repulsive bit of statuary. "You'll stay, of course." Dauntry grinned at the disconcerted expression on the lad's face. "You look famished. Been fishing, sprout?"

"Yes, sir. I brought you these because—you see, Uncle told me about—so I wanted—but you've guests, and there aren't enough, and Mama doesn't—and then they aren't very big, but then—"

"Guests who've been looking forward to meeting you." Disjointed communication when flustered ran in the family, did it? That Tommy was prey to it he'd never've suspected. "Come on in, lad. We're all friends here."

When Tommy started backing away, Dauntry seized his shoulder and pulled him into the house. "You're staying to tea. I insist." Then he turned to the fellows, whose expressions were at least as flustered as Tommy's. "Tommy, may I present Mr. St. Maure, Mr. Sinclair, and Mr. Threadwhistle? That sturdy one over there's Mr. Harnette, and this is Mr. Clough. Don't worry about remembering their names. You'll learn 'em soon enough.

"Fellows, this is Tommy Walters, the nephew of Coombe's vicar, Mr. Gardener. He and his widowed mother joined her brother here in '07, about the time Nappy invaded Portugal." That had the fellows' expressions clearing. They'd suspected the lad of being his by-blow, by damn. "He prefers to be called Thomas. I've been given a special dispensation to call him Tommy. Even his mother and uncle don't call him that."

"Those're fine trout, Thomas." Stubby Clough strode over with a grin, and made a show of examining the fish. "This one, especially. Too bad there aren't six, but maybe Quint'll share. I'm particularly partial to trout. Where'd you catch 'em?"

"Stream at the bottom of our garden, Mr. Clough." Tommy looked up at Dauntry. "I can't stay, sir. I wish I could, but Mama doesn't know I've come all this way. She thinks I'm just on one of my rambles, and wouldn't approve in the least."

"And so you are. Don't worry—I'll make it all right. Which shall it be, fellows—my father's library, or one of my mother's drawing rooms?"

"Library'd be cozier," Tommy blurted. Then he flushed. "Books always make a room seem friendlier," he explained at Dauntry's questioning look. "At least, Uncle's study is more comfortable than our parlor. One has to be on one's best behavior in a parlor, even if it does have nicer chairs, and not tell jokes or laugh or ask for seconds of anything. In Uncle's study it's different, so long as no one else is there. A drawing room'd be even worse than a parlor, I'd think."

"He has the right of that." Clough shuddered. "I quake every time Great-aunt Augusta arrives, and I'm forced to present myself. Always spill something or say something amiss, and mortify m'mother and m'self no end."

"The library it'll be, then."

Tommy's eyes turned up to Dauntry's, his expression wistful. "But how could you make it all right with Mama? I'd love to stay, but I mustn't."

"I'll send her a note telling her about the trout. Potts'll have one of the stableboys run it down, so you've nothing to worry about—especially as I'll take you home, and speak with your mother if needed. Don't worry—I'll have you there in time for supper. That's the rule in any well-ordered household unless arrangements're made in advance.

"Now, let's have Mayhew see to it these trout are placed on ice, shall we? They're too special to be permitted to spoil. I'll have them tonight. And, Mayhew, perhaps Nick could show Tommy and the fellows where they can wash off the grime of road and trout stream before our tea?"

Cook had contrived well.

While no delicate lady would've dignified the spread brought to the library as a proper tea—there wasn't a jelly or a *gâteau* or a cucumber slice in the lot, and both tea and ratafia were noticeable for their absence—it was precisely the sort of meal to appeal to four gentlemen who'd just completed a two-and-a-half-day journey in ill-sprung racing curricles, a fifth who'd accompanied them on horseback, and a boy who'd trudged three miles toting a gift of undersized trout.

As the food vanished, Dauntry wasn't certain in whom he felt more pride.

By the time they'd entered his father's library with clean hands and freshened faces, the quintet was playing adjunct uncle to Tommy, and he was regaling them with odd little observations on life in Coombe that were acute to the point of genius. It wasn't that Tommy was putting himself forward. Rather, they were drawing him out regarding nearby places of interest, local personalities, country celebrations, and the vexations of living in a vicarage. Odd, though—the fellows were keeping their eyes fixed on Tommy, and almost ignoring him.

If they didn't feel the gaffe, Tommy did, for finally he turned to Dauntry.

"Of course the Harvest Fair's grand, but the one all the countryside looks forward to is Combermere's big do. People'll be ever so disappointed if you don't have it this year, sir, though I suppose you can't with Lord and Lady Dauntry gone. That's a shame."

Pugs Harnette's brows soared. "What, and break with hallowed tradition?"

"Not have the Combermere do?" Ollie Threadwhistle grinned. "And disappoint everyone for miles about? How could you consider such a thing, Quint? Your ghost'd be sure to take umbrage, and you'd be in worse case than ever."

"Or is it too much for you?" Tony Sinclair prodded. "Probably nigh on impossible, a major celebration like that, for a disorganized, unimaginative military fellow like you."

Dauntry hadn't considered it until that moment. He'd intended to've decamped by then, the girl in white placated, but suddenly the prospect of coconut shies, three-legged races, tumblers, and all the other treats Combermere traditionally offered at its annual obeisance to entertaining the neighborhood had him smiling. Better yet, if he could manage it the fellows would encounter Cecelia Walters daily.

"We'll have the fête, Tommy." Best of all, she'd encounter them. Let her make her own decisions, since he was proving incapable of making them for her. "Of course it was the dowager viscountess who organized things. I suppose my mother's taken over now."

Tommy nodded, eyes wide.

"It requires a lady's touch if it's to be a success. It may not be up to snuff this year if I have to manage on my own, even with you and the fellows to help. I'd have to persuade someone to assist us for it to be as grand as you remember, and it's such a great amount of work that—"

"Mama'd help. She organizes everything for the Harvest Fair, and for Christmas and Easter. People say she's wonderful at it— even better than—well, that she knows how to do things in style at least expense without making people feel they aren't welcome because everything's so formal they daren't smile for fear of giving offense."

"But that would be a terrible burden to place on your mother, especially when one considers her parish and household duties."

"There's Mrs. Burchett and Miss Burchett. They always help whenever Mama asks, and Mama always asks. That way Miss Burchett gets to see Uncle, and they bring wonderful teas—almost as good as this one."

"Mrs. Burchett and Rebecca? They'd be perfect. Now why didn't I think of them?" Dauntry ignored the fellows' amused glances. Tommy could be quite the imparter of information others might've preferred to keep private. He could also be led to speak and act precisely as one would wish, all the while thinking it his own notion. "With their assistance it wouldn't be too great a burden for any. Mr. Nace must have records of some sort, and would lend a hand, of course." And serve Nace right for making a May game of the family, himself included. He'd explain the fête was being held so the girl in white wouldn't get up to more of her tricks. Nace'd get the point. "Do you really believe the ladies'd do it?"

"Mrs. Burchett's sure to say yes. Mama will too, if Uncle and Miss Burchett will be able to see each other. Mama loves fun as much as anybody. It's just she hasn't had much since Papa died, and sometimes she forgets how to have any."

After that the conversation turned general. Nick brought more lemonade. Dauntry retrieved the backgammon set and let Stubby Clough and Tommy have at it like the children they were. The others watched the backgammon wars for a bit, then escaped outside to blow a cloud, whispering to Nick they could do with more ale.

"Seriously," Sinclair said once they were out of earshot of the combatants, "what's happening here? This tale of a hoary ghost doesn't wash."

"My father's been remiss in his parochial duties. Someone became miffed, I'm not certain who at this point. If I didn't know it to be impossible, I'd suspect my great-aunt—the one who lives in Crete. She always considered my father neglectful. But there's no way she could've known about any of this."

"Might be in correspondence with some of the staff," St. Maure suggested.

"Or that squire Thomas mentioned," Harnette chimed in, "or the squire's wife."

"No, on all counts. Had she been, she'd've written me a scathing letter, and ordered me to Combermere posthaste."

"There's that."

"There is, indeed. Great-aunt Persephone doesn't believe in half measures, and her vocabulary tends to blister paper when she's irked."

"I take it that hoyden you encountered on the road's no longer a candidate?"

"No," Dauntry choked out, "I'm afraid not. Impossible."

The fellows leaned on the marble balustrade, gazing over the gardens and clearing their palates of the lemonade with gulps of ale. Heater puttered in the distance, no doubt complaining to his roses about the prospect of being forced to tend vegetables as if he were an insignificant gardener's helper.

"What about this Thomas of yours?" Ollie Threadwhistle turned, gazing steadily at Dauntry. "Seems a solid lad, though there're times when he expresses himself like a Cambridge don. Looks like one on occasion, too. His uncle the repressive sort?"

"Hardly. Had we found him early enough, Gardener would've joined our band."

"What, a vicar, eligible for North's Irregulars?"

"Mischief lurks at the back of his eyes. Totally engaging fellow, honest and caring as they come. Tommy adores him, and rightly so."

"The boy's mother, then?"

"Penniless widow dependent on her brother." That put them

on notice the easiest way possible. "There's something odd there, though, for they're closemouthed about her husband's family. Apparently grand sorts in London. At a guess, they cast her off when he died, if they hadn't already."

"Grand sorts in London?" St. Maure frowned. "What's her name?"

"Walters. Cecelia Walters, *née* Gardener. Parents were in modest circumstances, from what I've been able to determine, and're deceased. No inheritance, or if there was it's gone. Lady's husband was more than comfortable, though—big house, fair-sized property, lots of luxuries from the sound of it. No notion what his given name was."

"Gardener? Doesn't mean a thing. Walters? Something rings a bell. Let me write my mother. If there's anything havey-cavey about the Widow Walters, Mama'll know."

"I'll swear there isn't. More likely the husband's family, whoever they may be."

"Walters," Dabney St. Maure repeated, staring into the distance. "Seems to me there's a scandal of some sort, but I can't for the life of me remember what."

"It'll come to you, Dab," Tony Sinclair said with a chuckle. "Scandals always come to you. Usually it's a good thing."

Ollie Threadwhistle had been frowning through most of their discussion, paying little attention as a multitude of expressions flitted across his mobile features. Now he turned to Dauntry, eyes narrowed. "Y'seem a tad fond of young Thomas, Quint."

"I am. Very." He left it at that.

Six

Shadows were stretching long fingers across lane and field by the time Dauntry arrived at the vicarage, Tommy Walters perched before him on Argus. The lad had been silent the entire way.

"What's the matter, sprout?" He lifted the boy from the saddle, then handed him his crude fishing pole. "Fearing a lecture?"

"Mama doesn't give those. She just looks sad, and apologizes for what one's done. Then later she says how disappointed she is. That's worse. One feels terrible, even if one's done nothing wrong."

"And you give her many opportunities for such apologies?"

"Mama thinks I do. There're things she doesn't understand, like my helping Peter Croft muck out stables at the inn in exchange for a meat pie. She called it begging. I call it working. She's never mucked out stalls, so she doesn't know. I earned that pie, but she gave it to the Crays and told them it was a gift from the Twitchells. Uncle said it was best not to protest too much, and to leave the matter alone. He said mashed turnips and cabbage soup made a perfectly acceptable dinner. Well, they didn't."

"Your mother finds honest labor beneath you?"

"It's not that. Mama thought Mr. Twitchell gave me work out of pity, and she can't bear pity. He told her I'm worth my hire, but she wouldn't listen. She said I was too little to be of use. Now he's had to hire another boy because there's more work than Peter and the stableboy can manage if they're to have any time for fun. Mr. Twitchell says fun's one of the most important things there is."

"He's right."

Dauntry swung from the saddle and turned to face Cecelia Walters as she descended the steps to the pocket garden in front of the vicarage. Weariness lined her face, her frown hinting at an aching head.

"You're exhausted," he said without thinking. Then he turned to Tommy. "Off with you, sprout. I need to speak with your mother, and you need to scrub off the dust and comb your hair."

"Mr. Dauntry, I must apologize for Tommy's—"

"No, you absolutely must not," he said, as the boy scurried around the side of the house after a troubled glance at his mother. "Tommy brought me a gift in thanks for the riding lessons. That a lad his age should feel a sense of obligation is rare. You should be proud of him."

"Thank you, but—that is, Thomas has been told he mustn't be a bother to anyone."

"He isn't. Rather the opposite. Would you keep him totally from the world, and the world from him, for fear of his putting a foot wrong? Monastic isolation doesn't sit well with the young. They tend to run in packs. Certainly I did, and never suffered from it. Neither did the world, great or small."

She flushed. So that was it. Cecelia believed Tommy to be an inconvenience to everyone but herself. Amazing that she didn't have the lad apologizing for his existence. That was going to stop, no matter what it took.

"I've given Tommy permission to come visit at Combermere any time he wishes while I'm there." He smiled, but his tone was the one he'd used with junior officers who retained a tendency to dispute the wisdom of their elders. "Of course he'll come every day for his riding lessons, which I hope you'll attend, at least at first. I don't want you concerned about entrusting him to me."

"But I'm not worried—at least, not very. It's just that—" Then came another of those blushes. "You're excessively kind to offer, Mr. Dauntry."

"Then there's the matter of the trout. If he's to become a proper fisherman, someone's going to have to show him where the big ones are."

"Oh, but—"

"I intend to see to that, too."

"You're taking a great deal on yourself."

Hackles were rising again. What ailed her, for pity's sake?

"I like Tommy, and you and your brother're far too busy to accompany him on his rambles," Dauntry countered, trying a smile he hoped was disarming. "Besides, I have a few favors to ask in exchange. You didn't think I'd volunteer for infantry duty without requesting some form of recompense, did you?"

Her confusion proved he still had time to ease Heater's and Mrs. Ford's way.

"You know about the girl in white, of course."

"What has a spurious ghost to do with Thomas?"

"Nothing. She has to do with Combermere. See here, is your brother home yet? I'd like to discuss the problem with you both. I believe together you can be of assistance in banishing her, though not," he stressed with a grin, "by exorcisms or prayers. Something more direct is needed, Mrs. Walters, and you're just the lady who can manage it all for me with the least fuss."

Moments later Argus was tied to a tree at the front of the house. Dauntry and Cecelia were in the vicar's study. This time he paced rather than enduring one of the hard chairs, pretending he didn't notice Tommy sitting on the bottom step well out of his mother's and uncle's lines of sight, clothes brushed, hair combed, clean hands clenched in his lap.

"I understand I've you to thank for my sparkling lamp chimney," Gardener said.

"What? Oh." Dauntry flushed. "Something to occupy the hands while exercising the mind. Think nothing of it. I didn't."

"Any new information on your ghost?"

He shrugged and resumed his pacing. Gardener, given his grin, might prove an ally. Lord knew, he needed one. Cecelia Walters was entirely too acute for his comfort or her good. If she saw through his machinations, she'd become even more skittish, and he'd be in worse case than ever.

"I'm convinced it's one of the servants," Dauntry said finally, pausing in his forced march. "The girl, I mean. Which one doesn't matter as several are involved. I've seen to the major problems here and in the village, with your help. Now it's time to reward some of the clever scoundrels who called me home. Heater's distressed. You know Mr. Heater, the head gardener?"

They nodded.

"Seems my mother wanted more space to put in flowers for the house. He's had to give up his experimental plots. Heater's been trying new strains and methods. Don't ask me to explain, for I can't. Point is, would you permit him to set up here? I promise he'd be no trouble, but part of the bargain would be that you try his stuff, give him your opinion. Cook refuses to touch any of it. Heater'd keep the inconvenience to a minimum, though one of his lads'd have to come daily."

"Naturally, Mr. Heater is welcome." Gardener was leaning forward, gaze speculative. "Glad to be of assistance."

"But why doesn't he have new flower plots dug in Combermere's cutting garden?" Cecelia objected. "Surely there's space enough."

"Not enough time, as it's so late in the season," Dauntry returned, thinking quickly. "You've already got a plot ready, and while it isn't big he says it'd do once he clears it. If you don't grant him permission, he'll lose an entire year's work."

"Surely you've no objection, my dear." Gardener grinned at his sister. "Your vegetables aren't doing that well. Perhaps Mr. Heater can coax something to thrive."

She flushed and ducked her head.

"Next problem," Dauntry continued smoothly, "is Mrs. Ford. When my nephew was born, she hired on several new girls. Most of 'em've worked out, but there's one she's going to have to let go if something can't be done—a raw recruit of the clumsiest sort. Rose's willing enough, but she's a farm girl overpowered by a grand household. Needs extra training, and her manners smoothed. Worse yet, she's shy, homesick, and misses her brothers. Mrs. Ford hasn't time for that sort of nonsense, but she doesn't want to sack Rose. The girl's family has desperate need of her wages. A lot of mouths to feed.

"Would you be charitable enough to take her on? Mrs. Ford's convinced you could do what's needed, Mrs. Walters, though it'll take patience. Naturally you'd be compensated for your trouble, with no one the wiser, and Nace'd continue to pay Rose's wages."

"Surely you can't object, my dear," Gardener said. "I assume Rose is quite young?"

"Only fourteen, and at the bottom of the pecking order at Combermere. She wants a bit of encouragement, among other things."

"I may not be here all that long," Cecelia protested, "and I don't like to begin what I can't finish."

"We'll solve that problem when the time comes. If she's not ready for Combermere, I'll make other arrangements.

"And now, my biggest problem—Combermere's annual summer fête. Part of our ghost's complaint has been the changes that've occurred since my grandmother's death. I want her ways well reestablished before I leave, so I'll be here for a bit. I suspect if the fête's not held the ghost'll take umbrage, and treat me to a series of uncomfortable mishaps," he rushed on before either could interrupt. "Mr. Nace and Mrs. Ford have records of how things've been done in the past, but I need someone to oversee the whole.

"I was hoping you, Mrs. Burchett, and Becky would take it on, Mrs. Walters. Of course I'll help in any way I can, but organizing such things isn't a gentleman's province. I'd make a mull of it, which'd only make matters worse. I've been told you organize all the parish celebrations, and that the Burchetts are your capable assistants."

He turned to Gardener, overriding Cecelia Walters's flood of objections. "What I'd suggest is that the three ladies spend their days at Combermere. Much easier that way, as there's not much time. I'd be honored if you'd join us for dinner in the evenings, and for as much of the days as you find convenient. The squire, too. And, given your need to range the countryside, I'd appreciate your accepting the loan of a mount or a cart for the interim. You do ride and drive, don't you?"

"Passably," Gardener said, grin broadening.

"Otherwise, the project will come to naught, and Combermere's ghost'll drive me to distraction."

"But how can I train Rose if I'm not here?" Cecelia threw in. "This sounds like the veriest—"

"The mark of any well-trained servant is their ability to follow instructions without constant supervision. I'm sure you know that. It's part of what Mrs. Ford wants the girl taught—to show some initiative, and become more independent."

"I see. How kind of Mrs. Ford to take such an interest."

"You *have* been busy, Mr. Dauntry." Gardener was chuckling now. "Surely you have no objection, Cecelia? It's not only Combermere's ghost who'd be disappointed if the fête's not held. It's the entire neighborhood. Highlight of the summer."

She looked from Dauntry to her brother, hands twisting in her lap. "You said you wanted to request some favors, Mr. Dauntry. Instead, you're still conferring them, no matter how well you attempt to disguise the fact."

"Not a bit of it. D'you have any idea how irksome it is to be forever listening to Heater's and Mrs. Ford's complaints? I want a modicum of peace. This is the easiest way to achieve that. Will you take on the girl, help with the fête, and let Heater putter in your garden?"

"I suppose I must, mustn't I."

"Yes, Cecelia," Gardener said, "I believe you must."

"All right, Quint, let's have it." Dabney St. Maure set his empty brandy glass aside, propped his booted feet on the arm of the leather sofa where he sprawled on rearranged cushions, and grinned. "We've lionized your young protégé, bathed, done our bit to deplete your father's cellars, been fed twice—and a dab hand Combermere's cook is—and've settled into our quarters. The servants're long abed. No reason to avoid the issue any longer. There's a wager to settle."

"Two wagers, actually," Sinclair drawled from across the room. "Got one on your ghost's identity. Got a separate one on what it wants."

"Our first ideas about why your father'd sent for you were embarrassingly off, you were right about that," Ollie Threadwhistle explained, "so we've made some more. A ghost? No one'd've come up with that, not even Dab, and he's the most inventive of us when he makes the effort. Val's vicar got the first purse, since his poor box was closest. We want to know if any of us've won either of these, or if they'll go to Combermere's."

"It's complicated," Dauntry said.

"Ghosts generally are. Their specialty, in fact. Get on with it."

"Start with the legend, why don't you?" Stubby Clough suggested, eyes sparkling with anticipation. "When there's a ghost, there's always a legend, and it's nature's part of the bet."

"Yes, there's a legend, though most of it's fact, unfortunately."

"Well, out with it." Sinclair stretched, then helped himself to more port. "One would almost think you were reluctant to tell us."

"No. Yes. Perhaps. Part of it's vaguely amusing, though it casts my father in an unfortunate light. I've already told you that. The rest's as hoary as it is cheerless."

Dauntry watched a moth that'd fluttered in from the terrace hurl itself against the lamp on his father's desk, its pinging loud in the silence.

"The girl in white's your usual sort of tale, if a bit involved." He shrugged. "A local Saxon beauty—Elfreida something— thought she'd captured the heart and hand of one of my ancestors, Charles d'Auntré, heir to Baron Ranulph d'Auntré. Ranulph's father came over with William, lost an arm at Hastings, and was rewarded with Combermere. Hasn't been a Charles in the family since, by the bye. Or a Charlotte, or any other name beginning with a C, by birth or marriage, except for the name of the place itself. Considered bad luck."

He hadn't thought of that detail until this moment. Well, it didn't matter, did it, for he'd never be in a position to offer for Cecelia Walters. There were greater impediments than an unfortunate name.

"What the devil're you going off into a brown study for?" Pugs demanded. "Y'look like you'd just been ordered t'capture Nappy singlehanded."

"Nothing quite so drastic," Dauntry returned with a hollow laugh. He'd best get on with it, or the fellows'd suspect something. "Happened during the reign of the first Henry. Supposedly Charles gave Elfreida reason to believe she had—captured his heart, that is—but she wasn't well-enough dowered for his father, and she wasn't Norman, so Charles wed elsewhere—chit named Yolande de Chaumes—while Elfreida lay in the woods giving birth to his child. Elfreida's family'd shown her the door, of course, good Godfearing Christians that they were."

The moth'd given up on the lamp, and sought surcease in a candle flame on the mantel. The sizzle made him shudder.

Dauntry wandered to the French doors and stared across the terrace to the gardens, trying to imagine the beauty before him changed: serfs, and oxen, and tiny fields, ladies with oddly-shaped contraptions on their heads, knights riding about in armor, and soldiers guarding the battlements. No roses then, probably. Different trees. Different everything, except for the selfish streak that'd run through the Dauntrys since the beginning of time. Well, he was damned if he'd be guilty of it.

"Charles d'Auntré's Norman child bride adored Combermere," he continued, "and was revered as near to a saint in the area because of her attentions to the poor. Unfortunately, Yolande proved barren, and met with an accident.

"Charles'd established Elfreida in a cottage fairly close by. When his father died a few months later, he paid off or killed those who knew of his Saxon *inamorata,* wed her, and got her with child again. The night Elfreida gave birth to his heir, she crawled from her bed and flung herself from the same battlement his first wife'd fallen from. Right out there. No terrace, then. Just cobbles and dirt. Not even the same house, except for a bit of the cellars. This one was built over the ruins during Elizabeth's time after the castle, such as it was, burned. Nothing much but a keep and some walls. Elfreida died of her fall, of course. Her babe refused to suckle from the wet nurse, choked on a sugar tit, and followed her to the grave within days."

"Good Lord—it *is* complicated," Sinclair said.

"Gets worse. Ghost isn't the local Saxon beauty, as one would expect—dastardly Norman conquerors, and all that. It's the first wife. Barely fifteen when she died—or was pushed. That's why Yolande's called the girl in white, not the woman in white.

"Tradition has it when she's displeased with Combermere's inattention to those in need, Yolande'll appear. If she does, then the lord's wife—if she's still of childbearing age—or his heir's wife if she's not, will die in childbed. Often the heir, and *his* heir, too. They generally choke on a fish bone or bit of steak, though, not a sugar tit."

"Bloodthirsty chit," Sinclair murmured, a twinkle in his eye. "Thorough, too."

"Merely devoted to those she considers her responsibility.

Charles d'Auntré wed four more times. Each of his subsequent wives died just after she'd given birth to a son. Last one went mad first. Only male infant to survive was the child of Yolande's cousin. One tale says by then he'd had Yolande's remains taken from the family vault and buried in the woods, hoping to keep her away. Another claims he had what was left of her burned, and scattered the ashes. Said she was a witch. Either way, servants insisted they saw her every time one of his later wives was confined."

"Not just complicated. Infinitely convoluted."

"The men in my family've never done things the easy way, Tony, then or now," Dauntry returned with a touch of bitterness. "There's a streak of ruthlessness goes with the title. Even my father has it, and he's as good-natured as they come."

He grinned, shaking off the uncomfortable sensation of being watched by centuries of disapproving ancestors.

"Hair stood on end when Potts'd regale me with the tales of a stormy summer's night. Likes to give children the shivers, Potts does. Thunder and lightning made wonderful accompaniments. Then I'd have to make my way back to the house and sneak in through the secret passages—terrifying, until I hit on the notion that the ghost'd probably be more frightened of me than I was of it. Only a girl, after all. That made me braver."

"Secret passages? Better 'n' better. D'you have a priest's hole?"

"No. Family were staunch Protestants by the time those were needed."

"That's one tale I don't believe I've come across in Stowaker," St. Maure threw in, referring to the scandalous *Origins of the Great Families of England, Ireland, and Wales* they all suspected had been written pseudonymously by Valentine North's grandfather. "I'll have to check when we're back at Hillcrest."

"Not in it." Dauntry turned to his gossip-prone friend. "It's not the actual origin of the family. It's just something unpleasant that happened, albeit rather early. No interest to old Mr. North, even if he knew about it. Not salacious enough. Merely, as Stubby said, grim. Isaac Stowaker—or Chalmondly North—was never attracted to grim."

"Still doesn't explain why you're here. Course she's supposedly reappeared—you told us that."

"Terrified my sister-in-law, who's with child again. My mother was convinced both Selena and Bertram would die if they remained. The whole pack took off for Brighton. Once I arrived, my father went to join 'em."

"Bolted, did he?"

"Flew the coop with astonishing speed. Rather superstitious, my father—especially when he suspects he might be at fault. Oh, he's convinced the girl in white exists now—I've made sure of that—but in the beginning I'd say he understood what there was to do, and didn't want to deal with it. Much easier to pretend there's really a ghost, festoon the place with garlic, call me in, then blame me if things go amiss later."

"He's always doing that," Ollie Threadwhistle muttered. "Then, once you've extricated him from his latest sudsy bath, you might as well not exist until the next time."

"Of course it wasn't really my father who got me here. He was just a tool. It was the current ghost—my father's bailiff, probably, in collusion with Potts and Mayhew, possibly some others distressed by conditions in the neighborhood—which I'll thank you to keep to yourselves. If anyone beyond the vicar finds out I know who's behind this, I'll have to inform my father, and that'll be the end of my Combermere holiday. Cost my unholy trio their positions, too—an unfair reward for caring so deeply about the family's reputation, and the people who depend on them."

"But, why Nace? Why not some irate local?"

"Impossible. Easy enough to pop up if one knows where the passages are, but one has to know the warren like one knows one's own features. Moans echo wonderfully from certain spots. Makes one seem everywhere at once. I should know. Scared the maids often enough as a boy, though they never let on. Actually, they must've known it was me, for no one's claimed to see the girl in white for almost a century. Lowering thought—that while I believed I was terrifying them, they were humoring me."

"You did that?" Threadwhistle guffawed. "Always suspected you could be a devil when you wanted, but that's rich."

"Thing is, Nace'd know the passages," Dauntry forged on, trying to pretend he didn't realize his face had turned the hue of a boiled lobster. "Has all the architect's plans in his office. No one'd take bandy-legged old Potts for a slip of a girl. As for Mayhew, ridiculous. He's a strapping fellow, always was. Nace in sheets and veils just might pass. Light of foot, too, and quick. Quick'd be essential."

"All right, I'll grant you Nace. Why now?"

"Since my grandmother died, my father's been 'improving' the place while people starve, and church and vicarage crumble. Even cut the vicar's living by first a third, then a half, claiming what he retained was Gardener's contribution to having 'em re-roofed. Of course the roofs went begging, while my father's improvements didn't."

"Not an uncommon tale."

"At Combermere it is. Family's lived in terror of the girl in white since Charles d'Auntré's time, and done their duty with remarkably few lapses so she wouldn't rise up. Rather useful ghost, when one considers. Problem is, she'd been lying low for some time, and so my father'd dismissed the tales and gone about his business as if she didn't exist. His latest start was to enlarge the ballroom again. I've put a stop to that, given instructions for the estate's customary charities to resume, and had Nace start work on repairing the vicarage and church at the estate's expense."

"So, all's right and tight once more." Tony Sinclair glanced pointedly at Harnette.

Harnette shrugged. "I'm the closest," he said, "which is amazing as I never win anything, and I'm so far off the mark it's laughable. No, Quint, I won't tell you—not now, at any rate. Someday maybe, when y'want a good laugh. Meantime, both purses go to Mr. Gardener for the poor, Tony—appropriate, given what's really happened. Fat ones, too. Val's wagers were gargantuan, as always, Quint. Hope your girl in white appreciates my sacrifice, for I could claim 'em if one wanted to stretch things."

Sinclair nodded. "That's settled, then. God and the destitute benefit again. I'll concoct some appropriately saccharine tale for the vicar."

"Might better tell him the truth," Dauntry said with a grin. "He'd enjoy the joke."

"A vicar, enjoy this one? You're all about in your head." Sinclair's expression turned from contemptuous to curious. "Why aren't your bags packed, Quint? No need to rusticate now your girl in white's placated. You can scamper whenever you wish."

"I promised Tommy there'd be a fête this year as usual. Besides, I want to see what sort of trick our ghost'll pull next. You'll understand when you meet Nace."

"Who cares about a bailiff's tricks? And you aren't in the least needed for the fête. Vicar's sister and the squire's wife can see to that."

"I'm going to begin teaching Tommy to ride tomorrow. That's another promise I wouldn't care to break."

"Bear-leading the infantry turns dull in seconds. Minutes of it, and one's tempted to put quits to one's existence. Believe me, if my sisters' crawlers hadn't already taught me that, Val's wards would've. Forever asking unanswerable questions and expecting to be entertained, and that's on their good days."

"Tommy's not like that. Besides, if I leave too soon, all the good I've accomplished'll be undone."

"Fustian. This Nace fellow can tend to everything, so long as you convince your father it's essential. Bailiff'll be punctilious, given your suspicions."

"I don't want my father at Combermere this summer if I can manage it. Believe me, he'd put all back the way it was, and find a thousand excuses for doing so. Logical ones, too. No, I want inertia on my side. Next summer'll be safe enough. Besides," he added with a grin, "we daren't go back to Danescroft until Pugs's mother disembarrasses the place of marriage-minded frumps. Doing the pretty grows wearying far more quickly than bear-leading young sprouts."

"You're only too right about that," Harnette said with an unaccustomed edge to his voice. "Damned if I'll return sooner than the fortnight I threatened. Need to teach m'mother a lesson. This is the best way to do it."

"And then there's the vicar," Dauntry continued as the murmurs of approval subsided. "He'll be receiving his full living—including the arrears, as soon as I can devise a method for turning them over without insulting him or casting my father in a worse light than the one in which he already stands. Once that's done,

Gardener'll be able to wed the squire's daughter as soon as one last problem's solved."

"The destitute Widow Walters?" St. Maure swung his feet over the sofa's edge and sat, leaning forward with his elbows resting on his knees. "Been giving it some thought. Might be a daughter-in-law of the Countess of Marle. Family name's the same. Countess had a younger son who married to disoblige her, and then died. Gwynyth Walters is rumored to've made the poor woman's life a misery. If it's the same family, a remedy shouldn't be too difficult to arrange. There're other, more recent rumors about the countess, none of them to her credit, if I remember correctly."

"What rumors?"

"Not willing to specify until I've consulted my mother. She's always *au courant,* but I have a fair notion how things should be handled if I remember the *on dits* aright. Need to borrow North for a bit—he's the only one of us has the reputation we'd need—but otherwise it should be simple enough. Easiest'd be to wait until the Little Season. Countess'll be in Town, then. Could prove an amusing project, all told."

"Little Season'd be too late. Mrs. Walters is determined to find employment by September, and leave the field to her brother and Rebecca Burchett."

"Keep her from it, or rescue her later. Doesn't matter which. Point is, things couldn't be better if it *is* the countess. Mama's detested her since they shared their come-out year. Calling Gwynyth Walters a harpy's too kind. Vicious and unprincipled's more like it. Ruined the girl for whom Marle intended to offer, then slipped into her place. Tales were a hum, but she made 'em stick long enough to get what she wanted. Girl was a bosom bow of Mama's, took her own life shortly after. Dreadful scandal, hushed up as best they could. Marle's cringed under the cat's paw ever since. Always has her claws out, the countess does, and snarls when she's crossed. Mama's never forgiven her."

An odd look came over Dauntry's face. "She the restrained sort, or does she wear a lot of jewelry?"

"Rings on every finger, and more chains and necklaces than most women own. She's rather vulgar, for all she married an earl and moves in the highest circles."

Seven

The sun had passed its zenith when Dauntry headed for the stable block the next day, slapping his crop against his topboots.

Things were going well—almost too well. The fellows'd just sworn they'd solve the widow's problems, even if the Countess of Marle weren't involved. Stubby Clough'd proposed his Great-aunt Augusta as a potential employer. Pugs Harnette'd hit on the notion of Val North's wards requiring a governess.

And Dauntry hadn't had to say a single word. Not one. It was Tony Sinclair who'd done most of the talking, the others crowding behind him into the library, stumbling over each other in their efforts to convince Dauntry they could help.

The fellows hadn't caught a glimpse of Cecelia yet, and already they were riding to the rescue. Wait until they met her. One of them would tumble, and that would be that.

It couldn't be going better, could it?

He snarled wordlessly, wanting to curse until the devil himself protested. Instead, he snapped the head from a daisy as he passed. Altruism was fine in theory. In practice, it could be more painful than having a ball gouged from one's leg.

At least he'd finally managed to complete an acceptable letter to his father after the fellows went off to explore the passages, and one to Persephone Blaire, and had them taken to catch the Royal Mail in Chiverton. His father'd get his in a day or two at most. Great-aunt Persie? Hers he'd sent in care of her man of business, as usual. No way to know about that one. It might take a month to reach her. It might take six.

Dauntry rounded the outermost paddock with its permanent training jumps and headed for the stable block, forcing his features to neutrality. Potts would ask questions if he turned up sour-faced and surly. He wanted none.

It'd been a wise notion. His father's head groom was waiting by the innermost paddock, ostensibly inspecting the gate.

"Morning, Potts," he said, his false cheer grating on his nerves. "Fine day."

" 'S'afternoon, sir, case you hadn't noticed."

"Not by much. Anyone available to take one of the carriages into the village to collect Tommy Walters and his mother? If not, I'll borrow one of the fellows' curricles."

"No need. Been here two hours, and more. Walked. Vicar brought him, then went on about his business. No, he wouldn't take a mount or Miss Burchett's gig. Said they weren't needed. Lad's learning to muck out and curry. I know your opinions of those who can get in the saddle but can't see to their cattle."

Such as Dauntry's own father and brother, who never set foot in the stable block if they could help it—though Potts didn't mention that. "My opinions're those you instilled in me," Dauntry returned with a grin. "How's Tommy doing?"

"Mucks good. Learned at The Garter, so that's no surprise. The rest? Well's can be expected. The lady isn't coming. Vicar asked me to give you this."

Potts held out a note written on cheap paper. The handwriting was graceful. The message wasn't. Mrs. Walters regretted, but pressing duties at the vicarage prevented her attending Thomas's lesson.

Dauntry frowned. Then he grinned, and stuffed the note in his pocket. She wasn't going to avoid him that easily—indeed she wasn't.

"Send word up to the house," he said. "I want Cook to pack a tea that'll travel. Have the fellows informed I'll want them in an hour or two. They're to dress for paying a call on a lady. Now, let's see how Tommy's doing, shall we?"

He turned into the broad, cobbled alley between the ranks of stalls. Spotless, as always. Large, wise eyes regarded him with polite interest as he strode along, and elegant heads turned to follow his passage, while he looked for Tommy.

He spotted four Watford blacks. Not one, or even two. *Four*. Must've been in the pasture the few times he'd been in the block itself.

He'd have to speak to Nace, as well as his father's man of business. Watford hunters commanded a fortune. One was a luxury most men couldn't afford. That sort of extravagance had to end, right along with enlarged ballrooms and Gothic follies.

Tommy was in the last stall currying one of the ponies, crooning as he worked. Dauntry watched and listened unobserved, brows rising. This wasn't the first time the lad'd been to the Combermere stables. His technique and rhythm were too reminiscent of Dauntry's, as were the soft murmurings, all of which Dauntry had learned from Potts.

And the pony? Not only were it and Tommy well acquainted. There wasn't an ounce of fat on the animal. The only question was how expert a horseman Tommy had become under Potts's clandestine tutelage. The old fellow must be quaking in his boots for fear of being unmasked. Well, he'd play along with the charade for a bit. Why not? It should prove amusing.

Dauntry stifled a chuckle and strode to the stall door.

"Hello, sprout," he said. "How goes it?"

Tommy looked up, hands stilling. "Very well, sir, thank you. Good morning."

"See?" Dauntry glanced at Potts, who'd followed him down the alley. "It *is* morning. Even Tommy says so."

"Yes, sir," Potts muttered.

Dauntry turned back to the boy. "Ready for your first go in the saddle with no one to hold you on?"

Tommy nodded. "Where's Mr. Clough? He said he was going to watch, and Mr. Harnette, too."

"Exploring the old passages up at the house. The fellows've decided they're going to uncover the secret of the girl in white. Keeps 'em entertained, so I'm not complaining. If you'd rather, we could join them."

The boy blanched. "No, sir, I don't think so. I'd just be in the way."

"Some of the passages're narrow. Mr. Clough won't be able to get through. I doubt Mr. Harnette will, either. You could prove useful, though you might get dusty. I thought boys adored exploring secret passages. Certainly I always did."

"Mama said I wasn't to go up to the house, Mr. Dauntry, no matter what *you* said."

"Clearly another conversation's required with your mother. I'll take care of that later. Now, since we're confined to the stables, let's see how you handle saddling this fine fellow, shall we? First'll be the bridle and bit. That's the collection of straps hanging over there with a jointed metal rod between two of 'em."

Tommy fumbled at every turn, making a thorough botch of the process.

He tangled the pony's forelock in the headstall, neglecting to tuck it through. He let the reins dangle where the pony could've stepped on them had he not shortened them in anticipation of just such an error, and being corrected. He slid the blanket against the grain of the pony's coat. He let the stirrups down too soon, and left them dangling until told to loop them over the saddle before placing it on the pony's back, and then he dropped it—though not from very far—instead of setting it on lightly.

In fact, Tommy betrayed himself only once. He kneed the pony expertly in the belly without waiting to be told before tightening the girth the second time. Dauntry pretended not to notice.

In the paddock, the boy prepared to mount from the right—a gaffe not even a beginner would make unless he were so unobservant he might as well be blind. When Dauntry had him on the proper side, his attempts to mimic the awkwardness of a neophyte had Dauntry chuckling, especially when the animal turned its head in dismay and gave the boy a cautioning whicker.

"It's all right, Tommy, I already guessed. No need to torture the poor beast. He expects better of you, and deserves it. Scramble aboard properly, and show me your best. Here—let me unclip the lead." Dauntry glanced at the groom. "I assume it's safe to do so, Potts?"

Tommy froze, eyes terrified, staring from Dauntry to Potts. Potts shrugged.

"Safe as houses. Didn't use it beyond the first few times. Do

as you're told, lad," the old groom said. "No harm'll come of it,
I'd guess—at least to you."

"None to anyone, if you've done as well by him as you did
by me, Potts," Dauntry returned, grinning. "Have at it, Tommy.
Your very best, mind."

The display of youthful horsemanship that followed was more
than impressive.

"How long has he been coming here?" Dauntry said, leaning
against the paddock fence as he watched.

"Since he could walk the three miles from the village, and go
about without worrying Mrs. Walters—whenever his lordship
isn't in residence, that is. Comes through the woods, sometimes.
That cuts a bit from the trip. The lad knows the lines he can cross,
and those he can't. Everyone's been quiet about it for fear his
mother or uncle might find out, and not approve."

"A benevolent conspiracy of silence? You're all to be commended. Mrs. Walters certainly wouldn't've approved, even if
her brother did."

Potts watched as Tommy executed a series of intricate turns,
guiding the pony with only knees and shifts of weight, then
sighed.

"Lad's been riding only two years. Best I've ever taught, and
that includes you. Born to the saddle. Horses think he's one of
them, even his lordship's Watfords. Insists on helping in the stables when he can in exchange."

"I see."

"Brings me trout, too—scrawny undersized things. Can't
abide trout—no flavor, an' far too many bones—but I'd never
tell him that. Take 'em to the house with him tagging along. Cook
fries 'em up, makes a fuss over him, and gives him a grand tea,
and I choke 'em down somehow, and tell him how good they
are. Needs fattening up, Thomas does. He's a great favorite with
the staff. Old Heater even talks to him direct, 'stead of pretending
he's talking to his roses. Doesn't do that with many."

"He does? Now, that's interesting," Dauntry murmured, observing Tommy through eyes slitted against the bright sun.
"Don't worry—I won't inform on you, or Tommy, or anyone
else."

* * *

The expression on Cecelia's face when she discovered Dauntry at the vicarage door, accompanied by five strangers toting picnic hampers, had him chuckling. Her gaze flew to Tommy, proudly mounted on one of the Combermere ponies just beyond them, her eyes widening.

"Tommy!" she gasped, manners and injunctions forgotten.

"Good afternoon, Mama." The scamp doffed his cap and bowed in the saddle with the air of a polished Hyde Park beau.

"Oh, dear heaven—is he safe?"

"Completely so. Tommy's a young Pegasus—more horse than boy. Both mount and he grow wings when he springs into the saddle."

"But, how—I mean, he's never—"

"Born to it, Potts says. Tommy's quite amazing. Congratulations are in order."

"Dear heaven. George said he might the first time he—but Thomas was so young, and I didn't like—and then we couldn't—that is, I had no notion—"

"Now you do," he said, cutting through her distraught babble.

"Yes, I do, don't I? He sits a saddle just as his father did. Oh, dear heaven."

Were those tears to accompany the wistful smile trembling on her lips? And she had mentioned her deceased husband by name for the first time. So George Walters had been a horseman, had he? And placed his son in the saddle early? And Tommy had inherited his father's abilities.

It had to've been a love match, given her expression. Of course, he'd already suspected that. Well, they said a heart once unlocked could be unlocked again, if one held the right key. One of the fellows was sure to have it about him somewhere, for all he might not know it yet.

Dauntry mentally saluted the shadowy equestrian and moved slightly to block the fellows' view of her, granting her a moment to regain her composure.

"I decided you need a respite from all those onerous vicarage duties that prevented you from coming to watch Tommy's lesson," he said, tone light, "and one from the racket, too, so I've sent the workmen off to The Garter to drink our healths."

"We wondered why the noise'd stopped." She gave herself a shake, eyes still wide.

"Brought you a splendid tea, as well. Has Rose reported yet, or shall I have the fellows and Tommy see to the unpacking?"

"No, that will be tomorrow. Fellows? What—oh, my goodness, do forgive me."

She really hadn't noticed them then, all her concentration on her son.

"I've brought some very dear friends to meet you and your brother," Dauntry explained. "I didn't think you'd mind."

"The friends Thomas told us arrived at Combermere yesterday? Naturally not, Mr. Dauntry. They're being so kind as to accompany you does us honor. Thomas sang their praises from the moment you left until he sought his pillow."

That quickly she'd retreated to prim propriety. He refused to let it go on like that. Breeziness, that was what was needed. Informality. A certain ignoring of the conventions, while not overstepping the bounds. Otherwise they'd all sit around playing prunes and prisms and speak of the lovely weather, and nothing would be accomplished.

"Let's save the introductions until we're with your brother, shall we? There's a gaggle of 'em. No sense going through the roster twice. However—" He turned, spearing the fellows with his eyes. "This is Mrs. Walters, lads—Tommy's mother, as you've no doubt guessed."

Their grins were good-natured, their murmurs all that was correct, their expressions enigmatic. Dauntry shrugged. They could be counted on to play the gentleman when the occasion demanded—witness their treatment of Amelia North, even when they believed her a nameless nobody. He had nothing to worry about if he set the tone a hair closer to university lodgings than a vicarage.

"Why don't you alert your brother?" he said. "We'll tote all this into the kitchen and see to it. Where d'you want things brought?"

"The parlor, of course. It's on the right as you enter."

He stifled a grin, knowing Tommy's opinion of that room as a venue for jollity. Well, he'd turn that around too, no matter what it took.

"I know where it is. Been here often enough as a lad. Leave everything to me." He glanced at Tommy. "Tie your pony next to Argus, sprout, but not close enough they'll exchange kicks or nips, and lend us a hand. You'll know where anything we didn't think to bring's to be found."

In minutes they were ensconced in what had once been a gracious little drawing room, but now resembled the parlor of a poverty-stricken farmer clinging to his land while praying for better times. A few decent pieces had survived Lady Dauntry's raids, but chairs and sofa were threadbare, and the tables' finishes had been worn to bare wood. The fellows pretended to notice none of it.

Gardener joined them by the time Cook's lavish tea had been unpacked and spread about, grinning at the treat and welcoming the fellows as if they'd been the best of friends for years.

As for Cecelia, once she'd recovered from the shock of seeing Tommy astride a pony with no one to hold him on, she was like a brilliant butterfly emerging from its dull chrysalis. She sparkled, putting the fellows at ease, and turning their impromptu feast into something just short of a schoolroom romp. Never had he been so proud of anyone as he was of her in those moments.

It was a joy. It was a delight.

It was also a disaster.

The fellows treated her as they treated Val North's bride. No stumbling over flowery compliments. No thunderstruck looks. No bouts of abstraction. No flushes, or self-conscious incoherence. As for Cecelia, she treated them as if they'd just come down from school on holiday and stopped to pay a beloved former tutor their respects.

In sum, they were perfectly rational, every one of them. It didn't hit one like that—he ought to know. Shocking, that guilty relief could make one want to cheer.

Tommy was in a land of enchantment, no question about it, eyes wide, and—for him—silent, devouring sights and sounds rather than sand tarts and seed cake. This was a Cecelia the lad had rarely seen, Dauntry realized. Well, one way or another, he'd be seeing her constantly in the future.

Besides, perhaps he was the odd one. Perhaps it didn't strike everyone like a thunderclap. Perhaps he just needed to give them all some time.

Gardener was glancing around the room, grinning at them all.

"Got to thank you, Mr. Dauntry," he said. "Most fun any of us's had in years, myself included. You do know how to set things going."

"My p-pleasure," Dauntry stuttered, caught by surprise. "Thought you'd all find each others' company congenial."

"We do. You're to be congratulated on having such friends." Then he turned to his sister. "Cecelia, my dear, I think it's time we returned the compliment. What do you say to singing for our supper? I'm sure we'd all enjoy a ditty or two."

She blushed, but she didn't bridle, or complain of an inferior instrument far out of tune, or flutter her lashes waiting to be begged. She simply excused herself, rose from her place behind the tea table and crossed to the piano, opened it, played a few chords, then an arpeggio to limber her fingers, and launched into a lively Irish folk tune.

Dauntry couldn't drag his eyes from her as the silver notes cascaded through the air.

The late afternoon light streaming through the windows caught her perfectly, touching her chestnut hair with gold, and warming features he had always found distressingly pale from overwork. Dear God, but she was a beauty! And so without artifice, so lacking in the coy tricks of *ton* misses. The fellows had to be mad not to be planting their boots on each others' backs in a desperate scramble to reach her first.

"Told you Mama could sing like an angel."

Dauntry turned to Tommy, who'd tiptoed over to his chair.

"She can indeed, sprout," he whispered. "And play like one."

Tommy nodded, watching him with a hopeful expression. Dauntry turned back to face the instrument, praying his features betrayed only polite enjoyment of a skilled performance. Finally Tommy returned to his stool, shoulders slumped. Dauntry glanced at him. The lad appeared near tears—something he doubted happened often.

"Mrs. Walters is utterly charming," St. Maure murmured in Dauntry's ear under cover of the enthusiastic applause that followed. "No wonder you've no desire to quit Combermere."

"I—ah—that is, my father—and then, matters in the village—"

"Don't blather. Doesn't suit you."

Dauntry stood at the breakfast parlor windows, scowling at the limpid morning light, the first whispers of a breeze teasing his dark hair as the sun kissed the horizon.

The kedgeree on the sideboard behind him didn't appeal. Neither did the gammon or the eggs, or anything else. He was off his feed.

Ignoring Nick Beetle looming by the service door, he turned from the windows and stalked across the room. He was going to have to eat something—it didn't matter what. His face'd appeared gaunt in the mirror when he shaved, its lean planes exaggerated, the cheekbones prominent, and his coats seemed looser. That wouldn't do. Someone would notice. Given those at Combermere, that someone would then comment. He refused to risk inquiries, though he had the excuse of his leg should concern swell to impertinence.

He piled his plate with everything in sight, paying little attention to the odd jumble, capped the mess with a muffin, and took his place at the table.

"Lovely morning," he said, giving Nick a cheerful grin.

"Is indeed, sir."

"Going to be a fine day."

"Mostly that way this time o' year, sir, 'less the clouds build and it comes on to rain of an evening. Mr. Heater's partial to rain nighttimes for his roses, so long's there's sun by day. You be wanting coffee or tea, Mr. Dauntry? There's chocolate too, as Mr. Clough favors that."

"Coffee." Since his time in the Peninsula, tea carried the flavor of sickrooms and pain, and long convalescences. He could choke the stuff down when the occasion demanded, but that was about it. Still, Nick always asked.

The coffee arrived, very strong, very black, and hot as the devil, just as he'd requested Cook to prepare it. He attacked his plate, ignoring what he shoveled in his mouth. Everything tasted like dust.

A week had passed since the tea at the vicarage. With Cecelia, the squire's wife, and Becky in charge, preparations for the summer fête were well in hand. It would be held in two weeks without a single tradition slighted. The arrangements customarily cost his mother six months. Cecelia didn't vacillate, and she didn't change her mind once she'd made it up. Decisiveness was an enviable trait in a woman.

He had achieved success in other matters, too. Rose had reported to the vicarage. Cecelia's hands were softer, the slight crease above her brows fading. The vicar had given up his cavils at the loan of Becky's gig, and no longer mentioned returning home for the evening meal each night. Vicarage and church roofs were solid, the vicarage's interior in a fair way to being restored to its condition during the Killmartins' time. People in the region didn't suffer want unassisted. The girl in white hadn't reappeared.

Best of all, during all that long week Dauntry'd managed not to blather, as Dabney St. Maure had so inelegantly phrased it. Of course St. Maure had caught him off guard that first time.

Yes, everything was satisfactory. Entirely satisfactory. He couldn't ask for more. That was the point: Couldn't.

"Morning, Nick."

Dauntry glanced up. Ollie Threadwhistle yawned in the doorway, curly blond hair carelessly arranged, a Belcher handkerchief at his neck rather than the more conventional yards of starched muslin.

"Dear Lord, but you look grim, Quint. Sour stomach?"

"Stomach's fine. You're up and about early."

"So're you. Leg giving you problems? You look worn to the bone."

"No. Yes. I don't know. Went for a ride. Possibly." That had been preferable to staring at the ceiling while impossible visions whirled through his mind. Unfortunately, he hadn't been able to outrun them, not even on Argus at a full gallop. "Certain you should go about so informally? Ladies'll be arriving soon."

Threadwhistle shrugged, and ambled over to the sideboard.

"This is the country, not London. Going to be a hot day. Don't see why I should torture myself. They'll understand." He began inspecting what was available. "Ever notice how in summer it's they who go about fresh as daisies while we swelter, but in the winter they shiver while we're warm as toast? Fashion must be mandated by Bedlamites. A change's needed. Consider me in its van."

"I should think, out of respect for Mrs. Burchett, you'd—"

"So it's the squire's wife you're concerned about now? That's a twist!" He yawned again, and picked up a plate.

"And her daughter, and the vicar's sister—"

"The last being far from the least." Threadwhistle chuckled. "You've certainly become a high stickler. Totally unlike yourself."

Dauntry stifled a retort, fixing his eyes on his plate. Most everything was gone. Good. Nick'd see to it word traveled through the staff that he'd consumed a farmer's breakfast, and the troubled glances would cease.

"The others'll be down in a minute. When I left, Stubby was mangling his neckcloth. He'd do better if Tony wouldn't give him so much advice, though I suspect it's become a game between them now." Lids rattled as Threadwhistle made his selections. "Mayhew sent word a letter's arrived for Dab, which's why we're up and about at such an ungodly hour."

"So soon? It's been barely a week."

"Soon? It's been an eternity! Haven't you wondered what, ah—"

"Not enough to make a fuss over it."

Boot heels echoed from the entry, not-so-distant thunder presaging a storm, then halted. Dauntry signaled for his cup to be refilled.

Yes, he'd wondered. Of course he'd wondered. Every minute of every day, dreading what they'd learn from the indefatigable Lady St. Maure. She could've taken a year to reply, and he wouldn't have complained. Her response would be the beginning of the end. Once that began, it'd be over with a speed that would leave him gasping and plagued with futile regrets.

The lot streamed in, St. Maure's satisfied grin telling him it was indeed the all-important letter.

Unfortunately, despite the propinquity he'd encouraged—sending Cecelia out for strolls in the gardens with the fellows with the excuse she appeared fagged, enlisting them to play secretary while she labored over arrangements for the fête, rotating her partners at nuncheon and dinner—none had responded with more than disinterested friendship. That meant, no matter what the letter's contents, they'd present problems.

"I believe we could do with fresh pots of coffee and tea, Nick," he said. "No need to rush. Oh, and chocolate for Mr. Clough."

Nick, after a glance that spoke volumes, pushed through the service door and clomped off, letting it swing behind him.

"Certainly knows how to let the world know when he's miffed," Tony Sinclair chuckled. "Not sure you should permit him the luxury though, Quint. We're one thing. Your mother's an entirely different kettle of fish."

"Nick knows the difference. Always clomps when her ladyship's in residence, Mayhew's admitted, so as not to be forced to encounter her—no doubt because he doesn't care for the name she bestowed on him. Alphonse," he added at the inquiring looks, grinning.

"Preposterous!"

"Just so." Then he sobered. "I take it you've heard from your mother, Dab."

"Have indeed. It's quite a tale. Maria Edgeworth couldn't contrive a better." He slipped into the chair next to Dauntry's while the others crowded around the sideboard, loading their plates with the first items they happened on. "You want the whole thing, or just the essence?"

"Essence'll do for now."

St. Maure nodded, seeming to review the letter's contents in his mind and select among them. The sun's rays burst through the windows as he pondered, catching his shoulders and gilding his light brown hair, then streamed across the table to strike the fellows by the far wall. Dauntry's lips twisted at nature's imitation of the enlightenment he was about to receive. There were times when clear vision was far from welcome.

"Mrs. Walters *is* the Countess of Marle's daughter-in-law—got that right," St. Maure said finally, ticking the items off on his fingers. "Husband was the youngest son, name of George. Had that part right, too. Drowned—some sort of boating accident when he was out larking with friends. Then—"

"No, that's wrong," Dauntry interrupted. "He didn't drown, and he wasn't with friends. He and Tommy were rowing on a lake bordering his property. The weather changed, they overturned, and Walters swam to shore with Tommy, wrapped him in his coat, and rushed him to the house. Died of an inflammation of the lungs a few days later. Tommy told me about it."

"That's interesting. Mama's sources're generally reliable. Wonder if the countess had the other put about so there wouldn't be a hint of Walters's devotion to Thomas, and likely the boy's mother as well. Wouldn't surprise me."

The fellows filed to the table, Pugs Harnette plunking a mounded plate in front of St. Maure before he took his seat. A sea of plum compote lapped at yellow kedgeree shores, bits of rice crumbling away to form glutinous islands.

"Is this the best you could do by me?" St. Maure spluttered, staring. "Isn't there any gammon and eggs, or some kippers, or a bit of that sirloin we had last night?"

"Thought y'liked kedgeree."

"I do, but not every morning, not that much of it, and definitely not presented like this."

Dauntry rose as the pair squabbled, Harnette already digging into his more varied fare. He filled a plate with an assortment of stewed mushrooms, eggs, gammon, rabbit pie, grilled kidneys, muffins, and a thick slice of sirloin laced with the wine sauce St. Maure relished. Then he returned to the table, switched the plates, tossed a napkin over the rejected kedgeree, and sat.

"Get on with it," he snapped, cutting through their bickering. "Nick won't be gone all day, and the ladies'll be here soon."

St. Maure and Harnette threw him startled glances, flushing.

"Sorry," they mumbled.

"Apologies accepted. Do continue, Dab, if you'd be so kind?"

It wasn't easy to ignore the others' knowing looks. St. Maure devoured a buttery muffin, no doubt to fill the more annoying crannies, wiped the crumbs from his mouth, and leaned forward.

"All right," he said, "now for why Mrs. Walters is destitute when she should be excessively wealthy. Countess of Marle can't abide her. Had a much more elevated bride in mind for George Walters, even if he was the youngest son. He had his independence, though—a considerable inheritance, including a grand country place and a *pied-à-terre* in London—so there wasn't much her ladyship could do but grumble. Walters ignored her, and insisted his bride do the same. From all reports it was a love match, for all the countess tried to convince everyone Cecelia Gardener'd entrapped her son and was a fortune-hunting hussy. Mrs. Walters made a splash in Town—tickets to Almack's, invitations everywhere, given Lady Jersey lionized her—despite Gwynyth Walters's best efforts. Even gave her daughter-in-law the cut direct. Didn't do a bit of good.

"Then Walters died—how doesn't really matter, though it's interesting the countess lied about it. Gardener'd been named one of the lad's guardians, his paternal grandfather the other. Countess saw her chance. Had her husband's man of business seize everything as administrator of the estate. Wouldn't release so much as a farthing for food, or upkeep of their homes, or anything else."

"Good God," Dauntry muttered.

"Mrs. Walters had whatever remained of her pin money for the quarter, nothing more. Since Walters drowned—or died of an inflammation of the lungs—in March, that couldn't've been much.

"Countess summoned her daughter-in-law and grandson to London. Made Mrs. Walters an offer: If she'd turn Thomas over, swear she'd never attempt to see or communicate with him again, resume her maiden name, and repair to some out-of-the-way provincial town, she'd receive an allowance. Otherwise she'd not see a *sou* without a lengthy court battle and a tremendous scandal. Countess swore she'd ruin her son's widow. Mrs. Walters'd end up without her son, and as penniless as ever. Earl backed his wife up, though rumor has it he didn't like it much. Mrs. Walters turned the witch down flat, took her son, and fled before she could be stopped, my mother doesn't know where—but we know it was to Coombe.

"Walterses' only grandson, you understand. Nothing but girls from the older brothers back then. Still nothing but girls, come to that. As things stand, Thomas's in line for the earldom one day if he has the spunk to claim it, and the desire."

"That unrepentant—" Dauntry ground out, jaws clenched, balled fists shaking. "Anything else?"

"My mother's fulminations regarding the countess's character might be actionable if they were published," St. Maure returned with a grin, breaking the mood as he dug into his food. "Says she was a famous beauty. Arrogant, don't you see, and with unshakable confidence. Being a diamond affects some that way.

"There's some other interesting tidbits as well, but that's the heart of the matter. Word got out because of a gossip-prone footman. The countess denied everything when faced with it by Sally Jersey. Lost his position, of course, the footman did."

"Are you angry, sir?"

Dauntry glanced at Tommy as they turned in before the vicarage late that afternoon. Angry? What a pallid word. Clearly Gwynyth Walters wasn't a safe topic for consideration when those observant green eyes were about.

"No, I'm not angry, sprout." It was the truth. Even murderous was too phlegmatic a term.

"Because you've been looking like a thundercloud for the last mile."

"I have?" Dauntry forced a chuckle. "With good reason, don't you think? The trout were most uncooperative today."

"They're that way, sometimes." The boy shrugged and slipped to the ground, then handed Dauntry the pony's reins and unbuckled the basket containing a fat carp from Combermere's ponds. "Thank you for the wonderful day, sir."

"Wonderful? Despite not having a single trout to our credit?"

"My father always said I should learn patience when I complained of a poor catch. He said the beauty of the place should be enough."

"Then he was a better man than I. When I take time to trouble the trout, I expect them to reward my efforts."

"No, sir—not better. Just different. Fishing teaches one patience. Even Mama fished if the day was fine, and Papa teased her to come."

"And learned patience as well, I gather?"

"Infinite patience, Mr. Dauntry."

Dauntry whirled at the feminine accents and lilting laughter. Backlit by the low sun, Cecelia Walters was a vision from a folk tale, her unbound chestnut locks streaming across her shoulders in a shimmering cape.

"G-good afternoon," he managed. "I hope I find you well?"

"As thriving as I was this noon at Combermere. Rebecca was out of sorts, however, and so we played truant shortly after you all left for one of your secret streams. I hope you're not angry?"

"How could I be? It's you interrupting your lives for Combermere's sake, not I mine for yours. These things happen."

"Yes, they do—even to the most sturdy souls, and certainly Rebecca is that. No, no lasting trouble. She should be fine by morning." She blushed then, collecting herself as she gathered the rippling waves against the nape of her neck and twisted them into a loose knot. "Do forgive my informality, Mr. Dauntry. I took advantage of this wonderful weather to wash my hair, as I knew it would dry quickly. No luck today, I gather?"

"Either the stream lost its fish while I've been gone, or I remembered the best spots incorrectly. None of us caught a thing."

"A pity, but it happens. One can either choose the adventure of trying a new location and accept the risk of a poor catch, or one can plod along as one's always done, miss the adventure, and be assured of cooperative trout. I've always preferred adventure."

"Your intrepidity is an example to us all."

"Neither Thomas nor I have ever been accused of faint hearts." She smiled again and unlatched the gate, then turned to Tommy, smile broadening. "What a little ragamuffin! Are you attracted to mud and dead leaves, Thomas, or are they attracted to you?"

"We've already cleaned off the worst, Mama. Mr. Dauntry didn't want you to think he permitted me to run wild."

"He didn't, did he? One would never guess, but then I suppose opinions regarding a presentable appearance differ between ladies and gentlemen. Trot along to Rose. Once she's set you to scrubbing, tell her we'd enjoy some lemonade. I want to show Mr. Dauntry the miracles Mr. Heater's performed."

"I, ah—unfortunately, I must be going." Dauntry backed up Argus, dragging the reluctant pony, who'd been cropping daisies along the fence, with them. "I shouldn't like Cook forced to put off dinner on my account."

"Surely you can spare a few moments?"

Did she realize how irresistible she was in this guise, devil take her? Especially with those luminous gray eyes dancing as she gazed at him, the ghost of a smile lingering on her lips, the loose knot coming undone to let her hair tumble down her back in a silken river? She must, and yet he could hardly believe it, so natural she seemed. Evidently prunes and prisms were on holiday, despite her earlier blushes.

"Robert's in the garden, inspecting progress," she added. "He requested you join us, as you haven't stopped by since you brought that wonderful tea a week ago."

"Not much opportunity," he prevaricated, "what with one thing and another."

"Please, sir?" Tommy was staring up at him, eyes wide. "You should see it so you can tell Mr. Heater how nice it is. If you don't mention things that mean something to grown-ups, he'll think you're just repeating what I've told you."

"You're right, sprout." It was as good an excuse as any to do precisely what he wanted, Lord knew. He handed Tommy the pony's reins. "Tie Pansy to the fence, and then finish scrubbing up as your mother told you. Be sure to tell Rose that Cook's already stuffed the carp, and wrapped it in leaves. It only wants half an hour in the coals. Not a minute more, understand? I'll see to Argus myself."

Moments later he trailed after his hostess, determined not to study the slender figure leading the way. Tommy's earlier effusions had been accurate. Everything was cleaned and raked, flowers planted to either side of the entry and along the paths, as well. Combermere's cutting gardens must be suffering considerable depletion.

The area at the rear of the vicarage was equally transformed— shrubs and trees shaped, flowers everywhere, the kitchen plot thriving, sod covering the old patches of barren earth. Heater had lifted entire sections, complete with soil. Apparently the trick had worked.

Gardener sat by the stream which bordered the property, attention fixed on a water hen scolding a cat that crouched on the far bank. From the open windows came the sound of young Rose teasing Tommy about his hollow leg. Dauntry remembered the sweltering kitchen not so many days ago, and Tommy's serious mien the first time they met, and smiled.

"Heater's adjusted to vegetables, it would appear," he murmured, forgetting his company, then flushed.

"Only partially." Cecelia watched him from the corner of her eye, but otherwise gave no indication she understood the meaning behind his careless words, circumspection winning over what he didn't doubt was a pithy retort trembling on her lips. "Mostly he putters with the flowers, and leaves the vegetables to his grandson."

"Trained him to it, I suppose."

"He has? Amazing, for Billy constantly requires instructions. He's barely older than Thomas, though, so that's probably no surprise."

"No, it probably isn't. Heater's overseeing all. That's what matters to him."

"And there's nothing the least unusual about his cabbages, or anything else."

"Perhaps they're more resistant to rot, or pests, or something else not readily apparent to the eye."

"Perhaps."

Her low laugh had him flushing again. Today they skirmished in the old manner, it seemed, skill acknowledged and honor saluted, no matter how subtle the admissions. In the end, however, he'd win every engagement. He had to.

Gardener had risen and turned at the sound of their voices,

dusting off his breeches. "Afternoon, Mr. Dauntry," he called. "Forgive my abstraction. I was planning this week's sermon. That water hen and cat are perfect examples of maternal devotion in conflict. One mustn't blame the cat for wanting to feed her kittens, you see, or the water hen for denying her the privilege if she can. Is it to be trout tonight," he asked, striding over the sloping lawn, "or must we make do with the brace of duck you sent down?"

"The duck, to my everlasting shame, and a carp we brought with us."

Gardener grinned as he came up. "Thomas lectured you on the virtues of patience, I don't doubt?"

"Something along those lines."

"He learned the lesson early. My sister, on the other hand, learned it rather late."

"Please, Robert," Cecelia murmured, coloring as she struggled to bundle her hair back in its knot.

"Perhaps that's why she possesses the quality in such abundance now," the vicar continued as if he hadn't heard her plea, "along with not a little fortitude and a good deal of that maternal devotion of which I was speaking. Determination has always been Cecelia's long suit when the occasion demanded, however, no matter what cause she furthered."

"No wonder the fête preparations are coming along so well." Dauntry turned, gesturing at the garden. "I had no idea Heater could work such miracles so quickly."

"Not difficult when one moves an entire garden from one place to another at dusk so nothing wilts, and sets everything out by torchlight. You'll find the changes within as startling, if you have a moment? My new desk is a prime example, and Thomas's kite-making table has him in raptures, as I'm sure he's informed you."

"That he has."

"And you'll find you won't be crippled if you'll accept a chair, and a glass of the excellent sherry you sent over."

"How kind of you."

"You might even consider staying for dinner this time," Gardener continued with twinkling eyes. "Certainly you've provided us with a generous enough one for us to be able to play host without objections on your part. We can even offer you white wine with the fish, and burgundy with the duck."

Cecelia's hair tumbled down again. She gasped something incomprehensible and darted for the house, almost colliding with Rose and Tommy as they descended the kitchen steps, Tommy toting a pitcher of lemonade, Rose a tray of goblets.

"Why did she run off?" Gardener murmured, gazing after her. "Nothing in the least improper about issuing the invitation so late. You're among friends, here. There are times when I think I'll never understand my sister."

"She's a lady," Dauntry returned. "One's not supposed to understand them, merely appreciate them."

The familiar notes of a Bach invention cascaded from the newly tuned pianoforte, diminished by distance. Odd—that Bach, who was often a tinkly, convoluted sort of fellow, should hold such a hint of fury.

Eight

Behind Dauntry there was laughter as the game of lottery tickets ended, Tommy the big winner. In moments the evening tea tray would appear, a bit later the Beechy Knoll carriage, and so would end another of the speeding days. Precious few remained.

The fête was in three days' time. Everything, down to the favors for the tables in the main tea pavilion, was ready—an unheard triumph of common sense and efficiency.

The ladies would not be returning until the pavilions and booths were erected the day preceding the fête, the tents raised. Neither would Tommy, if he came then. Gardener insisted it was time their lives resumed a more usual routine. He was right, of course. That did not mean Dauntry had to like it.

He slipped onto the terrace and wandered toward the far end, pulling a cheroot from his coat and lighting it. If he felt very much alone, it was his own fault. He could be joining in the merriment if he chose. He couldn't bear to, and had given the excuse of pressing business earlier, then purposely entered the morning parlor too late to form a part of their game.

"Blowing a cloud? Think I'll join you."

Dauntry glanced back. Dabney St. Maure stood silhouetted against the light flooding from the morning parlor for a moment. Then he sauntered down the terrace, looking up at the star-studded sky in which the waxing moon gleamed like a Turkish scimitar. Somewhere in the night-shrouded gardens a band of crickets struck up, their song loud in the silence.

"You're being a fool, you know," St. Maure said, his voice

barely above a whisper as he reached Dauntry's side. "Val'd leap
at the chance to purchase you a commission, or establish you in
any other way you want. Then you could speak to—"

"No."

"Then approach your father, for God's sake, once the next
one's born. He's sure to see reason."

"Reason? You've seen Merlin's grotto." Dauntry leaned his
arms on the broad baluster, hands and cheroot dangling in the
void. "Credit me with enough sense to understand that my revered father being miraculously encumbered by reason's as ludicrous a notion as our beloved Regent adopting Byron's diet of
potatoes and vinegar."

"Then that great-aunt of yours. The one in Malta, or wherever."

"Crete. My brother's forever importuning her with his hand
out. Never gets a *sou,* of course. I refuse to descend to his level.
My aunt deserves better of us than that."

"Then how about—"

"Enough. Once all's right and tight, I'll see Val about a small
loan—just enough to get me to India—though I'll thank you to
keep that to yourself."

"India? Sheer lunacy."

"Should be able to make something of myself out there. Others
have, Lord knows. India's inconvenient enough that my father
won't be summoning me home each time my mother sneezes.
Besides," he said with a laugh, "by the time I got home, she'd've
stopped sneezing."

"You nodcock," St. Maure muttered. "She'd be having the
vapors about something else, and you'd still be stuck."

"Better yet, my father hasn't got any cronies in the East India
Company. If that's not far enough, I'll go on to New Holland.
They'd declare me deceased, not wanting to admit they had a son
residing in a penal colony, even if he was there by choice."

"Worse and worse. I've heard it called madness. Now I begin
to understand."

"Have done. I'll not put myself in the position of being labeled
a basket-scrambler, or cause Mrs. Walters to be sneered at for

succumbing to cream-pot love. If we're successful in London, that's how the world would view any offer on my part."

Dauntry shrugged and took a pull on his cheroot, continuing to stare toward his grandmother's rose gardens. "Heard from him again this morning—my father, not Val. Wanted to know when he could bring the family back. Brighton's proving deuced expensive, apparently. All those shops. Still cheaper than redoing the ballroom in the style he'd planned."

St. Maure chuckled, then sobered at Dauntry's sharp look.

"You wouldn't find it so amusing if you'd seen the want his spendthrift ways'd caused in the neighborhood," Dauntry snapped.

"I saw the vicarage. That was enough. How'd you answer him?"

"I told him not yet, though some progress'd been made."

Dauntry turned back to the gardens. A badger lumbered out from under a clump of shrubs and scuffled along the path directly below them, rooting with its nose, the scrape of its claws against the gravel clear.

"Said the ghost's still appearing all over the place—she is, for all I know—but that she's not moaning as loud and has stopped clanking her chains, which is a good sign, though not the best one, which'd be her not appearing at all. Informed him he'd be wise to take permanent lodgings, and count on remaining the rest of the summer—not that much of it left, after all—or else go on to some less fashionable spot."

"Think he'll agree?"

"With my father one can never be sure, but I suspect he may. He knows the district'd think him ten times a fool for returning in spite of the girl in white, given he decamped because of her. Strange as it may sound, he doesn't care to be thought a fool."

St. Maure nodded. "Most don't—especially those who suspect there might be some truth to the label. Sets their teeth on edge. Got a cousin like that. Hasn't so much as a dust mote in his attic. Hides it with an overbearing manner. Dreadful bore, Reggie.

"All's set in London," he continued after a moment. "Soon as she heard Gwynyth Walters had arrived, my mother sped to Town claiming she had a need to refurbish her wardrobe. Caused a bit of a to-do, as she hadn't alerted the staff. Holland covers everywhere. Left my father at Plaisance, which is all to the good. They sometimes brangle when she gets up to her tricks, though this time I believe he'd be cheering her on. All we have to do now is go to Hillcrest, and convince Val he's more needed than he's ever been in his life."

St. Maure leaned an arm on the baluster, back to the morning parlor. "Did we ever tell you what we found in the passages?"

"Not a word. I assumed all you got for your pains were faces full of cobwebs and filthy coats. Certainly that's all I got as a boy."

"Not quite, though we got those, all right. Besides the usual mouse droppings and dead beetles and what looked to be the remains of a squirrel in the gallery passage, there was a lantern, a tinderbox, some old shawls, and a length of chain. Those were by that door to the gardens. Left them where they were, since we didn't know what you'd want. We did find one set of footprints in a corner, but they were scuffed. Rest seemed to've been swept clean."

"The passages've been swept? Now that's odd."

"Not all of them. Just where your girl in white'd walked."

"Still odd. Of course Nace's a very careful fellow. Excellent sense of self-preservation. Glad you left her gear. I don't want her alerted we're in pursuit, though I imagine she must've guessed by now—hence the housewifery where one wouldn't expect it, and her silence. She's achieved her goal in any case, or at least Nace has."

At a sound, the men turned, and Dauntry broke into a broad grin.

"What ho, sprout?" he said. "Had enough of winning games for one evening, and want to join us reprobates?"

Tommy was staring at them, eyes wide. Then he gave himself a little shake.

"Mama asked me to tell you the tea tray's been brought in, sirs."

* * *

It had rained during the night—a perfect rain, cooling the air, lifting spirits, and soothing frazzled nerves. Not enough rain to muddy the paths or gather in low spots. Just enough to kiss Heater's roses and make them smile, to settle the dust raised by yesterday's frenetic preparations.

And frenetic they'd been, despite all Cecelia's planning, her assignment of the fellows as her deputies, and Becky and Mrs. Burchett's capable assistance. Last night's dinner had been silent, lids heavy, heads nodding. No suggestion of lottery tickets or jack straws, even from Tommy, who'd spent the day as his mother's messenger. No conversation, except for the occasional "Did you remember to—" The gentlemen had eschewed port and brandy, trailing the ladies to the parlor, the tea tray hard on their heels, the Beechy Knoll carriage summoned within minutes.

And now it was morning again. A sparkling morning. A perfect morning. One of those rare days when Combermere wasn't just an impressive country seat, but became an enchanted fairyland— so long as one didn't catch a glimpse of the house.

He was standing under the front portico, the slightest of smiles quirking his lips. A sea of tents, pavilions, and booths covered the front lawns devoted to the fête. Arriving vendors trundled overflowing barrows from the outermost paddock where they'd left their wagons, the price of their goods already met so none who came would need so much as a penny—Combermere's gift to its neighbors.

Dauntry kept his eyes strictly forward, a touch of the old excitement at the dawning of this crowning event of the summer coursing through him. Today was his, the only one like it he'd ever have. He'd permit no one to spoil it—not even Cecelia, no matter how she balked. And, she'd balk, at least at first. No question about it.

"Pleased with yourself?" Pugs Harnette said as four caterer's wagons from Chiverton pulled up and were directed to the back of the house by Nick Beetle.

"My grandmother'd be pleased, which is more to the point. Nace tells me the booths've run out of everything by midafternoon these last years—no doubt another of my father's economies at the expense of others. This time they won't."

"No, they won't. All of London could arrive, and there'd still be more'n enough to see you through." Harnette paused, glancing at him from the corner of his eye. "You look every inch the lord of the manor, you know."

"An illusion, believe me."

"Not so sure about that."

Dauntry held his peace. They'd been attacking him, front, rear, and flank, for days now. And inventive with it. An ambush one moment, a scout on a foraging expedition the next, a full-blown battle with cannons thundering and cavalry charging when he least expected it. God knows how it'd be when they got to Hillcrest. Probably no better. The fellows meant well—that was the best he could say for their efforts. Had even he seemed as bumbling to Val only weeks before? Probably—a dispiriting thought.

He grinned as the Beechy Knoll carriage appeared at the head of the drive, pausing every few feet to permit someone to pass while Tommy twisted on the box, peering in first one direction and then another as he chattered with the coachman. The lad finally sprang to the drive and dashed for the house, dodging through the throng.

"Good morning, sprout," Dauntry called. "What do you think?"

"It's glorious! Positively splendid! I'd no notion it'd be like this." Tommy arrived at the top of the steps, panting and grinning. "Wasn't ever before. Not half so much of anything."

"Oh, yes, it was—though not recently. All rested for the big day?"

"Slept like the dead last night, Mama said. Well, she didn't say it quite like that, but you understand. I don't remember, so I suppose I must've. Woke with the birds—before 'em, really—but Mama wouldn't let me come ahead no matter what I said. She insisted I'd be in the way. I wouldn't've. Really! I'd've been a help, not a hindrance, and wouldn't've bothered a soul. Took forever for the Burchetts to come, too, and even longer to get here. The lane's clogged with carts and wagons and people and I don't know what all, just as I knew it'd be. Thought we'd miss everything."

He paused, collecting himself. "Good morning, sir. Good morning, Mr. Harnette. I hope you're both well?"

"Top of the trees, Thomas." Harnette grinned at him. "Have you breakfasted?"

"Mama insisted I have some porridge. Didn't want it, so I gave it to the chickens when she wasn't looking. She let me eat outside, you see. Said I was too much of a chatterbox and was driving her to distraction, and Uncle suggested it. I wasn't being first cousin to a fiddlestick, though. Third cousin, maybe, but not first."

"Probably not even that. Now you're here, how about some gammon and eggs and muffins? There's a hollow in my leg big enough to sink all of Russia. We can see everything from the windows if we shift the table a bit. Be glad of the company."

"You're sure?" Tommy glanced from Harnette to Dauntry, then across the lawns. "I mean, isn't there something I should be doing, like showing people where to go, and handing them things, and helping with the flowers for the pavilions? Mama said—"

"No, sprout, you've worked hard enough," Dauntry broke in as the carriage carrying the Burchetts, Gardener, and Cecelia pulled up at last. "We all have. Go along with Mr. Harnette and fortify yourself. You're on holiday, with orders to enjoy yourself to the full. So's your mother."

"She won't listen."

"Today I believe I have the power to ensure she does. Wouldn't've been a fête if you hadn't raised the issue, and the family'd be in deeper disgrace with the girl in white than ever. If we were to be honest about it, we'd call it Tommy's do this year, and not Combermere's at all."

After a last excited glance over his shoulder, the boy accompanied Harnette into the house. Dauntry watched him go, then turned and descended the steps in time to hand the ladies from the carriage, complimenting Becky and Mrs. Burchett on their new bonnets and Cecelia on Tommy's enthusiasm and energy, as there wasn't much he could say about a made-over gown and a bonnet he'd seen dozens of times.

"I'd thought to manage things from the servants' hall," Cecelia told him as the others settled skirts and shawls and opened parasols, and Gardener and the squire donned their hats. "I hope that's acceptable, Mr. Dauntry. I can be found easiest there without disturbing your guests or household. Thomas has agreed to act as my messenger today as well, and so will be out of the way. He was quite good at it yesterday, and very quick."

"No." The one word, quick, firm, brooking no argument. He tucked her hand in the crook of his arm, gave her a smile, and turned to escort her up the steps.

"Where, then? Is there a side door of which people may be informed?"

"No."

"Then a table a bit out of the way that won't be mistaken for an amusement? Preferably in the shade? I hadn't realized you'd object to my being in the house."

She'd ducked her head, hiding beneath her bonnet's brim just as she had the first time he'd encountered her in Coombe. He knew she was blushing furiously, for all he could see only a curve of painfully rosy cheek.

"I have no objection to your being in the house, or anywhere else. You know that."

"Then what do you suggest, Mr. Dauntry?"

"I suggest you understand your part is done—other than having your health drunk at tonight's banquet, along with that of Rebecca and her mother, as the ones who've labored to make all this possible."

They'd reached the top of the steps, the others streaming in before them past Mayhew. He gripped her shoulders and forced her around.

"Look at it! None of this would be here if you hadn't agreed to help."

"Nace and Mrs. Ford could've—"

"They're excellent at following orders, but they're not the sort to initiate anything—with one possible exception," he added wryly. "You'll have to respond to the toasts, and once the dancing begins you'll probably have more partners than there are stars in the skies. That's a form of work, I suppose, dancing is. Certainly it's energetic enough. Nace and his crew'll see to everything else from here on."

"But I don't dance."

"Everyone does at Combermere's fête, from the oldest grandmother to the youngest moppet in its father's arms. You know that."

"We've always made our departure before the dinner and dancing. So has everyone from the village. Only the London guests remained for that, and a few of the gentry who'd been specially invited."

"The ones for whom all this is meant left? Well, they won't this time. You don't intend to make yourself conspicuous, do you? Because refusing to stand up is precisely the way to do it, if that's your goal."

"Of course not, but I'm a widow. My brother's the vicar. It wouldn't be proper for me to—"

"Forget circumspection, for once, Mrs. Walters—not that there's anything improper about deriving a bit of pleasure from life on occasion, as I'm sure your brother's informed you. Certainly Gardener intends to lead Becky out."

Best not to tell her she'd be opening the informal outdoor country ball that would cap the day as his own partner. Better to surprise her with it, and carry on from there.

She hesitated, marshaling her arguments. He wondered which would come next.

"But, I've prepared lists of what has yet to be—"

"The ones on my father's desk? I turned them over to Nace last night with instructions you aren't to be bothered, and he's to see to everything."

"Oh, but I—and then, Thomas—"

"I've handed Tommy the keys to the fair. It's more in his honor this year than Combermere's, truth be told. Don't worry—the fellows'll keep an eye on him." Dauntry gave her another smile he hoped remained within the bounds of disinterested friendship. "This is one day you'll not lift a finger, except to enjoy yourself. You've earned it, and more, so you'd best resign yourself."

"I'm not particularly adept at following orders." Her eyes were flashing now, her chin raised. "In fact, I'm known for precisely the opposite, Mr. Dauntry."

Blast her contrariness. Well, he'd expected it, hadn't he? And was prepared. There wasn't an argument she could raise that he couldn't counter. He'd anticipated them, having come to understand her character over the past weeks. She wasn't the only one who could make lists of challenges, and devise a solution to inscribe beside each.

"Did you really think I'd permit you to play servant while the countryside devotes itself to the enjoyment of a particularly fine day? If you'd prefer one of the fellows as your escort, tell me now. They were rather miffed that I intend to have you more or less to myself."

"Oh, no." She looked up at him then, features softening, gray eyes huge in her delicate face. "Not that they aren't pleasant gentlemen. Well," she said with a laugh that sounded forced, "rather more than that. But if I'm not to be permitted to proceed as I'd planned, then I believe I'd rather experience Combermere's fête with you. Perhaps we can join Rebecca and my brother. That would be best, I believe."

"I doubt they'd think so," Dauntry said with a chuckle. "No, you'll have to make do with just me, for I doubt not Tommy'll find the fellows' company more exciting than ours today."

He'd never felt such pride or contentment, Dauntry decided, as he had exploring the delights of Combermere's fête with this one lady on his arm.

It was a dangerous exercise. One could become too easily accustomed, and do precisely what one had sworn never to do. The temptation was constant to forget about Gwynyth Walters and London, sweep Cecelia to the far side of the maze where none would see them, pull her into his arms, and declare his life would be forever blighted did she not spend the rest of it at his side, waking or sleeping, that they'd make do somehow, penniless though they might be.

A good thing he and the fellows were leaving for Town on the morrow. When he returned all would have changed, and he'd be there only for a day or two at most in any case. He could resist irresistible impulse that long, at least.

The first minutes after they parted from the others had been disastrous, of course. She'd been self-conscious, and he'd been tongue-tied despite his best efforts at worldly urbanity. There was such a thing as caring too much.

Then Harry and Joan Twitchell from the inn had bustled up, Harry with Heather on his shoulders, Joan holding Peter's hand, and all had become natural thanks to the children's excited prattle.

"Tired?" he said now, gazing down into her luminous gray eyes and drowning. "It's a particularly warm afternoon."

"Not really, though my feet are, a bit. Tired, that is," she explained with a little laugh. "We haven't sat down once, and I've been cursed with a pebble in my boot for some time."

"Why didn't you say so? I thought you were limping. Of all the idiotish—" He picked her up, ignoring the curious glances of those around them, and carried her to a nearby bench set under a group of beeches while she protested the informal liberty. "Be still, and don't squirm so. I don't want to drop you."

"Then put me down!"

"I'm about to. Of all the foolish, unforgivable—"

He plunked her on the bench in disgust, and knelt to unfasten her boot. She jerked away, tucking her foot behind her where he couldn't reach it without creating a scene.

"This is totally unnecessary. I'm not helpless. It's a very small pebble. I can see to it myself."

"Then why didn't you?"

"Because I was having a wonderful time, and didn't want to make a fuss over nothing."

"My dear, take it from a soldier who's been on many a long march. Pebbles are nothing to laugh at. Infection can follow a cut swiftly. Now," he said, staring into eyes that had turned stormy, knowing his were just as threatening, "let me see that foot."

"No," she bit out.

Then her eyes widened. She peered at him, a startled look that had him flushing from the tip of his toes to the top of his head.

"Good heavens!" she giggled. "There's no question, though— none in the least. What you must've thought of me when we were introduced in the churchyard that first Sunday. No wonder you were so stiff and pompous one moment, and so sarcastic the next. I couldn't make you out at all.

"Poor man. The vicar's widowed sister, no less! You must've been at a complete loss as to what you should say or do. Thank you for deciding nothing was best. You made an excellent recovery, by the bye. At dinner you were completely natural, if a bit naughty and teasing."

"I beg your pardon?"

"It was you! And I thought you a vagrant, or worse. That wasn't a particularly elegant mount, you know. I scrambled through the ditch to escape you, remember? Your voice was unrecognizable later, and your face—you were quite disgustingly filthy, and extremely hoarse—but that Sunday I wondered if I hadn't encountered you before. You seemed familiar, but then I dismissed the notion as ludicrous.

"There can't be two gentlemen with such a concern for the slightest injury to a foot. Don't you remember? It was the day you arrived, near the Bittersfield fork."

Oh, he remembered. He remembered perfectly—every word, every incorrect assumption.

"The hoyden," he said, eyes twinkling in response to her delighted laughter. "The one I instructed to seek her keeper's assistance as she wouldn't accept mine."

"The very one. How funny!"

"Our secret?"

"Most definitely," she agreed with a grin. "When I think of the way I described you to Thomas and Robert, and later to the squire—well, let's just say I shouldn't like it known I'd so misjudged Coombe's savior."

"Neither would I, though I'm hardly that. How was the foot when you reached the vicarage?"

"A small blister. Nothing of consequence. A good rub with a slice of the lemon Rebecca gave me, and it vanished overnight."

"You were fortunate." He rose then, frowning at her. "You're turning the subject. Well, I'm not so easily put off. You've really hurt yourself this time, haven't you?"

"Not in the least. Merely a minor annoyance." She took a deep breath and smiled. It was a contrived thing if he'd ever seen one.

"I could do with a glass of lemonade, though, if you'd be so kind? I'm truly parched."

There was nothing for it. He strode off, cursing under his breath, spotted Tommy by the acrobats' stage, and made a quick detour on his way to the tea pavilion.

"Go to your mother," he ordered, seizing the boy's shoulder and forcing him to turn away from the spectacle of two females in spangled tights balancing on either end of a board set on a ball. "She's hurt her foot, and is on a bench at the end of this alley. No, nothing serious, but I want you to stay with her until I return. I'll require a report just as soon as I'm back with the lemonade she requested. If there's blood or the skin's broken, I want to know. It'll want washing and dusting with basilicum powder. Infections sneak up on one unaware, and can be dangerous. You're to obey me in this, Tommy, not her. Now, hop to it."

The boy nodded, eyes wide, and darted back the way Dauntry'd come. That wouldn't earn him any points with little Mrs. Walters. Well, that wasn't what mattered. Her health and safety were. He glanced about again, spotted a booth serving lemonade and gingerbread. Good. It was closer than the tea pavilion. Dauntry forced his way to the front, elbowing others out of his way with curt apologies, then crashing into Dabney St. Maure, who was at the lead of the line.

"For pity's sake, what's the matter with you, Quint?" St. Maure yelped. "I'm all over gingerbread."

"Mrs. Walters's injured her foot. Here you, give me a jug of that lemonade and a glass. Yes, an entire jug. No, I don't want any gingerbread. Just the lemonade, blast it. Hurry it up, will you?"

"Easy, Quint. I'm sure it's nothing serious. Need a hand?"

"Not in the least, just the lemonade. Says she's parched, but that's just an excuse to get me out of the way."

He seized the jug, said he'd return it later if he thought of it, plunked down a few coins to cover the cost of the jug if he didn't, and took off, St. Maure hard on his heels. Tommy was still there when they arrived, hands clasped behind his back, scrubbing the toe of his boot in the grass, eyes anywhere but on his mother.

"Skin wasn't broken, sir," he mumbled. "Just a tiny red spot that faded almost instantly. I'm sorry, Mama."

Then the boy took to his heels. After a quick glance at Cecelia Walters's tight expression, St. Maure murmured something innocuous and followed the boy's example, abandoning Dauntry to face the tempest alone.

He stared down at her, jug of lemonade in one hand, glass in the other, face red.

"What on earth possessed you?" she snapped.

"Don't blame Tommy. I told him to—"

"I'm perfectly capable of assigning blame, Mr. Dauntry. Issuing my son orders he feels compelled to follow isn't something I appreciate, especially when following them means he must disobey me. Such interference isn't to be borne. I've been patience itself regarding the riding lessons and fishing expeditions, but I permit no one to come between my son and myself. That includes my brother. It also includes you."

"I'm sorry. Would you like some lemonade?"

"No, I would not!" She surged to her feet, eyes flaming, and held out her hand. On it lay a speck barely larger than a grain of sand. *This* was the pebble, Mr. Dauntry. Not the Rock of Gibraltar—*this!*

"I am *not* made of crystal, sir. I do *not* shatter at the slightest touch. And, I'm not a complete simpleton. I'm a grown woman with as much experience of the world, in my own way, as you. A month before you came to Combermere I cut myself on a knife, and called for my brother's assistance. When he sent Tommy for the apothecary, I didn't argue even though paying him was a problem. It was a bad cut, and I knew it. This is the scar. Please keep that in mind in the future."

"I'll try. That is, I—oh, damnation, I told you I was sorry. It was just that I thought I'd noticed you limping, and I couldn't bear the thought of you, well—you see to everyone, and there's no one to see to you, and there should be."

The fury drained from her face. "There could be," she said, looking him directly in the eye. "Certainly there's an individual who makes the attempt on occasion, no matter how clumsily. I find those attempts touching, even when they anger me."

He filled the glass and held it out, refusing for both their sakes to acknowledge her meaning. After a moment she accepted it, shaking her head.

"I'm afraid I don't understand you, Mr. Dauntry. I don't understand you at all, anymore than I did in the churchyard."

"Sometimes I don't understand myself," he replied, setting the jug on the bench. "Friends again?"

She hesitated.

He prayed she'd forget circumspection for once, and speak her heart so clearly there'd be no pretending not to understand— though what he would do then he had no notion. Recklessly sweep her into his arms, thereby creating precisely the situation he was determined to avoid? Entirely too possible. As long as nothing was admitted openly between them she would have a future, even if he had none.

The breeze twined the soft folds of her gown against a form as lithe and graceful as a young sapling's. Voices faded to inconsequence, leaving them in a cheerless place from which there was no honorable exit—Tommy's Slough of Despond made visible in two pairs of eyes that met and spoke, though voices were still. It was all he could do to refrain from reaching out to touch her.

"If that's what you truly wish."

"Yes, it's what I wish. I won't interfere with Tommy again, I promise. That was unconscionable, though I hope you understand why I asked for his help. Let's not let a grain of sand spoil our day."

"It's not the grain of sand, as you know perfectly well. It's the principle of the thing. I wish you'd realize I'm not some fragile hothouse flower to be sheltered from the slightest breeze. I'm a sensible woman who knows her own mind perfectly well, and has never crumpled at the first sign of adversity."

"I'll try, though it may take some doing."

They stared at each other as the crowds swirled past, the words hanging between them like a barrier. He was never sure whether his eyes fell first, or hers. She turned away, gaze fixed on a juggler tossing sweetmeats to the crowd.

"Robert and I are keeping the matter quiet for the moment, but it's best you know I've accepted a position in Scotland with the family of an old schoolmate of his," she said. "I'm to report at the beginning of October. There's no sense your protesting. Robert arranged it at my insistence."

"You promised me you wouldn't do this—not until September."

"You commanded. I never agreed."

If this was an attempt to bring him to the point, it almost worked. October would be there so soon his head was spinning. He would have demanded Three Rivers back from Duncan in that instant if he could've, and to blazes with the rest of the world, or what it thought, or family harmony—except Three Rivers Farm would never serve, ramshackle as it had become, even if he was willing to face his father and brother down.

Reminding himself that he departed for Hillcrest, and then London, on the morrow, swearing Cecelia would never set foot in Scotland no matter what it took, he placed her emptied glass beside the jug, and tucked her hand back in the crook of his arm.

"October's a long time away," he said, managing a smile. "No, I won't attempt to prevent your departure, and I won't create a fuss. I'm in no position to, after all, and never will be. Now, let's forget Scotland, shall we? Would you like to try your luck at the coconut shy, or would you prefer to have your fortune told?"

It had been, all agreed, the grandest, jolliest fête ever. Nothing could've been more gay, more colorful, more delightful, or more enjoyable. Or, Mrs. Burchett murmured with a sniff, less stiff and off-putting. Why, it'd been precisely as it had in the old dowager viscountess's day. High time, too.

Now, visions of fireworks still sparkling behind drooping lids, they'd gathered in the morning parlor to await the arrival of the Beechy Knoll carriage. Exhausted smiles were many, words few. Squire Burchett emitted the occasional snore. Tommy leaned against his uncle, head nodding, eyes glazed, Becky on the vicar's other side.

Dauntry glanced around the room, avoiding the fellows' pointed looks.

Yes, it'd been fine. More than fine. Because her brother was to sit there, too, and the Burchetts and Tommy, Cecelia hadn't protested when the squire led her to the head table. And later, when Dauntry had risen from his chair as the musicians struck their first chords and requested the honor of the opening dance, she'd only blushed slightly and ducked her head as she placed her hand in his and stood to applause and cheers.

Cecelia'd danced the evening away after that, just as he'd intended—though the fellows hadn't needed to partner her after the first sets. No question about it: Cecelia Walters was as beloved in the region as her brother. As for himself, he'd made do with Becky, the squire's wife, Mavis Twitchell, and any other female his eyes lighted on, young or antiquated. He might permit himself one minor luxury, but not the luxury of a second dance which, in the country, would've heralded an imminent declaration.

Tony Sinclair coughed sharply. Strange, that a friend's cough could be an order, and not just a signal. Well, Sinclair was right. It was time, little as he liked it.

"We'll be leaving early tomorrow, the lot of us," Dauntry announced in the silence, keeping his eyes on his hands. "I've business in London which can't be longer delayed."

"You'll be missed," Becky said.

"Thank you, but my work's almost done here. I wouldn't want to outstay my welcome." Dauntry met her questioning eyes, forced a smile, then turned to the vicar's sister. "I've already conferred with Potts. Not tomorrow of course, as things'll be in confusion for a few days until Combermere's put back in order, but so long as you've no objection, Tommy's riding lessons will resume on Monday."

Cecelia shook her head, face expressionless. "You're most kind to think of him at such a busy juncture, Mr. Dauntry, but I'm not certain—"

"What," Dauntry snapped, "is your objection this time?"

"When his lordship returns—"

"He won't. Summer's half over, and more. A year from now, who knows what the situation will be? The arrangement is strictly between Tommy, Potts, and myself."

"Which is what still troubles me, no matter what my brother

says. It's not that I'm unrecognizant of the great kindness you've done Thomas, but Potts doesn't own the ponies, you don't pay his wages, and I doubt Lord Dauntry would approve."

"Well, the girl in white does. I have that on the very best authority, for he—she—told me so herself just today, and stressed the lessons should continue. You wouldn't want to anger her, would you? Certainly my father wouldn't, and so we can assume his agreement would be automatic."

Startled glances turned his way, the squire snorting, then coming erect.

"Y'know who it is then, Quint?" he said. "Someone from the village, I gather."

"I believe I may, Mr. Burchett, though I'm not about to publish the fact. We all owe her—him, use whatever designation you wish—an immense debt. Revealing her identity would be the poorest fashion in which I could repay it. Besides, there might be a need for her to surface again one day."

"There's that," the squire admitted.

"There is, indeed."

"Day your brother comes into the title," Mrs. Burchett fumed, "if not a deal sooner."

"Come now, there's not a cruel bone in Duncan's body."

"Nor a considerate one, either. As for feeling a responsibility to the neighborhood, or showing anyone genuine kindness, he's his father's son—which you've never been, if you'll forgive my plain speaking, Quintus."

"I'd forgive you just about anything, Mrs. Burchett," he replied with a smile, "including ordering me to take myself to perdition."

"If y'don't want Thomas coming to Combermere," the squire threw in, "I'd be glad to take him on, Mrs. Walters. Fair horseman myself—not that I hold a candle to Hiram Potts, or ever could. Best in the saddle I've ever known, and that's a fact."

"But you've no ponies."

"Doesn't mean I can't acquire one."

Nick arrived amid Cecelia's embarrassed protests, and announced the Beechy Knoll carriage was at the door. Under cover of the confusion of finding wraps and hats, Gardener told Dauntry not to concern himself, that he'd answer for Thomas's daily trips to Combermere's stables continuing as long as possible.

Then they were taking their leave of the fellows, the Burchetts issuing invitations to Beechy Knoll whenever they were in the vicinity, Cecelia blushing as they bent over her hand, wishing her well and telling her what a splendid fellow Thomas was. They were crossing the rotunda, at the door, descending the steps, saying their last farewells, entering the carriage, everything happening too quickly, the fellows lingering above in a pool of light. Dauntry closed the carriage door and latched it, just as he had every night during the past weeks, and nodded to the coachman.

"Take care of your mother, sprout, and don't forget where the big ones are," Dauntry called after them from the drive, and then, more softly, "Good-bye. God bless and keep you both."

The carriage rattled across the gravel and disappeared into the park.

"Y'want company?" Pugs Harnette called as Dauntry turned to circle toward his grandmother's rose gardens.

"Would you?" St. Maure's softer voice floated.

"Don't know. I might."

Dauntry turned toward the entry, trying not to see it. "Just going to walk about for a bit," he called back, ignoring the last of the tents, the workers scurrying about by lantern light. "Leg's stiffened up. No sense waiting for me, thank you all the same."

Then he was around the corner of the house, striking across the lawns without bothering with the paths, jaws clenched.

It was hard, far harder than he thought it would be, and he'd imagined a grimness that went beyond anything he'd ever experienced. And it wouldn't be the same when he returned. At least, he hoped it wouldn't. The notion of failure had a bitter taste, while success, unfortunately, would place Cecelia Walters and her son so far above his touch it was laughable.

He wandered for what felt like hours, sitting for a while by the pool at the center of the maze, trying not to think and making a distinctly poor job of it. Finally he returned to the house, let himself in, lowered the bar securing the main doors, and wearily climbed the stairs.

Someone had been busy. His traps were by his sitting room

door, closed and strapped, ready to be taken down in the morning. Only a single portmanteau remained in his bedchamber awaiting the last items, buckles gleaming in the light of the *veilleuse*.

He shrugged out of his coat and waistcoat without bothering to light a candle, pulled off his boots, then poured a glass of brandy from the decanter on his dressing table and gulped it in three swallows. The stuff burned all the way down.

Dauntry finished undressing, tossing his clothes aside without a care to where they landed or how, retrieved the glass and decanter, and crossed to his bed. If sleep wouldn't come naturally— and it wouldn't, not on this night of all nights—he was going to make damned sure it came unnaturally. He put the decanter and glass on the night table, snarling wordlessly at the neatly folded nightshirt. They were instruments of torture, trapping one's legs and binding one's—well, they were bloody uncomfortable. Why men wore them he hadn't the slightest notion, unless it was to pander to their wives. Well, he didn't have a wife, and never would. No reason he should don one of the blasted things if he didn't want to.

The nightshirt followed the rest of his clothes, flying through the air like a shroud to land by the cold fireplace. He laughed then, bitterly and long. The girl in white could have it. She could have everything, as far as he was concerned, and travel with it all straight to hell.

Naked as the day he was born, he sat, snuffed the *veilleuse,* picked up the decanter, unstopped it, and took a hearty pull without bothering to reach for the glass. Silly things anyway, glasses. Much too small, especially when one's goal was reaching a state of insensibility as rapidly as possible. He took a second pull, and froze. The hinges of the passageway entrance by the chimney surround were complaining. Good Lord—what now? He'd have Nace on the rack for this idiocy!

He set the decanter aside, grabbed his dressing gown from the foot of the bed, and pulled it over him as he dropped against the pillows, eyes slitted.

Ponderously, the decorative panel swung open. Even with only the glimmer of a lantern turned low in the passage behind her, he could see the girl in white well enough to tell she was small—

far too small for even Nace, and far too slight—for all her shadow leapt across the bedchamber like a giant on the rampage. If one hadn't been prepared, the effect would've been terrifying.

She moved into the room, trailing veils and shawls and God knew what else, wailing and sobbing as never before. He caught a few words in the midst of the incoherence, not many, but enough so that his mouth dropped open. The urge to tear Nace limb from limb died on the instant.

"I'll be back in a fortnight," he said, cutting through the ghost's lamentations. "I promise. Or if not then, very shortly thereafter."

Dead silence for a moment, except for a few gulps and sniffs.

"You will?" the ghost quavered. "You *really* promise?"

"I really promise. I'm not bolting. You can rest easy on that point."

"That's all right, then. I thought you meant to be gone forever." The ghost thought a moment, then gave a final, slightly mollified moan, and literally disappeared into the woodwork, the panel swinging closed behind him.

"I'll be damned. You little scamp." Dauntry tossed his dressing gown aside and went to the windows. "What in blazes've you been up to, and why?"

Clearly it wasn't just Combermere's stables with which Tommy Walters was acquainted, but what the devil did the boy expect to accomplish by resurrecting a hoary legend and scaring the family away? And who'd told him the tale, and why? And what else had they told him?

Most perplexing of all, what did Tommy require of him? Because there was no question about it: This girl in white had more in mind than needy villagers, impoverished vicars desiring to wed, and roofs in need of replacement. Nace? No wonder the poor man had seemed confused by Dauntry's hints.

As he watched, a small figure carrying a shuttered lantern emerged, glanced about, then darted across the lawns toward the park with as much speed as nine-year-old legs could produce. From below came the sound of the hidden door closing firmly, and a heavy bolt being shoved home.

"I'll be damned," Dauntry repeated in wonder, brandy forgotten.

Nine

London sweltered under oppressive skies, the miasma from the stews mingling with the stench of Mayfair's drains and the effluvia rising from the slow-moving Thames. Low tide was worst. The occasional showers didn't help, turning dust to mud that emitted more foul odors. Night brought no relief, heat absorbed by day radiating into air that hung like molten lead, refusing to cool.

"I hate this place in August," Valentine North grumbled as the Irregulars strode toward White's, intending to announce their arrival in Town with some deep play on North's part. Word would carry, even if the gaming was a charade, Harnette and Sinclair the assigned losers, no pounds actually changing hands. "Why the devil couldn't this've waited until fall? Little Season would've been soon enough, blast it. Still can't understand your rush."

"Mrs. Walters has found employment," Dauntry repeated for what felt like the dozenth time. "Amelia and your mother agreed it'd be best to put a stop to that nonsense as soon as may be, you'll remember. Could hurt Mrs. Walters's eventual marriage prospects, and Tommy needs a stepfather."

"Don't understand your interest at all, come to that. Your father may've caused most of the vicar's problems. The widow's certainly aren't on his plate."

"Don't like to see injustice permitted free rein, that's all."

Tony Sinclair's snort rang loud in Dauntry's ears.

"Besides, I'm damned if I'm willing to see Tommy Walters forced to hang on others' sleeves when by rights he's rich as a

Nabob," Dauntry forged on. "I have enough experience in that exercise to be acquainted with its more degrading aspects."

"Still don't see why this couldn't wait until October. Decent weather, then."

"Because in October she'll be in Scotland," Dauntry snapped.

"Worst of it is, I'm forced to concoct an excuse to call on old Burridge. He'll never believe business brought me. Neither will anyone else. I might come to Town myself—*might,* mind you, not would. Bring the rest of you? Ridiculous! Project's ill-conceived, and doomed to failure."

Dauntry held his peace as he swatted a mosquito that'd been buzzing about his ears for blocks.

Val North's objections didn't truly lie with the weather, or in calling on his man of business on a trumped-up excuse. They lay in leaving Amelia at Hillcrest, where he'd insisted she remain despite her pleas to join in the adventure of bringing the Countess of Marle low. London was unhealthy in the dog days of summer, no place more so. North had correctly refused to permit her the risk.

They turned in at White's and climbed the steps, shirt points wilting, sweat trickling down their necks to travel the small of their backs, teasing all the way. At least that's how it was for Dauntry. He assumed the fellows were equally uncomfortable.

He nodded to the porter and handed the waiting lackey hat, gloves, and walking stick.

"Thin of company, I assume," he said.

"A bit, sir. Mostly gentlemen forced to Town on family business, or—" The lackey hesitated, coloring up.

"Or visiting their convenients. I see. Thin, indeed."

White's was at Lady St. Maure's suggestion. It might prove useless. The notion of following the wagering-mad Countess of Marle directly into such hells as the Tinker's Bum, which she was known to frequent, had seemed a trifle obvious, however—especially given what they'd planned at Hillcrest.

Valentine North had always avoided hells, and North's reputation as an almost unbeatable gamester was the key. What they needed now was a fool with marginal entry to the *ton* and a taste for the less honest establishments, an evening of dicing or cards during which their gull won just enough to whet his appetite for more, and an invitation to accompany him into the Countess of Marle's customary haunts. Their resistance would be firm at first, agreement seemingly grudging, and long in coming.

He trailed the others into the main gaming salon and glanced about. The heat was still more oppressive than on the street. General Maitland, a fixture in all seasons, had abandoned his usual corner, though he appeared as sodden as ever. Hard to believe one of England's greatest strategists could have sunk so low. Only the tables closest to the open windows were occupied, those sparsely, the wagering lethargic. Coats, even waistcoats, had been discarded, neckcloths loosened, and not only to change one's luck, though that had doubtless been the excuse given for such *déshabille*.

"Good God," Dauntry murmured.

"Told you October'd be better, but you wouldn't listen." North surveyed the room. "Table between Lord Carter's and Marle's would be best, I think. Marle might carry word back to his rib. Can't help but wonder what he's doing in Town, though."

"Probably dancing attendance," St. Maure murmured. "You heard what my mother and Lady Katherine had to say about the countess."

"Ring in his nose, clipped wings, scorched posterior, and a tiger's paw in the middle of his back. Yes, I heard. Might as well go pay your respects to Maitland, Quint. Doesn't matter if he remembers you. Need to wander a bit, or someone'll suspect our game."

"In this heat? Their brains're fried. No one'll suspect a thing."

But he wandered nevertheless, his avoidance of the tables as anything but an observer too well known for a more direct role. Being reduced to depending on others since quitting the army was nothing new. It had always annoyed him. This time it galled.

He exchanged a few words with General Maitland—his courteous, Maitland's so slurred as to be incomprehensible—then ambled toward the farthest table, stopping short just before he reached it.

Chuffy Binkerton, by damn! Disheveled, in his cups, and complaining of his losses as usual, his "chuffing" exaggerated by drink. He'd recognize the sod anywhere, even from the back.

Well, they'd known Binkerton preferred Town during the Season, and detested the country at any time. No law said he couldn't still be here. Ignoring the toadying rotter was the only option.

Dauntry backed away, eyes fixed on the pudgy fop. Binkerton was rising from the table, waistcoat straining across his well-larded back. Bloody hell! There was no telling what North's reaction would be if he encountered this popinjay unexpectedly. They'd brangled too often in the past.

He strode down the uneven line of tables at a quick march, not caring if his unusual speed was noticed. Damned if he'd let the past interfere with the present.

"Yes, I saw him soon as we arrived," North murmured at Dauntry's caution, sweeping a pile of banknotes from the center of the table. Tony Sinclair or Pugs Harnette'd apparently just "lost" another small fortune. "We all did, I believe, except for you. Losing your powers of observation, old friend?"

"Possibly, or possibly he was hidden from where I stood."

"Or possibly you were distracted?" North grinned. "Wouldn't surprise me, given the fellows' descriptions of the Widow Walters. And her son, of course. Don't worry—I won't cause a stir. Binkerton just might prove useful, though. You know how his tongue flaps. Better yet, he frequents the lower hells. That's where we'll find Lady Walters when the time comes."

Then he turned as Binkerton, who'd spotted them and clearly wanted to avoid a confrontation, tried to scurry past unnoticed.

"What have we here?" North said loudly. "Do my eyes deceive me? No, I don't believe they do."

Binkerton skidded to an awkward halt as others glanced in their direction. After a moment's hesitation he turned toward their table, face glistening, eyes wide.

"Ah, er, North," he said, now traveling backward like a courtier taking leave of the King. "Gentlemen. Most pressing business elsewhere. Must excuse—"

"Nonsense," North interrupted, tone friendly enough, for all his eyes were arctic behind partially lowered lids. "Evening's early yet. In its infancy, one might say. At least *I'd* say it's in its infancy. Wouldn't you, Quint?"

Dauntry nodded. "Definitely in its infancy," he agreed, choking back laughter at Binkerton's terrified expression.

"Not fair to kill a fledgling before it's had an opportunity to

try its wings, Binkerton," North insisted, an edge to his voice
that had the other man paling despite the heat. "That'd be unconscionable. Why don't you join us? Plenty of room."

"Can't. That is, engaged elsewhere. Mustn't fail. Just not
done."

"Must be a lady, then."

"That's it—a lady. Promised to stop by. Promised the mater,
that is. Friend of hers. Not well. Not well at all."

"You, your mother, or your mother's bosom bow?"

"All of us," Binkerton bleated, maintaining a steady backward
scuffle. "Unwell. Most unwell. Didn't come over me 'til just now.
Must be the heat. Why I'm leaving. Y'wouldn't want to become
infected."

"I doubt your malady's contagious."

"It is, oh, it is. Might be, at any rate. They all are, aren't they,
one way or another?"

"What an intrepid soul you are." North shuffled the cards, an
idle, mesmerizing motion holding not a little menace in it. "I
quite admire your phlegmatic demeanor in the face of potential
debilitation."

The heel of Binkerton's pump caught on a chair leg behind
him. The chair fell backward. Binkerton landed on his broad posterior with a solid thump.

"Good heavens." North rose slightly, peering over the table's
edge. "The poor fellow. Won't one of you see if he's all right?"

Moments later, coat seams popping, unmentionables straining,
Binkerton was escorted over by Stubby Clough and Ollie Thread-
whistle, and plunked into the empty chair between North and
Pugs Harnette.

"Oh dear—I don't believe he can breathe." North's eyes were
dancing now. "Loosen his neckcloth and unbutton his waistcoat,
Ollie. Stubby, I believe he wants some brandy as a restorative.
Y'may have to hold the glass for him."

An hour later Chuffy Binkerton wove from the room assisted
by a pair of lackeys, his pockets a trifle heavier than when he'd
taken his tumble, his expression fuddled. North watched him go,
brows raised, nostrils flaring.

"That," he said, "was deuced amusing." Then he glanced at
Dauntry. "We've just taken the first round, my friend. No need

to go a second tonight. Tomorrow's soon enough. Mustn't rush things." He tossed the cards aside and swept his "winnings" into the steel mesh-lined pockets of his coat. "Y'know, this project may not be as doomed as I thought."

"There's more to it than we knew."

The fellows and Lady St. Maure turned at Valentine North's hard-bitten words. Their discussion regarding that evening's excursion to Vauxhall, and where the Countess of Marle would most likely disport herself the day after, died on the instant. North loomed in the family parlor doorway at St. Maure House, a grim twist to his mouth, blue eyes as cold and hard as Dauntry had ever seen them.

"So here you are at last. Thought you intended to spend the least time possible with Burridge," Stubby Clough said. "You've been hours at it."

"Intentions go hang. Besides, I wasn't there above an hour. Spent most of my time trying to confirm Burridge's tattle as best I could. Figured Quint'd want that."

"You discussed Mrs. Walters's problems with your man of business?" Dauntry rose, hands balled into fists. "Of all the officious—"

"Stubble it. You'll be thanking me in a moment." North closed the door. "No servants in earshot?"

"None." Dauntry subsided. "We wanted to be private."

"Give me a moment, and I'll explain. Chattering with the sorts in Town at this season's debilitating. Rather less than half a brain among the lot of them."

North strode to the library table where a cold nuncheon had been set out, slapped some gammon between slices of bread, poured himself a tankard of ale, stalked to an empty wing chair, put his plate on the table at its side, and sat.

"You will not believe what I've learned," he ground out as he leaned forward, elbows on knees, white-knuckled hands gripping the tankard.

"I will," Lady St. Maure murmured. "When Gwynyth Walters is involved, nothing's impossible."

"Can't prove it, of course. Possible it's someone else," North conceded, "but—"

"Well, don't just sit there looking like an avenging angel." Pugs Harnette set aside the list of gambling hells he'd been making using an old copy of *La Belle Assemblée* as a portable desk. "Tell us."

"I thought it'd be useful to know a bit more about Walters and his family," North admitted with a shrug. "Asked the old fellow if he'd ever heard of them. Said a friend of mine'd encountered the widow, and was in a fair way to becoming entangled. Sorry, Quint, but that seemed easiest."

Dauntry decided he'd developed the art of dissimulation to a fine degree. No flush about the ears this time. No warming of his face. No ducking his head. Instead he looked North directly in the eyes and said, "Whatever serves, Val." Perhaps he was becoming accustomed to the constant hints, the sympathetic glances.

"It served very well, as it happens."

North took a long pull of the ale, set the tankard aside, bit into his sandwich and chewed, frowning.

"Well?" Dauntry demanded, then colored up at the looks the fellows, and even Lady St. Maure, threw him.

"Claimed what little I knew of her tale was so bathetic it went beyond the bounds of credibility," North said finally, "and I was fearing a take-in. Even suggested to Burridge the widow very possibly wasn't, well, wasn't one, if you understand me.

"Again, my apologies, Quint. Didn't like portraying you as a dunce and Mrs. Walters as a cozening vixen, but that seemed easiest, too. Burridge has a knack for hearing things. Ears to the ground, or the wind, or whatever. Courts those in his profession with a reputation for loose tongues when in their cups, gleans what he can at the expense of a meal and a bottle of port, and trains his hirelings to do the same with their clerks.

"Mama warned me about him when my father died. The pater found Burridge's bent for learning all he could about those who weren't his clients both amusing and useful. Family tradition, apparently. My mother's always suspected Burridge's father and grandfather're where my grandfather acquired some of—enough of that. Immaterial. Close-mouthed about his own clients' business, but as for the rest? No old woman chatters as avidly while eliminating the names of those involved."

He paused, clearly great with news. Then, "She had an agent in their household," he announced, and took another bite of his sandwich.

Lady St. Maure surged to her feet, head high, eyes stormy.

"Valentine North, I've known you since you were a noxious adolescent with spots on your face. I've been on the friendliest of terms with your mother almost as long, and am well acquainted with your tricks, both from personal experience and from her tales."

She moved North's plate and tankard well beyond his reach, then stood in front of them blocking access, arms crossed, sun glinting on light brown hair frosted with silver. North gave her a wink, flushing slightly.

"If you persist in doling out scraps as if they were a rare elixir to be dispensed by the drop," she threatened, unmollified, "I'll find a birch rod and lay it smartly about your shoulders. This is one instance when your teasing ways go far beyond the irritating, and verge on the despicable. The details, *Mr. North,* if you please. Immediately. There's no way you'll charm yourself out of it this time."

He grinned, then sobered at her firmed chin, her lips drawn in a flat line.

"All right, my lady," he said. "For the sake of your friendship with my mother, if not for Quint's sake, here you have it—if it *is* the same family—and old Burridge was merely talking in suppositions, mind you, with no names mentioned, so it may not be—Lady Walters bribed a retainer at Grafton. That's the name of the place George Walters inherited—Grafton Lodge, up in the Lake District. Walters'd drawn a will naming his wife's brother—Gardener, your vicar in Coombe, Quint—the guardian of any children. Lord and Lady Walters weren't even mentioned in Walters's will. You can guess the rest, given Lord Walters ended up as one of Thomas's guardians, and his man of business the trustee and administrator."

"I'll see that beldame in hell," Dauntry ground out.

If what he felt was rage—and there was no other applicable term he could think of—it was unlike any anger he'd experienced.

This wasn't hot. Yes, it burned, but it was as icy as a winter storm in the Hebrides.

"She'll get there without your assistance, Quint."

"I intend to usher her in, however."

"Rest easy. We all do, myself most of all now I've learned the whole."

"A forged will." Lady St. Maure sank into her chair, cheeks pale. "So, *la* Walters was up to her old tricks. That's how she ruined my friend and landed Marle—forged letters 'proving' Camilla anticipated her vows with one of the infamous DeVille tribe."

"Makes sense."

"Told Marle on their wedding night, once she'd done her duty and an annulment was impossible. Laughed. I wanted to kill her. So did Marle, but he's lost the inclination since. I haven't."

"Wouldn't've helped. Won't do the least good in this instance, either. Now, may I be permitted to stave off starvation before continuing, Lady St. Maure? The rest is details, and I'm so famished there're stars dancing before me."

"What? Oh, yes, of course. If there's something you want that's not there, Valentine, Dabney has only to ring and ask," she replied absently. "Poor Mrs. Walters."

North retrieved plate and tankard and set them beside him again, then took another bite and chewed thoughtfully while the others waited.

"It's not her I feel for the most," he said after a bit. "It's George Walters. If ever a man had the right to rest in an unquiet grave, he's the one. Were my mother to pull such a trick on Amelia, I'd see her burned at the stake and her ashes scattered to the four winds."

A look of profound understanding passed between Dauntry and North.

"Well, let's have the details," Dauntry said.

"Not much to it, really. Countess supposedly paid her solicitor handsomely for drawing up the new will after the boy was born," North explained with a shrug, "then signed it herself, mimicking her son's hand—a talent she'd apparently cultivated. The Grafton retainer in her pay substituted the false for the genuine, and that was that. Countess summoned the widow to Town once the forged

will was read, and offered her the choice of perpetual poverty or
giving her son up and vanishing into well-financed country re-
tirement. Mrs. Walters refused, and disappeared with her son on
her own account, which you already know."

"I want Gwynyth Walters brought low in this house," Lady
St. Maure insisted, tone venomous, ignoring the startled glances
of North's Irregulars. "Before my eyes, at my contrivance. It
won't be enough, but it'll be something. When it's over, it's my
face I want her to remember, and no other."

"Mama!" St. Maure gasped.

His mother gave him a sweet smile, though her eyes remained
hard.

"I never was your usual milk-and-water miss, Dabney. Leop-
ardesses don't change their spots to appease their cubs. Please
remember that."

Then she turned to Dauntry. "I'll give a card party. The end
will come here, not in some hell. There's a lady I'd like to include
in the planning with your permission—and old friend, Lady
Cheltenham—if she's in Town. Daphne doesn't care for summer
house parties, so I assume she is. We'll need a few others of
irreproachable character present when the time comes. She can
help there.

"More to the point, she and her husband were among the few
who insisted Camilla Ethridge couldn't've done the things those
letters purported to prove against her. No one would derive greater
pleasure from seeing Gwynyth Walters served up a bit of her
own bitter broth than Daphne Cheltenham."

"Then definitely, let's invite Lady Cheltenham to join us."

Though with far different intent, they'd dressed for Vauxhall
with as much care as if they'd received invitations to Carlton
House.

Outré without being obvious, Lady St. Maure had instructed
before they departed for North's Wilton Street town house. Nothing outrageous. Merely, in each case, sartorial details that would
cause them to be remarked at the time, and remembered later.

That was, after all, the goal: to have their presence noted and, if possible, North's prowess at the tables brought to mind. Even the wariest trout would respond to a well-baited line, Lady St. Maure insisted, once it was flicked within striking distance.

They'd done their best to accommodate. Colors clashed with studied subtlety. Threadwhistle sported too many fobs, North a showy quizzing glass his mother had presented him as a joke. Tony Sinclair's borrowed walking stick, however, was the crowning touch. Its malaca shaft was a fine one. The knob—a naked woman fashioned primarily of silver, her legs clasping the stick's head, her breasts sprouting a pair of garnets—was also a fine example of its sort.

They'd come by carriage, then made their way through the crowds to the box Lady St. Maure reserved after sending a groom to make discreet inquiries of one of the countess's footmen. Across the way, the box she'd learned the Countess of Marle had hired for the evening remained untenanted.

"Wish your mother'd come with us, Dab," Clough complained as they selected seats offering the best view of promenaders displaying their wares. The muslin company was out in force, the decorative lanterns hanging from the trees casting a flush on their rouged cheeks and brassy curls. "Dull on our own."

"Told you before, Stubby—Mama invited Lady Cheltenham to join her for the evening. Sent a note 'round soon as Val'd opened his budget. You know that, too."

"They both could've come."

"And ruin our pose as North's Irregulars, on the strut and bent on deviltry? Come, now!"

"Still dull. And look at the sorts disporting themselves. A bit lower than below the salt, unless I know less of the type than I believe I do. Vauxhall's not quite the thing best of times. Now? Phah! Nothing but Cits, Cyprians, pimps, and tradesmen."

"Stop grumbling like a constipated cleric." Ollie Threadwhistle stretched his legs out and tilted his chair back. "Besides, Lady St. Maure has the right of it. We shouldn't be seen in her company until what she terms the endgame. Dab, yes. He's her son, after all, could even stay there if he wanted. The rest of us can't so much as stop by until it's time."

"Dull," Clough insisted, slumping as he watched the ragtag crowds.

"I'm sorry you're bored, Stubby." Holding his temper while the fellows turned a serious venture into a spree, squabbling all the while, wasn't as easy as Dauntry had expected. At least Val North and St. Maure appeared committed to the project, but the others? If he hadn't known better, he'd've sworn only the amusement they could derive from the situation attracted. He couldn't understand it. They'd met Cecelia, gotten to know her, even taken her about. As for Tommy— "Maybe you should consider returning to Hillcrest with a report for Lady Katherine and Amelia."

Clough came erect at that, spluttering protests.

"At ease, sprig." Sinclair's eyes narrowed. "I do believe our prey's in sight."

"By Jove, will y'look who's squiring her?" Pugs Harnette crowed.

"Pretend you don't see them. Make him come to us," North ordered. "Signal a waiter, Dab. All the usual stuff. Be sure to tell him we'll want some sort of flaming dessert. Doesn't matter what, so long as there's a great fuss made preparing it at table. Chatter, the rest of you. A bit bored, if you please, and conscious of slumming it, but willing to be amused."

Dauntry examined the party across the way from the corner of his eye, unable to help himself, as Dab gave instructions to a waiter and the others blathered about nothing.

So this was the woman who'd cozened Cecelia, and slapped Tommy so hard her ring sliced his cheek. The Countess of Marle dripped jewels St. Maure's mother claimed were paste, the genuine Marle gems having been sacrificed to her passion for the tables.

He took inventory with the precision he'd used in the Peninsula when assessing an enemy position: A high forehead. A narrow nose, delicately formed. Fine dark brows. Finer carmined lips. Hair of an improbable dark brown, not a silver thread in the lot that he could tell, styled in a curly crop suitable to a girl in her first Season. A feathered turban festooned with pearls. A gauzy silk gown so crusted with beads and spangles he had no notion the color of the bodice's fabric. Several shawls whose deep fringe writhed like slender snakes in the light breeze.

St. Maure was right. The countess verged on the vulgar, though it was a costly vulgarity just shy of true elegance. The surprise was her height. Diminutive wasn't accurate. Lilliputian would've been closer. That so much viciousness dwelt in such a small—and not totally unattractive—package startled him. He'd unconsciously anticipated the traditional villainess of the romances, thick-waisted and hawk-nosed, the evil writ clear on coarse features.

Binkerton, of course, was Binkerton. The other two dancing attendance had the look of ivory turners—a bit down-at-the-heels, a trifle foxed perhaps, definitely anxious to please.

Well, the gullers were about to be gulled, though they didn't know it yet.

"Quint," North hissed, "that's enough. Eyes front. Might be wise to turn your chair so you can't see her. Easier that way."

He didn't bother to protest. North was right. While he wasn't certain what he felt at finally sighting his quarry—hatred, contempt, the need of a horsewhip, the desire to cry havoc—it couldn't help but show in his eyes. She mustn't be permitted to see that, not yet.

North pulled a deck of cards from an inner pocket and began dealing a hand of patience. "I'm accepting all bets," he announced a trifle more loudly than necessary.

Harnette shoved a few of the pound notes North'd given him earlier to the center of the table. "I say y'won't unbury the ace of spades," he declared on cue.

"And I say I shall," North drawled. The ace of spades was, as prearranged, the third card he revealed. He swept up his "winnings," "shuffled" the cards, and dealt another hand. "Any takers?"

Tony Sinclair, who'd been assigned outlook duty, absently tossed out a few guineas at the snapped reminder without bothering with his lines.

Instead he murmured, "Binkerton's spotted us. Gabbling like a gander. Now the countess's glancing our way. Brows're rising. Nose in the air—and what a lovely little nose it is. Doesn't look half her age. Maybe she's made a pact with the devil? Now she's turning away. Binkerton's still chattering."

North looked up, pretending to inspect a nearby lantern surrounded by moths.

"I see 'em. Good. Dab, when the food arrives, make a fuss

about something not being right. Claim the punch's too sweet.
Insist the ham's not shaved fine enough. Doesn't matter what.
Just be loud about it. Stubby, slip out the back way. Time for
your reconnoitering expedition. Don't get caught."

"I still say I'm the one should go," Dauntry protested as
Clough, no longer bored now he had a part to play, rose and
clattered down the rear steps. "More experience."

"And too likely to raise precisely the sort of suspicions we
don't want. If he's caught, Stubby has the look of an innocent in
search of adventure. You don't."

"Damn and blast," murmured Sinclair, the only one directly
facing the countess's box. "Stubby's been trapped by a bit of
fluff. Hanging all over him. Now he's being jostled by a lout with
a neckcloth so high it hides half his face. Fellow must be taking
lessons from Prinny. Now Stubby's pockets're being picked. Now
the trollop's dragging him toward the dancing pavilion. No way
for him to get away, but dear Lord, is he trying! Precisely the
sort of fracas we didn't want."

"No—he's creating a diversion," Dauntry said after a furtive
peek. "Give him credit for inventiveness in the face of disaster.
You'd best turn 'round. Everyone else is, and it'll be remarked if
you don't. Stubby could do with a bit of rescuing, I believe. His
part's over, though—you've the right of that, Tony."

With a triumphant glance for North, Dauntry rose, slipped
down the rear steps, and made his way through the shrubbery to
the edge of the promenade at the far end of the boxes. Quite a
crowd had gathered around Stubby, some cheering the trollop
on, some jeering Stubby as a cawker lacking any notion how to
enjoy Vauxhall's more elevating entertainments. The fellows had
just quitted their box, North charging the crowd as he ordered it
to make way, Sinclair brandishing his walking stick.

Dauntry turned his back on the uproar and sauntered in the
opposite direction, pretending bored unconcern. Then, with a
quick glance over his shoulder, he slipped into the bushes and
sneaked behind the opposing rank of boxes, footsteps silent,
counting until he reached the one holding the countess and her
party.

There was laughter, which he'd expected, then a woman's voice
sneering she had no notion how such an out and out bumpkin

could be the famous Valentine North of whose prowess at the tables she'd heard so many reports. Her voice didn't match the rest of her, grating on Dauntry's ears like steel scraping slate.

"Not the one with the doxy," Chuffy Binkerton protested. "Just a friend of North's, name of Stephen Clough. Ain't a bumpkin, though. Great-aunt's Lady Augusta Farnsworth. Certain you've heard of her, even if you ain't acquainted. Don't know why North puts up with him. Rather less than half the usual furniture in his attic. North's the tallish one with the quizzing glass." Then he giggled. "Will you look at the walking stick Anthony Sinclair's laying about? A work of art."

The box shook from a loud thump.

"I believe it's time we left," the countess snapped over her companions' laughter. "This isn't at all what I expected, or am willing to endure."

"Well, y'aint never been here this time o' year before, Lady Walters," Binkerton explained. "Sides, now the celebrations for Wellington's Vitoria triumph're about done, there's not as many respectable sorts about. Novelty's worn off, y'see."

"I say we go on to Mother Hinchey's," a high-pitched man's voice suggested. "Always deep play at Hinchey's. Pretty hostesses, too."

"Tinker's Bum's got better refreshments," a lazy, lower-pitched voice insisted, "and the play's just as deep, and the girls as, ah, welcoming. More to the point, her ladyship's luck runs better there."

"But we got to stay for the fireworks," Binkerton whined. "The countess wanted to see 'em particular. Besides, we'd never find North either place. Doesn't frequent hells."

"Bother North! I'll meet him one day if he's all they say he is, Mr. Binkerton, and you'll be the one to bring him to me. When you do, you'll learn he's considerably less than the rest of you imagine." Chair feet scraped against the flooring. "You may do as you please, gentlemen," the countess snapped over the fading sounds of the ribald confrontation on the promenade. "I'm leaving—by the back way, as I've no desire to become embroiled in that low-bred farce."

Dauntry backed into the shrubbery and squatted, still watching and listening.

There were more protests from Chuffy Binkerton, all of them countered. It didn't take long, though the horde of mosquitoes buzzing about Dauntry's ears and nipping his neck made it seem an eternity. He could smell her heavy scent as she passed, something redolent of musk. Binkerton stumbled behind, still complaining at their departure, wondering what would become of the supper they'd ordered and extolling the glories of the special fireworks in celebration of Vitoria. Then they were gone.

Dauntry stood, staring after them. "The Tinker's Bum," he murmured with a slight smile, "just as we thought. And she wants at Val. It couldn't be better."

Ten

The invitations to his mother's card party had been delivered that morning, Dabney St. Maure reported on his return to North's town house just before the dinner hour.

Lady Cheltenham and his mother had conferred long and hard regarding the guest list, for Town was so thin of company half their more promising candidates were unavailable. The ones they'd decided on were sorts who likely wouldn't take umbrage at receiving an invitation a mere two days before the proffered entertainment. Five acceptances had already arrived when he left. The chances of any refusals were slim. There'd be sufficient tables that the countess wouldn't become suspicious.

"Best of all, Maitland'll be there," he announced. "Lady Cheltenham vouches for his presence, and promises to have him sober as a judge and as formidable as when he helped get Malta out of French hands. An old friend of her husband's, Maitland. Lady Cheltenham has the oddest acquaintances. I've arranged with Rundell and Bridge to have one of their best men on hand, and Mama's already conferred with our solicitor. He'll be there too, with both documents ready for Lady Walters to sign, so everything's in place."

He pulled a black scarf from his pocket and tossed it to Dauntry, who caught it in midair.

"My mother wants to know if this is what you had in mind, Quint."

Dauntry held the length of fragile silk gauze to the light, examining it closely.

"Too easy to spot," he said. "My guess is Lady Walters possesses quicksilver fingers and an avaricious soul, and better eyes than even Pugs, and he can see better in the dark than any I know. The blindfold the colonel I unmasked was using had only peepholes for the eyes, not a broad band, and the fabric was stiffer—a black neckcloth, not a silk scarf. Too easy for this to slip, or see through even without benefit of pulled threads. I hate to ask your mother to begin again, but—"

"She did this one, too. Lady Cheltenham's suggestion, as she suspected the other wouldn't serve—though how she knew that I haven't any notion. Sent you her compliments, and said to tell you she's looking forward to making your acquaintance. Anyone who foils the rapacious of the world's a hero in her book."

"Very kind of her, but I was merely doing my duty," Dauntry returned, flushing.

While the second scarf was silk as well, and wouldn't seem out of place in a lady's possession, it was heavier, and possessed a subtle grain that would keep it from slipping. There were only two small areas of alternating drawn threads.

Dauntry held it before his eyes, watching as St. Maure wandered to the drinks table and helped himself to claret.

In full daylight—the sun still streamed through the library windows, even at this hour—it was no problem, for all the image seemed at the end of a dark tunnel. In a candlelit drawing room? Colonel Forcythe'd had lanterns strategically positioned, his tent glowing like a beacon in the stifling Spanish night. That wouldn't be possible. Everything had to appear normal, given the only gull would be on her mettle, and perfectly capable of causing a scene if things weren't to her liking.

He handed the scarf to North, who was seated across from him on the other side of the cold fireplace.

"What d'you think, Val? Can you manage it?"

North held the scarf up, turning his head first one way, then another.

"Not impossible, but whoever ties it'll have to get it right the first time. A bit of embroidery as a guide wouldn't be amiss. No opportunity for adjustments, and I won't dare touch the damned thing. Sure to be called on it."

"Lady Cheltenham recommends we spend the evening practicing. Binkerton's been trying to find you, by the bye, Val. Left several messages at White's. Surprised he hasn't stopped here, unless he doesn't dare. Playing least in sight until tomorrow night was an excellent notion. Whets their appetite."

"At your Lady Cheltenham's suggestion." North draped the blindfold over the arm of his chair, and picked up his glass. "Wonder how she'd like to sit around being bored for an entire day."

"She was right. If you were too easy to find, it'd almost seem as if we wanted you to be found—which we do, but they aren't to know that. Lady Cheltenham also provided these. Said it wouldn't do for me to acquire them. Too likely to be remarked on, and tales born where we wouldn't want."

St. Maure tossed two decks of used cards on the table beside North.

"She got them from a bit of stews bait named Tom the Toff, and no, don't ask how she knows someone of that sort, for I have no idea about that, either. She seemed rather proud of his acquaintance, though, and he was clearly in awe of her. Decks're marked. There'll be five identically marked sealed decks at Mama's, also thanks to the Toff. These're for practice. We're to burn them when we're done with them."

"I can hardly wait to meet this Lady Cheltenham of yours." Dauntry reached for the top deck. The cards were indeed marked, and expertly at that, for all they were quite worn, and sported lewd faces.

"Tiny thing, always bang-to-the-mark," St. Maure enthused. "Everyone's favorite confidante, looks like butter wouldn't melt in her mouth. Sounds odd given her age, but I'd term her a minx. Says she's bored now her niece's happily wed and her nephew's stormed off to his country place in a fit of the sulks. Thanked my mother for bringing her into this, and swears she's the best assistant we could've found."

"I suspect she's hit the target dead center."

Dauntry rose, returned the cards to the table beside North, then strolled to the open windows giving on the pocket garden behind the town house, glass of sherry in hand, to stare beyond the rooftops toward the horizon. It didn't matter that it was the wrong horizon. Any would do.

Dear Lord, what would Cecelia say if she knew what they were up to? Gardener wouldn't be best pleased, either—not because it was dangerous, for it wasn't, or because it would cost North dearly, for it wouldn't, but because it was so deuced underhanded. Would he consider the game worth the candle? Doubtful, even with justice on their side, and visions of Rebecca Burchett meeting him at the altar.

And Tommy? The lad'd be disillusioned. That's the word the sprout'd use, too. No infantile expressions for young Master Thomas Walters. He might caper with a child's abandon on occasion, but his mind worked on an adult level.

"I'm not sure about this," Dauntry muttered.

"What's that, Quint?"

He turned at the sound of Ollie Threadwhistle's voice.

"I'm not so sure about all this," he repeated.

Silence greeted his words.

"It's underhanded," he insisted. "What would Gardener say if he knew? And Mrs. Walters? I doubt they'd approve, no matter how laudable our goal. As for little Tommy, what sort of example are we setting him?"

"Fine time to be having doubts," North snapped.

"What we intend is every bit as unscrupulous as what the countess contrived. We're counting on the worst aspects of her character leaping to the fore."

"While she used Mrs. Walters's best qualities against her. For pity's sake, Quint—"

"No, he has a point," Stubby Clough broke in. "Depends on how you look at it, don't you see? We're playing the countess's game, even if it is in reverse. I can see how that'd stick in Quint's craw."

Dauntry stared at the taffy-haired sprig in surprise. One expected the occasional grumble from Clough. One expected pranks of the more juvenile sort. One expected lack of comprehension if a joke was too involved. One even expected the rare flashes of insight of an *idiot savant*. One didn't expect reasoned arguments.

"No need to look at me like that. What you're ignoring, Quint," Clough forged on, head cocked as if he were listening rather than speaking, "is that if the countess was an honest woman, we'd lose. She's got to cheat at least twice—once at cards, and again when she offers jewels that're nothing but paste and glass as a pledge against solid gold guineas. Ain't the first time she's pulled that trick, from all reports, and that doesn't count all the other times she'll fuzz the cards. If she doesn't cheat at the tables, and if her jewels're real, she's home free. Point is, she'll cheat, and they won't be."

"Hear, hear," Sinclair said with a grin.

"I ain't quite the fool y'take me for. Seems to me if it were an enemy fortification you were facing, y'wouldn't waffle like this, Quint. Been thinking about it a lot, because at first I didn't like the notion either, even if it did sound like a grand joke. One doesn't treat ladies that way, only the countess ain't a real lady, not by a long shot. She's the reverse. George Walters didn't even mention her in his will. That ought to tell you something.

"It's a sort of a joust, don't you see, like they had back when knights wore armor and took insult at the slightest thing, and they decided where justice lay by fighting it out and counting on God to help the right one. Val's Mrs. Walters's champion, even if he ain't got a favor to tie on his lance. His play'll be honest so long as the countess's is.

"So, let's have no more of this nonsense. Things go ahead as planned. If you've got too many qualms to be part of it, Quint, one of us'll take your place. After all, there's no need to tell anyone but Gardener precisely how we managed it.

"Now, where's our dinner? I'm famished, and we've got a lot of practicing to do. Not just Val, either. Every one of us has to try our hand at it."

The next day they drove past Tattersall's unremarked—not that that was so unusual in late summer.

They went on the strut along Bond Street to no avail—which was unusual, given Chuffy Binkerton's predilection for haunting fashionable establishments.

Val North ordered a waistcoat from Weston, and even stepped in at Nugee's, shuddering at the fabrics before making his escape.

Ollie Threadwhistle was measured for Hessians at Hoby's.

Pugs Harnette inspected the beavers at Locke's.

They stopped by a carriage maker's, where Tony Sinclair made inquiries regarding progress on his new racing curricle, which was to be delivered in the fall.

They ambled by Hatchard's on Piccadilly to acquire *An Improvident Providence,* the latest *roman à clef* by the author of *To Take or Not to Take,* for Amelia, and Ackerman's Repository to thumb through the prints.

Dauntry tried his hand with a perfectly balanced hair-trigger pistol at Manton's, and North went several rounds with Gentleman Jackson himself at the famous boxing establishment.

They stopped by Cribb's Parlor for a pint, and Gunter's for ices.

They called at a toy shop, where the fellows purchased a kite and a miniature creel and fishing rod for Tommy.

They even strolled through Hyde Park at the proper hour despite the sodden heat, and then continued to White's on Saint James Street, sweltering all the way.

And they did most of it afoot, rarely resorting to North's open carriage.

Not anywhere did they catch a glimpse of Chuffy Binkerton, despite making their progress as slow and obvious as possible.

"So much for your Lady Cheltenham's plotting," North grumbled, stuffing several nearly illegible scrawls in his coat pocket as they climbed the stairs, his carriage sent back to Wilton Street with their purchases of the day. "Not near so clever as she thinks herself."

"We acted precisely as gentlemen on a dash to Town in midsummer would," St. Maure insisted. "That's the crux."

"They've lost interest, and we've lost our best chance. Told you this project was doomed."

"What the devil ails you, Val? Haven't ever seen you like this. Binkerton left more notes. Porter gave them to you not a minute ago. Besides, he's not the only idiot who might tempt you to a hell, no matter what your reputation for avoiding them."

"Best one, though, especially as her ladyship's put him on

orders to present me for sheering—not that I've any intention of being so accommodating. This lamb's never gone contentedly to the slaughter."

"You might answer one of those notes you just crumpled if you're so deuced anxious to get on with things."

"Not that anxious. Still need more time with the blindfold. It's awkward. Difficult to make out the marks on the cards. Not sure I can bring the thing off."

"Mama's card party is tomorrow evening," St. Maure reminded him.

"I'm aware of that. Only thing you could speak of all the blessed day. Stop carping. It's not your reputation'll be on the line. It's mine."

It had to be the weather making them so peevish, Dauntry decided as he trailed the others into one of the smaller parlors available at White's if one wanted to be private—another suggestion of Lady Cheltenham's as relayed by St. Maure. Even when they were where they might be expected to perch, they mustn't make it too easy, she'd insisted.

Yes, the weather must be at fault, or the waiting, or the uncertainty of the outcome, or the fruitless day spent ranging the Town on the chance of encountering Binkerton. Or, it might be all of those, or any combination, or even something else entirely, though for the devil of him he couldn't think what. Customarily the fellows had the sunniest of dispositions—even Sinclair, who'd refined the cut direct to an art.

They arranged themselves around the table, North taking a seat as far as possible from St. Maure. From the look of him, it wasn't far enough.

"We'll want bowls of water, soap, and towels," North snapped at the waiter who followed them in, head bobbing like a woodcock's. "London's filthy, and we've been on the toddle all day. And lemonade. Several pitchers. Yes, with ice, like children. And a bottle of rum, unlike children, and another of blue ruin. Send out for that if you must. The combination makes a tolerable cold punch, and cold's what we want in this weather. Once you've brought those, we'll order.

"Now," he said, as the waiter scuttled off, not bothering to hide his opinion of North's eccentric list, "not another word from any of us until we've washed off the blasted sweat and dirt and consumed at least two glasses of my concoction. That'll humanize us, if anything will."

Then he leaned back in his chair.

"Was there ever such a damnable day," he muttered.

"I can think of a few," Dauntry retorted, eyes steel as they clashed with North's. "And we'd best not consume too much of your punch. Sounds calculated to lay the hardest head beneath the table. We'll need our wits about us if all goes well."

North opened his mouth, then seemed to think better of it. The others shifted in their chairs, looking anywhere but at them. The minutes stretched uncomfortably, the silence as leaden as the sky, across which occasional lightning flickered, too distant for the thunder to be more than the hint of a rumble.

"Damn, but I wish this weather'd break," Clough complained at last, then flushed at the look thrown him by North. "Worst I've ever known it. Doesn't do a bit of good to keep quiet, Val. We're all in foul tempers and worn to the bone, myself included. Might as well admit it, and get on with things. The way you're acting, you'd think we were the worst of enemies instead of the best of friends.

A file of stone-faced lackeys chained through the room, depositing towels, soap, and a basin in front of each. Coats and neckcloths were discarded, shirts unbuttoned as they plunged their hands and faces into the cooling wonder, snorting like walruses.

Minutes later, North's restorative punch soothing parched throats and settling uncertain tempers, they were digging into a better than average club dinner. The turkey was golden, the veal cutlets flavorful, the poached trout succulent. Even the mushroom fritters had more of the woods and fields than the saucepan of a clumsy chef to them.

They destroyed North's iced punch. They destroyed the dinner, taking their time about it. They destroyed three bottles of claret, a good portion of a Stilton soaked in port, a bowl of early pears, and as many nuts as their waiter would provide, rejecting only the oversweet plum tart as beneath interest. While they waited to be found, they wandered in and out of the card rooms, perused the journals in the reading room, returned to the card rooms, then wandered back to their private parlor only to resume their profitless circuit after giving it half an hour.

"He's not coming," North growled when they finally were in the parlor again, sprawled around the table. "Might as well go home. Sun'll be up in a bit."

"It's barely midnight. Evening's young yet," St. Maure insisted. "We should try some of the hells. Stubby's got the list. A pity to waste Mama's card party. I have no idea what we'll contrive if you do."

"I'm known for never frequenting hells. That's the whole point of this."

"One more round." Ollie Threadwhistle clapped him on the shoulder. "Maybe you should join a table. Sure to be someone in there you can cozen into inviting us to accompany him elsewhere. All you need do is complain the play isn't deep enough. Think I saw Bertie Scanlon. He's known for frequenting the worst places. We'll make sure it's the Tinker's Bum he proposes, and make him believe it was all his idea."

"Binkerton's bad enough. I will not consort with the likes of Bertie Scanlon," North spluttered.

"This time you will, if he's the best that offers." Sinclair tossed down the dregs in his glass, and rose. "On your feet, Val. If the mountain refuses to come to Mahomet, we'll take Mahomet to the mountain, or some such."

"Besides, it can't've been he. They'd never admit him."

"Would if he arrived as someone's guest, and that someone was elevated enough. What would Amelia say? Why you came to Town, after all—to set things right. Sooner you get the job done, sooner you'll be back at Hillcrest, Thomas'll have ponies of his own to ride, and Mrs. Walters will be rescued from a life of drudgery."

"I, ah—" North's shoulders slumped. He glanced at each in turn, eyes falling before Dauntry's concerned expression. "Fellows, I haven't won at cards in weeks, not even against Robby. Don't know what's happened, but—"

"Doesn't matter. You'll be playing rigged hands," Dauntry said.

"Not against Lady Walters at the card party, I won't."

"Not to worry. She's just a cheat. You've foiled her sort dozens of times."

They'd managed it, though at first Bertie Scanlon had been oddly reluctant to offer them the hospitality of the slums, claiming the play at White's was as deep as anywhere. It took North losing several hands and over twenty guineas to convince the greedy little rotter he'd happened on a rooster ripe for plucking, and that the plucking would be easier in less formal surroundings.

Seven Dials stank of refuse and worse. An ideal location for the lowest sort of hell, Dauntry supposed. One guarded one's back, and prayed one would be quick enough to fend off the attacks that were inevitable if one lingered too long.

He glanced behind him at a sudden noise, hesitating as he followed the fellows up the worn steps of Mother Hinchey's in Catspaw Alley. Nothing but a rat, thank God, scurrying across broken cobbles with something writhing in its jaws. Suppressing a shudder, he took two more steps, keeping well clear of the greasy railings.

A raindrop splattered on his forehead. Another struck his cheek. It was just possible they'd be blessed with a deluge tonight, and wake to a Mayfair cleansed of dust and foul odors, though not even Noah's flood would wash this backwater clean.

"One of the best places, if deep play's what you want," Scanlon enthused on the stoop above him, linking his arm with North's. North shook him off. "Entertainment upstairs is even better. Girls're clean, too."

"How good of them," North murmured, lips curling.

A tough opened the door at Scanlon's odd knock, cudgel grasped in a meaty fist.

"Now there's a fine, welcoming sort," Clough hissed. "Sight of him warms my heart."

"Evening, Badger." Scanlon drew himself up, puffing out his chest. "Brought some friends. Hosed and shod, every one of 'em.

Wouldn't've brought 'em otherwise, knowing how the mother regards the other sort. Thought we'd try our luck."

"If the place suits," Sinclair threw in, a edge to his voice, "which I doubt it will, given its Cerberus. You've got odd tastes, Scanlon."

"Wish we'd thought to bring pistols," Threadwhistle muttered. "Good Lord, what a hovel. Calling it a hell's granting it too much dignity."

The air was heavy with the stench of unwashed bodies, cheap perfume, and cheaper wine, the light dim, the straw-strewn floor filthy. In a far corner a pair of figures writhed in the shadows, their sex indeterminate. Whether they fought or coupled it was impossible to tell.

A quick glance proved the Countess of Marle had chosen to avoid this lowest infernal ring. Scanlon continued to sing the hell's praises, but only with half a heart, his gaze anxiously wandering the low-ceilinged room as they watched from the doorway, fending off malodorous doxies intent on luring them to the floor above. A thick-necked lackey lumbered up, proposing free blue ruin and seats at the tables, something in his eyes threatening swift retribution should they refuse his invitation.

Pugs Harnette slipped him a coin and murmured, "Just want to watch a bit before trying our luck, don't you see? Not much sense joining a table if we aren't going to stay, and if we don't it isn't right to accept your hospitality."

The lout tested the coin with his teeth. "Can't have yer standin' by t'door, nohow," he muttered. "Might make others think they can do the same. The Hinch'd flay me."

"A few moments only, and then we'll be at a table or gone."

"A few moments here is a few moments too many," Stubby Clough grumbled.

With a final glance, North muttered, "I don't much care for your choice in places of entertainment, Scanlon. Pugs, you wasted that coin," and flung the outer door open.

"Well, it is a trifle raw," Scanlon admitted, scrambling to keep up with North's long strides, "but y'said y'wanted deep play, and the play's the deepest at Mother Hinchey's of any place I know."

"So's the degradation, and the invitation to disease."

"Y'can't have everything."

Behind them a shot rang out, echoing in the low-ceilinged room.

"Quickly now," Dauntry ordered, speeding Scanlon's scrambling retreat with a firm hand between the shoulders. "We wanted deep play, not shallow graves."

"That ain't never happened before," Scanlon panted. "Don't think I'll be coming back."

"A wise notion."

"We'll go to the Tinker's Bum. Y'll like that. Much better sorts there."

The cobbles glistened, slick from the failed shower, as Dauntry followed the rest from Catspaw Alley. They cut around Old Sedgewick House, dodging shapeless piles of human refuse huddled against the crumbling walls.

"If the Tinker's Bum is of the same stamp, you can take yourself off Scanlon," North snapped. "There's a deal of difference between seeking out the unusual and descending to depths even the most callow youth would disdain."

"Tinker's Bum's different," Scanlon insisted. "Elegant, even. You'll find ladies there."

"With a name like that? I doubt it."

"Don't claim they're of the highest elegance, but some of 'em even got titles."

North snorted.

"Hope Val doesn't overplay his hand just to seem reluctant," St. Maure muttered as they broke onto what passed for a main thoroughfare in that area, and headed for the hackneys they'd hired outside White's. "All we need is for Scanlon to take insult and abandon us to our own devices."

"We'll muddle through if he does. Don't fuss," Dauntry returned with a shrug.

"It isn't your mother's gone to all this trouble."

"No, it certainly isn't." The thought of the vaporish Delilah Dauntry exerting herself on behalf of someone so inconsequential as a country vicar's sister was laughable. "I appreciate her efforts, believe me."

Dauntry followed St. Maure, Threadwhistle, and Harnette into the second hackney, knocked on the roof with his walking stick, then sank onto the rearward facing seat.

"What do you think?" he said, as they clattered off.

"Of Mother Hinchey's? A stews crib with pretensions." Harnette wiped the sweat from his face, then stuck his sodden handkerchief between the squabs. "I doubt even the countess would sink so low as to show herself there, not even in domino and mask."

"I'm of like mind. If the Tinker's Bum isn't a deal better—"

"Oh, it's better. Scanlon has the right of that. Don't let the name put you off. It's by way of a joke."

"You don't say. And how would you know so much?"

"Been there." Threadwhistle colored up at the looks thrown him by the others. "That time I was sent down to rusticate. Several of us wanted a tad of dissipation before facing our fathers. Rebellious youth, and all that. Wine's not watered, place doesn't smell quite so much of clogged drains and old sweat, floors're clean, and the girls have only half the stains on their gowns. More to the point, they permit private gaming so long as the house receives its fee."

Threadwhistle was right, Dauntry decided as he followed the others into the main salon at the Tinker's Bum not above half an hour later. The distance between the two establishments was measured in far more than miles. If the risqué wallpaper was a trifle obvious, no snarls filled the air, and hands didn't constantly seek weapons concealed in waistcoat or sleeve.

Scanlon was on the prowl, relieving North of more pounds clearly forgotten, gaze coming to rest on a table at which a voluptuous blonde whose décolletage left little to the imagination held both court and bank.

"Ah—friends I should join. Promised earlier, y'understand. You'll be able to see to your own entertainment, I'm sure," Scanlon murmured, eye alight, then scurried away.

"Carlotta Leighton, by damn." North's brows soared. "She may be notorious, but she's received by all but the highest sticklers. Maybe there's a chance of Lady Walters gracing the Bum with her presence, after all."

"Binkerton's by the supper table, so I'd say your chances of being right're better than average," Sinclair pointed out, "but whether she's come and gone, or is yet to arrive, there's no saying."

North gave the room a quick inspection, nodding. "Could even be tending to nature's demands. That's a need hits the most refined lady as hard as the lowest slut, even if she's a bit more circumspect about answering it. Find tables where they'll invite you to join in, and start your play. See if you can learn anything of Lady Walters. Tony and I'll get to work."

A female glided over, scarlet gown advertising sagging wares that were hardly worth the effort, her smile practiced, her eyes flat. "Need some pointers, duckies? Introductions I don't do, as that ain't the style here."

"My friend and I have a private score to settle," North explained. "Any corner'll do. The others'll find their own levels, though a hint as to personalities might be in order. Names aren't necessary so long as your guests can cover their bets, but none of us cares for types who claim one's fuzzed the cards if they don't win, and turn their fusses into meetings at dawn if one dares disagree. Dead bores—in more ways than one."

She tittered, recognizing the intention of a joke, if not its point.

"I'm their proctor," Dauntry said to forestall comment about his non-participant status, "here merely to make sure all's right and tight."

"No arguments, no raised voices, no challenges, no mills, and no pistols," she recited. "This is a genteel establishment. Y'cause trouble, and you're out on your bums." She pointed to a pair of thick-wristed footmen by the entry, then others doubling as waiters, deformed ears and noses proclaiming their previous calling.

"Don't intend to cause any."

"Think I'll watch for a bit as well," Clough said. "You don't have any rules say one must be constantly wagering, do you, madam?"

Again, the smile that didn't quite reach hard eyes. "Y'don't play, y'll find it flat, ducks. Don't talk much in the gaming rooms. If conversation's what you want, we got all kinds abovestairs. Reasonable, too."

"Perhaps later," Clough choked out, slipping the woman a

pound note. "For now I'll just toddle about, if that won't discommode you overly."

This time the smile reached the eyes. "Don't mind a bit, ducks." She shoved the note deep in her cleavage. "Help yourself at the buffet table on your way. Got most things you toffs're partial to. Y'want something y'don't see, y've only to ask."

The others sorted themselves out as North and Sinclair followed their hostess to a small alcove whose draperies had been pulled back, creating a miniature stage on which was set a small gaming table, four chairs, a serving cart holding decks of cards, paper, a standish, and a bouquet of flowers wilting in the heat.

Nothing could've suited their purposes better, Dauntry decided, trailing after. As with the four other alcoves, candelabra burned brightly within, while beyond the lighting was dimmer. They'd receive the attention they wanted when the time was ripe.

Eleven

North swept up another jumble of bills and coins, the total well over a thousand pounds. His expression was impassive unless one caught his eye. Then one knew: Valentine North, for all his earlier complaints, was enjoying himself hugely.

" 'Nother hand, Tony?" he said, leaning back and lighting one of the superior cheroots provided for the guests.

Sinclair nodded. "Luck's got to change," he claimed for the benefit of the footmen, one in the alcove ensuring the house got its fee, the other just outside playing the role of guard, who would spread word of their deep play when sent on an errand. "A few hands to me, then a few to you. That's how it usually goes when there's just the two of us. Don't know what's happened tonight. Y'seem unbeatable. Thing of it is, I know you're not, for all you're having the devil's own luck."

North chuckled, took a few notes from the pile before him, slipped them through the slot in the baize, and into the locked coffer bolted beneath the table.

"We could do with more wine," he said, laying his cheroot across the shallow basin provided for ashes, then shuffling the cards. "Wouldn't mind a few mouthfuls from the buffet table, either. Nothing that's been sitting out too long, mind you."

He shoved a banknote in the footman's direction without checking the denomination. The footman palmed it, then snapped his fingers. The lackey just beyond the alcove scurried off.

It was going well, Dauntry decided from his post by the wall. The Tinker's Bum had provided. Wherever she'd been, whatever she'd been doing, the Countess of Marle—festooned in shawls despite the warmth of the evening, and toting a capacious reticule to hold her winnings—now honored a table that included her three cicisbeos, though Binkerton and the one with the high-pitched voice stood and watched rather than sat and participated. According to Stubby Clough, the stakes at her table were almost as high as the ones for which North and Sinclair were ostensibly playing, and far beyond the reach of all but the deepest pockets and most reckless souls.

Success swung first one way, then another, the countess losing more often than she won, Clough had murmured before wandering off again, but only over so many hands she appeared not to notice when luck or skill—or something else—went against her. There was more trickery at that table than honest play, the house turning a blind eye and a tidy profit. Her ladyship was living up to her reputation as a rapacious addict, though who was most skilled at fuzzing the cards among her fellow players remained a good question.

The other three were hard at it, losing the pounds North had provided, though not with such rapidity as to expose themselves as easy marks. Even Harnette appeared to be holding his own. Certainly he'd been at it longer than he customarily managed.

Clough was pausing by Harnette now, murmuring in his ear. Harnette glanced at them over his shoulder, then responded to a question or comment from one of his fellow gamesters as Clough wandered off again. Good. Word of the battle in the alcove would spread, reaching the countess without any of them being directly involved. That was essential if they were to pull this off.

Several hands later, Dauntry decided the worst of it was attempting to appear interested when he knew the outcome of each hand the moment it was dealt thanks to North's and Sinclair's signals. His eyes burned. The skin was tight across his face. His throat was raw from the smoke of North's and his own countless cheroots, trapped in the alcove like a noxious fog. His leg had taken to complaining again.

It was a monotonous litany. He wanted his bed. He wanted dreamless sleep untenanted by Cecelia or Tommy. He wanted to cough, and mustn't. Above all, he wanted for it to be over.

Well, he'd have the first soon, and eventually the last, for good or ill.

It seemed to take hours, but at last a crowd alerted to the high stakes game began to gather, just as they'd planned it, only a few stragglers at first following St. Maure's lead, then more and more. The bleary-eyed arc swelled until it was many gamesters deep, more flocking to the fringes, their *sotto voce* comments, indrawn breaths, side bets, and demands for information a counterpoint to the flat, almost bored voices of North and Sinclair. North was "winning" steadily now that their audience had arrived, sweeping up what amounted to a small fortune with each turn of the cards.

Dauntry scanned the faces. He spotted Scanlon, Clough well behind him and off to the side, but the one they wanted remained missing. Dauntry lifted his brows in inquiry. Clough shrugged. So the countess was still at it, and unlikely to cry "enough" soon.

Sinclair stood, complained of his ill luck, removed his coat, made a show of turning it inside out, donned it again with the lining on the exterior, then circled the table backward three times, insisting those stratagems would change his luck. North led the laughter, called for brandy, and dealt the cards.

And then there was a stir at the rear of the crowd. Heart racing, mouth dry, Dauntry glimpsed the men from Vauxhall. Binkerton was doubtless back there somewhere, and the countess. It was now. He coughed.

"Drink up, Quint, and stop fidgeting," North grumbled, alert on the instant. He shoved the mountain of banknotes and coins before him to the center of the table, and made a great show of yawning. "Lord, but I'm tired. Can you cover that, Tony? I'd as soon have done with this. No challenges. No surprises."

"If you'll accept my vowels."

"Never caviled before. Shan't start now."

The footman retrieved paper and standish, and placed them before Sinclair.

"Here you, make way for the lady," Ollie Threadwhistle's voice sliced through the buzz. "Come on, now—let her through. She's a slip of a thing. Isn't as if you won't be able to see over her head."

In the strong light flooding from the alcove the countess was attractive enough despite pointed chin and hectic flush, her feath-

ered turban of cloth of gold slightly awry, her myriad shawls
trailing past her hem to the floor. The famous Marle jewels, as
at Vauxhall, gleamed among others that must form her private
trove.

Dauntry imagined her without the silks and jewels, and saw
a harridan where the rest of the world undoubtedly saw a diminutive lady of considerable presence and fire. It was all in the eyes,
which were as hard and unforgiving as granite, and as calculating
as those of a counting house clerk.

"Let's be done with this. Just scribble you'll cover it, Tony,"
North drawled. "I trust you. We'll have an accounting later, as
usual."

Sinclair wrote the requisite words, scrawled his signature
across the bottom of the page, sanded it, waited a moment, then
blew the sand away and tossed his vowels on top of the jumble
of bank notes and guineas. "I'll shuffle this time," he said.

North shrugged, smiled, leaned back, and took a sip of his
brandy. "You can shuffle, cut, and deal for all of me, or do none
of it. I'll triple the odds, should you win—which you won't. The
only question is how quickly you'll lose."

Moments later North swept the mountain in the direction of
the footman as Stubby Clough, Pugs Harnette, and Ollie Threadwhistle entered the alcove. "You'll watch these three gentlemen
tally this, and determine the house's fee. Be quick about it."

"The only reason this Valentine North wins so handily is he
plays children's games against inferior opponents," the Countess
of Marle hissed from the front row.

The murmurs died away. North took a last draw on his cheroot,
crushed it in the basin, then shifted in his chair and inspected
the countess from feathered turban to spangled sandals, his face
expressionless.

"I don't believe I've had the pleasure," he said at last, turning
to Chuffy Binkerton, who hovered at her side babbling she had
better have held her tongue and considered with whom she had
to do.

Binkerton bungled the presentations. North waited him out.
Then, one brow raised, he nodded without rising. "I'm honored,
my lady," he said.

"No, you're not. I've caught you out." She waved her fan with a courtesan's indolence. "Gentlemen don't like that. Unfortunately for you, I was just the one to do it."

"Really? Fascinating." North's drawl was becoming thicker by the word.

"What would you do should news of your lackluster gaming get about?" she taunted. "Not quite the image you desire others to hold of you, I'd think."

"Ignore the prattle as beneath notice."

"Here now, I won't be having trouble," the red-gowned hostess called from the back of the crowd. Then she shoved her way to the front, a pair of her louts clearing her path.

"Trouble? There's none I recognize as such." North refilled his glass, eyes never leaving the countess's. "Your guest and I are merely indulging in a pleasant exchange regarding our fortunes at play, madam."

"I consider myself something of an expert," the countess insisted.

A veil seemed to descend over her features. She fluttered her fan. She donned as close to an innocent air as was possible for a female displaying herself in a venue hardly commensurate with innocence—one who, moreover, would never see the sunny side of fifty again. She cocked her head, offering a coquettish pose. North remained impassive.

"The evening's been disappointingly dull," she complained with a moue that emphasized the lines ringing her lips. "If you're as invincible as you claim, Mr. North—and are vaunted to be, which is why I've wanted to try my luck against yours forever— then you'll play a round or two with me now, and see how you fare against a superior opponent. Unfortunately, meeting you was impossible until tonight, given you're known never to test yourself in venues where ladies are welcome."

Dear Lord—the countess actually appeared to be trying to flirt with North. Certainly she was almost simpering at him.

"Far be it from me to disappoint a lady," North returned, downing the last of his brandy, yawning, and rising, "but it's almost dawn. Time for devoted gamesters such as you and me to retreat to our several beds, Lady Walters, and recoup our forces for tomorrow's encounters. Otherwise our play will be below its customary standard."

"Tomorrow, then? Perfect. I'd begun to fear you tended to the capricious. Shall we say earliesh, when we're both at the height of our powers? We might even consider requesting a private room, and having supper brought in from Grillon's."

"Impossible, deeply as I regret being forced to say you nay. I'm already bespoken at a private entertainment. Courtesy demands I not fail my hostess."

"The day after, then," she pressed, gaze darting to the bills Clough, Harnette, and Threadwhistle were counting under the watchful eye of the footman-*cum*-guard, "at a place and time of your choosing. My home even, if you prefer. My chef provides passable refreshments, and my husband's cellar holds nothing but the best."

"Most gracious of you, but I intend to depart for the country the following morning, and will be unavailable."

"Surely you can put off your departure to please a lady?"

"Not when it would displease another lady to whom I owe higher allegiance. The separation from my bride wasn't by choice, and will be ended as quickly as I have it in my power to do so."

Binkerton buzzed in her ear. The countess slapped him away with her fan, breaking several spokes. "A paltry excuse. Of course luck, as any gentleman here will attest," she said, softening her continued insults with a laugh that was itself just short of insult, "is known to be a lady, and favors her own. It's no wonder you're reluctant."

North bowed, but held his peace.

Ollie Threadwhistle slapped down the bills he'd been counting, face purple, timing his ire to perfection.

"I won't stand for Val North being slandered this way," he blustered. "Never heard of such a thing—never! It's as well you're not a man, Lady Walters. If y'were, he'd've drawn your cork by now—if he hadn't already taken a horsewhip to you for impertinence, that is."

"My, how ferocious," the countess murmured, eyes still fixed on North's. "I'm all aquiver."

"If you're so anxious to try a hand or two against him," Threadwhistle forged on, "why not join us at the whist party Dab's mother's giving? Certain Lady St. Maure won't object. Anything to accommodate a fellow enthusiast."

"Lady St. Maure and I are not on visiting terms," the countess snapped, drawing herself up.

"I'm certain Mama would understand the circumstances," St. Maure threw in on cue. "Rather fond of Val. Wouldn't care to see him maligned any more than the rest of us do. In fact, I'll pledge myself to her accepting your presence, if not accepting it gladly."

"What, reluctant, Lady Walters?" North drawled. "I apologize if you find the notion repugnant, but meeting at St. Maure House appears our sole option. Is it possible you don't actually desire to test your skill against mine, and merely wish to make it appear you do?"

The silence was deafening.

"St. Maure House, then," the countess conceded, "not that it'll be a pleasure. Madeleine St. Maure is an unprincipled Jezebel given to ruining reputations as blithely as she ruins gowns. The prospect of finding myself in her company holds no attraction. I warn you, Mr. North: Expect to play exceeding deep, or be known as a *poseur.*"

She skewered St. Maure with a stiletto gaze. "Have your mother send me an invitation. Should she fail, I'll ensure all my acquaintances learn Valentine North is a poltroon with pretensions." She smiled sweetly, the smile not reaching her eyes. "My acquaintance is extensive, and includes many luminaries."

Then she was gone.

"So this is the famous Major Quintus Dauntry!" Daphne Cheltenham's eyes sparkled with the brilliance of those of a young girl. "Sir, your championing George Walters's widow and son does you proud. We forget injustices too easily."

Dauntry bowed low over the petite dowager countess's hand, instantly charmed. She radiated intelligence rather than cunning, kindness rather than polish. She was no taller than the Countess of Marle and of almost the same generation. None could've presented a greater contrast to that despicable witch.

"An honor, my lady, but I'm afraid it's plain Mr. Dauntry, now."

"Plain? Hardly, and perhaps not for long. Yes, Dabney's mentioned a thing or two. There's a military friend I want you to speak with, one with no ties to your father, General Maitland. You should receive some recompense for your altruism, and my friend's head—when he's not in his cup—is one of the longest I know. Maitland may prove of use to you."

Her silvery laugh as she gazed up at him proved he hadn't been quite as quick to hide his reaction as he'd thought.

"I understand you're already acquainted with the general, but not with the man I've known these many years, only his shadow." She tucked her hand in the crook of Dauntry's arm, leading him slightly away from the others. "Shadows can be deceptive. Beware of them. Now, I've a question of a personal nature, though I'm convinced I already know the answer, more's the pity"

So he was to be subjected to an inquisition regarding Cecelia Walters. Blast St. Maure, and his gossiping tongue!

He threw the fellow a withering glance. St. Maure smiled and shrugged, and continued to play butler beside a tray of decanters and glasses.

"You were wounded at Salamanca, I understand," the dowager countess said, throwing Dauntry off guard. "First, my congratulations on your recovery from what I'm informed was a potentially crippling wound."

"Hardly so serious. Say rather uncomfortable and inconvenient."

"Yes, that's what my nephew insists, and *he* lost an arm there. Were you perhaps acquainted? Henry Beckenham. Like yourself, a major who sold out shortly afterwards."

"Salamanca?" Dauntry thought back, then shook his head. "I'm afraid not. It was a confused time, and I was among the ambulatory beyond the first few days, which your nephew wouldn't've been. The more fortunate among us fended for ourselves until we could be sent to the rear."

"I see. Not even a passing acquaintance? Most unfortunate. I'd counted on your proven good nature to assist in blasting him from his doldrums once all this was seen to, if you had a few spare moments—one of the reasons I was delighted to involve myself in your project." Then she patted his arm. "Don't worry. We'll get him through it, somehow. Let's see about testing the lighting, shall we? That must be done before the others arrive."

The task he faced, North complained once they got to it, was close to impossible. Over and over he practiced drawing the crucial last card, the draperies closed to simulate the night that would've fallen by then. Over and over he got it wrong. More candelabra didn't help. Neither did fewer, nor repositioning them. Even without the blindfold, he rarely succeeded in drawing the higher card, not even when the deck was marked and the lower was merely a deuce or a trey.

"I'll do the best I can," he sighed after a final failed attempt, "but that's all I can promise you. Tony might better take my place, or even Stubby."

"That woman's expecting to play against *you*," Lady St. Maure snapped. "It's the only reason she's coming."

"You don't meet her at the tables, and she'll suspect something's not as it should be." Lady Cheltenham's chin was up, her smile encouraging. "Besides, you should do well enough in regular play. Skill always triumphs over cheating, especially as you've more than one way to foil her at that. Only the final hand's in doubt."

"And there's the rub," North sighed.

"Nonsense! When the times comes, you'll be adroitness itself."

But they all knew it wasn't nonsense. North had claimed two nights before that his luck had changed with his marriage. He might have the right of it. Even his skill at *léger-de-main* when faced with a dishonest opponent appeared to've deserted him. Determination wouldn't necessarily be enough to see them through this time.

Again relegated to the role of observer, almost wishing he were absent, Dauntry escorted the man from Rundell and Bridge, Lady St. Maure's solicitor, and her man of business to the parlor of her private apartments on the floor above as soon as the trio arrived, and saw them settled and provided with refreshments. There they'd be safe from discovery until their presence was required.

A rapid perusal proved the documents Skipworth had drawn were as specified, and would ensure Cecelia's and Tommy's futures—so long as North could pull off the essential coup. One phrase even hinted at the substitution of the false will for the real, and the potential for prosecution should the countess prove recalcitrant.

Dauntry glanced at the solicitor. "You've located the scoundrel, Mr. Skipworth?"

"Mr. Tisdale has, in a manner of speaking, sir. Why he's here."

"We've traced him to his departure for the American Colonies," Lady St. Maure's man of business explained. "Venality being what it is, a few coins sprinkled here and there keeps such trails fresh, even after some years. Unfortunately, there's no assurance Screed is alive. We're hoping the mere fact that we know of his existence will suffice, should the countess refuse the jump at the last moment."

"Lady St. Maure is determined young Thomas Walters won't be cheated of his birthright." Skipworth accepted the documents from Dauntry and slipped them back in their leather pouch. "We all are, come to that."

"I see," Dauntry said. "You're all enjoying this, aren't you?"

"A worthy project, and an intriguing one." Tisdale beamed and winked. "Far more intriguing than totaling accounts in a ledger."

"Yes, I suppose it is." He'd never thought of it that way. Too close to the problem, perhaps. For him it wasn't a game. It was a matter of desperation. "I wish I could recompense you personally for your efforts, gentlemen."

"Adequately recompensed already, though we would've been delighted to be of assistance *pro bono*. Success will be the true compensation. The Countess of Marle has a certain reputation in our world, as well as the one she bears in yours."

Dauntry nodded, then turned to the man from Rundell and Bridge. "All set?"

The bespectacled Kulp indicated a small black leather case set on a table before the cold fireplace. "Entirely, sir."

"And enjoying yourself, as well."

"Shall we say Rundell and Bridge is aware of the variable nature of Lady Walters's gems, sir, and has suffered from that nature more than once, given scandal must never attach to the firm."

"I see."

Apparently the famous jewelers had their own motive for seeking justice here. Amazing—that the woman had been able to play her games so long, and so successfully. It would've taken only one victim standing up to her to spoil them. Others would've flocked to their side on the instant.

When Dauntry returned to the drawing room, all but one table were filled. The candles had been lit again, their glow reflecting on the carpetless floor for which Lady St. Maure had earlier apologized, and vying with the setting sun whose rays streamed through open windows. The sky was leaden, the underbellies of the clouds tinged red, the slit through which the sun peeked incandescent gold. Distant thunder rumbled like heavy artillery, echoing from cloud to cloud. The slit closed. A sudden gust of wind sent the draperies billowing, followed by a flash and a closer peal.

He accepted a glass of wine from a footman and wandered to the windows. Town equipages clotted the torch-lit courtyard, the teams restive, grooms at their heads murmuring soothing nothings. As he watched, the first fat drops splattered against the cobbles.

It appeared they'd get their storm at last. With the Countess of Marle yet to make her appearance, the timing couldn't've been worse.

Dauntry quitted the open windows and wandered the drawing room, pausing occasionally to watch the fellows' play. North was holding his own, but only barely, a preoccupied frown creasing his forehead. At another table, Pugs Harnette enjoyed an unusual streak of luck, the best of hands falling to him and his clever partner. Or, were the audacity and skill Harnette's, rather than Daphne Cheltenham's? Certainly his air of abstraction was deep, almost as if he were following instructions unheard by others. The brilliance he exhibited in both bidding and play were so uncharacteristic that it was as if the North of a few months ago sat in his place.

Harnette glanced uncertainly at the others after leading his last card, a deuce none could cover. "And that's the hand to us, I believe."

"It is indeed, and the rubber." Lady Cheltenham's laugh was delighted. "I don't understand why you apologized when we drew each other. I doubt even my husband could've beaten you, and he was the most adept player I've ever known."

"This ain't like me at all, that's all I can tell you." Harnette spread his hands wide. "Even with good cards, I generally cock up my toes."

"A likely tale." General Maitland, who was partnered by an elderly lady with a formidable bosom, chuckled. "You've been diddling us, young man, that's what. Excellent strategy, but it won't work now we're on to you."

Turning away with a shudder as the raillery continued, Dauntry wandered to the refreshment table and helped himself to several triangles of pastry holding bits of heaven knew what in a savory sauce. He devoured the lot mechanically, then accepted a fresh glass from a footman and returned to the windows. The first spatters had given way to a steady downpour, the wind now blowing toward the street. Cobbles glistened. Torches sputtered. Coachmen and grooms huddled under tarpaulins, shivering in the sudden cold. The weather had indeed broken, the temperature plummeted.

"Anxious?"

"What do you think, Pugs?" Dauntry snapped, not bothering to turn.

"Don't be. It's an odd night. I feel it in my bones."

"Where you feel it's your purse."

"Yes, it's considerably heavier than when I arrived. Already slipped North his stake, and enough to cover his losses to Scanlon at White's, and I'm playing on my own now. Wonder where the nearest church is? Poor box'll receive a tidy sum if things continue as they've begun. No accounting for it—no accounting at all—but I'm not about to complain. Tony's not faring any better than Val, by the bye, but Stubby can do no wrong most hands, and he's almost as much of a clunch as I am. As I said, odd night."

"Why aren't you still at it, then?"

"Others said they were gut-foundered. They're loading up their plates. Then we'll go at it again. I couldn't eat a bite—not if my life depended on it. Feel off, somehow."

A closed town carriage pulled through the gates, the horses' heads bent into the wind, the coachman's neck drawn like a turtle's between hunched shoulders.

"And there she is at last, by damn," Harnette murmured. "Was beginning to fear she'd thought better of it, and we'd have to find another way."

A pair of footmen appeared, toting umbrellas. A third was opening the carriage door. A figure that had to be the Countess of Marle descended, muffled in a hooded cloak. Three men followed her onto the cobbles.

"Damnation," Dauntry muttered. "She's brought her entourage. Lady St. Maure'll never stand for that. Best warn her."

"Don't worry," St. Maure, who'd just joined them, murmured, craning to see into the courtyard. "Mama knows how to depress pretensions. Binkerton may just make it past the door. The other two'll cool their heels in the carriage."

He was wrong. Moments later the countess of Marle, gowned in long-sleeved, heavy jonquil silk, once more festooned in shawls, sporting every jewel she owned and toting her oversized reticule, swept into the drawing room on Binkerton's arm, followed by her Captain Sharps and a red-faced Lady St. Maure.

"What the devil?" St. Maure muttered.

"Used numbers as the excuse," Harnette said. "Sure to've. She didn't bring her tribe, there'd be three forced to sit out each round. Odds are she's going to insist one partner her, the other Val, and Binkerton take Val's place at the other table. Damned clever. She'll win, no matter how the cards lie."

In the event he was proved wrong. The countess cared nothing for upsetting the numbers, permitted no partners, no others at the table, and wanted none of whist. Her game, she insisted, was *vingt-et-un*—with her as dealer, North her sole opponent. The shill for the Tinker's Bum took his place behind North, Binkerton to one side, the fellow from Mother Hinchey's on the other. There was nothing they could do about it.

When North swiftly lost two of the first three hands, Dauntry went to stand behind the countess, prepared to determine if her play was honest.

She shrugged. She twitched. She actually squirmed as if something were crawling up her back, and resettled her myriad shawls. Then she treated Dauntry to a cold-eyed stare.

"What do you think you're doing back there?" she demanded.

"Observing the play."

"If you want to observe, go stand behind Mr. North."

"As he already has a sufficiency of observers, I thought you could do with one."

"I don't permit anyone to stand at my back," she snapped. "Ever. Go away. Shoo."

She flicked her fingers, in the process sending the deck lying on the table to the floor.

There was nothing to do but give in. Dauntry went away, ignoring the spilled cards, the shills, even Chuffy Binkerton, who had the grace to throw him a nervous glance. North was going to lose, no matter what the reason. That was the essential.

What seemed hours later supper was announced. The fellows gathered at the windows while their seniors flocked to the freshly burdened refreshment table, exclaiming over the cold soups, ices, intricate meat dishes, hothouse fruits, and delicate pastries.

"Not going well," North admitted at their anxious babble, then turned to Dauntry. "Warned you in the beginning it mightn't, but nothing would satisfy anyone but for me to come where I'm not the least use. I'm willing to continue as Mrs. Walters's champion if you want, Quint, but it won't accomplish a thing. Up to you. It's your project, after all."

"Anyone would fare better," Clough muttered, "even a scullery maid. She fuzzing the cards, Val?"

"Something's off. I could understand losing, even consistently, but not every hand. One would think my cards were face up, but if those louts are giving her signals I can't catch them. It's not skill with the pasteboards that's wanted. It's better eyes than I possess, and nerves of steel. Who's faring best tonight?"

All turned to Pugs Harnette.

"No," he protested. "No, I tell you. Out of the question. A fluke, that's all it's been. I'd lose, too, and then we'd be in worse case than ever."

Twelve

In the event, Harnette had no choice. The countess glided up and seized his arm in jeweled talons.

"I've run your friend off his legs. He's become a bore," she pouted. "Nothing but chicken stakes now. Definitely not up to the standard I warned him to expect." She threw North a triumphant look. He shrugged.

"Oh, but he—" Harnette stared wildly around the drawing room, eyes finally locking with Dauntry's. "That is, Val don't generally—"

"I detest being bored, and I'm most dreadfully bored. I understand you're this evening's big winner, and might present a worthy challenge," the countess cooed. "Your partner'll accept Mr. North in your place, I'm sure. It's early yet, but the weather's so foul I have no desire to seek more exciting entertainment elsewhere."

"That's a pity, my lady. It's just that—"

"Your name? I never play against those to whom I've not been introduced, though introducing themselves is the usual thing."

"B-but, you should give Val a chance to—" he spluttered. "I mean, it just ain't gentlemanly not to permit him to—"

"But then I'm a lady, not a gentleman with a taste for infantile codes. What, no bottom, young man?"

"It's all right, Pugs." Only Dauntry caught North slipping Harnette a flat packet of thousand-pound notes. Harnette slid them well up his sleeve as if he'd been doing it all his life. "You can take my place, and welcome. Lady Walters, may I present my country neighbor, Percival Harnette, better known to his friends as Pugs?"

"Mr. Harnette," she murmured, resettling her shawls, and holding her hand out to be saluted, gracing them with what she apparently considered a winsome smile.

Dauntry trailed them as she propelled the luckless fellow toward the table where she and North had battled, mouthing her usual drivel about wanting to test her skill against a superior opponent, praising his and denigrating her own now that she had her latest victim in her clutches. The men from Vauxhall flanked them, a guard of dishonor.

Harnette sent Dauntry a warning glance. Dauntry stopped in his tracks. Odd. The fellow didn't look the least like himself, and he was overplaying the bumbling country mark to an alarming extent. Amazingly, the countess didn't appear to recognize the parody for what it was.

Then Harnette winked. He'd never seen the fellow wink before, not in all their lives—claimed he'd he couldn't do it, any more than he could lift his ears. As stunned as he was confused, Dauntry retreated a few steps. Harnette gave a slight nod, expression more his own, then turned to the countess, chattering about something that obviously flattered her. She posed. She simpered. She patted Harnette's cheek with a sauciness more appropriate to an experienced *demimondaine* than a grandmother.

The entire evening had been off so far. No reason for that to change.

Dauntry rejoined North at the depleted buffet table, nerves singing. He wanted it over, the last farewells said, himself on his way to wherever. That couldn't happen soon enough, but he could make it sooner rather than later.

"Got a favor to ask of you," he murmured, "if you don't mind, that is."

North snagged a glass from a passing footman, downed it, and set it on the table behind them, all the while studying Dauntry's face.

"Dab's all ready informed me of your latest start," he said finally. "I'll purchase you a commission, Quint, and gladly. I've already offered more than once. I'll *not* finance a foray to India, or the Antipodes, or any other such place."

"But—"

"Don't try to sound like Pugs. He can get away with it. You can't."

Their eyes clashed. At last Dauntry's fell.

"It seemed a logical solution. I've got to do something. The price of passage is far cheaper, dear though it is, and the prospect of debt terrifies me. Rather face a battery of Nappy's best single-handed. The less I incur, the better."

"Well, it isn't logical."

"I can't abide having others act for me when by rights I'm the one should be taking action."

North's arm descended on Dauntry's shoulders. "You've been a superior general. Content yourself with that. Wellington does, after all."

"Only thing I did was at Vauxhall. It wasn't much, and it was by accident. Even you'll admit that."

"I will? Think again. You uncovered the problem. You marshaled the forces. You ran the reconnaissance. You laid the plans. That's the essential." North sighed. "This entire thing's rested on your shoulders from start to finish. Even Wellington employs scouts and spies, and has others act as his hands."

"This is different. I should be at that table, not Pugs."

"Only in your own mind. Now's hardly the time for self-doubts—not if you really care what happens to Mrs. Walters and her son. Besides, your part'll begin as soon as they've played a few hands, and the harpy's lost more than she's willing to lose."

Dauntry could feel his old friend's eyes boring into him, and almost flinched. He sounded like a whining whelp, at least to his own ears. It seemed he couldn't help it, which was as odd as the look Harnette had thrown him earlier. Even odder was the fact that North, who rarely lectured anyone no matter what the provocation, was treating him to a superior example of the art.

"You've borne more than most of us could," North insisted, "and you've borne it with a patience not one of us would've shown. Ghost, indeed! See here, old friend, you've been felled. *Bon courage,* as the Froggies say. Don't let the fact turn you into as much of a cawker as it did me. I'm hardly the *beau idéal* of how a gentleman should comport himself under such circumstances."

"You think I'm being a fool."

"In a manner of speaking, and only in one respect, which is better than I managed. You might follow Lady Cheltenham's suggestion, and confer with old Maitland. Certainly she's opened that door wide. When you're ready, I'll be waiting."

"I'll consider it."

"Don't just consider it. Do it. Maitland's quitted the tables. He'll be sodden soon, and Lord knows when Lady Cheltenham'll manage to have him more than a shadow of his real self again."

"No, not now. My problems can wait."

"Not so sure about that. More than one game's playing itself out tonight. No reason to be entirely uncooperative."

"What the devil do you mean by that?"

"Not sure myself," North returned with a shrug. "Just know they've got to be won, every last one of them, or you'll regret it for the rest of your life."

Lady St. Maure came over under the guise of telling the servants to clear away the debris and restock the table with lighter fare for those who might find themselves still peckish after a hand or two.

Harnette was, she whispered between louder instructions, winning. Not by much, but winning. For all she suspected he was well above par, given the wine and brandy with which the countess's henchmen were plying him. That was better than North'd done, though it was possible the countess was merely playing cat to his mouse, and intended to pounce once she'd lulled him into cup-shot overconfidence.

Then she glided off, making the rounds of the tables as she acted the gracious hostess. If she lingered longer where Harnette and the Countess of Marle skirmished, the countess made no comment beyond throwing her the occasional cold look.

North and Dauntry remained by the refreshment table, which seemed as good an observation post as any. The other guests by now had sensed something unusual was occurring. Play was desultory, chatter brighter than would've been the case under normal circumstances, trips to acquire a tidbit or two to stave off starvation more frequent, the route selected invariably passing by the countess's table.

"His luck's changed, hasn't it?" North murmured to Lady St. Maure some time later when she included them in her latest circuit. "Bound to happen. Wish I could figure out that woman's tricks. She's up to something."

"I'd swear the cards aren't those I provided," she said, "though they appear identical. All those shawls, that dreadful oversized reticule, and those tawdry louts! This grows tiresome. Do you know," she said, gracing Dauntry with a smile, "I believe I'm a trifle thirsty. No, not the champagne. Not emphatic enough. The raspberry fruit cup. An excellent notion—to have Cook use claret for that, and include more raspberries than customary, though at first she thought I'd gone mad. Well, I hadn't. Not to worry—we'll bring all right in a bit."

"She wouldn't!" North watched, brows rising, as Lady St. Maure wandered off, a certain light in her eyes that would've given the Countess of Marle pause had she noted it. "I mean, I can't believe she'd dare—"

"I do believe she would," Dauntry countered, breaking into a grin. "Now I understand why she had all the carpets removed, and has spent the evening apologizing to everyone for their not being returned in time for her party. By damn, but Dab has a mother in a million!"

"She's enjoying this."

"She is now. I believe I am, as well. She's speaking with Maitland. Doesn't appear half so sodden as he did a moment ago. Not sodden in the least. Must've been a ruse so he'd be free when the time came. Look at those eyes! Enough to set one quaking, just as the tales claim. Never believed them until now. Well, who would?"

"Over there, Quint—Lady Cheltenham's rising. See? Just behind Lady Walters. Still conversing with those at her table. Wonder what *she's* about?"

"Wellington'd better look to his laurels. That, or enlist this trio to devise his strategies. Direct action? I believe I'm about to be exposed as an amateur."

General Maitland approached the countess's table, steps unsteady, puffing mightily.

"Here, you," he bellowed, words slurring. "Yes, I mean you blackguards. Want a game?" He lurched into the Captain Sharps, grabbing their arms and pushing them away. "Boring, sitting over there by m'self. Give an old fellow a game, will you? Not quite at *point-non-plus* yet."

They tried to break away, protesting they'd merely come to observe, and perhaps pick up a pointer or two. He laughed, and continued his importunings. Lady St. Maure ambled over to the countess's table to watch the play, fruit cup almost to her lips. Lady Cheltenham, still chattering, emphasized her point with a sweeping gesture. She turned, outflung arm colliding with Lady St. Maure's shoulder. Purplish fruit cup deluged the table, soaking the pasteboards and streaming toward the Countess of Marle's jonquil gown. The countess squealed, springing to her feet and overturning the table to avoid the dribbles.

"You vixen!" she shrieked "Look what you've done! Do the contents of your glass *never* stay where they belong? I'd've thought you'd outgrown such ungainliness."

"My fault entirely," Lady Cheltenham insisted as Lady St. Maure handed her emptied glass to a footman and took refuge at Maitland's side. "Not our hostess's in the least. Oh, I'm so sorry! Is that a spot on your gown? Oh dear, I do hope it's not ruined. Salt—that's what's wanted, and lemon juice. Do someone fetch salt and a lemon. A pity—to ruin such a lovely gown."

She gazed in dismay at the overturned table as if noticing it for the first time.

"Goodness, there's no way to tell what the wagers were, is there, or who held which cards? What a shame! You'll have to replay the hand. At least there's no need to determine who'd won what. All your winnings landed quite neatly with the exception of a guinea or two."

"They must've rehearsed that," North murmured in admiration.

Servants scurried up with basins of water, rags, and a substitute card table perhaps a trifle sooner than might've been expected, and Lady St. Maure's abject apologies and Lady Cheltenham's soothing manner were belied by their laughing eyes as the mess was whisked away. A footman presented the Countess of Marle with a silver tray holding three fresh decks still in their wrappers.

She protested. She argued. She all but succumbed to the vapors at the thought of being forced to continue the game with any cards but those with which they'd been playing, and which she'd doubtless provided from somewhere within her shawls or the depths of her capacious reticule. Finally, cursing lustily at her unwarranted fuss, General Maitland grabbed the center pack and tossed it on the table, grabbed a second pack and forced the lady's three escorts to join him at an empty table some distance from hers or be labeled lily-livered mice.

After that, things went better, the tide turning slowly in Harnette's favor as reckless wagers, uneven play, and the lack of her accomplices steadily shrank the stacks of bank notes and guineas in front of the countess. At last, considerably poorer than when she arrived, her ladyship yawned and declared herself un-utterably wearied. It was time she sought her bed, she declared, as there was no one present possessing sufficient wit to make the evening other than unbearably tedious.

She rose, gathering shawls and reticule, and the remains of her funds.

"B-but, this ain't right." Pugs Harnette blinked, slurring his words. "Not in no way is it." He stared from her to his considerable winnings in dismay. "Can't be so ungentlemanly as to take advantage of a lovely lady. Can't in the least, but I can't just return your losses. Not done, not even in a friendly game. Might as well play for imaginary stakes the way the infantry do, and have done with it."

She bridled at the compliment, eyes darting to the jumble lying before him.

"How punctilious of you. It's not that much. I'll never breathe a word." She opened her reticule and reached out to sweep away the majority of the banknotes. "It'll be our secret."

"Got to bet it all," he insisted, shoving the whole to the center of the table with both hands before she could appropriate what she wanted, adroitly slipping the small fortune North'd earlier passed him into the mishmash without her noticing, just as they'd planned and practiced. "That's how it's done. Y'saw that last night. Turn of a card, and winner take all. Best I can offer without ruining us both. Word'd travel, we did it any other way. Y'wouldn't want that. Neither would I. Wouldn't be able to show our faces in Town for a month o' Sundays, and the country's a dead bore."

Maitland strode up at the same moment as North, Dauntry, and Lady St. Maure.

"Deciding the evening by the turn of a card?" he barked. "Fine old tradition. Done blindfolded with a fresh deck, and others doing the shuffling. Y'got something we can use as a blindfold about the place, Lady St. Maure? Needs to be black, and soft."

"I'm certain there must be something in my dressing room that'll suffice."

Lady St. Maure waylaid a footman and requested that her abigail be told to bring a black scarf to the drawing room. The countess of Marle opened her mouth, then apparently thought better of it and shrugged.

"I can't cover such a sum," she said. "Will my vowels suffice?"

"A gentleman's word's his bond," Maitland said in a considering tone. "I assume a lady's is the same? No objection I know of unless this young fellow has one. You object, Harnette? It can be counted once you're done if that's needed, with witnesses to make sure someone doesn't miss a bill or two. Be enough if her ladyship simply says she'll cover the lot, whatever it may be, right? Then we can get this over with, and return to our own games. Evening's young, yet."

By then the rest of the guests were joining the throng around Harnette and the countess.

"What the devil's going on?" Sinclair hissed. "The old fellow's playing your role, Quint."

"And doing a masterful job. Leave him to it. I suspect they decided I was too inconsequential to intimidate her ladyship, but didn't care to inform us for fear we'd take insult. Maitland in wolf's clothing'd intimidate anyone."

A footman appeared, this time with a tray containing five

sealed decks. Maitland seized two, then put his hands behind his back, the decks hidden. "Choose, my lady," he ordered, facing her.

"Left," she snapped.

"Stand well back from the table, if you would. Yes, you as well, Mr. Harnette. And the rest of you. No crowding about. This'll be done properly, or it won't be done at all."

He handed the deck in his right hand to the footman, slit the seal of the one in his left, fanned the cards onto the table backs up, then expertly flipped them so the faces showed. "All there," he said. "Everyone satisfied they're all there? Good. Now, let's get this under way."

He slid the cards into a neat stack and pointed to a lady in puce silk and garnets. "We'll have you begin, I believe. Lady Doncaster, isn't it? Please shuffle the cards. Once only, faces up."

When she'd done, he repeated the process four more times, each with a different guest shuffling, the last two times with the cards face down. Then, still at random, he selected five more to cut the deck, the faces against the baize tabletop, as the countess impatiently tapped her toe and protested at the silly ritual he was making of it.

"Take your places," he ordered Harnette and the countess, ignoring her complaints. "Yes, the same seats y'held before. Nothing's to change. Y'want to reverse your coat, young fellow, that's allowed. Y'can turn your turban front to back, Lady Walters, if you want—not that it'll do the least bit of good. Lady draws first, of course."

He accepted the blindfold from Lady St. Maure, made a show of inspecting it, then moved behind the Countess of Marle to tie it over her eyes.

"Let me see that thing," the countess snapped.

"Y'don't trust me?"

"Not in the least."

General Maitland handed her the blindfold.

"Good God—what's he doing?" Sinclair muttered.

"I haven't the slightest notion," Dauntry admitted.

"I don't like this."

"I don't either."

The countess unfolded it, held it to the light, grudgingly returned it to the general. "I want Chuffy to blindfold me," she said, as Maitland refolded the scarf.

"I'm not your friend, or this young fellow's. Never met either of you before tonight. A friend might leave you a peephole. I won't leave either of you anything, not being prejudiced one way or the other," he said, tying the blindfold securely over her eyes. "Now, hop to it. This ain't supposed to take all night."

As Dauntry watched, heart in his mouth, the countess groped clumsily, fingering the cards, hesitated, appeared to select one toward the end, and flipped it over. Dauntry gasped along with the others, though not for the same reason, for all it was the ace of hearts. She tore the blindfold off, laughing in triumph as she started to pull her winnings toward her without looking to see the value of the card she'd revealed, or waiting for Harnette to take his turn.

"I ain't drawn yet, my lady," Hamette protested as Maitland retrieved the blindfold and eased back.

Her brows soared. "There's only one card can overtake mine," she said, still not looking at the card she'd supposedly drawn.

This time Dauntry'd caught it. The ace of hearts had been palmed, slipping adroitly from her gown's long sleeve to join the others on the table an instant before she "selected" it. The woman was a master.

Dauntry gave a violent sneeze, then a series of three choked coughs, made a show of accepting a glass of wine from Sinclair, and held his place behind Harnette. Only he heard the poor fellow's moan.

"Still got to draw," Harnette insisted, squaring his shoulders. "That's how it's done. I won't give up the field that easy, my lady."

"Draw if you wish. You won't be walking away any the richer. Your luck's turned." She drummed her fingers on the table at the shocked glances thrown her, rings flashing in the candlelight. "Go on—draw if you must."

"The blindfold, General Maitland, if you'd be so kind, sir?"

Maitland, who'd eased to the back of the throng circling the table, forged to the front, blindfold in hand.

"I'll inspect that, if you please." The countess extended her hand as she brushed the importuning Chuffy Binkerton away.

Maitland gave it to her with an expressive shrug, murmuring, "Can't understand why that demmed female insists on exposing herself at every turn," just loudly enough for those closest to the table to hear him.

The countess turned pale, but she held the silk scarf up to the light, unfolded it, and turned it this way and that.

"Satisfied?" Maitland growled.

"No, but it'll have to do, I suppose."

Maitland accepted the blindfold from her and moved directly behind Harnette, shoving Dauntry out of the way. The exchange of the scarf in Maitland's hand for one in his coat was so swift, so dexterous, so totally hidden from all but himself it left Dauntry stunned. Where the devil had the old fellow learned *that* trick?

Then what had to be Lady St. Maure's carefully prepared scarf was over Harnette's eyes, the general tying the ends securely at the back of his head. He gave Harnette's shoulder a bracing clap.

"Go to it, young fellow," he ordered, "and may the best man— ah, *person*—win. You've been far more gracious than's necessary, y'know—*far* more."

Harnette hesitated, reached out, appearing to grope blindly. His fingertips touched a card. The blindfold slipped. Dauntry stifled a groan, jaws rigid. Then Harnette's hand shifted to the center of the fanned arc.

"Please, heaven!" he murmured, drew a card and turned it face up, then tore off the blindfold at the indrawn breaths around him.

Dauntry grinned in triumph as Maitland swept up the deck before the glaring countess could retrieve her ace of hearts, and slipped the fifty-three cards in an inner pocket along with the scarf. Pugs Harnette's card was the ace of spades.

This must be what it would feel like were one trapped at the bottom of a deep well, Dauntry decided a few minutes later as St. Maure slipped off to fetch Tisdale, Skipworth, and Kulp. It was an odd sensation, not the triumph of moments before, but something else entirely, almost as if he saw through another's eyes.

He glanced about.

General Maitland was standing guard as two of Lady St. Maure's other guests, selected by a draw in which all but the Irregulars and the Countess of Marle's escorts had participated, counted the piles of banknotes and stacks of guineas. Harnette stood behind one, gulping the champagne he'd been presented, the Countess of Marle behind the other, her face turning first crimson, then pale.

Of the Irregulars, only he remained, unable to tear himself away. The others had already retreated to the library for fear of giving the game away.

"It can't be half so much," the Countess of Marle protested when the astonishing total was announced.

"It's so easy to lose track, Lady Walters. One wager leads to another without one noticing," Lady St. Maure commiserated. "At least I've always found it so, and am later dismayed by the sums that've changed hands. Surely you've experienced the same?"

"And I say it's impossible. That's far more than I brought with me."

"You played against Mr. North as well as Mr. Harnette. Surely that makes it possible? You did empty Mr. North's purse. That must be the reason for such a vast sum."

"Course it is." The general threw the countess a narrowed look. "Happens all the time. No one complains when they leave with more than they brought. It's only when it's the reverse trouble starts, and y'learn who's an honest gamester and who's not. If you can't pay, y'shouldn't play, madam."

"There's no way anyone could cover such a sum immediately," the countess snapped.

"Debt of honor. Y'got to cover it. Plunge your good husband in the suds if y'don't. Be chased from his clubs when it got about, which it'd be sure to. Fair number in attendance. Wouldn't please him in the least, that wouldn't. Y'got until tomorrow."

"As well demand a turnip produce blood, if guineas are all you'll accept. May I suggest an alternative? These diamonds are worth much the same," she said, indicating several bracelets, a necklace, a brooch, and three rings. "I'll leave them as a pledge, and redeem them later if I can."

"How much later?"

"Shall we say a month?"

"Y'that patient?" Maitland turned to Harnette. "By rights, she's got until this time tomorrow unless you agree otherwise. No reason y'have to. Not in the least customary. She don't redeem 'em, you'll be stuck."

Harnette seemed to consider the matter, eyes fixed on the countess. "I'll be glad to accommodate her ladyship," he said, then turned to Lady St. Maure. "Is there somewhere we could be private to formalize the arrangement? It's really not the sort of thing for your drawing room—this counting house stuff."

"There's the library. It's at the back of the house."

"That'd do nicely."

"I'll see you there, and show you where my husband keeps the writing supplies. I assume you plan to accompany them, General?"

"Of course. Someone's got to see all's right and tight. Young fellows have a habit of letting the ladies run roughshod over them when there's not the least reason for it, and every reason to see it doesn't happen."

"Misogynistic lout!" the countess hissed.

Maitland laughed. "Unfortunately, madam, I can't return the compliment now. Later maybe, when we're private. No, no," he said, as Binkerton and Captain Sharps made to follow them, "ain't a need for any of you. Not principals in the matter. You'll wait in her ladyship's carriage, which's where you should've been all along given not a one of you was invited, and Lady Walters was only here on sufferance. Our hostess's been more than gracious in letting you to foul her house this long."

The Countess of Marle's complaints at General Maitland's high-handed officiousness availed her nothing. Lady St. Maure's butler and three oversized footmen saw the men from the drawing room and escorted them to the front door, faces impassive, handing them gloves, capes, hats, and walking sticks, and forced them on their way with the minimum of fuss as the others watched from the head of the main staircase. That easily they were rid of the interlopers.

"Y'see how it's done now, young fellow?" Maitland murmured too low for Harnette or the countess to hear as they followed St. Maure's mother to the rear of the house. "Cheating ladies're a deal more difficult to deal with than cheating colonels. Yes, I've heard about it. Y'did well that time. You wouldn't've this—not without help. Gave you a good example to follow. Next round's yours, as there's little you can do to botch it. See y'don't, or I'll have your head on a pike."

"Yes, sir," Dauntry murmured, ears reddening. "I won't botch it."

"Y'don't, and we'll talk later. Not always the ladies who need rescuing from their folly, or even the follies of others."

"No, sir."

"Glad you recognize the fact."

"Recognizing it, and doing something about it, aren't necessarily compatible, sir."

"Y'were inventive enough for another's sake. Do yourself the same favor." The general slipped Dauntry the deck with the two aces of hearts. "Don't be afraid to use these if y'must. She's a downy one, and as dishonest as they come. Steel yourself."

And then they were filing into the library, much to Dauntry's relief. North's lecture had been difficult enough to stomach. General Maitland's had verged on impertinence, if one didn't take rank and age into account—and, he supposed, caring.

Tisdale, Kulp, and Skipworth were in a far corner hidden in the shadows, backs to the others. The countess didn't even notice them, so intent was she on complaining about the Irregulars' presence.

With a sunny and general "You'll find paper in the third drawer on the left. Pens and standish are on the top, as you can see," and a whispered "Only the fun remains," for Dauntry, St. Maure's mother slipped from the room, leaving them to themselves.

Dauntry, with a quick glance at the general, strode over to the long table in the center of the library and pulled out a chair at one end. "Lady Walters," he said.

It wasn't a request or an offer. It was an order holding not the slightest trace of courtesy or deference. She glanced about, then obeyed, head high, lips clamped, expression disdainful. The others took their positions, Harnette in the chair to her right, General Maitland by the door, the rest blocking any potential avenues of escape.

Dauntry set a leather tray lined in deep blue velvet before her. "Remove the jewels in question, if you please, and place them here."

"What have you to do with this?" she protested. "You didn't play a single hand tonight. By rights—"

"The jewels you wish to pledge, my lady."

Slowly, clearly uneasy, the countess removed necklace, rings, bracelets, and brooch, and tossed them on the velvet in a careless jumble. Dauntry tipped the tray toward the light, studying the assortment for a moment, then carried it to the far end of the table where he set it at the opposing place.

"Mr. Kulp," he said, "I believe the stage is yours. Please ascertain Lady Walters isn't pledging jewels whose value is in excess of her debt."

The countess half rose from her chair as Kulp came forward, followed by Tisdale and Skipworth. "Here now, what's all this? What're those men doing here? This sort of thing's always conducted in private."

Harnette laid a hand on her arm. "I wouldn't want to cheat you, my lady," he said. "Couldn't live with myself if I did. Maybe just the necklace'll suffice."

She sank back, eyes round and blank, color high, clenched fists lying on the table.

"Good evening, Lady Walters; a pleasure to see you again." Kulp bowed low, set his case on the table beside the tray of jewels, and took his seat. "Please move that lamp closer, Mr. Dauntry, and bring another. I want stronger light."

Dauntry did as requested, then went to stand behind the jeweler. First Kulp selected a ring, circling it with his other hand so it was in shadow. The thing failed to give off the sparkle a diamond would've even when deprived of direct light.

Next, retrieving a thick square of glass with rounded sides, Kulp drew the edge of the stone across the surface, then peered at the square under the light, twisting it this way and that. The glass remained unmarred.

The rest of Kulp's examination didn't take long. He turned to Harnette at the end of it, ignoring the countess.

"All the stones're glass, sir," he said. "This stuff's without value except for the settings, which're almost worthless as they're mere copies—in inferior silver—of the white gold originals. Ten pounds would be a far too generous estimate for the lot, given the shoddy workmanship. Fit to be melted down—nothing more."

"I'll see you're chased from your position, Kulp," the countess stormed, surging to her feet. "Of all the scurrilous lies—"

"I'm here at the request of my superiors, Lady Walters," Kulp interrupted, smiling slightly. "I doubt they'll be calling for my resignation as a result of tonight's doings."

"These, then," she said, tearing at an emerald and diamond necklace and tossing it down the table toward the man from Rundell and Bridge, and following it with a pair of ear bobs.

"I won't even trouble myself. They'll be of a piece with the rest."

"I demand another expert," she blustered.

"It seems you've got nothing to pledge that'll cover your debt, my lady." Harnette's voice was harder than Dauntry'd ever heard it. "I'm afraid I've got to demand payment by this time tomorrow, or expose your inability where it'll do you the most harm."

"I've never been so insulted! I should've known how it would be, coming to this cursed house. It's a conspiracy, though what you think to gain by it I've no notion. It's criminal—that a lady should be beset by such scoundrels. My husband will call every one of you out."

"I doubt it. If he does, we'll refuse to meet him."

She spun toward the door. Maitland advanced a single step.

"Resume your seat, Lady Walters," Dauntry ordered. "If you please, of course. You may remain standing, if you wish." He pulled Maitland's deck of cards from his pocket and placed them on the table well out of her reach. "Shall we see who's been cheating? And provide Lord Walters with the evidence? He'd grant us redress, even if you won't. Might beggar him temporarily, even make visits to Town impossible for either of you, but he'd do it."

Taking his time, leaving the aces of hearts—which were on the bottom—until last, Dauntry turned over the cards, one by one. When he revealed the second ace of hearts, the countess stiffened.

"Merely a faulty deck."

"I'm afraid not. The cards may look much the same in poor light, but they won't stand up to closer examination."

"You're in league with the devil," she muttered, sinking into her chair. "Must be cheats yourselves. Only way you'd've known. Wonder what people'd say if I told them. Your word against mine. Gentlemen'll always believe a lady."

"Not quite always. I wonder what would be discovered if your reticule and shawls were examined. Be glad to have your husband do it. He's at Brooke's tonight, not White's. We had him followed." He gave it a moment. "Of course, there's another solution—which would cost you nothing, and leave Lord Walters none the wiser. All you need do is inform him you've experienced a change of heart regarding a certain widow and her son."

Her countenance darkened, and she frowned. Then her eyes widened as she realized who he meant.

"He'd know it for a lie. I *never* experience changes of heart."

"Which would make this one all the more impressive. Mr. Skipworth, if you'll provide Lady Walters with a copy of the documents you've prepared, so she can review them? Mr. Skipworth is a solicitor, Lady Walters, and knows what he's about."

Skipworth rose, pulled the documents Dauntry had examined earlier from their leather pouch, and set them before the countess.

"Might I suggest, Lady Walters, that we know all about a certain underfootman," Tisdale threw in. "And can produce him, if necessary? He's anxious to make a public confession regarding several transgressions against master and mistress to those who can best take action against the instigator of those transgressions."

"I haven't the slightest notion to what or to whom you're referring."

"You don't? Odd. Jamie Screed certainly knows and in detail."

"I'll claim entrapment. I'll claim—"

"You'd catch cold, my lady," Dauntry snapped. "Too many heard your demand to try your luck against Val at the Tinker's Bum. There's no way for you to deny you were the instigator of tonight's doings. He refused at first."

"That final turn of the cards was rigged," she raged. "I know it was. When I turned over my card, I'd won."

"When you slipped it from your sleeve to the table, don't you mean? How many doors do you think you'd find closed to you if that detail got about?"

"This isn't over, no matter how much you think it is."

"Oh, it's over. It's entirely over. If you wish, we'll have your husband brought here to witness the ending. Wonder what he'd say."

"Set her aside at last, the way he should've in the beginning," Maitland murmured in the background. "Even a jellyfish'll stand for only so much."

The countess paled beneath her rouged skin. "That little country nobody has no right to my grandson, or anything else. Young Thomas must be trained to his future position. She's incapable." She held out her hand. "You might as well give me pen and ink now. But, be warned—you'll pay, and you'll pay mightily, if you force this. You've one last chance to save your skins."

They regarded her coldly, unmoving and unmoved.

"Be reasonable," she said after a moment, hand dropping. "George was always a fool for a pretty face and a winning manner. So're the rest of you. Well, you've been cozened by as clever a little vixen as it's ever been my misfortune to encounter. It's time this idiocy ended."

She turned to the general, eyes swimming in tears.

"You're ruining everything," she pleaded. "That harlot entrapped my son, as anyone with the least sense will attest. The son of an earl, wed a vicar's sister? Unheard of—unless he's taken complete leave of his senses.

"You're a man of experience, General. Surely you understand, even if these impudent young fools don't? I was desperate, but I'm only a frail woman far past middle-age, lacking any resources or assistance, and not nearly as clever as a man would've been.

There was only one solution I could find. For my grandson's sake, for my son's, don't permit this travesty. In a more reasonable century, I would've had Cecelia Gardener burned as a witch and been applauded for it."

"Not quite, madam," he returned.

"Thomas belongs with me," she snapped. "I can ensure he becomes worthy of an earldom. She'll squander his inheritance, and make mice feet of the entire thing."

Dauntry placed the standish before her. "Your signature's all we require," he said. "Explanations and excuses are useless."

"Who are you? What business is this of yours?" she demanded, staring up at him as he turned Skipworth's documents to the signature pages.

"I've merely been acting for another," he said with a smile. "No, that individual's identity is not for you to know. A caution—any attempt to go back on your signed and attested word will result in full disclosure of both tonight's doings and the forged will. Is that clear, my lady? Any attempt against any of us, or our families and friends, will have the same result. The first one to learn the truth will be your husband, the second a magistrate."

"Well done, Major," Maitland murmured, returning to guard the door.

Thirteen

Only Dabney St. Maure accompanied Dauntry to Combermere once they'd deposited North at Hillcrest, the others at Pugs Harnette's neighboring estate, and regaled Lady Katherine and Amelia with the tale of their London triumph.

The celebrations, at Hillcrest as at St. Maure House, had been gay and filled with laughter, Dauntry alone remaining abstracted despite his best efforts to join in the fun. He'd been desperate to get on with it. No questions remained, no dilemmas, no doubts. If one were to mount the scaffold, best to do it swiftly, tread firm, head high, shoulders squared. That was what mattered.

At least he'd kept his promise to a non-existent ghost, cup-shot though that promise'd been. Soon George Walters would rest peacefully in his grave, secure in the knowledge his wife and son would never again suffer privation.

Dauntry's lips twisted as they trotted past Merlin's grotto and his father's gothic folly. Maybe Nace would inform him of their fate once young Bertram was out of leading strings and intent on adventures neither nurse, hysterical mother, nor vaporish grandmother would be able to forestall. If the lad's head were half as hard as Duncan's, the things would soon have to be torn down.

Then he scowled.

Old Maitland had forced a brief conversation on him once Lady St. Maure's other guests departed, and they held a more private celebration of the countess's downfall. A commission and reinstatement at his former rank were his if he wanted them, so long as he could come up with the ready. So was posting to his old regiment, currently encamped near the French border. North'd twice tried to press the funds on him the night they laid the Countess of Marle low. He'd refused both times.

Even if he'd been willing to accept North's generosity, he was no more willing now to offer Cecelia Walters the privations and uncertainties of a life following the drum—and the possibility of a second untimely widowhood—than he had been in the beginning. She and Tommy deserved better. A brief adieu, and he'd be gone, and to the devil with his father, Combermere, and everything else.

They trotted up the drive, mounts still fresh, the afternoon sun dappling the verges where late summer flowers bloomed.

Nace had been busy. The lane between the village and the Bittersfield fork had been leveled and scraped at last. By now repairs to tenant cottages were doubtless completed, and the vicarage once more possessed the aspect and furnishings of a gentleman's residence. All was well. Rebecca Burchett and Robert Gardener would soon wed, Cecelia and her son would return to the big house by the lake, and a life of comfort and ease. No more nonsense regarding a post as governess or companion. No more girl in white.

"You seem pensive," St. Maure said at his side.

"Always am when I come here. Nothing surprising about that."

They broke out of the woods, the sunshine warm on their backs, and continued to the house. No grooms dashed up. Not even a footman appeared at the door, let alone Mayhew. What the devil?

"Guess we'll have to see to ourselves," Dauntry grumbled. He swung from the saddle and dropped to the drive, led Argus to the steps and looped the reins over the baluster. Then he unbuckled his portmanteau and the bundle containing the gifts for Tommy. "Can't think what'd cause this, except we're in no way expected. Hope nothing's wrong. Sorry about this, Dab. I'll have a word with Mayhew later."

"Not to worry. I rather enjoy it—like arriving at an enchanted castle where everyone from lowliest potboy to most elevated dresser sleeps."

"Fustian. When the cat's away, the mice'll play—even well-regulated mice."

Together they climbed the steps and let themselves in. The rotunda was deserted.

"What the deuce?" Dauntry dropped his portmanteau by the door and leaned the bundle against the wall, glancing about. No garlic or crucifixes this time. Instead, flowers everywhere.

"Maybe the family's returned despite your warnings."

"See those?" Dauntry pointed to a clumsy bouquet in which Queen Anne's lace and daisies vied with his grandmother's roses. "My mother can't abide wildflowers. Calls them weeds. Won't permit them in the house, or roses either. Considers those too showy. Only person who likes any of them is—but that's impossible. She's in Crete."

A distinctive, full-throated laugh echoed from the terrace, through the library, down the hall, and circled the rotunda.

"By Jove!" Dauntry broke into a broad grin as he tossed crop, hat, and gloves on top of his portmanteau, troubles forgotten. "Come on, Dab. You're in for a treat. No, don't worry about your appearance. Aunt Persie's above that sort of nonsense, though what the devil she's doing here, I haven't the slightest notion. Her last letter mentioned nothing about a return to England. Rather the opposite. Heaven knows how she got here so fast."

Then he was dashing across the rotunda, down the hall, and through the library. He broke onto the terrace with a whoop, descended on a tall lady with iron-gray hair, pulled her to her feet ignoring the mutts surrounding her, and whirled her about.

"Aunt Persie, by all that's holy," he crowed, still grinning as the mutts leapt around them, tongues lolling, tails wagging, barking in delight at the new arrivals. "What the devil're you doing here?" Then he set her down, and bowed. "A pleasure to discover you in residence, Aunt Persephone. I hope I find you well?"

"Scapegrace," she returned, laughing. "Yes, I'm well enough, though what you've just done to these old bones should earn you a birching."

"Nonsense. Does 'em good to be shaken up a bit, and you, too. What *are* you doing here? Your last letter said—"

"I'll explain later. In the meantime, hadn't you best redeem yourself by greeting my guests and presenting your companion, now you've exposed yourself as a mannerless rogue?"

Dauntry glanced about. With the exception of the kitchen staff, every last one of the indoor servants was on the terrace. So were Cecelia, Mrs. Burchett, and Rebecca. Stifled grins were the order of the day, both among servants and guests.

"Oh, dear Lord," he muttered, coloring up nicely. "Never saw a one of them."

"Tell me something I don't already know," his great-aunt returned with mock severity. "Well, don't stand there like a bumpkin. Make your bows and present your friend, Quintus—unless you've forgotten how, that is?"

He got through it somehow, unable to meet even Rebecca's dancing eyes. As for Cecelia Walters, he'd rather've faced a firing squad than her amused glance. Thank God for the fuss of presenting St. Maure to his aunt, and for her explanations regarding the mutts—a curly-tailed "Carthaginian Puff-ball," a rangy "Portuguese Stews-scrap," and a perpetually drooling "Pyrenean Ankle-scratcher"—all rescued from the depredations of war. At last they were seated again, glasses of lemonade in hand, Nick Beetle sent off to alert the kitchen there'd be two more for dinner, and the stables that a pair of mounts awaited attention on the drive, before settling them in their old bedchambers.

Somehow he'd ended up between Cecelia and Mrs. Burchett, not quite certain how that trick'd been managed, for his intention had been to put as much distance as possible between the vicar's sister and himself. Instead he couldn't't've been closer unless he'd been sitting in her lap, while Mrs. Burchett's chair was at some distance from theirs, and far closer to the others. Damnation!

"I hope you were able to conclude your business in London successfully," Cecelia said under cover of the general conversation.

"Very well, indeed. That is, not much to it. I mean—well, it's done. That's what matters."

"Yes, I suppose it is. You intend to remain at Combermere for long?"

"A few days at most. Need to finish things up. The girl in white, you know. Have to see to it she's put to rest for good. Then I expect to be on my way, unless Aunt Persie has a need of me. Can't imagine she would. Very independent female."

He glanced at Cecelia—not at her eyes, which he didn't dare meet, but her hands, her face. She'd lost her air of perpetual exhaustion, and her hands were smooth, what he could see of them. Good. Step one, which had been begun even before the fête, accomplished. The morrow would see to the rest.

"Things going well in Coombe?" he said. "Work completed at St. Martin's and the vicarage?"

"It's all lovely except for the window over the font, whose restoration is yet to begin—and yes, before you ask, Rose is proving a more than adequate student, both in the kitchen and about the house. Indeed, I find her cookery far superior to mine. Nothing seems to intimidate her, not even French sauces. I can't imagine what fault Mrs. Ford found with her."

"Smaller household's obviously worked miracles. Mrs. Ford suspected it might. And your garden—that's faring well? Old Heater not proving too much of a bother? He can be something of a fusspot on occasion."

"No, he's a delight. So're his roses and his vegetables, and his grandson's taken to helping about the house with the heavier work as well. We're all quite spoiled. I hardly know how to pass the time, there's so little left for me to do. If it weren't for arranging the harvest fair, I'd be almost without occupation."

He nodded, staring into the distance. Dear God, but this was torture of the sweetest sort. How many more times? Not many. Once, maybe twice. Then he and St. Maure would be gone. So would she and Tommy, and life would resume an even tenor—he despised even tenors.

"Tell me about London," she said, breaking through his abstraction. "Did you encounter any old military friends?"

"Not a one. They're in the Peninsula for the most part, otherwise occupied. I hope your brother's well?"

"Exceedingly so, and enjoying the use of the horse and gig from Beechy Knoll. Was it hot there?"

"What?"

"Was it hot?" she repeated.

"The Peninsula? In summer, yes. In winter the mountains rival Scotland's for harshness."

"No," she said with a chuckle, "London. I asked you how you found London."

"Oh, sorry. Dirty and malodorous. It always is at this season, and rather thin of company, which is to be expected. The schoolroom misses have yet to descend for the Little Season's nonsense."

"And how was the weather?"

"It broke on our last night, but otherwise? A foul, disease-ridden place in the dogdays. I was glad to be quit of it."

Her brows rose, but she said nothing. A silence that stretched to uncomfortable lengths had him considering impossible conversations, real ones.

Then she said, "I believe it's your turn to ask a question now," eyes twinkling. "You might follow my lead, and inquire how the weather here's been. I should inform you it's been excellent for the most part, though we did have two days of rain and one of drizzle."

"How's Tommy faring?" he blurted for something to say. "You've permitted his riding lessons to continue?"

"My brother has. That's where Thomas is now—down at the paddock with Mr. Potts, unless they're cantering about somewhere. They do a lot of that now Thomas's expertise has been exposed to the world. He quite enjoys it."

"I see. Good. Gets him out in the sunshine. He needs that."

"Oh, yes," she said with a smile, "and even if he doesn't, he likes it excessively. You've become his hero even more than before."

"Before?"

"I suppose that does constitute a question, even if it's but a single word. Thomas collected every tale about you there was to be had in the village," she explained, "and brought them all home. He could even recite the mentions of you in dispatches and the dates of your promotions, and I don't doubt he knows almost as much about Salamanca as you."

"Good heavens," Dauntry muttered, flushing. "Well, in this instance he chose his object of veneration poorly. I was only peripherally involved in that action."

"Not according to Thomas, or the dispatches. Heaven knows where he acquired the information. Thomas has always been as inquisitive as he is resourceful. He'll be in despair at having missed you, for he was invited to tea, as well."

"How's your brother keeping himself?" he said to turn the subject.

"Very well, thank you."

"Good. I'll need to confer with him as soon as may be."

She colored up, gazing first at him, then her hands. "Robert is always delighted by your visits," she murmured.

"A business matter," he specified.

"Oh—a business matter. Yes, I suppose some might term it that."

Dauntry squirmed, then glanced up from his study of the dust on his topboots. His aunt watched them, just as he'd suspected. She broke into an enigmatic smile, then turned to Rebecca and Mrs. Burchett, who were rising. The fuss of departure began, the collections of reticule and shawl, the summoning of the Burchett carriage, the interminable messages to be carried to the squire and the vicar, the arrangements for tea at the vicarage two days hence, and dinner at Beechy Knoll following services on the coming Sunday. At last they were gone.

"She's utterly charming, just as I suspected from your letter," Persephone Blaire murmured as they watched the Beechy Knoll carriage roll down the drive. "You couldn't do better, Quintus, and her son's her equal—an engaging rogue with all a schoolboy's graces, *and* lack of 'em. Puts me in mind of you at the same age, though you were hardly so bookish."

"Unfortunately, she couldn't do worse."

"She couldn't? Dear heaven, what a nodcock you are!"

"Merely a man of considerable sense and practicality. Somebody has to show some."

"She's as enamored of you as you are of her."

"She'll get over it. If necessary, I'll make sure she does."

"It's clear you've raised certain expectations, you know."

"Then I'll depress them, or events will."

"Idiotish! You could do with being a little more natural with her, though. Barking out responses as if you were at a military review definitely isn't the thing. Neither is losing the thread of a conversation, or asking her twice how her brother does. At least they weren't in my day. Neither is bearing the air of a man about to be pilloried."

"That bad?"

"Worse. Had I not known better, I'd've believed you held Mrs. Walters in dislike, and merely endured her presence for the sake of convention. A more stilted conversation it's never been my misfortune to witness, though she certainly did her best. Get your wits about you, boy!"

The carriage had disappeared into the park. Still he stared after it. His aunt chuckled, and whistled her dogs to heel.

"In case you're wondering, your last letter's what brought me to Combermere," she said. "Too many inconsequential details about Mrs. Walters, and far too few that mattered. Made me suspicious. Well, my suspicions're confirmed. You've tumbled top-over-tail at last. As it happened, I'd just arrived in London, so coming didn't take that much once I settled my most immediate affairs, which took a bit of doing. Must've passed each other on the road."

"But you said you were fixed in Crete," he protested, ignoring the rest.

"Crete's a trifle uncomfortable for a lone Englishwoman at the moment, given the activities of Bonaparte's agents. I departed within days of sending your letter off with a rug merchant who promised he'd post it when and where he could. The trip to England was quite an adventure. I'll tell you about it at dinner. The dogs're the least of it. I've also got an entire family, from crabbed grandmother to newborn babe, with me, complete with donkey, goat, and some chickens—all Spanish, except the chickens. Those're Moroccan. Left the lot in London. They'll make passable servants eventually, I suspect, if they're still about when I return. The family, I mean, not the livestock.

"You," she commanded, fixing him with her eyes, "will return the favor by telling me what you were doing in London at this season. After all, if I entertain the pair of you with my tales, it's only fair for you to entertain me with yours. Can't imagine what sort of business took you there if it wasn't the obvious one of putting your affairs in order, especially with little Mrs. Walters and Thomas to keep you firmly fixed here."

That night, following a dinner sauced with tales of Persephone Blaire's adventures that had them laughing until tears rolled down their cheeks—she'd even shared a meal she characterized as inedible with the Earl of Wellington, and crossed the Channel in the company of smugglers ferrying brandy to Cornwall, and those incidents were the least of it—Dauntry retired early to his bed-chamber to watch for his little ghost. He waited until on toward dawn, lids drooping, leg aching now it'd stiffened up again, but the gardens remained deserted except for the badgers, the owls, and a single nightingale serenading the moon with liquid trills.

"What a slugabed," his great-aunt scolded when he appeared in the breakfast parlor the next morning as she and St. Maure were quitting it. "One would think you'd been up half the night, given the smudges beneath your eyes. Uncomfortable with your decisions?"

"Not in the least." He kissed her soft cheek, then squatted to make a fuss over the three mutts capering about his ankles, their tails wagging as they yipped for attention.

"It's his leg," St. Maure explained, ignoring the furious look Dauntry threw him.

"What about his leg?"

"You know—Salamanca. Keeps him up sometimes if he over-does. Then he's sour."

"Well?" she demanded, turning to Dauntry.

He shrugged and rose stiffly from his crouch. "Three-day ride from Hillcrest," he admitted. "We took our time, but it's com-plaining, nonetheless. Stuff Potts gave me hasn't touched it. Should be fine once I walk it out."

"It's been a year, and more."

"These things take time, Aunt. Probably would've healed quicker had I remained in the army. The activity would've been good for it."

"Unless it left you a cripple. Your father may've done you a favor despite himself. Why didn't you come by carriage?"

"Haven't got one."

"I'm sure your Mr. North does, and offered it."

"I hate being cooped up, dammit," he exploded. "The trip from London to Hillcrest was more than enough. Besides, I'd ridden one of my father's mounts down, and had to bring him back. Now, have done. I'm not in leading strings."

"I begin to think you should be, however. One of these days that cursed pride of yours'll prove your downfall, if it hasn't al-ready."

She spun on her heel and quitted the breakfast parlor, back rigid, gray curls bobbing, trailed by her motley canine assortment.

"That wasn't well done," St. Maure said, giving Nick Beetle—who lurked by the sideboard, ears flapping—a nervous glance.

"No, it wasn't." Dauntry let out the heavy breath he'd been retaining. "I'll apologize later. We're always coming to cuffs, Aunt Persie and I. Doesn't mean a thing. She comes to cuffs with everyone, mostly because she's forever putting her nose where it's not wanted, and trying to make decisions for others which they're perfectly capable of making for themselves."

"I haven't come to cuffs with her. I find her refreshing. So will my mother. I've already arranged for her to visit us in London."

"Refreshing? In small doses, perhaps. You're not her nephew. Like as not she did have to leave Crete, though experience suggests it was the locals rather than Nappy's agents she'd riled. Probably tried to arrange a marriage they considered inappropriate, or trod on elevated local toes in some other fashion. Only woman I know of who contradicted Mrs. Drummond-Burrell, and emerged triumphant. Bearded her at Almack's, no less, right in front of Lady Jersey. Of course that tale's apocryphal, but I suspect there's a deal of truth to it. Aunt Persie would've made an excellent field commander. No good for much else. She was born in the wrong century, and into the wrong family."

He loaded a plate without paying attention to what he put on it, and took the third place at the table. St. Maure wandered to the windows, which were open on a day as bright and fair as any they'd had that summer.

"Beautiful place in this season," he said.

"Yes, it is. Out with it. It's clear you're great with news."

"Your aunt and I had a long conversation after you retired last night. About that business we saw to in London."

"Said she'd have the whole from me. Quite the interlocutrix, isn't she? Tale amused her no end, I don't doubt."

"Yes, in fact it did. Said our solution had a neatness she admired, though we'd best ware our backs. Doesn't trust our opponent not to try a trick or two, given certain reputations."

"Then we'll ware our backs. Aunt Persie's rarely in error on that sort of thing."

"That's what she said. Wanted to know who came up with the notion. I gave you full credit."

"And none to your mother or her friends? For shame! As for the endgame, Pugs deserves considerable admiration for his cold-blooded determination, a characteristic for which he's not generally known."

St. Maure shifted uneasily at the window, turning to gaze back at the table—though at any place but Dauntry's. St. Maure in a uncertain mood was a rare event.

"Don't worry," Dauntry said, returning his attention to his plate. More than half gone, now. "If she hadn't gotten it out of you, she'd've gotten it from me. Doesn't matter in the least."

"She seems to think it does."

"She's wrong, unlikely though you may find it that such a redoubtable female could ever be wrong about anything."

"This time I don't believe she is. Rather canny lady, your Aunt Persephone."

"Have done, Dab." Dauntry looked up, his expression hardening. Well, and why not? Those he loved were making his life damned difficult—hardly a act of kindness. "My decisions're made. I'll be speaking with Nace this morning and Gardener later, turn all over to him, take Tommy fishing one last time—though he won't know it's the last—and that'll be the end of it unless Gardener's more of a fool than I take him for. We'll be leaving in the morning."

"Why the rush? I'd think you'd want to spend some time with your aunt. Came to see you, after all. Bolting's a bit boorish, don't you think?"

"Not if it saves us from exchanging unforgivable insults. I happen to be rather fond of the old thing, and would rather that didn't happen. If I stay, it will."

"But what if the vicar's unavailable, and you have to put off your discussion?"

"Then I'll guard my tongue, and we'll leave the day after."

"Did it ever occur to you there might be other parties with a right to a say in the matter?"

"No." Dauntry turned to Mayhew's nephew. "Nick, I could

do with a fresh pot of coffee. Hop to it, will you? And a rack of toast."

The would-be footman gave Dauntry a hard look, then clomped off, heels striking the floor like hammers, the service door swinging behind him like a rectangular pendulum gone mad.

"See, even Nick doesn't approve," St. Maure said, returning to the table. "If he could've slammed that door, he would've."

Dauntry shrugged, and continued consuming the food before him. "He'll live."

"They'll want you here for the wedding. Given the part you've played in making it possible, Gardener'll probably ask you to stand up for him."

"He can ask all he likes. One of you can take my place."

"Stubborn. Where'll we go?"

"You? Wherever you wish. To perdition, if that's your choice. Harnette's might be a better notion."

"I? To Brighton, where I'll give my father a full report, and warn him Aunt Persie's back. That should keep them away the rest of the summer. Might even keep 'em away permanently. He's terrified of her, and it's in my grandfather's will she has a right to live at the dower house if she wants. Nothing he can do about it. So far she hasn't wanted, but now I suspect she may, even if she does have her own place in Kent. Always has loved to devil my father. Says it keeps her young. That'd devil him to a fare-thee-well."

"Brighton? Well, that won't be so bad. Fellows could join us there."

"For a single night? Don't be ridiculous. Then London, briefly. After that, either Bristol, Dover, or Portsmouth, depending on what I decide. Doubt any of you'd find them all that interesting. Antipodes, India, or possibly Jamaica," he added at St. Maure's questioning look. "Haven't made my mind up yet. Probably work for my passage, as I'm damned if I'm willing to incur that much debt."

"Never knew insanity ran in your family. There's no reasoning with you? Val'll have my head, if Tony doesn't chop it off first."

"No, they won't. They'd just like you to think they would. Why can't a one of you understand I don't require a keeper?"

"Perhaps because you do."

"And you've appointed yourself my guardian?"

"We thought you'd find my presence the least onerous, as I'm the most restful of the lot."

Dauntry growled wordlessly, and continued to make short work of the contents of his plate as St. Maure stared at him steadily from his place across the table.

It was difficult to ignore those penetrating gray eyes. They reminded him too much of another pair that'd held precisely the same air of concern the afternoon before. The only difference lay in the fact that there wasn't a trace of confusion in St. Maure's. Neither was there reproach, or a silent plea he had to ignore or go mad.

The sooner he quitted Combermere, the better. He'd been within a inch of forgetting honor and duty and declaring himself the afternoon before. This was one instance when the devil couldn't be permitted to take the hindmost—not if he cared for Cecelia Walters half as much as he knew he did.

Nick's appearance with coffee and fresh toast was a blessed relief.

"Gardener—good of you to stop by. I know how busy you are." Dauntry seized the vicar's hand, pumping it as if he'd been absent from Combermere for a decade rather than less than a fortnight. "How've you been keeping yourself?"

"Well. And yourself and Mr. St. Maure?"

"Exceeding well. The other fellows're well, too. Sent you and your sister their regards, which I neglected to mention to the ladies yesterday. I can only plead my aunt's unexpected arrival as an excuse. Discovering her here rather knocked me off my pins. Thought she was in Crete." It was true enough as far as it went. Having Cecelia where he'd least expected to find her hadn't helped, either. "Sent their regards to Tommy, too—and a kite and some fishing gear I'll turn over to you before you leave, which is more to the point where the infantry's concerned. Quite taken with Tommy, the lot of them were."

"How kind. He'll be delighted—and no doubt try to devise a

method of sending them his first catch unspoiled by way of thanks, accompanied by an essay on the joys of flying a kite."

"In Latin, I don't doubt," Dauntry returned with a sudden and very genuine grin.

"He'll make the attempt, at least—probably in execrable verse. You have the right of that. Your friends didn't accompany you, from what Mrs. Burchett says, except for Mr. St. Maure?"

"Stayed on at Harnette's, once the London business was concluded. Only came here in the first place because they were curious about the girl in white. Foul at this season, London. They wanted a touch of the country, and a deal less traveling about than returning to Combermere would've required. Dab was deputized to accompany me for your sake. He insisted he had the best of it. You'll be the judge of that."

"I gather your business in London was successfully concluded?"

Dauntry nodded. "That's why I asked you to stop by as soon as was convenient."

"Then why don't we cut through the formalities? No need for Mr. St. Maure to vouch for you. You have my approval and permission, for what they're worth. You might better ask for Tommy's. He'll give them on the instant."

There was no way to pretend he didn't understand the vicar's meaning. "I'm afraid you mistake my intent," Dauntry said, flushing. "I asked you here regarding a business matter, not a personal one."

Gardener's mortified flush was at least as deep as his own. Not a good beginning.

"Oh, I see. Sorry," the vicar mumbled.

"So am I. You'll understand in a moment."

Dauntry led the way to a group of three chairs clustered around a low table, and gestured for Gardener to sit.

To either side draperies stirred at the bank of French doors giving on the terrace. The documents assuring Cecelia's future—and making Gardener's marriage to Rebecca Burchett possible—lay on the table, still hidden in their dark leather pouch along with letters of explanation and exculpation from Lady St. Maure, Mr. Tisdale, Mr. Skipworth, Lady Cheltenham, and General Maitland. They'd covered every contingency they could think of before departing for Hillcrest.

Gardener sat as requested, hands on his knees, clearly distressed and ill at ease. "All right, then—how may I be of assistance?" he said.

"Not the first time you've asked me that," Dauntry said with a shaky smile.

"Ah yes—your first visit to the vicarage."

"This time I hope it's I who's been of assistance. We'll want Dab, for my word won't suffice. Even Dab's won't. Well, they shouldn't, as you're personally acquainted only with us, and we were merely a few among the principals. You'll want confirmation from others who were involved. Got letters to take care of that. One's from Dab's mother, another from a rather redoubtable dowager countess. Then there's the general's, and ones from a solicitor and a man of business. You should trust their word, even if you find the rest of us less than credible."

"A countess and a general? But—"

"Our London exploits've changed everything. I don't mean to sound mysterious, but it's better if you get it all at once. A bit here and a bit there would serve nothing, and probably drive you to distraction."

Dauntry strode through the open French doors and over to the terrace balustrade. St. Maure and Persie Blaire ambled among his grandmother's roses, the dogs romping about them on the smooth, sun-struck path. It was the tag end of summer now. Fewer heavy-headed blooms nodded in the soft breeze, and the light had a thinner, lemony quality. Shadows held a hint of chill, harbingers of the coming winter.

He stood there a moment, watching. It might almost be his grandmother out there with St. Maure, so closely had the sisters resembled one another. Like stature, at least, and like features and air. And, when details were stripped away, like characters, for all they expressed themselves far differently. Neither had ever suffered fools gladly.

The pair paused, gazing back at the house as the dogs pelted up the twisting paths and broke onto the lawn below the terrace in a frenzy of barking. He waved. St. Maure nodded, squinting into the sun, then turned, said something to Aunt Persie, and bowed. She seized his arm, holding him back a moment speaking rapidly, then summoned the dogs with a schoolboy's whistle just as they reached the steps leading to the terrace. The tatterdemalion trio whirled and gamboled across the beds to their mistress as St. Maure took the more conventional route.

How many endings could an impossible dream have, Dauntry wondered as he handed the legal documents to Gardener moments later, offering no more explanation than he had before. Many, it would seem. This was like watching a bucket in which a hole had been poked. The water leaked, sinking into the sand, each drop a small death.

"I'm to read all this?" Gardener said in dismay as he tore his gaze from the sheaf of papers. "It'll take forever, and I won't understand half of it. No head for the legal profession or its convoluted rhetoric."

"Every word, if you're so inclined." St. Maure gave him a reassuring smile. "You'll understand it clearly enough, and you won't find the perusal displeasing. Or, you can skip to the signature pages. They contain summations that slice through the legal flights. There're two. You'll understand why once you start reading, as the cases are somewhat different, though they're definitely linked."

Dauntry nodded at Gardener's questioning glance. "Get on with it," he muttered, then flushed at his own lack of courtesy. "If you'd be so kind," he added.

Gardener bent his attention to the first document, which regarded his sister, as Dauntry paced the library, jerking books from shelves only to return them to their places unopened moments later.

"Dear Lord in heaven," the vicar whispered after struggling through the first page.

He glanced at Dauntry, who'd paused by the fireplace. Dauntry forced a smile. The vicar tore through the rest, face pale, hands shaking, reading only the final page with care.

"Dear Lord in heaven," he repeated, grabbed the second document and skipped to the final page. "What angels of mercy managed this?" he breathed, staring from one man to the other, eyes wide, as he set the document regarding Tommy back on the table as if it were made of flames. "More to the point, *how* did they manage it?"

"Mostly it was Quint. The rest of us marched to his tune. You may not approve entirely," St. Maure cautioned, handing over the first of the letters, which detailed the fate of Camilla Ethridge years before, and set the stage for Skipworth's letter detailing the countess's forgery of a second will. "This one first, if you would. It explains my mother's involvement, and her determination to ensure success. No, hold your questions until you've read them all. More likely you'll consider us minions of hell than angels from heaven once you know the whole."

Since vicars never cursed, it couldn't've been curses Gardener was muttering under his breath as be tossed Lady St. Maure's letter aside following a breakneck reading, and held out his hand for the next. As Dauntry watched, St. Maure passed him Tisdale's, which told of Jamie Screed and the forged will. That time there was no question regarding the vicar's vocabulary. His bishop might've been shocked, but he would've probably also understood.

That letter was followed by Lady Cheltenham's and the general's explanations, and finally the one from Skipworth putting the legalities in terms even an idiot would've understood. Gardener was no idiot.

At the end of it he gazed from one man to the other, still clutching Skipworth's recital of the terms and conditions of the Countess of Marle's capitulation in the face of certain ruin.

"Underhanded," the vicar managed.

"Yes," Dauntry admitted, resuming his place across from Gardener. "What of it? If Lady Walters hadn't cheated North, and attempted to cheat Pugs, we'd've let her off and figured something else out. It was that palmed ace of hearts sealed her fate. Don't forget what she did to your sister and nephew."

"Vengeance doesn't belong to man. It belongs to God."

"For pity's sake, forget you're a vicar. There wasn't any vengeance in this," St. Maure protested. "We could've exposed her for what she is, and brought charges. That would've constituted revenge. We didn't. We merely saw justice done. Mr. Tisdale'll see all through to the end, unless there's someone you'd prefer? He's ready to confer with Marle and his man of business once you agree, and he'll see to Thomas and Mrs. Walters's interests with a devotion that'll earn your approbation, that I can promise you."

"But, *why?*" Gardener almost bleated. "This isn't at all what I suspected you wanted. How could I have?"

"Josh Burchett would've seen to things for Becky were he still alive. Consider me his agent. As for the rest, the girl in white required it of me," Dauntry answered, "though she didn't specify methods, just results."

"I didn't cut my wisdoms yesterday," Gardener spluttered.

"No, I'm serious. I'm convinced it's one of the reasons she reappeared after so many years. She didn't like the idea of your sister enduring a menial's life any more than she approved Mrs. Walters's and Tommy's unnecessary dependence on you." He flushed under Gardener's steady gaze. "And then, I've become rather fond of Tommy," Dauntry admitted, trying to meet the vicar's eyes, and failing. "His grandmother robbed him of his birthright. That can't've pleased his father, and they say displeased fathers rest in unquiet graves. You could say I've merely been doing my Christian duty. Tommy'll make an excellent earl one day, given half a chance."

"I don't know whether I should curse the lot of you, or cheer."

"Cheer, of course. Cowper said it best: 'God works in a mysterious way,' sometimes," St. Maure insisted with an unrepentant grin, " 'His wonders to perform.' Don't protest that in this instance He employed the unlikeliest of assistants. We're very reputable most of the time. When we're disreputable, we are so in the grand manner, and always in an excellent cause."

Gardener nodded, breaking into a slow smile.

"You are, at that—though I'd've done my best to stop you if I'd known. As it is, you have my everlasting gratitude. You know what this means, of course." He rose, a new light in his eyes. "Dare I request you hold yourselves ready to attend a celebratory dinner at Squire Burchett's this evening?"

"Of course you may." Dauntry held out his hand. The vicar shook it. "By the bye, the sum withheld for roof repairs will be yours on the day your fondest hopes are realized. Already arranged it with Nace and my father—another of the girl in white's preconditions to returning to her place of rest."

"If you're sure there's nothing else?"

Dauntry hesitated. "No, there's nothing else," he said.

The girl in white was a excellent excuse for everything, Dauntry decided. Gardener crammed the essential documents in his pocket and made his farewells with a speed more commensurate with his heart than his calling or common courtesy would've suggested—Tommy's kite and fishing gear and the crop Dauntry'd acquired for the boy in the village near Hillcrest forgotten.

"Well done, lads," Persephone Blaire said, striding in from the terrace as soon as Gardener dashed for the entry, coattails flapping. Dauntry and St. Maure turned to stare at her in surprise. "Yes, of course I listened to the whole thing. You thought I wouldn't? Admirably performed. You should be on the stage, both of you. Not the least need for me to involve myself, which I first suspected there might be. Young Gardener has a spine of steel, for all he's a sunny fellow most of the time. If he'd truly taken umbrage at your methods, you'd've been in the suds. As it was, placing the onus on the shoulders of your ghost solved everything.

"Now, Quintus, we're going to have to see what this girl in white can do for you, as she's solved everyone else's problems so neatly."

Fourteen

Dauntry made for the paddocks without regard to his aunt or St. Maure, both of whom insisted he should wait for the news from Beechy Knoll that was sure to arrive as quickly as one tired horse could cover five cross-country miles in one direction, and a fresh mount five miles in the other.

It was too late for a true fishing expedition, but he'd take what he could get. The trout pond just below the ornamental falls would suffice. They could talk there, and Tommy could try out the gear that would turn him into a true fisherman, at least in *his* youthful eyes. He'd store up memories of the lad, play cousin or uncle, or whatever it was he'd been playing, one last time, watching for hints of the man to come in the boy that was.

Then, perhaps from Bristol, a short letter containing a partial explanation of his sudden departure not just from Combermere, but from England itself. Months later, a few last words from a location the lad would consider exotic, accompanied by some trinkets he'd treasure for a bit before they found themselves at the back of a drawer. Cecelia might even be remarried by then, Tommy with a new father more worthy of him than a scarred veteran of the Peninsular campaigns. He'd have to be careful what he wrote.

Dauntry broke out of the shrub-lined path leading to the outermost paddock, gasped, and eased back. Creel, rods, and bundle slipped to the ground unnoticed.

Tommy wasn't mounted on one of the ponies.

He was bareback astride one of the great Watford blacks, taking the jumps at an easy canter, hands buried in the mane. No one was about, not even Potts. It was hard to admire the lad's skill when all Dauntry could see were the flying, iron-shod hooves, the powerful muscles, the great neck.

They took a jump, then another, Dauntry's heart following them over, lodging in his throat each time, only to leap again as great muscles bunched.

The boy was too small. The horse was too big. It would end in disaster, this beautiful thing he was seeing, and then how would he face Cecelia? How would he face himself, dammit! It would be his fault, all of it. Even the grooms had difficulties with the blacks, perfectly schooled though they'd been when they arrived at Combermere. His father and brother'd taught them bad habits, Potts claimed. If they had, no evidence of it remained, at least with this one.

Another jump, and then it was over, the hunter slowing to a steady trot as he circled to the center of the ring, then a walk. At last he stopped, a living statue of flawless ebony, neck arched, ears proudly forward, as if he knew his own magnificence and wished to display it to the world.

The boy slipped to the grass, flinging his arm over the horse's neck and crooning as he offered a windfall on the flat of his hand.

"Dear God, I'll kill him!" Dauntry muttered, knees like water.

The black whickered, and turned its elegant head. Wise eyes regarded him from twenty yards away. Tommy glanced over his shoulder, then seemed to shrink within himself as he spotted Dauntry.

"Come here, Tommy," Dauntry managed, keeping his voice low. "Out of the paddock. Now!"

The black's ears flattened. Otherwise it remained unmoving, still regarding Dauntry steadily.

Shoulders slumped, head hanging, Tommy dragged his feet across the grass, then the track, then the verge, and scrambled over the fence. The thing of beauty, wild and free, had vanished. All that was left were a frightened boy, an arrogant hunter, and a man so relieved he was almost speechless, his limbs still shaking uncontrollably.

"What the devil d'you think you were doing in there?" Dauntry roared. "I should take a horsewhip to you! Of all the irresponsible, idiotic, *brazen—*"

"I wouldn't've hurt him," Tommy pleaded in a voice so small Dauntry could barely make out the words.

"Hurt *him?* Is that what you—my God, it's a miracle he didn't kill *you,* dammit!"

"But we're friends, sir. I always bring Hephaestus an apple. One time he told me to climb on, and so I did. We always have a grand time. He likes me as much as I like him. He doesn't bite, or kick, or blow up his belly anymore, either. And he doesn't balk at jumps."

"The horse told you—devil take it, Thomas Walters, I will *not* be made a game of!"

"I'm not. Truly, sir."

"You are not, ever, under any circumstances, to get back on that horse. Is that understood? Not today. Not tomorrow. Not next week. Not ever!"

"But—"

"Ever!" Dauntry thundered.

Tommy nodded, eyes huge.

Dauntry dropped to his knees and gathered the lad against him, still shaking. "Not ever, Tommy, please," he whispered. "You could've been killed, or worse."

"No, I couldn't. He *likes* me, I tell you."

"Swear it, sprout," Dauntry groaned. "Not ever."

"But what about the others? Mr. Potts says his lordship ordered them put down if they can't be taught better manners. There's three more, and I haven't had a chance to make true friends with them yet, or to—"

"They'll not be put down—I promise. If nothing else, I'll arrange for them to be sent back to Chronicle Watford for additional schooling, and tell his lordship the girl in white insisted. It wouldn't be all that far from the truth, and Twin Oaks isn't that distant. Just a matter of a day or two."

He managed to let go of the lad and stood, heart slowing. "Did Potts know of this?"

"No, it was to be a surprise. He likes the blacks, too."

"I'm sure he does."

"You not angry anymore?"

"With my father and brother, perhaps. Not with you. I never was."

"Well, you sounded angry."

"No, sprout," Dauntry sighed, "what you just heard was the sound of sheer, blind terror. I'd rather relive Badajoz or Salamanca than the last few minutes. Anger's entirely different. Don't confuse the two."

Tommy regarded him for a few moments, eyes as wise and old as the black's.

"I didn't mean to frighten you," he said finally. "I'm sorry, sir. I promise I won't do it again."

"No, I know you won't," Dauntry agreed, adding silently, *Not intentionally, and then only because I won't be here to see you do it.* "I think it's best to keep this escapade from your mother."

Being a parent had to be an impossible task. No wonder Cecelia tried to shelter Tommy from every bump and bruise. He was no less guilty. It had been obvious from the start the black and the boy had a strange bond. Tommy had been in no danger, not really, except for the possibility of a untoward accident the black would've done everything in its power to prevent.

"I think that's best," Tommy agreed. "She wouldn't understand."

"No, she wouldn't. I'm afraid I don't, either. You have far more sense than to attempt something so foolhardy. Promise me in the future you'll think before you act."

"But I did—think, that is. What I thought was, if I didn't do something they'd be put down. I couldn't let that happen."

Dauntry glanced at his feet. The creel containing their picnic tea had spilled onto the grass, the flagon shattering against a rock, the lemonade soaking their sandwiches before seeping into the ground.

"There are always other solutions. You could've come to me."

"You hadn't arrived yet when his lordship got so angry. Hephaestus had nipped him on the—well, he'd nipped him."

"Then you could've told the squire."

"What could Mr. Burchett've done? Lord Dauntry wouldn't've listened. He probably wouldn't even've received him."

"Then you could've told me *after* I arrived."

"You were too busy worrying about everything else."

"The point is, Tommy," he sighed, "making everything right with the world isn't your responsibility. You have to learn to delegate. That means letting others help, even do the most important part, and being satisfied with playing the role you can. It's not as exciting, but it's usually more effective than trying to solve things single-handed. Do you think Lord Wellington could win battles without the rest of us to help him, and follow his orders?"

Listen to yourself, a small voice jeered inside him. Then it became more serious. *Listen to yourself, blast you!*

He shrugged it off. Schooling a lad in the road he should follow was one thing, especially when there was little time to do it. The world changed when one became a man.

"I think you'd best be getting home," he said, glancing at the level of the sun. "I'd thought we might go fishing, but it's getting late. Your mother'll be wondering where you are." He picked up the bundle holding crop, kite, rod, and miniature creel. "The fellows sent you this. There's something from me in there, too."

"Oh, my," Tommy whispered, taking them. "How awfully kind. What is it?"

"Undo it when you get home."

"I'll need to write them to say thank you."

"Your uncle has their direction."

"Tomorrow?"

"If you can. Things may be very different tomorrow."

"Why would they be? Nothing ever changes in Coombe."

Dauntry gave a noncommittal grunt.

It was his last chance. "I'll walk you to the gates," he said.

The invitation to Beechy Knoll had already arrived when Dauntry returned to the house, the Burchett groom been sent off with the customary acceptance after Persephone Blaire and Dabney St. Maure had him join them in drinking the healths of the vicar, Rebecca, the Irregulars, and everyone else they could think of, including the girl in white.

So, it had begun. This was the true endgame. He'd already admitted to Tommy he didn't intend to linger long at Combermere, though he hadn't mentioned the morrow as his date of departure. Clamped lips and stiffened shoulders had met his announcement, almost as if he'd struck the lad. Well, he'd soon have other thoughts to occupy him.

By now Gardener would've returned to the vicarage and told his sister the essentials. Very shortly Tommy would know he was no longer a pauper. Creel, rod, crop, and kite would fade to insignificance beside a future earldom. Cecelia would welcome her son home with tears of joy, and insist he smarten himself for the coming evening. Either way, she'd be putting on her prettiest gown and her most elegant air. Wealthy widows had a right to some airs, especially ones who'd suffered poverty when there was no need, and had the beauty and character to carry off airs with aplomb.

Dauntry accepted a glass of champagne from his great-aunt.

"To the girl in white," she crowed, raising her glass. "And to you, you dear, misguided fool. She must be delighted with you."

He lifted his in return, managed a slight smile, then downed it.

"All's seen to, I gather," he said, placing the emptied glass on the table at his side.

"Banns'll be read for the first time on Sunday," St. Maure announced with a grin. "We're to stay for that at least, and we're all invited to the wedding, including my mother, Lady Cheltenham, and the general. Miss Blaire says she won't quit Combermere, though she may take up residence at the dower house. You're to stand up for Gardener. His bishop'll probably perform the ceremony. Gardener's note was a bit incoherent, Mrs. Burchett's even more so, but that much we managed to decipher."

"So joy reigns supreme in every heart."

"Not quite," his great-aunt returned, "but you may be sure it will be if I have anything to say about it."

"Not unless you've become a sorceress." If there was more determination in his tone than the words called for, so be it. He glanced about the terrace. "Where're the dogs?"

She laughed, expression clearing. "Celebrating canine style in the kitchens while we celebrate here. Cook promised them a treat of uncommon delicacy. I've ordered wine and champagne to be served in the servants' hall tonight, by the bye. Mayhew agreed it would be appropriate. I hope you don't mind?"

"No, an excellent notion."

"How was your reunion with Thomas?" St. Maure asked, helping himself to more champagne and refilling Dauntry's glass as well. "Is the kite still in one piece?"

"Not even unwrapped. Deliver me from ever becoming a parent," Dauntry returned with a genuine smile. "I learned some home truths this afternoon, among them that I'm in no way suited to that task. Raw recruits're bad enough. The infantry's impossible. Believe themselves immortal, I suspect."

"No one's ever prepared until faced with it. Look at how well Val's going on with those wards of his, now he's been forced to make a beginning."

"With his mother's and Amelia's assistance. I was there, too, you'll remember. No, I'd make a muddle of it. I'm far better as I am."

His great-aunt ignored the pointed look he gave her. Well, she'd accustom herself as well. They all would, and in the end they'd admit he'd had the right of it.

"What in heaven's name've you done now?" St. Maure threw into the sudden silence. "Thomas is still in one piece, I hope."

"That's between Tommy and me, though I've learned why his mother shudders at his escapades. George Walters must've been something. With any luck, Tommy'll remember the lecture as well as the tone of voice, and that both were infused with deep affection. If I frightened him a bit as well, that's all to the good. It'll keep him safe for a week or two."

"Catch him aboard Argus?"

"No, nothing like that. As I said, it's between us."

Within minutes they'd separated to change for the gala dinner at Beechy Knoll. An early departure was needed. Seven miles at a staid trot by the lanes in a carriage would take far longer than five cross-country on a horse, and neither Dauntry nor St. Maure was willing for Persephone Blaire to endure the tedious trip with only herself for company. For a miracle, conversation in the carriage was innocuous the entire way, if one didn't count the occasional pointed glance from his great-aunt or knowing one from St. Maure.

When they arrived, Beechy Knoll was *en fête,* lights in every window, bowls of flowers on every surface. Rebecca and Gardener glowed as brightly as the setting sun.

Dauntry left the first effusions to his aunt, who proved more than equal to the task before moving on to join the squire and Mrs. Burchett. Then he took her place, bending to kiss his childhood playmate's cheek and shake Gardener's hand. "There's no need for me to wish you happy," he said. "One look at you tells the tale."

"Little did I think, when you first stopped by the vicarage, that such a end was possible, let alone that it would come so quickly," Gardener beamed. "When I think of what you've accomplished for my sister and Thomas, it takes my breath away, and Rebecca and I owe you everything. I doubt any other could've managed it."

"Quint's always been quite the wizard," Rebecca insisted with a sunny laugh. "I've always thought we should dub him Merlin."

"Deliver me! I haven't the beard for it, and mossy grottos are at the bottom of my list of desirable residences. Much too damp. No, give all the credit to the girl in white. That's where it properly belongs."

"Ah, yes—our mysterious girl in white," Gardener returned, eyes twinkling. "Now all's resolved, won't you reveal her identity? I'd like to reward her, if only privately, as I'm certain she'd want her identity to remain officially secret. Not all would appreciate the good she's accomplished unrecompensed."

Dauntry smiled slightly, and shook his head. "She's her own reward, strange as that may sound, but in a sense she's already been more than adequately compensated for her good offices. After all, each of her complaints has been dealt with, as well as a few that weren't immediately obvious. That's all she wanted, I believe. Besides, I'm still not convinced of her identity, and content it should remain so. There are some things one's meant to know, and others one's only meant to suspect."

"If you insist. You will stand up for us? Once all was settled between us—"

"Which took perhaps five seconds, as explanations came later," Rebecca interrupted. "Robert's precise words were, 'We can at last. Which date suits you best?' "

"—that was the first thought that came to us."

"The first? Really? And I'd never taken either of you for a slow-top," Dauntry responded, breaking into a full-throated laugh. "I see I'll have to readjust my thinking." Then he sobered. "I'd be honored, if it's possible. Who knows what another month will bring, given the evidence of the last two? Actually, I intend to quit the neighborhood soon, as the work I'd been summoned to accomplish is done."

"But surely you can put off your departure, Quint?" Rebecca pleaded. "For Josh's sake, if for no other? It's not to be a month, though. We're to be wed in six weeks, as Mama insists we'll need that much time for bride clothes and such, and of course the bishop's convenience must be considered. If all else fails, you could return."

"We'll see," was all he'd say, and moved on, ceding his place to St. Maure, who twirled Rebecca about, bussed her heartily, then clapped the vicar on the back, imparting the congratulations and best wishes of the rest of the Irregulars, and their sure promise of attending the nuptials whenever they took place.

Dauntry glanced about the familiar parlor. Mrs. Burchett and Aunt Persie had their heads together, discussing the relative merits of various London drapers as the squire good-naturedly complained he intended to marry off a daughter, not equip a palace. Tommy, spruced up indeed, sat well away from the celebrating adults, shoulders hunched, eyes fixed on the floor.

"Thomas says you intend to make your departure soon, Mr. Dauntry," a soft voice said behind him.

Dauntry took a deep breath, schooled his features, and turned. She was exquisite. The gown was one he'd seen a thousand times—a slight exaggeration, but not by much—this time furbished up with simple knots of ribbon, a scrap of lace no doubt donated by Rebecca or Mrs. Burchett, and fresh flowers to give it a new look.

"Mrs. Walters," he said, giving her a deep bow.

"Mr. Dauntry." She curtsyed mechanically, eyes fixed on his face. "Thomas didn't mistake the matter? You do indeed intend to quit Combermere almost immediately?"

"My work here is done," he said, shocked at the harshness of his tone.

"That's a pity. You'll be greatly missed. You do intend to return for the wedding, of course? Rebecca and Robert are counting on you."

"I doubt that'll be possible, unfortunately."

"Oh."

Just the single word, so soft, almost inaudible amid the joking and laughter of the others. And the gray eyes, clouded, dark, almost stormy. He glanced away, refusing to acknowledge the question in their depths.

"I have a life to get on with," he snapped.

"You don't sound entirely pleased by the prospect."

"If I'm not, I should be. It's time and more."

"Yes, I suppose it is. Your friends told us enough for me to understand that. I wish you well in your new ventures, whatever they may be, and wherever they may take you."

"Thank you."

He bowed again, and made to join the group now clustered around his aunt. Cecelia laid a graceful hand on his arm, holding him back.

"As I may not have another opportunity," she said, "I must take this one to thank you for what you and your friends have done. We'd considered the situation beyond remedy, as my brother and I agreed in the beginning scandal was to be avoided at all costs for the sake of my husband's memory."

"The merest lark." He managed a smile that grew far warmer than propriety would've condoned, or circumspection. "A prank, believe me. We enjoyed every minute—when our hearts weren't in our mouths for fear of failure. Happened more than once. All came right in the end. That's what matters."

"It wasn't a lark. I know Lady Walters too well to permit you to shrug off your accomplishments in this manner. It took courage, inventiveness, and not a little effort. The only one I've ever known to best her was George, and he did it by the simple expedient of ignoring her. I hadn't that option."

"A mere bagatelle," he insisted, "and infinitely amusing. Not the first time we've played similar tricks in a good cause. Likely it won't be the last. Keeps us from becoming bored. Life can be exceeding tedious on occasion."

"I'd like to reimburse you for any expenses incurred," she said after a moment, "once that's possible."

"Out of the question. We were amusing ourselves, I tell you."
He paused. She shook her head, regarding him steadily.

"I won't permit you to make nothing of it," she insisted.

"And I refuse to permit you to make too much."

"Why must you be so difficult?"

The hand was still there, holding him back. "The point now is to get on with things," he said. "What are your plans?"

Her hand fell. She sighed. "We'll remain at the vicarage until Robert and Rebecca are wed. Then I'll return to Grafton with Thomas, so they may begin their married lives unencumbered. It's a bit isolated, and will be exceeding lonely after the vicarage, but we'll accustom ourselves."

"It will, however, be far more comfortable for you."

"Comfort isn't everything. Happiness and companionship count far more."

"You'll find both. In the end, Tommy'll see to it. I'm convinced of that."

Her eyes rose to his, then. "If you believe that, you know far more than I do. It would seem our best hope of either is determined to vanish."

It was a bold hint for so circumspect a woman. Neither was it her first one. Desperation, he decided, could take many forms. Well, it wouldn't serve. He'd see her through despite herself.

Finally her eyes dropped, though not her head. Shoulders squared, she moved off to join the others, and Dauntry was left to consider the joys of pride, and the rewards of a rigid code of honor that took only itself into account The look his great-aunt sent him would've leveled the strongest fortifications.

Dinner was announced. The squire led the way, Persephone Blaire on his arm, followed by St. Maure and Mrs. Burchett. Dauntry, Cecelia, and Tommy trailed after the newly betrothed couple, all three silent and preoccupied.

It was a good thing there was a wedding to plan, and the tale of the Irregulars' London adventures to be told and retold until not one detail remained unexplored and uncommented on. St. Maure handled that part with good humor, constantly referring to Dauntry so only his great-aunt noticed how silent he remained, going so far as to kick him sharply beneath the table when he failed to respond with enough alacrity to satisfy her. Finally, for the sake of his shins, he began to pay attention to what went on about him, though not to what lay on his plate.

Tommy remained pale, almost listless, despite the squire's good-natured jollying, his food as untouched as Dauntry's. Cecelia Walters, for all she mimicked the gaiety suitable to such a happy occasion, appeared equally out of sorts and distracted, her contributions to the conversation too often at variance with the subject at hand. Strangely, only he seemed to note the discrepancies and contradictions. That, or there was a conspiracy of silence regarding the trio whose spirits were so at odds with the rest.

He should've taken to his heels after that first Sunday, Dauntry decided, holding his glass out for more wine, and to blazes with his father, female hysterics, garlic necklaces, and the girl in white.

Then, smiling slightly, he glanced at Tommy from the corner of his eye. No, never to blazes with the girl in white.

He longed to explain, but it couldn't be done. One day Tommy would understand, if he even remembered the incidents of his final summer in Coombe. Children forgot things easily at his age, and learned to accept what remained incomprehensible. It was better that way. Explanations encouraged protest. It had been an accident, all of it. Better it should all fade away.

At last the toasts to king, country, and master of the hounds were drunk, the interminable meal over.

Foregoing the ritual of port and cigarillos, the gentlemen followed the ladies directly to the parlor—the vicar, Rebecca, Persephone Blaire, the squire, and his wife continuing their discussion of wedding plans, St. Maure offering suggestions that had them laughing until their sides ached. Even Dauntry's lips twitched at the notion of a trout-fishing contest in lieu of the more conventional dancing. As for fireworks in midmorning, and a triumphal arch in the Roman style at the village's edge through which the bridal couple could drive following the ceremony while being pelted with flowers and sweetmeats, only St. Maure's proposal of a hunt breakfast—before a mounted game of catch-as-catch-can in which capturing bride and groom took the place of running the fox to ground—exceeded them.

A leaden weight in his chest, Dauntry eased back from the hilarity, wondering if this was the post to which he'd relegated himself for the rest of his life. Grim it certainly was, and infinitely lonely.

"Cecelia, my dear, would you favor us with an air or two?" Mrs. Burchett called from her seat at the center of things. "We'd be ever so honored. I can't think of a more perfect expression of our joy than your lovely voice."

With nod, and a smile that held very little that was joyous in it, Cecelia went to the pianoforte on the far side of the room and began to leaf through the music. At last she sat, ran her fingers over the keys, then began to sing. Was it his imagination, or had her voice just cracked? Impossible.

He turned away just in time to notice Tommy slip into the moonlit garden. The boy's expression had been woebegone.

There was just so much one could bear. A quick glance at the others proved no one would miss him.

Dauntry went through the French doors and stood on the terrace, looking down at the gardens. It took a few moments for his eyes to adjust. At last he spotted the boy huddled on a stone bench in the shadows cast by some tall hydrangeas whose blooms shone in the moonlight. He frowned. This wouldn't do, not at all.

It was only a few steps to the gardens, and a seat on the bench. Tommy turned his back.

"You don't mind my joining you for a bit, do you, sprout?" Dauntry said. "Stuffy in there, and I'm not one for interminable discussions of lace, flowers, and menus."

Silence greeted his words. He pulled out a cheroot to excuse his presence, making a great fuss of lighting it to permit the lad a chance to regain his composure. Soaring voice and rippling arpeggios flooded from the house, the song holding far more longing than joy. The voice cracked again, then stilled, only the liquid notes pouring into the liquid moonlight, vying with it for beauty. He'd never forget this night—not ever, no matter how long he lived. He doubted if its pain would ever lessen.

"You must be looking forward to returning to the home you remember as being such a beautiful and happy place," he said after a bit, trying again, "especially knowing Grafton's yours now, just as your father intended, and the lady with all the rings can never hurt you or your mother again."

Tommy shrugged, back still turned.

"Certainly you must be delighted your uncle and Miss Burchett are free to wed." Dauntry took a long pull on his cheroot, watching the smoke spiral upwards, kissed by the moonlight. The music came to a crashing finale, the notes trailing away at last. The selection had contained a disturbing element of fury, even desperation. Cecelia could've chosen better—at least she should have. When passionate Beethoven had replaced simple country air he wasn't certain. "You're extremely fond of your uncle, after all."

The boy nodded.

"And you must be delighted your mother won't have to clean any more lamps or scrub any more floors."

Tommy shrugged, then nodded again, grinding the toe of his boot in the gravel.

"Got to be," he said. "Thank you for the crop, sir."

"You're welcome."

Dauntry took another pull on his cheroot, watching the glowing tip as it brightened, then faded. Interesting, how the things were like life—dull for the most part, with occasional flashes of beauty, leaving only ashes in the end.

"Lovely night," he said to fill the silence, watching Tommy's averted face from the corner of his eye, and making his tone as light as possible, and as matter-of-fact. At least Cecelia was no longer attacking the pianoforte as if it were her enemy, responsible for all the sorrows of the world. He couldn't've borne another such wrenching performance. "You ever learn to identify the constellations? That's Ursae Majoris up there, clear as can be."

The lad was close to tears, no question about it, and refusing to give in to them.

"What's the matter?" Dauntry said gently. "And don't try to tell me everything's wonderful, because I know that's not true."

"It doesn't work," Tommy said after a moment, "no matter what Uncle says."

"What doesn't work?"

"Praying. It all happened just the way I asked at first. You came, and you took care of a lot but I didn't get what I wanted most of all."

There was an uneasy silence. Then, "And you're going away again," Tommy accused, "only this time you aren't coming back, are you? Not ever. You're going away very soon, and we're going away, too."

"I don't belong here, Tommy. Combermere is my father's, and will be my brother's one day. I can never come except as a guest."

"You weren't a guest this time."

"No," Dauntry admitted with a rueful smile. "I was ordered here to catch a ghost. While I never quite caught it, I don't think it'll be troubling anyone at Combermere again, do you?"

"No," Tommy replied in a small voice. "D'you think that's why I didn't get it?"

"Because you were the ghost?" Dauntry said, drawing on his cheroot.

There was a soft shifting of the gravel behind them, no doubt some intrepid woods animal foraging for its supper. A mouse scurried across the path, little more than a silver streak in the moonlight. So that'd been it.

Thomas looked up at Dauntry, eyes wide.

"You knew?"

"Not in the beginning. You were very clever. At first I thought it was Potts or Mr. Nace, or possibly even Mayhew. How did you learn about the passages?"

"Mayhew let me play in the gallery when it was wet and cold outside, and I discovered the big one. It was easy after that. Only when the family wasn't in residence, though. You're not to scold Mayhew, sir. He was only being kind."

"But why the ghost? I suppose Potts told you the tale, or Mrs. Ford."

"Actually, sir, that was Mayhew, too."

"The old reprobate." Dauntry barely managed not to chuckle at the thought of the twists the butler had given the tale when he was a lad. The old fellow had been so anxious to gloss over its less attractive bits that only a confusing hotchpotch had remained. It'd taken Potts to make all clear. "You don't impress me as the sort to play pranks that terrify ladies who've never done you any harm."

"I'm not. They were silly to think I was real. But," the boy gulped, "I knew they'd think I was, even his lordship, and that's almost as bad, isn't it? Only I had to get you here once Potts told me about you—something kept telling me to, and when something tells me to do something, I do it, just like riding Hephaestus, because it carps until I do—and it was the only way I could think of. Took years, too. I cheered when Lord Dauntry made you sell out, even if it was unfair. Spain was much too far."

"Something talks to you? Oh, your conscience, of course. I suspect, as with the blacks, it could do with some additional training."

"No, not like that. One's conscience can be uncomfortable. This is different, like a friend, and tells me to do things, not to *not* do them."

"Incessantly, I take it."

"Yes, it does. It never gets nasty, but, well, it *insists*. His lordship always calls you home when there's a problem. Potts told me so. Like when he made you sell out when your brother got thrown and didn't wake up for the longest time, and almost died like my father did. I didn't want to kill anybody, or make them sick, and being the girl in white was the only thing I could think of."

The whisper of a breeze touched the branches behind them, a soft sound very like a human gasp, the leaves stirring with a silken rustle. In the distance an owl hooted. There was a squeal, high and despairing. Suddenly the owl swooped past them, the rush of its wings ghostly in the night, something writhing in its talons.

"And," Thomas said, ignoring the small drama, "you always make everything right. Potts said that, too, and so I knew you were the person who could fix it all. And then you called me Tommy, and I was sure of it. Only you haven't."

"The villagers are seen to, and your uncle. So is your mother. Her future's assured now, as well as yours. Why, you'll probably be a earl one day."

"Don't want to be."

"Which is precisely why you'll make a extremely good one. What else is there to fix?" Dauntry said, taking a pull on his cheroot.

"Why don't you like Mama?"

"But I do. Very much indeed. Well, rather a bit more than that, actually."

"It must be me you don't like, then. Is it because of Hephaestus?"

"Oh, Tommy," Dauntry almost groaned. "No, I like you far above half, too. Your father was infinitely fortunate in both of you."

"But you don't like us enough."

"Enough for what?"

"To be my father. Well, my stepfather. I know you can't be my real father, because you didn't beget me. Uncle explained all that a long time ago because of Peter Croft, when Mrs. Croft married Mr. Twitchell at the inn. And to be Mama's husband."

"Your mother is quite a wealthy woman, now. That's what we were about in London. Situated as I am, I've all I can do to keep myself, and must watch the pennies and guard the crowns or I'll sail up the River Tick on the fastest sloop afloat."

"She wouldn't be wealthy if you hadn't done something about it, so that shouldn't count. She'd still be poorer than you are."

"It does, though. The world would hold me in contempt were I to offer for her, Tommy. Good Lord—I'd hold myself in contempt."

"Why?"

"A second son? Landless, without a profession, forced to hang on his father's sleeve so his mother won't suffer palpitations and take to her bed each time she imagines she's vexed or been insulted? That's going to change, but my purse'll be lighter than ever for a long while. Come now, sprout—you have intelligence enough to understand the impossibility of such a situation. Certainly you will when you're a man, and would despise me then were I to do what you think you want now."

"You would've had a profession if your father hadn't made you sell out. And Three Rivers Farm should've been yours. Potts said so. He says it's not your fault, any of it, any more than Joshua Burchett's death was."

"He does, does he? I see I'll have to have a word or two with him concerning his loose tongue before I leave."

"Potts said it was infinitely unfair to you, too. Please, Mr.

Dauntry, won't you forget all the silly stuff, and marry us and be my stepfather, if you like us above half? Because we like you far, far above half."

"I can't, Tommy."

"Yes," a voice whispered behind them, "please Mr. Dauntry, if the silly stuff is the only impediment, won't you marry us? We *would* like it infinitely, both of us."

"I can't," Dauntry repeated on a strangled note, rising and crushing his cheroot on the gravel path. Dear God—how long had she been there? Since the furious notes ceased spilling from the piano? "Don't you see that, Cecelia? I *can't*." Slowly he turned to face her. "You're a wealthy woman," he insisted. "You can have your choice of anyone."

"And if my choice is you?"

"It won't do."

"Why?" mother and son chorused.

Dauntry stared at them helplessly, his heart in his eyes, then glanced up at the house. They had an audience, at the fore one silhouette that was clearly his great-aunt's, another Dabney St. Maure's. The rest were a jumble of black against the golden candlelight.

"Damn them!" he muttered. "Can they never learn when to leave well enough alone?"

"I can see I'm doomed to perpetual widowhood," Cecelia murmured, "and Thomas to never having a father. Ah well, while it's a pity for us to tread solitary paths when there's no need for it, I hope you'll at least permit us to think kindly of one another as we totter toward infirmity? It seems a dreadful waste, but if that's what you prefer, then I suppose there's very little either Thomas or I can say to change your mind."

Dauntry cursed with the inventive vocabulary of a seasoned officer.

"Of course, there is another option," Cecelia interrupted, a glint in her eyes. "We could hire Nace away from your father to run Thomas's estate, and Potts the stables, and Mayhew and Mrs. Ford to manage the house, and retain the services of Lady St. Maure's man of business to oversee everything. We'd find a place for Nick Beetle, too. Then I could give you your colors as a wedding present, so long as General Maitland remains willing to lend a hand."

"How d'you know about that?" Dauntry thundered.

"Don't try to frighten me. You can't. I know about a lot of things."

"Blast them," he growled.

"Then the three of us could follow the drum. If you insist, I'd even permit you to repay the sum when you can, and we'd touch Thomas's inheritance only for his schooling. Would that suit your sense of the conventions?"

"You don't know what you're asking. It's a cursed hard life. You'd find it intolerable."

"I've told you before I'm well able to determine for myself what I can and can't tolerate," she said, head high, "whether it's a pebble in my boot, or how I wish to spend my life. There's no need for you, or anyone else, to make such decisions for me. Besides, these last years have been most instructive. I do know how to clean lamps and sweep floors, even if I'm not very good at it. The one thing I simply cannot tolerate is the prospect of life at anyone's side but yours."

"Your husband would despise and curse me."

"Oh, no," she countered with a shaky laugh, "George would cheer us on, were he able. You're precisely the person he'd've chosen as Thomas's stepfather and my husband, had he the opportunity. He described you to me before he died, though only in very general terms, and told me not to be a goose when the time came, but to make sure I had the perfect husband, and Thomas the perfect father. You're not allowed to say no, you see, or dear George will never leave any of us in peace."

With a strangled gasp, Dauntry stumbled forward as if pushed, seized her in his arms, and kissed her in the moonlight, Tommy and their audience forgotten.

"Dear heaven, what have I ever done to deserve this?" he murmured at last, gazing down at her in wonder.

The entrancing gray eyes were dark no longer. Instead, they shone up at him with the radiance of a thousand stars.

From somewhere within him the notion occurred that he'd never sought his own good at the expense of others. Dauntry dismissed it on the instant, laying all credit at the feet of a di-

minutive and determined ghost garbed in shawls, and the rene-
gade retainers who lent him a hand.

And so the second of North's Irregulars succumbed to the im-
peratives of a conquered heart.

The celebration, when Dauntry, Cecelia, and Tommy came
up from the gardens at last, held a strong element of self-
congratulation to it. Certainly both Persephone Blaire and Dabney
St. Maure made no secret of having informed Cecelia where her
son and Quintus Dauntry had taken themselves while she struggled to sing through her despair for the delight of the company.

It had been she, Miss Blaire declared with no little satisfaction,
who bodily escorted Cecelia to the French doors and shoved her
onto the terrace when all else failed, then blocked the way so it
was descend to the gardens or sit on the steps, and informed the
young widow she had a choice between pride and happiness, as
her nephew had unaccountably transformed himself from reasonable man to stiff-rumped dolt. Being an eminently practical
woman—just as she'd suspected, Miss Blaire crowed—and one
of no little fortitude, Cecelia had determined pride to be a useless
commodity, and seized the future with both hands, just as any
woman of sense would. It hadn't taken that much encouragement,
either.

The rejoicing was universal when news of the dual betrothals
traveled through the countryside. There was no need to wait for
banns to spread the word. One look at the five joyous faces—
Tommy Walters's perhaps the most joyous of all—told the tale
to any who happened on them.

While a wedding wasn't quite the sort of ceremony Lord Harald
Dauntry'd had in mind to banish the girl in white when he sum-
moned his younger son to Combermere, six weeks later Quintus
Dauntry and Cecelia Walters were married by her brother an hour
before his own wedding, the squire and Tommy giving the bride
away, and with Persephone Blaire, the Irregulars, Lady Amelia,
Lady Katherine, Lady Cheltenham, Lady St. Maure, and General
Maitland in attendance at both weddings. Then the new bride

stood up for her soon-to-be sister-in-law, the groom for his new brother.

Contrary to Lord and Lady Dauntry's desires, the wedding breakfast was held at Beechy Knoll, and was far too informal and rollicking an affair for their tastes. A hint that it was the wish of the girl in white, however, caused them to hold their peace and to behave with as much graciousness as it was possible for them to evidence, Lady Dauntry suffering but a single attack of the vapors at the horror of being forced to forego her younger son dancing attendance whenever it suited her, and Lord Dauntry complaining not once of his gout.

Cecelia they welcomed as Dauntry's wife, excepting they pleaded with her to change her name to Griselda, or Sophronia, or anything that didn't begin with a "C". She was, after all, excessively wealthy. Quintus, they agreed, had done far better for himself than could've been expected. Best of all, he'd assured them that the girl in white would rest quietly in her grave, so long as Combermere's attentions to the neighborhood continued.

Persephone Blaire didn't settle in Combermere's dower house, as all expected. Instead she—and the Spanish family, complete with livestock, "Carthaginian Puff-ball", "Portuguese Stews-scrap," and "Pyrenean Ankle-scratcher"—returned to Kent following the wedding, where the doughty old lady took a sudden and deep interest in the property that would have constituted her dowry had she wed. From a rundown embarrassment to all under the supervision of an inferior bailiff, it soon became a thriving place, and the envy of the neighborhood.

She did, however, make unannounced visits to Combermere, each time threatening to remain permanently. Those she leavened with occasional visits to Dauntry and Cecelia, and she was with them in Brussels at the time of Waterloo, where Dauntry distinguished himself. Something had mellowed great-nephew and great-aunt, for by then they no longer brangled, perhaps calmed by Cecelia's soothing influence, perhaps by Tommy's impish ways, perhaps by Miss Blaire's terror that Dauntry would predecease her, and Dauntry's realization that she would not always be with them.

Some years later, Quintus Dauntry was stunned to learn he hadn't been quite so without prospects as he'd always believed.

It was the '20s, King George III and the Corsican Monster deceased, Thomas just down from Oxford with a degree in classics, Duncan sporting the title of viscount, Bertram a stripling who far exceeded his father in sense. By then a colonel, Dauntry sold out for the second time, and he, Cecelia, and their three children retired to Persephone Blaire's property in Kent.

And the improvements caused by the girl in white in Coombe and its environs while seeing to matters of more immediate concern to her? To this day, mindful of the tale of Baron Charles d'Auntré and his six wives, and the reappearance of Yolande d'Auntré's restless spirit shortly before the end of the Napoleonic Wars, the Dauntry family, now elevated to a earldom, sees to tenants, parish, and parishioners with a generosity and devotion that makes them an example to all. The house, during both great wars, served as a convalescent home for the wounded, and in the summers now takes in children from the modern successors to the slums where Dauntry and his friends sought the Countess of Marle, offering them a vision of a better and happier life most take to heart.

Was there truly a ghost at Combermere that long-ago summer, or at least in the village of Coombe, haunting a simple vicarage rather than a great house, and trailing after one small boy whispering suggestions and issuing commands only he could hear? Or was it a case of the only people in whom Tommy Walters had dared confide—the retainers at the great house—protecting him, and encouraging him to think and act in ways that might solve the insoluble problems of one they cherished?

One thing is certain: following the marriage of his mother and Quintus Dauntry, Tommy Walters no longer heard the voice in his head that commanded him to do things, only the one that told him what not to do.

About the Author

The girl in white was inspired by tales of a ghost who supposedly inhabited the 200-year-old house where Monique Ellis's husband lived when they met. If the ghost existed—and there are those who claim to have both heard and seen her—that restless spirit had a decidedly romantic bent. Every young Air Force officer who moved into the house moved out for one reason only: to meet his bride—whom he first encountered while living there—at the altar.

Monique lives in Arizona with her husband of almost forty years—Jim Ellis, a gifted artist and popular watercolor instructor.

She's the award-winning author of six other Zebra Regency novels: *The Fortescue Diamond, DeLacey's Angel, The Lady and the Spy, The Marquess Lends a Hand, The Colonel's Courtship,* and *An Uncommon Governess,* as well as five anthologized novellas: *Lady Charlotte Contrives* (in *A Mother's Delight*), *The Schooling of a Rake* (in *Rogues and Rakes*), *The DeVille Inheritance* (in *Lords of the Night*), *Three Nights at a Country Inn* (in *A Winter Wedding*), and *The Year Father Christmas Came Calling* (in *Underneath the Mistletoe*).

Monique is currently researching several future projects. In the meantime, she'd like to know how you enjoyed a tale written from the hero's point of view, and whether you believe there was an actual ghost in addition to the girl in white.

She loves to hear from readers, and can be reached at P.O. Box 24398, Tempe AZ 85285-4398. Please include a stamped self-addressed envelope if you wish a response.